The Lore Wielder

By Leslie Montaño

The Light-Wielders Series: Book One

Copyright © 2026 by Leslie Montaño

Content warning: depression and suicide

The Lore-Wielder is a fictional novel. Names, places, people, and events were written from the author's imagination.

All rights reserved. No part of the publication may be copied or reproduced without permission from the author.

Cover design, map, and character art by Leslie Montaño.
Edited by Leah Taylor and copy edited by Genevieve Mumford

ISBN: 979-8-9943852-0-3

First edition 2026.

Printed in the United States of America

Dedicated to my daughters,
Gigi and Zio, and to anyone
who has ever believed they don't belong.

TUNDRA
NW
NE
W
E
SW
SE
S
Channel Frost
Mt. Nea
Cedra
DESERT
Wisptale
Province of
Avarlyn
Fal'Eron
Misty Lale
Madrielle
Southern Mountains
Duelle
Anvel
Da'Shinar
Sea of the
Suns
STEPPE

Wisptale Butter Tea Recipe

<u>2 Servings</u>
2 cups of water
2 cups of milk
2 bags of black tea
½ tsp ground ginger
¼ tsp cinnamon
¼ cloves
6 dashes of turmeric

Simmer ingredients together on the stove for 5-8 minutes.
Pour through a fine strainer, and add ½ tsp butter to each cup.
Enjoy!

We plea for healing
On bones we continue to break.
Who chained our giving hands?
Was it ships across the sea?
Instructions were laid at our feet.
Did we carve our own destruction?

~Galio, Elowynnite herald, year 325

Table of contents

Before you read my story,
I have one piece of advice. *Pay attention...*
Hope glimmers in unexpected places
and death is not what it seems.

~Opal

Prologue

"THE LURE IS GETTING STRONGER," she whispered into the dark as she stared at the black water breaking on the rocks below them.

"I know. I saw it in Opal's eyes tonight." He followed her gaze to the lake, an unusually cool breeze reaching into his core. They could feel as much as see it—a mind-gripping lure into darkness. His hand grazed the hilt of a knife, but he knew weapons were useless.

"I don't know if I can stop her, and we're running out of time." Gravel crunched beneath her boots as she turned to meet his eyes, sorrow etched into her own. He studied her face a moment before clenching his eyes shut. It was agony balancing on the brink of life and death, but they didn't have much choice.

"You know what our father said..." he answered, holding her gaze once more, but the words caressed the darkness, weak and hollow. Where was their father when tragedy was rising like a storm?

She blinked twice before diverting her eyes to the cliff below them again. "Of course, but my heart is breaking." Her voice caught. "What if she chooses that path of rescue?" She covered her mouth with her hand, tears ready to spill down her cheeks. He gently touched her shoulder, forcing her to look at him once more.

"Let it break." His voice pierced the black veil around them as a bright light broke overhead. "We can't unbreak this world, but we can bring the broken pieces into the light."

One

TODAY, I COULD DIE. IF I *fail, they'll try to save me—at least I've been told they'll try—but what kind of outcome is that?*

Despite myself, despite the task I'd dreaded since childhood now staring me in the face, I hummed softly. The words were a faded bit of art, coming in and out of focus. *A song from the beginning forever abides. An echo of all the beauty ever known.* It sang to me through the wind and trees sometimes, as far back as I could remember. *Listen, beloved, for its melody guides you home.*

"Are you ready?" the Herald asked, pulling out a piece of cloth and tearing me from the melody drumming through my head. A blindfold. I nodded, a torrent of butterflies choking back any words I might form as we bobbed on the boat. His kind brown eyes were set in a tan face, and he wore a loose-knit shirt. One small braid peeked out from behind his right ear, denoting his place as the Herald—an Avarish religious leader.

The Lore Wielder

The bright sky, the town keepton's back and the lake vanished as he tied the blindfold, and I gripped the middle seat where I sat between the two men, trying to orient myself on the row boat. The Herald was my only comfort now, and it was small. Maybe it was because he'd known me since I was born. Maybe it was because my village gathered to listen to his readings every week like little children sitting around their appa for a bedtime story. Maybe it was because he accompanied all the middling girls on the Gilding. I squeezed my eyes shut. All my hopes of purpose and belonging hinged on what would happen today.

While I waited in darkness, my mind drifted to the conversation with my sister I'd had only this morning. She'd earned the gems for her own daggers two years ago when she was fifteen and knew what awaited me today.

"Tell me again. How do I know which geode to choose?" I asked, tracing the knots imprinted in the white oak of the table with my fingertip.

"You don't. Just pick one you like. Or the one closest to you," Alana said.

"But what if I choose the wrong one?" I swallowed, looking away and folding my arms.

"There is no 'wrong' one." She rubbed the sleep from her eyes and straightened to look at me. "I know you're worried about the prophecy, but that's not how it works."

I knew she was right. Ultimately, it was always chance that determined the gems—the color and shape which gave them their meaning. That would have been the only thing on my mind if it weren't for the tunnel.

"What if I can't make it through the tunnel?"

"You can. It is hard. And scary. But if you keep going, you'll be all right. It's not as long as it feels.

"I wish you could do it for me," I murmured, looking at her with pleading eyes.

"I almost wish I could."

But Alana was not here. I was alone, forced to navigate this without my sister. The Herald's question played over in my mind. *Am I ready?* How could I be ready? A light weight brushed my shoulder as the wind danced through my loose strands of hair, and I smiled despite myself. Even without my sight, I knew a metallic blue dragonfly rested on my shoulder, one that only I could see and hear. Nevma. My eyelashes brushed against the blindfold as I turned my head in his direction.

Where were you? I asked in my head. He usually never left my side.

On a morning adventure. As are you. Nevma replied.

I turned my face away, thoughts of what I was about to do stealing the warmth Nevma offered. *Don't remind me.*

Is the Gilding so important to you?

Frustration at his question churned inside me. *Of course it is. It's the mark of my new place as a middling.*

A mark is only a sign. You are already a Lore-wielder without it.

But if I don't succeed in the Gilding, I'll be the only one without my daggers decorated. I'll be different and marked a failure—not a wielder.

According to whom? There are other ways to decorate your daggers.

My grip on the seat tightened at his audacity. *I don't want another way. I want to find my gems like every other middling girl in Wisptale.*

The Lore Wielder

Sometimes what we don't want is what we need. His voice was gentle, but I clenched my jaw. He couldn't understand what this meant to me. He might be my dearest companion, but he was only a dragonfly after all.

By the time I was spoken to again, my back ached. I stretched, wondering how far Keepton Thorn rowed us from Wisptale and the marina.

"All right. You can take off the blindfold now," the Herald encouraged. The splash of the oar stopped. I swallowed the butterflies in my throat and slid the cloth off, almost wishing I could stay in the darkness. My eyes ached in the bright light as I rubbed them, trying to focus. How far had we traveled? Maybe a league? I recognized nothing but the shore behind us—Wisptale not even a speck on it. A small, rocky island rose from the lake that otherwise engulfed us, gleaming white in the summer sun. The lake itself stretched leagues across a vast reach, hemming Avarlyn into the mountains, away from most of the world—Wisptale perhaps the most remote of its towns.

"There," Keepton Thorn began. A gray beard edged his comely face, and he was swathed in a cloak colored in twilight, buttoned nearly up to his chin. My eyes followed his crooked finger. A dark crack marred the white cliff looming before us as we bobbed in the waves. From here, the low cliffs hindered any glimpse of the island beyond. Chilled by the wind sweeping across the surface, I held my arms close.

"You swim to the cave mouth, and it will narrow into the tunnel," Keepton Thorn continued.

"It's not as long as it feels," the Herald added. "Don't stop until you see the light."

How long is the tunnel? Has anyone died? I blinked, forcing the questions out of my mind. The Herald untangled the long end of a rope from underneath his seat. I stepped forward so he could tie it securely around my waist. I fingered the thin rope, shivers etching into my bones.

"Yank on this to signal you need help. Five times. Do you understand?" Keepton Thorn found my eyes as I struggled to hold his gaze.

"Five times," I murmured back, dropping the rope and balling my fist. I knew about the rope, but now that it was tied to me, I wondered who had discovered the need for it and if they survived.

"You'll see the tree," the Herald cut in with a kind smile. "The geodes grow from its branches." He put his hand on my shoulder. "It's okay to be afraid, and every middling girl is to some degree. But you have to choose what to do with that fear."

I nodded again, barely hearing his words, staring at the cold water that was about to greet me. The wind sucked my breath away, and numbness crept in.

"Whenever you're ready," the Herald said, watching me with a gaze that attempted to calm my racing heart. It didn't work.

"I'd like to get back before dinner time, though." Keepton Thorn offered a half-smile in my direction. I shook off his comment, focusing on the water once more. It was so deep here I could barely see the bottom that threatened to swallow me up. Nevma clung to my shirt, and I realized for the first time he would not be able to go into the cave with me. As if he knew my unspoken thoughts, he answered.

Don't doubt where I will go with you. Nevma darted into the air. I let go of the boat, resigning myself to the whims of Misty Lale. Cold water enveloped my body as I sank. *What if this is the last time I resurface?* I kicked upwards until my head broke through to the air above, gasping from the chill.

The Lore Wielder

As I retreated from Keepton Thorn and the Herald, the opening in the rock yawned like a mouth, wanting to consume me. Nevma circled my head, and I submerged again, opening my eyes. The bottom of the lake was only about fifteen arms below me now, sandy and strewn with shells. Behind, an underwater cliff plummeted, and ice trickled down my spine.

The ominous cave narrowed into a tunnel. The passage ran about eight arms long, according to Alana, but I was met with nothing but darkness. My chest throbbed as I returned to the surface, treading water. It was now or never.

Filling my lungs once more, I propelled myself down and swam into the darkness, into oblivion. I reached towards the sides of the tunnel, barely an arm wide.

Soft blue light appeared ahead, but my lungs burned. There was no escape—no resurfacing until I reached the cave at the end of the tunnel. My body, paralyzed at the thought, refused to move forward. In a flurry of bubbles, I pushed against the walls and swam back towards the bright blue behind me. As soon as I reached the surface, I gasped and clung to the rocks jutting out from the cliff. Water droplets blurred my eyes, and I wiped them away, refusing to acknowledge the boat bobbing ten arms away.

My body raged against my mind, and I cowered beneath the battle—my hope, a broken blade. Reluctantly, I released the rocks, running a hand over the knotted rope as I treaded water. It was still secure. Nevma hovered just a few arms away. He buzzed over my head before diving straight down into the water.

"Wha—" My voice caught in my throat. I could see him moving towards the tunnel beneath the surface. My pulse quickened as I submerged. He was glowing. Bubbles escaped my lips with my shock as his light glanced off the cave walls.

My courage stoked once more, I swam into the mouth of the tunnel. It was cold and eerie as a starless night. A chill, not born of the water surrounding me, flooded every nerve in my body. The end was still beyond my vision, and its narrow endlessness whispered death to me. I clenched my teeth and shut my eyes as I swam after Nevma's light, but a desperate ache spread through my chest.

Air. I had to get air. I kicked hard against the tunnel's wall, shoving myself backwards, but instead of out and up, I hit the other side. Frantically, my last breath escaping me, I yanked on the rope. *One. Two. Three...* But I could no longer move as the pain in my chest burst. Water shoved its way into my mouth, gripping my throat, yet instead of more pain, numbness rushed over me. Then calm, an eerie calm, as my body glided back through the water, my mind in darkness.

<div align="center">~~~</div>

BRILLANT YELLOW DOTTED THE FIELD around me, and I stepped gingerly through the grass, careful not to trample any of the dandelions.

"Wait!" I cried after Alana, but she and Ilynn disappeared into the woods. "I'm coming too!" I sighed, forgetting about the flowers and raced after them. But my five-year-old legs could only run so fast, and my sister was determined to get away from me. Tears pricked in my eyes, and I was glad no one was there to see me cry. Why didn't they want me?

I spun, wondering what to do and where to go. Our turf home poked through the trees in the distance, but it was so far. I brushed a tear away and plopped down in the grass. All I could do was wait until they returned. I drew my knees to my chest and rested my head on them. Honey bees flitted from the clover to the dandelions and back. *At least they are here with me*, I thought. The yellow was interrupted by bright blue as Nevma landed on a dandelion. I smiled, holding out my finger, and he alighted there.

"Aya," I whispered, drying my cheeks with my other hand. He watched me with dark eyes, his wings fluttering. "You won't leave me, will you?" I asked.

Never, came the familiar reply in my head. I smiled as his presence melted my sadness away. **You are my dandelion, more precious than you'll ever know.** He shifted his body to face the woods where Alana and Ilynn went. **It won't always be this way.**

I raised my eyebrows in disbelief. "When? When will they want me around?"

Do you trust me?

I nodded.

He sighed—if a dragonfly could sigh. **Often, others are too busy worrying about themselves to look someone else in the eye. Until they learn to open their eyes, I will be here, and I will remind you what is true.**

~~~

THUNK! MY CALM EVAPORATED. THUNK! Pain jolted me conscious. *Thunk!* Force stimulated my muscles to expel the water. It flew out of my mouth, and I wearily picked my face up off the bottom of the boat.

"She's up. She's breathing!" The Herald's voice patronized my throbbing head, and the weight of his hand left my back. I sat up, trembling. "Are you all right?" He searched my face. I sputtered more water, my eyes stinging, and did my best to nod. I was alive, that much I knew.

"We haven't had to drag anyone out in years." Keepton Thorn dropped into his seat with a huff. He closed his eyes
~~~

and put a hand on his forehead. I hugged my knees, staring at the water pooling in the boat. The water I'd aspirated. I drew in a breath and dropped my head back. I'd failed. Not only that, but I'd needed rescuing.

Three vivid black moths caught my eye as they skimmed over the water. Wings of dark fluttered around my head as a sudden sadness rushed through me. I was worthless. Weak. How could I ever feel joy again? I blinked as the foreign thoughts pierced my mind. Never before had I thought of myself as worthless or feared losing joy. Yet the void grew in my chest until Nevma attacked the moths, scaring them away along with the tantalizing feeling. The weight lifted from my heart, and I finally raised my eyes to the two faces scrutinizing me as we rowed back to the marina. Whatever had just come over me wasn't wholly wrong. I *was* weak.

It was one thing for Nevma to bear witness to my failure, but another thing entirely to face the disappointment from my family. From the whole town.

Two

THERE'S A PART OF EVERY story told that isn't real. A narrative that buds with truth but lives separate from reality. A tale that exists only to expose the truth about oneself—and she was one of those stories.

She lived countless lives, died countless times but never ceased breathing, the deaths only lingering in the shadows of her mind. She had been cracked to her very core for one purpose—to descend into the shards of a world she was protected from as a beacon of hope—a guiding star of light.

Noura didn't rush to the edge of the ship to glimpse the lakeside village tucked into the cliffs guarding Misty Lale. She'd already seen it—from the sky. She inhaled the warm summer air tainted with the scent of damp wood and freshwater as she gathered her belongings.

The Lore Wielder

A leather bag, a book with flowers and leaves painted across the front, and her shoes. Noura had a particular habit of neglecting to wear her shoes. She slipped them on as the ship glided into the marina in Wisptale, the shouts of the sailors making her smile. They had given her a difficult time about her complexion, but she would miss them. She tugged on her sleeves and retied the handkerchief adorning her neck before her hand slid down to the locket she always wore. Her connection, not just to home but something beyond it

She'd boarded only two days ago, but since it was her first time on a ship, she really had made the best of it. Once her shoes were secure, she straightened her cream-colored skirts and reached for her bag and book. No one around her noticed, but her usually calm eyes fluttered. No, this wasn't the first time she'd been on a ship. The memories flooded back to her more real than the sun-kissed air and people shuffling around her. The storm. The terror of being the only survivor in the wreckage.

She jerked her head to clear her mind. But it *hadn't* been real. The only real story was the fear—surviving when everyone around her did not. *Fear of death is only a distraction.* She'd passed that test, but for reasons she did not yet understand, the memories were allowed to remain.

Noura stepped off the gang plank and on to the shifting docks of the marina. When she'd seen Wisptale from the sky, her heart had swelled with anticipation. Not only was it her first mission outside the Rim, but she had been drawn to an undeniably beautiful place.

Another man exiting the ship bumped her arm.

"Excuse me," she murmured, but he merely grunted as he hurried by. She smiled to herself. Of course. When fear seeps into every moment of one's life, there is no time to consider others.

She let her eyes drift around her, mostly to the other sailors and a few merchants working at the docks. She readjusted her grip on her bag and strode towards the village itself. A good portion of it was built directly on docks floating on the water. The other part, as she noted before, clung to the cliffside in many stacked buildings and staircases.

A market peeked at her from around the corner, bustling and vibrant with life. The moment she rounded the corner, wonder rose in her middle. It wasn't the smell of baked goods or fresh fruits. It wasn't even the flower cart a few arms away. It was the people. They were why she was here, the souls the very essence of the tug on her heart.

Noura bought a cardamon roll and sat down at the small table beside the shop. It was adjacent to the main pier stretching through the middle of the Misty District. Noura glanced back at the large yellow-trimmed window where she had purchased the roll. The woman working there had eyed her even more warily than the sailors, questions brimming beneath her light eyes.

Noura bit into the warm, sweet roll, settling back at the small round table tucked under the shop's awning, observing the other residences of Wisptale. The woman had remained silent. Noura almost wished she had asked about her complexion. Whatever tale the woman concocted in her head about Noura was most certainly untrue. Especially here, in a village almost entirely of the Refiner sect. They not only took the unexplainable out of their religion, but feared beauty for beauty's sake.

A group of middling girls, probably between fourteen and seventeen, passed by. Instead of dresses like the one Noura wore with a long-sleeved bodice, their skirts were divided. But most intriguing of all were the daggers woven into their braided buns. Noura rested her chin on her hand watching them. Lore-wielders came from all over the province of Avarlyn, but this was the first time she saw a group of them. The tradition was dying out in larger cities, but here, it lived on. Still a heartbeat of the culture to present their young women as competent defenders.

Noura finished her roll and stood. She could people-watch for hours, but that would not provide her a place to stay, nor would it help her open a tea shop. She paused, running her fingers over the cover of the book she carried. *Remedies for The Heart.* She knew it cover to cover of course, but it was more than a book to her. Its pages held the presence of the author himself, even though his name was not written on the cover.

She slipped it under her arm once more, inhaling. Her first mission in Wisptale was to find the home of someone she only knew of from stories. Mari. Mari had lived outside the Rim for over fifty years now and had grandchildren and great grandchildren of her own.

"Fair morning." She stopped by the flower cart. "Do you happen to know where the home of Mari and Ignolian is?"

The florist crossed his arms. His shoulders were broad, but he wasn't much taller than her, and grey streaks flecked his dark hair. "Maybe. But who are you, and why do you want to know?"

Noura reached back into her memories from the Unreal, the most common place she'd encountered untrusting people. "They are expecting me. I am family, of a sort."

"Family, aye?" The florist eyed Noura with a raised eyebrow. "You aren't anyone I've seen before."

"No," Noura started. She couldn't tell him where she was from. She glanced at the flowers, cut and resting in buckets of water in a neat row. "Will you tell me if I buy a dozen daisies?"

The florist's face slowly broadened into a smile almost as bright as the yellow shirt he wore. "Their home is at the edge of Old Town. On Pine lane. Follow this dock all the way to the land, and you can't miss it."

Noura dug in her pocket for coinlets and dropped them into the florist's hand. "Thank you!" she replied, gathering up a dozen pink daisies and taking the man's directions.

In her haste, she nearly stumbled into someone else. *Heavens*, she wasn't used to crowded places.

"I apologize," she said, glancing up at the man. He stood a head taller than her, two hands gripping a cart. Sweat leaked down his white-bearded face as he grinned at her.

"S'all right," he replied, with a dip of his head. His gray hair was pulled into a bun, and his clothes spoke of toil and adventure—and not enough washing. Noura stepped aside, eyes flickering over the wagon he pulled. Chunks of ice were tucked under a thick blanket, and a trail of water dripped down the dock behind him. The local iceman. When she looked at him again, he was still watching her. Noura brushed her hair behind her ear. She was used to people staring, but his look held something else.

"First time on this side?" he asked in a low voice.

Noura caught her breath. "If you mean Wisptale, yes."

The man's eyes crinkled in a smile before he looked away. "I won't tell anyone." He grasped the handles of the wagon, and the wheels creaked to life again.

Noura stared after him before turning to leave. Her forsaken complexion. She glanced down at the hand clutching her book. She'd never dimmed before, but now she couldn't wait for it to happen.

Mari's house would be safe from prying eyes though. It would be hard to set up a shop from scratch and gather all the supplies, but she needed a solid cover for being here. Refiners' questions could lead to dangerous places.

Noura peered at the water rippling below her as she made her way down the pier and away from the market. Dangerous places indeed. These people were far closer to what they feared than they knew, even in collaboration with it. This mission couldn't be a coincidence either. No one had been chosen to guide another soul in forty years—and what had been bound in the dark so long ago was stirring. It would escape, and when it did, Noura would be ready.

I HAD NOT BEEN OUT since I failed my Gilding. No one else knew that I even attempted it, but I felt as though the failure was stamped on my forehead. Alana smacked me with a pillow three times before I relented to show my face.

"Come on! We're going to be late."

I squinted at my sister, cinnamon curls framing her tilted green eyes. "Good. I don't want to go at all." I threw my flower-embroidered quilt back over my head.

Everyone. *Everyone* would be at Memoir Day. My stomach growled, but not even hunger pains could drag me out to face the world. Not yet anyway.

"I know you're still shaken up from the Gilding, but it was only your first try." She wrestled the blanket from me. "You can try again."

Try again? The mere thought was a threat in my mind. "Did it take you two tries? Did you nearly drown?" The rhetorical questions tasted bitter on my lips.

Alana sat down next to me on my bed, which was shoved into the corner of my small room. "No, Opi, it didn't take me two times, and I didn't almost drown." She put her hand on my arm, trying to sympathize with me. "I know it scared you and that you're disappointed, but you can't stay in this room forever. You have to face your fear one way or another. And besides, I know you'll make it next time." She lifted her hand to the blonde hair spilling over my shoulder. "Come on, let me fix your hair. You already slept through breakfast." She rose, searching for a hairbrush.

I gritted my teeth. I would have to face my failure today, tomorrow, and for the rest of my life if Alana was wrong.

Once Alana finished braiding and securing my hair, she left to finish getting ready herself. I ran my fingers over the braids. It was rare that women ever appeared in public with their hair down. Braided hair was not only a sign of discipline but of modesty. I rose from the sunken place on my bed and grabbed a clean shirt from the chest at the foot of it. After I shed my night clothes, I peered into my looking glass. It hung on the wall, and light from the window beside it cast the morning's glow at me. I blinked. Alana had piled and pinned my two blonde braids on top of my head, but my eyes were not on her work. A dark spot stained the area above my heart.

I wet my fingers and leaned closer to the looking glass, rubbing off the mark. It didn't budge. I looked down at my chest, dark purple veins spreading out of the center. Was it a bruise? I pressed my fingertips against my skin, but no pain answered my touch. I furrowed my eyebrows. It was just a bruise from the tunnel at the Gilding, surely.

I threw on a blue shirt with loose, billowly sleeves, pulling the strings up the middle tight and tying them over my collar bone. If anyone else saw the bruise, the only explanation I had was my failure.

I peered back as a spiral of smoke swirled up from our chimney. The structure, built of stone and wood, grew a thick layer of grassy turf on the roof, tucking it snugly into the hillside. Deep forests rolled into mountains behind it, and a wooden fence encircled the house. Yellow curtains rippled in the opened windows. The comforts of a solitary morning at home reached out with warm arms, but I forced myself to look away. There was no excuse for missing Memoir Day. Only grave sickness. Or death. I smirked to myself. My yemma probably hadn't missed a Memoir Day since I was born.

Clover, our work-dog, chased us as far as the edge of town. I stopped to scratch his ears before reluctantly turning to face the sloping dirt road that wound all the way to the lake. The wide grassy hilltop on my right nodded grimly at me as it disappeared, and we descended into the heart of Old Wisptale, which clung to the side of the cliff. Vibrant yellows, blues, and oranges stained the shops and homes as the town descended the bluff. We wound through the narrow passages and uneven staircases edged with windows graced with flower pots.

Long, wide docks ran from the shore all through the Misty District where the town center was, floating on the water. It always bustled, small cargo ships making anchor to sell their goods to the vendors, and it was quite a sight, balancing gracefully on the edge of the great lake, Misty Lale. The lake's namesake had melted away, and the sun was shining brilliantly off the glassy water. Even though this was a walk we were well acquainted with, it never grew old in its beauty. It didn't matter that we trod it every week.

"Seeing Ilynn will cheer you up," Alana said, descending the staircase beside me. "You know she'll ask about it."

I sighed, the weight of making my failed Gilding known beyond my family caving in on me. "I know. I'm not ready for her to know. Not just yet." I glanced at my sister and realized she was still watching me with a heavy gaze. I cleared my throat. "You're fortunate you see Ilynn almost every day now." Alana and Ilynn had just started at the local school. I would attend in two years, but for now I studied at home, dutifully milking Maiz and Mizzy, our sheep, every morning.

Alana's eyes crinkled in a smile, and she indulged my need for distraction. "Yes, but it comes with a lot of work. The courses at Wisptale Commons aren't easy. Ilynn and the others are trying to do well so they can attend Arlo's Fellowship next year." Selfishly, I hoped Alana would never leave, and the idea of her and Ilynn traveling fifty leagues for a tour of Arlo's Fellowship in two weeks set me on edge.

"You like it though, right?" I looked out again at the pier crowding with people below us. "I would be so nervous going to the Commons."

My sister shrugged. "I like learning and doing some things on my own. I like growing up."

I grimaced, glancing away and clutching my gray divided skirt in one hand. I couldn't relate. And I didn't want to. "Well, are there at least any cute boys there?" I joked.

Alana scoffed. "Just the usual rabble." She grinned before we reached the bottom step of the staircase. A wide, well-worn wharf ran parallel to the cliff with three sturdy piers jutting out into the bay beyond. Floating docks stretched between them, creating pathways over the water.

There was no going back now. I unconsciously placed a hand over my heart where the mark lay hidden beneath my shirt.

"Aya!"

We both turned at the familiar voice. It took us only a second to pick out Ilynn's long black braid and dimpled smile as she made her way towards us through the small crowd blocking the wharf. She greeted us with a kiss on the cheek.

The Lore Wielder

"Anything sailing?" Ilynn looped her arm through Alana's. Once we were on a floating dock, everything gently swayed and bobbed as we headed to the town center.

"Just the usual," my sister answered as half the traffic walked, and the other half floated by us in boats.

"And you?" Ilynn looked over her shoulder at me, where I was taking up my usual place behind them. I bit my lip, searching for a way to make sure the conversation never neared the Gilding.

"Better than you two. I heard there are no cute boys at the Commons."

"Oh and you've found one, have you?" She returned the remark with kind humor in her eyes.

"When the sun stops shining again," I laughed, joy I couldn't explain spreading through my middle. Ilynn was not my blood sister, but she might as well have been. Though the memory of her and my sister abandoning me in a field of dandelions would never fade, it was now surrounded by a thousand beautiful moments of friendship. Over the years, she had become a soft glow by which I could see the world and myself in a less harsh light.

We wound our ways through the various floating pathways that all intertwined until we reached the town center. The Memoir reading gathered a moving crowd, just like the platform it was held on. Those passing by would stop for a few minutes and listen before going on their way, and the children ran about in their own little worlds. Then there was us. We were always part of the ones sitting close by to hear the histories. Ilynn could not have been caught anywhere else. Her appa was the one reading.

The Herald opened the small, long box in front of him, his fingers grasping a flute. The tune that pierced the air was both beautiful and haunting as a hush quieted the crowd, gentle as a wave. It was the call to come and listen, the call to come and be a part of something greater than the tedium of everyday life. I breathed it in, glancing at the sky. Nevma flew high over everyone's heads, as if lifted by the music.

Another level of quietness fell over the people as the song ended and Ilynn's appa opened the book. The pages of the *Book of Memories* fluttered a moment in the breeze before he read out in a clear voice:

Memoir One

"870 years ago, Nedea brimmed with untold beauty and life. It existed for one reason—as a simple delight for its Creator. No other intelligent form knew of it, nor could lay eyes upon it. But then, the Other was broken. Another world in another time, scarred to its core. Tragedy marked its existence. A tragedy that became the beginning of our world as we know it.

A glimpse of what could be, a sanctuary, was beheld in the eyes of the Heir of all things. The potential for our world to be a place of extraordinary importance. And he planted a garden in the beautiful terrain with divine delight and tender hands—a garden full of beauty, life, and purpose. Who should enjoy the handiwork of a world meant to be only good, and safe, and lovely? The Heir looked deep into his heart and saw them. He beheld those who could not be in the Other, those too full of light for the brokenness of that world, and knew that what had been given him was meant to be a place for them to belong and to dance in their light."

"With his own blood, he created the seedlings of the Flowers of Loy. And each tiny form that the Heir brought from the Other was cradled in its red petals and sustained. The children grew and thrived in the new world. They drank sweet water from the

river and played with the Heir every day. Their joy was endless. Yet the fate of Nedea was still intertwined with the Other.

Demons from the Other were cast into the great void. In darkness they fled, in fear they searched. They searched for a new host. It was to Hesith, a naiad and the Keeper of the Sweet Water, that they came, binding his will and inhabiting his body. The Heir banished Hesith and weaved a wall of trees around his garden to protect his children, but the naiad, controlled by the demons from the Other, still whispered to them through the branches. He whispered of freedom. Freedom that lay only outside the walls.

Then came the rebellion. Merely two generations later, the children forgot who they were. Though they walked with the Heir every day, something in the Hesith's whispers convinced them. They left their sanctuary. The Sweet Waters turned bitter, and the sun ceased to shine."

Though the voice of the Herald flowed on, a melodic river through the passage, my attention was diverted when my eyes caught sight of someone. He stood a few yards away, reddish curls hanging in his eyes and his hand spinning a long paddle.

Alius's family moved to the Western Province years ago, but returned to Wisptale only last week. I had vague memories of playing with him when we were little, our yemmas chatting over butter tea.

My cheeks warmed, remembering his dimpled smile when he asked Ilynn and me if we wanted to join him and the other middlings for a game out on the water the week before. I'd lost, of course, but I could have sworn he looked remorseful after I fell into the cold water.

He caught me staring and nodded in my direction. I shifted, anticipation rising in me as I watched him and the other middling boys picking up their paddle boards.

Shouts tore my eyes from him, filling the air and turning all our heads in the direction of the commotion. Both Alana and Ilynn leapt up, Alana slipping her arm through mine.

"What is going on?" My yemma approached from behind.

"I don't know, but it doesn't look good. We should go..." Alana began to push us both in the other direction.

A group of men were coming down the dock—no, *running* down the dock after someone. I squinted my eyes to see who they were chasing. It was a young man, no more than thirty, his white tunic and long hair flying behind him. My fear stuttered into disgust as realization came over me. An Elowynnite. Now that we could see the situation, none of us moved or intervened as the group of men caught hold of him, shoving him.

"What are you doing here?" they demanded. He cowered in front of them, holding his hands in front of his face, but more angry men continued to shout.

"Return to whatever boat brought you here!"

"Aye, your kind don't belong here!"

Despite their intensity, the men were right. Elowynnites considered themselves part of our religion, but their ideas bordered on heresy. They were dangerous, and most of those who practiced their ideas left Wisptale more than a century ago. The last known Elowynnite in Wisptale was a lighthouse keeper, and he had killed himself.

Someone jumped in the middle of the mob. My eyes widened, my grip on Alana tightening. It was a woman, long brown hair stirred up by the wind and her passion.

"Leave him alone!" Her voice cut through the growls of the others. Her presence did not disperse them, but they stopped shoving the Elowynnite and turned to stare at her. Who was she? I didn't recognize her. I caught my breath and stood on my tiptoes trying to see as an angry man took a step towards the young woman. She held her ground.

"Stop this!" Keepton Thorn swept past us. "This isn't the way we handle things." He ran into the mob and scattered the red-faced men before they hurt anyone. Half the onlookers rolled their eyes at Keepton Thorn's deescalation, wanting to see justice play out. Appa and the Herald found us moments later and ushered us away, wordless.

Once the crowd dispersed and we were out of earshot, the tense silence broke with the questions building underneath the surface.

"I don't know if it was brave or just plain foolish for that man to show up here." Appa shook his head.

"Well everyone knows Wisptale is Refined. We don't put up with heretics here," Yemma added, shaking her head.

"Why would he even come?" Alana asked. Her hand gripped mine, dragging me along even though I still looked in the direction of the chaos and the fiery young woman.

"I'm not sure. Wisptale does have some ancient Elowynnite sites," the Herald added, glancing back. "He is dressed like a pilgrim though."

"A pilgrim?" Ilynn asked her appa as we continued to distance ourselves from the situation.

"Pilgrims are those who set out to try and find The Lost Garden." He answered his daughter in a matter of fact tone.

The garden planted by the Heir at the very beginning of our world.

I laughed. "Why? It's called The Lost Garden for a reason." The others chuckled and my cheeks warmed. I *had* meant to be funny, but I usually kept those comments to myself unless only Alana and Ilynn were around.

Ilynn's appa smiled in my direction. "Because they seek their own honor. Imagine the renown of someone who did find it." He paused. "But, it is a forbidden quest. If the Heir hid The Lost Garden, we shouldn't try to find it." The Herald's face grew thoughtful. "Not to mention, it's believed to be in the Southern Mountains. Not many can survive a trek through there."

"What happens if someone tries to go on the Pilgrimage?" Alana asked.

"If you, a Refiner, tried to go, you'd be deemed a heretic," Appa answered. "And locked up until you gave up the notion all together." He glanced at the Herald for confirmation, but the Herald's face was set forward.

"There are worse things out there than our wayward brothers and sisters." The Herald sighed.

"Well, I hope the Keepton packs that man's bags and sends him on his way. Aren't there Elowynnite majority villages somewhere in the Southern Mountains?" Yemma looked at Appa.

"Four. I reckon they settled there because it's closer to the Rema Soul," Appa explained.

The Rema Soul—stream of Honey. The gift from the Heir after the rebellion.

Three

THE MORNING SLIPPED BY in quietness—not of sound but of words, making the early hour easier to bear.

I gulped down a warm cup of sheep's milk, a feeling akin to being wrapped up in a cozy blanket all over again. Yet the coil of fear in my stomach did not melt. I stared at the empty cup in my hand. When I'd looked at the mark over my heart last night, it hadn't changed. This morning though, I could have sworn it was bigger. I set the cup down with a thunk on the wooden crate next to me.

The mark growing had to be my imagination. Just the manifestation of my own fears. The bruise would heal in a few days, and this uncertainty gripping me would be forgotten.

Maiz and Mizzy nuzzled me appreciatively as I stooped to carry the buckets of milk to the house. Once Clover saw me, he dashed in circles, nearly tripping me, ears flopping and tail flying. The black and white work dog was desperate to be chasing runaway sheep, but unfortunately for him, Maiz and Mizzy never ran away.

My yemma poked her head outside. "I was about to come out and see what had become of my milk!" Her cheery voice danced through the morning. Normally, I would have replied with a clever remark or quote from *The Prince's Bride*, but not this morning. My failure of the Gilding was still dampening my spirit like the fog that rolled off Misty Lale.

I removed my dew-and-hay-covered boots before daring to enter the house. Yemma ran a tidy and homey household, but one could quickly fall behind her in cleanliness and get swept out along with the dirt.

After filling a bowl of porridge and dropping a chunk of butter into my milky tea, I sat down to eat on the floor cushions surrounding our low table. The tea's rich ginger smell wafted towards me as I wrapped my hands around the warm cup. Nevma, who had decided the wet weather was not fit for flying in, perched on the rim of my cup for a moment before settling on the vase of flowers. Fortunately for Nevma, only I could see him. Otherwise, Yemma would have chased him out the window with a hand-towel. I tapped the butter, watching it melt and the oil swirl into the tea as my sister came staggering into the kitchen. She joined me, wordless, at the table. I knew better than to say anything to her in this state. Resentment crept through me. She was supposed to be up and ready for the Wisptale Commons. That's why I'd taken over the morning chores.

Fortunately for me, the chore of gathering the fertilizer was not solely my responsibility. Appa worked beside me, shovel in hand. I dug my own shovel into the pile of sheep manure and tossed it into the cart behind us.

"Thanks for doing this with me." Appa paused, leaning on the handle of his shovel. "You know, if you're too big for small jobs, you're too small for big jobs."

The Lore Wielder

"That was especially profound," I joked as I threw another shovel full of manure into the cart and found the next pile. Mornings like these made attending Wisptale Commons seem not so bad.

"I'll finish up here. You take the milk sheep to join the others in the upper field." Appa returned to his work.

"They have names you know!" I chided and put away my shovel, wandering over to stroke Mizzy while Appa took the cart to our small garden. She pressed her head against my side.

"You're a good girl, aren't you?" I looked at her blissful face as she munched on the grass.

"Do you always talk to yourself, Scout?" A voice came from behind me.

"*Forsaken Other!*" I spun around to see the last person I expected standing just over the fence, dimples and all. Alius approached the fence and leaned against it, barefoot and covered in sweat even though the sun had yet to dissipate the mist.

I suddenly became aware of my dirty clothes and messy hair. "What are you doing here?" An urge to be charming, tangled with the stranger urge to tell him all my thoughts at once, left me dazed. "You—you scared my sheep."

He laughed as if pleased with himself. "Well, Scout, I'd say I was here to see you. But that wouldn't be true," he said casually.

What should I say? I tugged at my messy braid, not knowing where to look. He was watching me, waiting for me to say something, but I avoided his gaze.

He took my silence in stride. "I'm training for the competition in the Summer Festival. I've been running up the mountain path every morning." He nodded towards the woods where the path disappeared up the hillside.

"I never noticed you before," I replied, approaching the fence, not realizing the implied accusation.

"Okay," he admitted with a smile, "maybe not every morning." He placed one foot on the bottom rung of the fence. "I do think I have a good chance at winning though."

"Really?"

He raised an eyebrow. "You doubt me?"

I shrugged. "How should I know?"

He looked away, considering my comment. "True. Maybe we should be friends. Then I could prove it to you." He unconsciously put his hand closer to mine. I immediately moved my hand away and stepped back from the fence, afraid of the curiosity growing inside me. He appeared unfazed. *Friends?*

"I don't have many friends," I found myself saying.

"Well, I guess you have one more," Alius replied. "It'll be fun."

I hesitated at my next thought but spoke it aloud anyway. "Like old times?" Something about that drew me to him. He wasn't just any middling boy.

"Sure, like old times." He studied me for a moment before his face softened to amusement. "Are you going to run away and hide behind your sister every time I try to talk to you?"

I stole a glance at him before looking away from his green eyes again. "I might."

"That's why I always called you Scout." He shook his head, a grin pulling at his lips. "It took you two seconds flat to scout out your sister if she left your side."

I blushed at his words. He really did remember me.

"Aya! Is that Alius?" Appa's voice echoed over the field.

"Aye, sir." Alius moved another step away from me.

"I heard your family is back in Wisptale."

"Yes, we moved back three weeks ago." The conversation veered towards his appa's occupation in the Western Province and what he was doing here now.

I found a wild daisy thriving just out of Mizzy's reach and picked it. When I looked up, I saw Alius glance at me before looking away again. The daisy now decapitated, I stood awkwardly, wishing one of the sheep would lean against me so I had somewhere to hide my hands. What does one do with their hands?

"Send your family our greetings," Appa said and waved as Alius turned to finish his run up the mountain. I watched him go, with a twinge of. . . something. I didn't want him to leave. Appa returned to his abandoned cart.

"I like Alius, but tell me if he comes to see you again."

"Again? He didn't come to see me," I reiterated, turning away quickly from Appa, not waiting for his reply. "Come on, girls." I followed behind the woolly sheep as they scampered in circles, Clover herding them along, ecstatic to be nipping at their hooves. Alius might not have come to see me, but he did want to be my friend. I pressed my lips together, trying not to smile. A new friend today, maybe something more tomorrow. I flinched at the thought. No, I couldn't let myself go there. I might never find my way back.

The drums beat steadily, intertwined with the sound of a lyre as I moved through the steps of the dance. Portraits hung on the walls, mostly of famous Lore-wielders, and the wooden floor creaked beneath our feet. Sunlight from the windows flashed through my vision as I spun. I no longer needed to picture myself stepping through the shapes of the triangles on the floor. The motion was innate now as I rehearsed the defensive stances. My hair was braided and wound tightly in a bun, a leather-clad dagger woven through the middle to hold it in place. My divided skirt swished around my ankles, and an overskirt, parted in the front, hid the second dagger strapped to my outer thigh. The significance of the real daggers weighed heavily as I moved, reminding me that the festival performance was only a week and a half away. So far, none of us had injured ourselves in our first lesson with real blades, but the day was not yet over.

The music crescendoed, and I jumped forward, first feigning left before spinning right and removing the dagger in one fluid motion. My braid unwound and fell over my shoulder as I landed, blade poised ready to strike, its sheath gripped in my other hand. The other girls landed beside me in perfect timing, daggers glinting in the light.

"Masterfully done!" Mistress Rendell clasped her hands together in approval as she observed us. "And no blood was spilled today!" Her slight yet strong form crossed before us and we knew to prepare for one of her speeches. "As you prepare for the festival performance, remember it is a demonstration in front of all Wisptale of your bravery and worthiness to wear your daggers. And, maybe even more importantly, it is a testimony that the skill has not and will not be lost." She held her own daggers out for us to see. White gems glistened in the pale bone handle, and a twinge of despair coursed through me. If I didn't attempt the Gilding again soon, I would lose my daggers the very same week I'd received them. And if I lost them, I'd lose my place among the Lore-wielders, which I'd fought so long to have.

"I've made preserving Lore-wielding my life." Rendell's voice continued. "And I think our ancestors, who bravely stood up in the face of the war with Da'Shinar, deserve that honor. They hung up their aprons, and some even left their homes all for the love of their families, their lives, and their country." She stopped, looking each of us in the eyes. "Bear your daggers well, my dears. It is not simply a tradition, but a heritage that is ours and ours alone as women."

I looked down at the glass blades, the weapon of the Lore-wielders for over four hundred years now. I'd thought receiving the real ones today would make me feel braver, but all it did was taunt me, reminding me of all the strong women in my heritage who I would never live up to.

I slipped the blades back into their sheaths and scoffed to myself as I crossed the floor and paused in front of one of the portraits hanging on the wall by the door. We weren't really defenders anymore. Wisptale had enjoyed safety for so long that the foundation of the art had been turned into a dance. The essence was the same, but the purpose had morphed into something merely shiny, no matter what Mistress Rendell claimed.

I tilted my head at the portrait before me. Dark hair framed a solemn face, but her bright eyes spoke of mischief beneath their surface. Winnie of the Wildedge lived four hundred years ago, but I didn't wonder if this was how she really looked. She was so revered by the Avarish people—both Refiners and Elowynnites—that I doubted her image was lost to time. What color were her gems? They must have meant something wonderful. Maybe *fierce protector*. Or *hope-bringer*.

When the tree and geodes were discovered inside the Gilding Island, a geologist had written down the meaning of each color and shape. The words became so powerful that no woman could become a Lore-wielder without first understanding what her gemstones meant. How could a defender face the darkness of battle without words of life to cling to?

I rubbed my shirt where it covered the mark on my chest. What if I failed because there were no words of life for me? I shuddered.

Eighty years ago, the magic of the Gilding had cast a girl named Lindi from the Lore-wielders through smoke and haze. We knew her as Lindi the Forsaken. I hadn't given much thought to her story until now.

I turned, looking around the room once more. The chatter and laughter from every other girl in the class cut me like my own dagger. It filled the room so sufficiently that there was no place left for me. What if Lindi and I were not so different? The thought coiled cold and heavy in my chest.

Wisptale Commons was just across the waterway, but I felt Alana and Ilynn's absence as if I were missing a limb while I waited for them just inside the door. My eyes trailed the pier before me, its wood creaking against the shifting lake below, before glancing up to the girl who stood on the other side of the doorway.

Faelle wound her fiery braid into a bun once more and secured it with her dagger. Words danced on my lips, but I swallowed them as I did every week. I didn't know Faelle. I pretended to readjust my own dagger as she left with her sister, before dropping my hand back to my side, frowning. After the festival, there would be no more Lore-wielding classes and no more chances to speak to her.

A breeze outside beckoned me to follow it down the dock, and I stepped outside, the sunlight washing me in its warmth. I closed my eyes, allowing it to suppress my despair, if only for a moment. The other girls would be taking their daggers to the jeweler's today to be studded with gems. Mine would remain empty.

I crossed my arms and chewed my cheek, unsure if I should continue walking or stay put. The market, huddled along the middle pier lined with shops and carts, was only a few minutes' walk away. I threw a glance back at Wisptale Commons. Its two-story frame rose from the corner made by one of the piers and the wharf below the bluff of Old Town. A sloping wooden-shingled roof graced the top, and two bright red doors marked the entrance.

"Excuse me," a man said, brushing past me. I stumbled, moving out of the way, and he shot me a confused look. What had I been thinking, wandering off alone? But before I could run back to hide under my sister's wing, the tingle of someone watching me crept up my neck. I caught my breath, searching for them over my shoulder. My eyes flew over her once before settling on the woman leaning against the side of a canopy-covered boat. It bobbed in the water on the edge of the market. *Noura's Shop: Tea, Spice, & More* was painted in large white letters across the side, and I gaped when I recognized her. It was the same woman who had jumped in front of the Elowynnite to save him. I swallowed, lowering my head and walking the opposite direction. Maybe she was simply daydreaming. I threw a cautious look back, but her gaze was still on me, and this time, she waved. *Forsaken Other*, what does she want?

"Hello!" Her voice tumbled in echoes over the water. I stopped retreating, coldness washing through my middle. It would be rude to ignore her. The moments slipping by were as heavy as cargo in my head. Was it too late to reply with a simple hello? I crossed one arm as I approached the floating shop.

The Lore Wielder

"You must be coming from Lore-wielding practice," she stated, motioning to the dagger in my hair. She leaned her slight frame on the side of the boat as a breeze ruffled the green scarf tied around her neck. A gold locket glinted on the bodice of her brown dress a few knuckles below the scarf.

My craving for a warm, sweet butter tea grew stronger now that I was only paces away, the smell of spices drifting by.

"Yes," I answered, removing the blade from my bun, leaving the sheath to hold my hair in place. My hands itched for something to fiddle with, and a dagger would more than suffice.

"It's quite beautiful." She nodded at the unusual glimmer of the blade. When Lore-wielding was created, all steel and bronze were taken for the main army. No metal could be found to forge weapons for the Lore-wielders.

"The glass blade is reinforced with snow-oxide," I explained, an unusual pride swelling in me. "And the handle is carved from bone." What once were scraps created something unique and beautiful.

Noura's rich brown eyes crinkled as she smiled at me. "Where I come from, I could have been a weapons master, and truly for good, but I chose a different path." Her smile softened. "But that's more than enough about me. What is your name?"

My gaze flickered back to her. "Opal," I answered before stifling a gasp. Her face, in the right light, glimmered, like faint glints of gold swam beneath her tan skin. I blinked hard.

"A pleasure to meet you, Opal. I am Noura." She studied me for a moment, and my cheeks warmed. She'd seen my reaction to her complexion. "Is there anything you would like to drink?" She prompted. Of course. She wanted to sell me something. I stepped back, pretending to look at her list of teas, knowing my pockets lay intentionally empty of coinlets.

"I—I don't know." I shifted uneasily under her gaze, glancing back at the Commons. Nevma, who had been happily darting through Noura's herbs hanging in the back of her boat, landed on my arm. His presence set me at ease, though he didn't give me an answer to her question.

Noura raised an eyebrow. "How about I make a proposition. There is a specific tea leaf combination that I have been wanting to try, and you can be my guinea pig."

I flipped my dagger, catching it by the handle again before nodding. She spooned a mixture of dried herbs and powders into a cup, and poured piping hot water over it to steep. Noura returned to the edge of the boat. "Now, be honest when you try it. Sometimes my ideas need tweaking before they are right."

Nevma alighted on my shoulder, and my muscles relaxed. I might still be out of my depth, trying to talk to a stranger, but at least I wasn't alone. When the tea was ready, Noura strained it into a smaller mug and handed it to me.

"Thank you," I finally remembered to say and blew gently on the hot liquid, a sweet and citrusy scent rising.

"I've never seen a Lore-wielding performance. I assume you will be graduating at the festival?"

"Aye. I just need to earn my gemstones first." I took a scalding sip of tea.

"It's the Gilding, isn't it? It's spoken of in rather hushed tones here," she relayed, placing her elbows on the railing of her boat with a curious half-smile lighting her face. The Gilding island had appeared when the first Lore-wielders stepped into their role of defending the Avarish Province from Da'Shinar, the land across the lake.

The Lore Wielder

I nursed a burnt tongue, brow furrowed. "We keep the location hidden."

"Because—" Noura contemplated, resting her chin on her palms, "if others found the gemstones, the island would be stripped of its beauty, and nothing would be left of your tradition?"

"I guess. Something like that," I answered, grimacing at the thought.

Noura smiled. "Concealing beauty for preservation. I like it. Now," she paused, "how is your tea?"

I looked down at my nearly empty mug, relieved by her question. "It was very good." When I raised my eyes, she was still looking at me, but it no longer made me uncomfortable. Something unnaturally kind bloomed behind her eyes. "Thank you."

Noura took my empty cup back with a silent nod. Part of me wanted to stay, but my search for words was to no avail.

"Well," I said, looking down at the dagger still in my hand, "my sister is probably looking for me." I turned to leave, flipping the blade in my hand but missed the handle. The sharp edge came down on my palm, and I caught my breath as a line of red appeared along with a throb of pain; the dagger clattered to the ground, blood dripping down my fingers.

"Wait—I can help you." She began to rummage around in her boat. Heat drained from my face as my gaze went from Noura to my hand and back again. I knew what was coming. Darkness crept across my vision.

"I think... I think I'm fainting," I managed to get out as I stumbled towards a post on the dock to steady myself. Blood. Why did I always faint at blood? Vaguely, I sensed Noura directing me to sit on the ground. Liquid splashed onto my hand, and then the cloth pressed on my wound. My consciousness edged back in along with pain. I winced at the pressure, but Noura did not react. She was calm but determined. It took me a few moments to realize she was talking to me. My ears rang.

"...there, and can you hold this, and put pressure on it? Then I can find a salve to protect from infection and help with any pain." She continued, and I realized she was probably only speaking to encourage me to stay awake. She lifted the reddened cloth. "Not deep enough for stitches—just needs a nice bandage."

"I'm so sorry," I said, my embarrassment rising. When I finally looked up, I noticed a few people had stopped and were watching. All the color returned to my face and then some.

"Don't bother your head about it, love. I'm glad it happened here so I could help." After a minute, she removed the cloth and, taking a thin wooden spoon, spread a thick layer of green salve over the cut. Cool relief trickled through my palm. "How is that?"

"Better," I croaked.

"Good. And your color is back. I'll just wrap it up here." She put a clean white strip of cloth over my hand and tied it. "And here is some salve to take with you. Change it twice a day."

Still in a fog, I accepted her gifts and warily tested my balance. "Thank you, I don't... know what to say."

"It's all right to not know what to say. Just come back and see me." Noura clasped my good hand in hers.

Two things were running through my head as I crossed the waterway back towards Wisptale Commons. One was how humiliating the incident had been, and the other was that I felt almost no pain in my hand. I wiggled my fingers.

Whatever was in the salve was working. If only there were a salve to make people forget it ever happened.

I frowned, knowing I had to explain my bandage to Alana and Ilynn. And Appa and Yemma. It wasn't the anticipated joking I dreaded, but the confirmation in their eyes. I was not like them, and it wasn't just in my head. Carefully, I wove the dagger back into my hair.

"What happened to you?" Alana asked as soon as she laid eyes on me. She walked towards me trying to mask some of her concern.

"Where were you?" Ilynn added. "Are you all right? We were waiting for you."

My sister took the salve and bandages from me and put them in her bag.

I folded my arms, not meeting their eyes. "I was talking to the lady at the new tea shop," I answered, "and I managed to cut myself the first day using real daggers." I gave them a sheepish look, hoping to win their sympathy instead of their condemnation.

"You went by yourself?" both of them exclaimed at once, and I let a small smile cross my face. At least they were focusing on that and not my hand.

"You actually spoke to her? *Actual words?*" my sister reiterated.

My smile vanished as I glowered at them. "Aye, and if you keep making a big deal about it, I may never do it again."

"Sorry. We're just trying to get over the shock!" Ilynn grinned, linking arms with Alana and me as we stepped off the dock into Old Town and headed for home. Ilynn was spending the day with us, and the thought revived the smile on my face.

As soon as we greeted Yemma and Appa and deposited our things in the house, we raced outside, stumbling down the path towards the chatter of the river. Vines taunting to entangle us draped the trees along the bank.

I waded barefoot into the cool water as Alana and Ilynn pushed the rowboat into the creek. The leafy ceiling made no accommodation for the sun; only rays of light here and there forced their way through. Our stream, a tributary of Snow Cap Creek, was wide and over my head in places, its water as clear as the sky. The spring it flowed from was hidden far in the mountains that overshadowed the Avarish countryside. I bent down to put my good hand in the water, the current drawing me in.

"We're headed down to the cove." The sound of Alana's voice lifted my head. The Cove. My favorite place.

"Can I come?"

"Sure. You can tag along." Alana braced the oars against the riverbed to keep the boat from floating away. I climbed in and settled myself on the bottom. She pulled the oars up, and I was caught in the current once more. The green canopy drifted by above, and I closed my eyes, letting myself go, a sense of belonging nurturing my spirit.

Nevma alighted on my sleeve, and I cracked my eyes open at him.

I told you things would change.

Aye, you were right. As always. I answered, watching his wings flicker. I had found my place of belonging right here between my sister and Ilynn.

Now it's your turn to open your eyes. Nevma reiterated what he'd said to me long ago.

I glowered at him. *That's not funny.* Nevma was talking about Alana and Ilynn abandoning me in the field of dandelions. *Who do I need to open my eyes to see?* He didn't reply but zipped into the air above us.

I slipped my hand out of my pocket, stretching my fingers again, testing my injured hand. All traces of pain were gone. I hesitated before unwinding the bandage and dipping my hand into the water, washing away the dried blood and salve. There was nothing left of the cut except a pink scar running across my palm. I touched it, feeling no sensation beyond my own fingertips.

I sat up, rocking the boat. "Look!" Alana and Ilynn gasped, grabbing onto the sides until it leveled out again, but I ignored them. "Look at my hand!"

"What is it?" Alana asked, taking my hand and studying it for a moment. "It's impressive that it healed so quickly."

"You don't even need a bandage anymore," Ilynn added. "What did she put on it?"

"I don't know." I shrugged. Ilynn paused thoughtfully, still facing us as we drifted into Snow Cap Creek. I could see it widening and rushing in a thousand ripples into the cove. "I've heard of herbs working to heal, but that's really unusual. How deep was the cut?"

"She said it didn't need stitches," I answered.

"I don't know, Opal. Did you ask her where she came from?" Ilynn said.

"No."

"Well, be careful. Someone with talent like that is either blessed by the Heir, though I've never seen anything like it before, or—the opposite."

"What do you mean?" I asked.

"Don't you remember the Memoir? We've heard it a hundred times. This world is tainted. And people can be tainted too."

Leslie Montaño

A chill entered my middle, and I rested my hand on my chest. Tainted. What Ilynn said about Noura unsettled me, but even more so, it forced me to ask the same question about myself. What if the mark hiding beneath my chest didn't go away?

The river had cradled us in its current all the way to the cove, and now it gently let us go into the calm stillness of Misty Lale. The cove itself was not wide and had low cliffs on one side. Wisptale bobbed gently in the distance, bathed in mid-afternoon light. Far across the lake, gray clouds billowed on the horizon. They rose gloomily, a stark contrast against the summer sky, the whispers and smell of a storm beyond.

I splashed out into the water as Alana walked the length of the boat and climbed out onto the pebble-strewn shore, not wanting to dampen her shoes. The cove—my favorite place because it swirled with memories of us. Its wild beauty stayed my breath as we walked below the cliffs running along the shore, the many colorful layers a natural mosaic. An old abandoned boat was run aground, splintered against the rocks and marring the shore. Its dark doorway would have stirred hesitation in me if it wasn't for the burnt circles on the ground and paintings covering its side. They were our mark on the place. Alana and Ilynn found the boat abandoned years ago, ridding it of any demons and making it our sacred place.

Gingerly, I walked barefoot across the rocky beach, searching for hardened clay rocks. Ilynn crouched by one of the blackened circles, trying to catch wood and dry leaves on fire with her match. Alana had disappeared into the boat. Once my hands were full of dull orange, pink, and dark chunks of rock, I joined Ilynn. Sweat beaded on her face as she fed the faint orange glow with her breath. Small flames sparked through the leaves, and before long, we had a crackling fire. I removed a long, flat stone from under the boat, pressing the clay rocks into powder. Mixed with water, I could use it to add more paintings to our hideout. I always chose my rocks carefully, knowing that shiny black rocks or ones colored too brightly were dangerous. Just inhaling the crushed powder could render one sick. Alana brought out our stash of nuts for roasting over the fire.

"So." Ilynn leaned back against a boulder, dusting off her hands. "Are you ready for the performance at the Festival?"

I swallowed, knowing I could not keep that I had failed the Gilding from her any longer.

"Well, I thought I was," I replied, glancing at the scar on my hand. "I couldn't swim through the tunnel."

Alana, listening quietly, lined up a row of nuts on a long stone we'd found and placed them in the fire, the popping sound yet another voice in the conversation.

"You still have time." Ilynn straightened, tossing a bit of bark into the fire.

"That's what I told her," Alana added. "She was pretty shaken up though."

"What happened, Opi?" Ilynn slid over and sat next to me, studying my face. I blinked, refusing to allow any more tears to fall over the Gilding.

"I—I panicked in the middle. They had to drag me out by the rope. I just remember waking up in the boat with your appa," I said, the memory of water sputtering out of my lungs haunting me. Ilynn put her arm over my shoulder..

"No wonder you were shaken up, Opi!" Concern was etched into her tan face. "What are you going to do about your daggers?"

"I'm not sure."

She drew back, determination rimming her eyes. "You can't give up. Take your second chance," she encouraged, as if the choice was that simple. "How do you feel about being in front of everyone, though?" Ilynn pressed.

I ran my fingers through the grainy dirt and threw little bits into the fire. "Even if I am able to perform, I don't really want to," I said, my eyes flickering away from hers. Part of me did want to perform. I wanted to do well. But dread suppressed the tiny desire struggling to bloom inside me.

"You'll do just fine, Opi. At the Gilding and the Festival."

I forced a smile. "Well, if they take away my daggers, I won't have to worry about either one."

Ilynn's eyes narrowed at my cynicism. "Keepton Thorn will only take your daggers if you refuse to complete the Gilding. And I know that's not what you really want; it's just an easy choice you're hiding behind. Opi, if you are afraid to do something, there's a good chance it's exactly what you need to do. And you've grown and changed so much over the last few years. That's all people will see when you graduate," Ilynn said with a graceful tone of finality. My spirits warmed for a moment, admiring her audacity to challenge my spiraling thoughts.

I hugged my knees to my chest as my gaze settled on the popping fire again. I was older, but was I stronger? In many ways, I felt weaker. More lost. Once, there was freedom in the commonality of childhood. Friendship was simple. Something changed—I wasn't sure what—but I was becoming someone who did not fit in any friend circle, except the small one in front of me. And even then, I wondered if I only belonged out of sympathy. Proximity.

The shadows inside the boat met me as I slipped into the hold through a crack in the hull. Inside, it was small and not much bigger than our shed. I ran my hand along the ground until I reached the handle of a basket and lifted it from its hiding place. The tattered basket was old, but it made for a good place to store my paintbrushes and a little glass jar. When I first found it, we didn't realize what it was until it was brought into the light. It wasn't just an old forgotten basket. It was a binding basket—an Avarish wedding tradition where the bride and groom weave together the last section to signify how their lives become intertwined.

Once I ducked outside again, I dipped my brush in the dark paint I had crushed and mixed from the rocks and brought it thoughtfully to the weathered side of the boat. Large dark clouds swirled across it, brought to life with each stroke. I painted what I saw. Blue sky, birds, and new flowers springing up from where the foreboding rain fell in my imagination. An interdependence. A purpose for the storm.

Alana and Ilynn's laughter echoed off the water. They had taken the boat out onto the lake, floating a hundred arms away. I tore my gaze from them, returning it to the painting before me as a sigh escaped my lips.

The air thickened as the storm grew nearer. Nevma took off down the shoreline, and I set my paintbrush down to follow him.

Where are you going? Maybe the weather would hold off for a little while longer. I knew every knuckle of this cove, but as I walked alone over the broken pebbles below the cliffs, something different caught my eye. Something new. Vibrant vines the color of life itself were growing on the cliffs. I glanced back, keeping my eye on the clouds. I was about fifty arms from the boat. Alana and Ilynn were already paddling back to shore.

What caused me to linger, more than the new foliage, was the glow. The vines crept into the water, and once submerged, they let off a soft leafy light. Nevma hovered over it. Slowly, I waded into the water. My feet lost the ground in mere moments as the sand tumbled away into the deep water below the cliffs. I swam towards the glow, placing my hand over the water and wondering at the light bouncing off my skin. Nevma alighted on my hand before diving in. I inhaled and plunged after him. The glow went all the way down to the lake bottom, revealing what lay there. Tucked away nearly hidden in the sand were two little clam shells, a rarity in this part of the lake.

Lungs burning, I resurfaced into a soft pattering of rain. The gray clouds overwhelmed the sky now. I ought to leave, but desire flitted through my mind as I watched Nevma skim across the water. What if they held pearls? Pearl Cove was leagues from here, and I always admired the harvest brought to be sold in the market. I propelled myself down to the sandy bottom, the water pressure punishing my body as I grabbed hold of the clams and came back up into the storm.

Alana and Ilynn had grounded the boat and were pulling it onto the shore as the wind whipped around them. I glanced back at the vines from the shore once more before catching sight of the lighthouse in the distance, faded behind the light layer of rain. It had been empty as long as I could remember, and the tales of its last keeper swirled in my mind. Since his suspected suicide forty years ago, the rumors deemed it haunted.

I stopped walking, even though the storm was gathering its breath around me. The lighthouse wasn't empty any longer. A shiver crawled over me when I saw the door at the bottom ajar and movement in the glass windows at the very top. A dark figure stirred about the massive beacon.

"Opal!" Alana yelled as the wind picked up. "What are you doing?!"

The Lore Wielder

When she approached from behind, I grabbed her arm, pulling on her shirt. "The lighthouse. There is someone inside." She followed my gaze, staring up at the craggy cliff with the lone building gracing its top.

"It's probably just the wraith that lives there," Ilynn joked from behind, and I nearly jumped.

"I doubt anyone from here would take up that job. Looks like we might have a foreigner in town," Alana mused. I ran my hand over my wet braid, my cheeks warming. Wisptale was not a place many foreigners came to, especially to stay. Whoever it was in the lighthouse either had no idea of its history or had a specific reason for coming to Wisptale.

Four

NOURA TRIED TO LAY LOW since throwing herself between the townsfolk and the Elowynnite. It was enough that she was a foreigner. She didn't need to press her fate with these people, but the incident still made her smile. She shifted her bare feet on the deck of the boat. Everyone had been so thoroughly shocked by her actions, actions that had been ingrained in her from her first breath—*to love is the fiercest weapon and fear of death, only a distraction.*

Childhood had ingrained it in her, and the Unreal had proven it immoveable.

She'd already cheated death in a way, and pain was temporary. As a healer, she knew it was real, but it shrank before the eternality of love and sacrifice. Some might even mistake her as immortal. She studied her hands that no longer glowed. Before coming to Wisptale, she had never dimmed, but it was proof of her mortality and a relief to finally appear normal.

The Lore Wielder

Noura breathed in the heavily spiced air around her and watched steam waft from the kettle she kept perpetually warming. Yes, she was mortal and glad of it. It meant a time existed when brokenness would finally lose its grip on her life.

"Excuse me." A voice Noura had been expecting for days drew her from the playground of her mind. She found the green eyes of the speaker and whispered a silent prayer before replying.

"Fair morning. How can I help you?" Noura studied the long red hair and freckled faces of the girls. They must be sisters with hair like that. The one Noura had been waiting for tilted her head, taking in all the spices and jars of tea leaves.

"I'll have lavender orange and—" She turned towards her sister who was a step behind her. "Have you decided yet?" Her sister nodded before murmuring a reply. Noura reached for the jar of dried lavender but continued to observe them both. The girl answered a moment later. "My sister will have the same."

The girl deposited coinlets on the counter as Noura set their cups down.

"You two haven't come by before," Noura commented, drying her hands on the cloth wrapped around her flowy skirt.

"No, this is the first time," the girl answered, handing one of the cups to her sister before taking her own.

"What are your names? I like to remember my customers." Noura rested her elbows on the side of her boat. This was her favorite moment. Finally putting the name to the soul who'd drawn her here.

"I'm Faelle and this is—"

"Klarene," her sister answered, giving Faelle a glance. Noura held back a smile of amusement at their dynamic, remembering her own brother.

"Well, it is lovely to meet you two." She nodded at them just as two other people appeared. She glanced up, noting the red hair of the woman who walked fifteen arm lengths ahead of the man. Both their faces were stony until they saw Noura and their daughters watching them. The sisters' yemma absentmindedly smoothed her hair and folded her arms, waiting for her husband to catch up. They turned to greet their parents, but not before Faelle's eyes glazed over with despair. Noura's heart ached. They were a family, but something was broken, and she couldn't put her finger on it—not yet.

Not long after Faelle and Klarene disappeared down the dock, a small brown creature popped its head out of the water next to the boat. She grinned when she saw the large round eyes and soft fur of the freshwater otter. To her amusement, it held a little bottle in its hand.

"Hello, little friend," Noura said, watching it roll onto its back, hugging the bottle to its belly. "What have you got there?"

The otter lifted its treasure towards her, so she slipped her shoes back on and stepped off the boat onto the dock. She reached down to take the bottle from its outstretched hands. A note was inside. Noura had forgotten the villages living on the coast of Misty Lale used otter mail. She uncorked the glass bottle, slid it out, and unfolded the small paper.

Look behind you

Mouth parted, she glanced over her shoulder. Who had sent this? She scanned the dock across the waterway as she rose to her feet.

"Dion!" She exclaimed, crumpling the note in her hand and dashing across the connecting dock towards the man standing in the shadow of a building. "What are you doing? Why are you here?"

Her brother grinned, holding his arms open for a hug. "For this," he answered as she hugged him back. After a moment, he spun her around into a choke-hold.

"*Dion!*" Noura shoved at his arm across her neck, but when he broke into laughter, she couldn't help but smile. She should have seen this coming.

He released her, and she spun to face him again. "But what are you doing here? I thought you were scouting at the border of Cedra."

Dion pocketed his hand, his smile faltering as he watched his younger sister. "I was. But Father needed someone here."

"But you're a Guardian."

"Yes," he replied, his dark eyes drifting to the unseen land across the lake. "I think it's worse than we thought, Noura. That's why I'm here."

Noura tilted her head, studying her brother. She hadn't seen him in a year. Part of her was irritated that he'd shown up. Did their father think she couldn't do this alone? Noura folded her arms. No. He'd chosen her for this.

"I didn't know you missed me *that* much." Noura's eyes twinkled.

Dion chuckled. "If it makes you feel better." He disarmed her comment. He nodded towards her floating tea shop. "What's this?" he lowered his voice. "Your cover? It's not that great considering you do, in fact, work with herbal remedies."

Noura rolled her eyes. "And what would you suggest? I get a job as a maid?"

Dion raised his eyebrows. "There's an idea. I did run out of clean socks six months ago."

Noura batted his arm. "Dion! That's disgusting."

He faked pain, crinkling his eyes. "Aye! I'm kidding."

"Do you want to see it?" Noura nodded towards her tea shop. "Mari, the lady I'm staying with—"

"I know who Mari is," Dion interrupted, rolling his eyes.

Noura scoffed, finishing her thought, "—she helped me find a tea-leaf supplier and paint the side."

Dion made a face as they approached the small canopy-covered boat. "You probably should have let her do all the painting," he commented, stopping on the dock in front of the boat. Noura looked away, trying not to roll her eyes. She might be annoyed that he was here, but it would make things more fun. He brought her into a real hug this time. "It's wonderful, Noura. And when I get my new place in order, you can come stay with me."

"Really?" Noura pulled back, looking up at him. "Where are you staying?"

He grinned. "It's a surprise."

THE TOWN CENTER CLIMBED UP around us, its colorful buildings like pastel gems. *Rosin's Rum Cakes. Wisptale Inn & Pub. Calian's Cloaks & More.* The sweet smell from the rum cakes floated from my right before mixing with the dense smell of the marina, barely visible between two moss-colored buildings on my left. I crinkled my nose as the breeze swept some of it away. Alana and I had just taken our seats on the benches before the small stage. Ilynn hugged us from behind before squeezing in to sit between us. Alius sat two rows behind me, but I didn't dare glance back. I bit my lip, still dazed that he wanted to be my friend. He would talk to me today, wouldn't he? I brushed the rosiness from my cheeks.

Noura leaned against the wall of Rosin's Rum cakes, one of them in her hand as she waited for the Memoir to begin. She caught my eye, and I returned her smile, thinking about what Ilynn had said about her. And my perfectly healed hand. The glow in Noura's skin was completely gone now as if it had never been, but I knew it hadn't been my imagination. What *was* she?

The melodic sound of the flute began as the people settled in for the next chronicle.

Memoir Two

Our world lived in darkness and frozen terrain for more than two moon cycles. The moon was faithful to reflect its light, yet it was not enough to sustain life. The Heir mourned his lost children and the chaos of his world, and the world mourned him. The garden was no longer safe for new life, and he hid it away in the mountains. Instead of it being the people's home, it was now a lost memory.

The naiad, Hesith, told the people that the darkness and the bitter water were a small price to pay for their freedom and that the Freebirds—now hunted down by the malicious Harfares—were mere coins in exchange for the gold of sovereignty. The people reveled in their freedom, blaming the Heir for punishing them with this darkness. But not all. There were some left who regretted what they had done, and every night, when the stars were their brightest, they would look to the sky and plead for the Heir to come back.

The Lore Wielder

First, came the gray streaks in the sky. Then a river. A river of sweet water tumbling down the mountain. And finally, the Heir himself. He came back for his own.

Hesith tried to rally his rebels, a dark mark marring each one, but this time, his lies died before they had a chance to be heard. The Heir, in all his glory and strength, bound him to the bottom of a lake where the whispers of the demons could no longer be heard. But a warning remained from the Heir. Though the sun returned, though the Naiad was bound, darkness had marred this world too. Our world. He commanded us to share the Sweet Water before he returned to The Lost Garden. There were still new children to be brought from the Other everyday.

Even though he left, something akin to his spirit infused the world, from the flowers in the field to the creatures that scurried through the forest. A love, his love, would never cease to permeate the world around us as long as there was faith to see it.

The crowd who had gathered to hear the memoir began to stir, but I was still lost in the pages of the *Book of Memories*. It had taken some discernment, but the scholars eventually discovered why the sun ceased to shine for two moon cycles. The land had originally been somewhere nearer the equator, but when the world was without its Heir, it changed its rotation so that the land was at the very top, tilted away from the sun. Somehow, the very core of the planet knew its Heir and could not be set right until he returned.

"Hey, Opi." Alana leaned closer to me. "I read that it was this lake, our lake, that Hesith was bound in. The naiad could be under us *right now.*"

A chill trickled down my spine as I gaped at her.

"It's true. I read it in a book at the Commons," Ilynn added, but there was a sparkle in her eyes.

"Stop it! You're making it up." I huffed, jumping to my feet and eyeing the waterway only a few arms away. The lake that imprisoned the Naiad remained unknown. Yet even if they were messing with me, the possibility still lingered. Both my sister and Ilynn bit back their smiles. I squinted my eyes, annoyance prickling me. But I couldn't be truly upset. Not at them.

Though the thought of the possessed naiad kept me awake some nights, the Harfares haunted my dreams. The corrupted creatures still tainted our skies with their razor sharp talons and thirst for blood. It was they who caused so many birds to go extinct, and while a sighting was rare, it held a bad omen. Seeing a Harfare meant death whispered behind the next corner.

After we returned home from the memoir, I retreated to my room. Alius hadn't so much as acknowledged my existence. I sighed, biting my cheek. What if his idea of being a friend was different from mine?

I paused before the two shapes on my desk. The clam shells. I'd forgotten about them.

Open them. Nevma prompted.

"Should I?" I answered Nevma in a low voice. Part of me was afraid of being disappointed. For some reason, I needed to find something inside. The vines were so strange and their glow so warm. They led me to the clams, didn't they? I worked to pry one open. It fought me only a moment before the shell gave way, and there, tucked away barely visible in the clam's flesh, were three glistening pearls. I threw a glance at Nevma.

"You knew all along, didn't you?"

Maybe.

The Lore Wielder

I set to work on the pearls in the quiet corner in my room. It took a little while to work them out of the clam muscle, but when they did finally squeeze out, I stared at them with wonder. They were smooth and shiny, the color of a raindrop resting on a leaf. I cracked open the other clam shell, and found the same.

Carefully, I strung each on a string along with shells I'd found to make a bracelet. It wasn't much, but I wanted to wear them. I wanted them near, maybe because Nevma helped me find them.

Appa knocked on my door frame. "Opal?"
"Aye?" I answered, squinting my eyes in concentration as I clasped the bracelet on my wrist.

"Maiz and Mizzy need to be taken to the upper fields. What are you working on?"

I rose from my chair and approached the door. "I was just making this," I said, holding out my wrist. "I found two clams at the cove the other day."

"So far from Pearl Cove? I bet that's a story."

"Aye," I mused, "it is."

"Well you did a good job. Maybe I'll quit working at the wheel shop and you can sell jewelry."

"Who will take care of the sheep, then?" I asked, brushing past him.

"Good point. We could make them into mutton chops instead of using their milk and butter."

"Appa!" I cried, holding back a smile. He knew how much I loved our sheep, but I still wasn't convinced he wouldn't serve them for dinner one day.

Clover nipped at Maiz and Mizzy's hooves whenever they paused to nibble at a fresh patch of grass, and Nevma buzzed high over my head. The upper field was a ten-minute walk from our home, and I breathed in the summer air, admiring the mountains rising before me. In their grandeur, I was small. Wisptale was small. The mountains and trees reached out to me with their untouchable, steady beauty. Even the *Gilding* was small.

I opened the gate and let Clover chase the two milk sheep through. Up here, away from everything, my failure diminished. I could just be. The light glinted off the pearls on my wrist, and I ran my fingers over them again. Maybe there was still beauty around me, I'd just forgotten to open my eyes.

A soft breeze hummed through the field around me, familiar words beckoning me to some other home replaying in my head. *An echo of all the beauty ever known—its melody guides you home.* Maybe it was an old Avarish lullaby. I sighed as the melody drifted away from me before losing itself in the trees creeping up the hillside.

Nevma flitted through the air. **Did you hear it?**

"What? The song?"

The invitation.

Invitation? *To what?* "I'm already home, Nevma," I answered, squinting at him as he darted about in the sunshine. *Could he be a part of the Heir's spirit infusing our world?*

Taking one last look at our turf house and Misty Lale sparkling beyond, I sat down in the tall grass. Clover jumped into my lap, licking my face. I grimaced, about to shove him away before he curled up into a ball beside me. I scratched behind his ear. Trees rimmed the grassy hillside, a dirt path winding near the edge of our land and disappearing into the woods. Daisies and dandelions bloomed all around me, and Nevma landed on one nearby. Following a childish impulse, I wove a few of the dandelions into my braid. I'd never forgotten what Nevma said about the flowers, even though I didn't understand it. *You are my dandelion, more precious than you'll ever know.*

Clover's ears twitched.

"What is it, boy?" I asked, burying a hand in the long fur on his back. In response, he barked in the direction of the path and leapt up. I squinted. The shadow of someone moved along the path. My grip on Clover tightened. We lived on the outskirts of Wisptale, and not many people walked through here.

When the figure waved, I rose to my feet. Clover paced in front of me, and I had to blink twice before I recognized Alius. I sighed with relief but grimaced at the cold flutter in my middle. I'd wanted it to be him, I realized with a small shock.

"Aya, Scout!" He slowed to a walk. The sheep watched him with wary eyes, and Maiz let out a pathetic bleat.

"Aya," I replied, first fiddling with my bracelet and then clasping my hands behind my back. He rested his hands on his knees taking in a few long breaths. He was training again.

"You spend an awful lot of time with sheep." Alius glanced up, grinning.

What could I say to that?

He rose and folded his arms. "You're just about as chatty as they are too," he joked.

I tucked a loose strand of hair behind my ear. "Sorry," I answered, still floundering for words. "Their company is better than most."

Alius laughed, and I found myself smiling too. I unclasped my hands and stooped to pick a daisy. He watched me for a moment, one red curl dangling in his eyes.

"What about mine?" he glanced at me.

"Your what?" I asked, bending down to pat Clover.

"My company," Alius scoffed, looking away.

I hesitated. A smile still pulled at his lips, his eyes hiding a twinkle. "Well, I suppose you're still under trial. I haven't decided yet," I answered.

"I didn't realize being your friend included a trial," he replied, shaking his head.

"I—"

"It's okay," he interrupted, leaning down to stroke Clover who'd wandered over to him. "The truth is, I like a challenge."

"What do you mean?"

"You," he replied, shifting his weight to one leg and pocketing his hand.

I furrowed my eyebrows.

"I can be friends with almost anyone, Opal. But when I think about you, I'm not so sure."

Was he questioning our friendship already? What had I done wrong? "Why?" I asked, crumpling the flower in my hand.

"I don't think you've let anyone in, other than your sister. And maybe Ilynn." He said all this lightly, but he was echoing some of my deepest thoughts. "That's the challenge. Am I friends with the *real* Opal?" He met my gaze, and color warmed my cheeks. I wasn't sure if I should feel embarrassed or happy he still wanted to be my friend. Even in his seriousness, a playful shadow danced in his eyes. How did he do that?

I opened my mouth to reply, but nothing came out.

Alius nudged my arm with his. "No worries, Scout." We both peered at the water glinting far away for a moment. "You'll officially be a Lore-wielder soon," he added, glancing at me.

I froze, words hovering on my lips. I wanted to tell him everything, from my failure to the mark on my skin. I rubbed the neckline of my shirt. "I suppose."

"You suppose?" He raised an eyebrow.

"You know me—" I forced a smile, flying through a myriad of diversions in my head. "I'd rather drink day-old mead than be on a stage."

To my surprise, Alius laughed at my comment, and I almost joined in, a small bubble of joy usurping the butterflies in my stomach.

An amused expression crossed his face as he watched me. "I feel honored."

"Why?" I wondered, twirling the end of my braid around my finger.

"I've only seen you laugh around your sister," he explained. My blink faltered as I searched for what to say or where to look, but when I did finally meet his gaze, the butterflies relented. He was just a boy who wanted to be my friend. For the first time, maybe I could have a friend. Friendship that was all my own.

"What's this?" he asked, picking one of the dandelions out of my hair. "Are weeds the new fashion now?" He gave me a half-dimpled smirk.

"No," I answered. All the butterflies I'd thought had left flooded back, and I took a step away from him. He didn't mean anything by his comment, but it still felt like I'd been struck in the stomach.

Clover's bark made us both jump as he dashed towards the path, scattering the sheep.

"Clover!" I started after him, glad of the interruption. "Stop that!" What was he barking at this time?

"Aya, Opal!" Alius yelled after me. I spun around. He ran a hand through his hair, his eyes darting between the woods and me. "I'll see you later. Don't lose any of the sheep."

What? He was leaving so soon? I nodded and waved back even as the disappointment washed through me.

He jogged backwards. "Say hi next Memoir day—" but his words were interrupted by a muffled howl. He stumbled into a nearby tree and tumbled to the ground with a groan. He scrambled to his feet again before muttering, "Blasted tree—" and peering back to see if I was watching.

I covered my face with my hand, trying not to laugh. "Are you okay?" I called back.

"It's not funny, Opal!" Alius shook his head and gave me one last grin before disappearing into the woods.

When I looked up, Noura was walking towards me, a basket brimming with foraged plants over her arm. She waved as her purple skirt rippled in the breeze, a smile breaking across her face. I threw one last look over my shoulder where Alius had vanished into the trees and tucked an escaped strand of hair behind my ear.

"Fair afternoon, Opal!" Noura's voice drew my gaze back to her, and I hugged my arms around myself. "Do you live near here?"

"Aye," I answered, pointing. The grassy roof of our home was just visible through the trees.

Noura breathed in, closing her eyes, her long dark hair falling around her shoulders. "It's beautiful." She set her basket down and knelt in the long grass. I shifted uncomfortably before sitting next to her on the ground. Noura tucked her legs under herself, running her fingers over the dandelion before her. "Have you ever been foraging?"

"No—not for anything important, at least." I answered. She continued to study me before blinking and turning away. "There's nothing quite like it. You never know what you might find."

The way she relaxed, letting the sun warm her face, set me at ease. She didn't want anything from me. She didn't expect anything from me. The silence drifted kindly between us.

The Lore Wielder

I pulled the dandelions from my braid and rolled one of the stems between my fingers. "Can I ask you something?"

"You can ask me anything." Noura's eyes smiled, pushing back on my fear.

"The other day, at the Memoir reading—" I paused, averting my eyes to the sheep who munched happily on the fresh grass a few arms away. "You... you tried to help the Elowynnite. Why? Weren't you scared?"

Noura shifted her legs to the side, absorbing my questions. "I helped him because I saw someone who needed help. It doesn't matter to me if someone is an Elowynnite or a Refiner." She searched my eyes. "And no, I wasn't scared. Not nearly as scared as the men who were shouting."

"I don't think they were scared." I almost laughed at the idea.

"No?" Noura raised her eyebrows, but her face invited me to finish my thought.

"No, they were upset. Angry. Those types of people don't live here anymore." I was surprised at my own assertion and how easily it spilled out of me.

"People fear what they don't understand," Noura began slowly, "and they bury their fear under hatred."

Hatred? The word felt wrong. We didn't hate people.

"My yemma said the Elowynnites have their own villages. So they don't have a reason to come here," I added as I harvested seeds from a head of grass.

"In the Southern Mountains, yes. I've been through them. They are beautiful. Full of old traditions and religious sites. Did you know they have a Pilgrimage?"

I wrinkled my nose. "The one to The Lost Garden?"

"Yes. I think it's a beautiful idea."

"It's forbidden here," I replied, remembering what my Appa said.

Noura raised her eyebrows. "Forbidden?"

I expected her to say more, but she looked away. Afraid I'd offended her, I asked, "Have you seen the Rema Soul?" It flowed right through the Madrielle itself, a magnificent waterfall rushing like a thousand jewels into Misty Lale. I'd heard stories and seen paintings, but never witnessed it in person.

"I have. And I've tasted its water, and I must say, the water from Snow Cap Creek is a good deal sweeter—to me at least," Noura said.

"That's a shame." I wanted to ask why the water wasn't sweet anymore, but the question felt too big. I blinked away the question tainted with doubt.

"It is a shame." Her gaze lifted to the snow-covered mountain above us. Mount Nea. Its peak lay behind leagues of low mountains and forests, a dagger of white against the summer sky. The sunrises that spilled over its summit every morning were unmatched. I shifted, hugging my knees.

"What's that?" Noura noticed the light glinting off the pearls on my bracelet. "May I?"

"Sure." I held my wrist out so she could look at the shimmering pearls and the shells.

She brushed the pearls gently with her fingers. "They're beautiful."

"Thank you. Nev—I mean, I found them." No one else could see Nevma. My cheeks warmed.

"There is something distinctly you about pearls. Their softness. Their shine. Do you know what the colors mean?" Noura asked, but I shook my head. I didn't know pearls could have a meaning. "Maybe you should find out." Her eyes glinted, and I wondered if she knew herself.

"Do you know what they mean?"

The Lore Wielder

"Sort of. I read about pearls and their colors somewhere, but I can't remember exactly what their meanings are. And I don't want to be mistaken. Besides, learning for yourself is a journey all its own." The silence between us returned, soft and gentle, like a mountain gale dancing through the wildflowers. I stole a glance at her face, dark lashes rimming her eyes and high cheek bones brushed with pink. She couldn't be more than ten years my elder. In some ways, she reminded me of my sister. When Noura looked up at me, the feeling only grew stronger.

As I undressed for bed that evening, I paused. For days, I'd avoided looking at the mark on my chest, hoping that it would simply disappear. *Please, please be gone,* I pleaded, turning to face the mirror with shaking hands.

My vision faltered in the candle light. The purple mark was twice as big as it had been, its veins fingering out like vines across my chest. My heart. I sank to my bed, trembling. What was wrong with me? If it continued to grow, it would be visible on my neck within a week or two. I threw on my night shirt, holding the collar closed and shut my eyes as thoughts of Lindi the Forsaken slithered into my mind. What if this mark was part of the magic of the Gilding? I rolled my eyes beneath their lids, returning to the first day I'd seen the mark. It was mere days after I failed the Gilding. My head spun, and nausea tainted my stomach. I lay back on my bed. Lindi was ousted from the Lore-wielders nearly a century ago. I couldn't be the only one who had failed since her. She was ousted through smoke and haze. Not a mark.

I slid under my covers, even though I knew the peace of sleep was a star glimmering out of reach, and lowered my eyelids. If only I could go back to before the Gilding, before my failure. I blew out the candle beside my bed.

My eyes flew open again. I stared into the dark as a line from the Memoir echoed through my bones. *Hesith tried to rally his rebels, a dark mark marring each one.* I sucked in a breath, trembling. I pressed my palms over my eyes and rolled to the side of my bed, afraid I might throw up.

Lies grow best in the dark, Nevma's voice whispered.

I didn't open my eyes but filled the dark with my heavy breathing. This wasn't a lie. It was real. My pulse sped as I laid a hand over my chest. I could see it with my own eyes.

Nevma's scratchy legs tickled my arm as he crawled to my chest and curled up there. **But even into the dark, I will go with you.**

Five

EVERY TIME I THOUGHT ABOUT the Summer Festival, my heart sank. I was out of time.

"Are you sure you don't want to go today?" Yemma peeked into my room. I shifted to face her from my position on the bed. "It's the last rehearsal before the festival." Tomorrow marked the beginning of the festival, and I was no closer to becoming a Lore-wielder.

"I can't go to the rehearsal. I didn't do what I needed to do," I droned, not looking up. I couldn't bring myself to face the darkness of that tunnel. I couldn't fail again. It was almost better not knowing if I could do it than finding out I really wasn't capable. Yemma sat down beside me.

"Did they really say you can't dance at the festival without your gemstones?"

"That, and Keepton Thorn is going to take my daggers," I replied, frowning.

"Well, I think you should go anyway. It's your last day in the class. Won't you miss Mistress Rendell?" she asked.

My jaw tightened at the cheer in her voice. It didn't matter if she was right. She would talk about it all day until I agreed to go.

"Fine. I'll go." I relented. So far, I had put off revealing that I'd failed the Gilding to everyone but my family and Ilynn. Going today would seal my fate as soon as the other girls saw my empty daggers.

I reluctantly got dressed, slipping on my divided skirts and braiding my hair. I stepped back from the mirror. I was just missing my daggers. And my pearl bracelet. I'd left it on the windowsill... Or at least I thought I did. When I went to retrieve it, it was gone. I searched for it until Yemma's voice came down the hall saying we were going to be late. My heart sank a little more. I didn't want to leave without it. Even though I made it only a couple of days ago, I was already attached to wearing it. I sighed, opening the box where I kept my daggers.

The box lay empty. I'd misplaced my daggers as well. I shook my head; tears of anger mixed with shame trembled in the corners of my eyes. I shouldn't be surprised by any of this. Not with the strange things that were happening to me. Not with Lindi's forsaken legacy haunting my every step.

"What's going on?" Alana pushed my door open. I slammed the box shut and tossed it on my bed.

"I can't go. I don't want to go. I can't even find my daggers." I shook the braids out of my hair. "Can you tell Yemma I'm not going?"

"No," she said slowly. "I agree with her. You need to go anyway."

"Didn't you hear me? I don't. Have. My. Daggers!" My cheeks flushed with anger. Why couldn't they understand? Alana only smiled at me, holding something out to me in her hands. I resisted the urge to glance down a moment longer

The Lore Wielder

"What are you smiling about?" I demanded, giving in to my curiosity. She held two daggers, hilt out. For a moment, I thought they were mine before I saw the purple glint.

"Take mine." She pushed them into my hands.

"What?" I murmured, taken aback. Daggers were personal. "I can't."

"Just for today. They will get you through rehearsal." She put her arm around my shoulders. "You're going to be just fine." *Does she really believe that?* I wondered, afraid to let the warmth of her confidence melt the fear in my bones. I blinked away my tears. She didn't know that I was marked. Even worse, she and Ilynn would be leaving me in a week for Madrielle, a city sixty leagues away. They wouldn't be attending Arlo's Fellowship yet—it was only a ten-day tour—but it would be a taste of what life would be like without Alana. And I wasn't ready for it.

It was strange using her daggers. The look and weight were the same, but I felt even more like a fraud. I wasn't brave and beautiful, like her prophecy said. I didn't know what I was. I was the furthest thing from Winnie of the Wildedge, the first-ever Lore-Wielder. Her story of taking out a whole unit of Shinarish men was legendary. How much of it was true didn't matter. She not only belonged but was beloved. What did that feel like?

I flew through the motions numbly, grateful Mistress Rendell hadn't put sparring on the agenda. The dance was easy to step through, but fighting the other girls required focus—the right steps, posture, and balance to land a hit or kick. I spun, arching my foot high over my head, all the time wishing for rehearsal to end. And waiting, waiting for someone to notice I had Alana's daggers and not my own. But no one asked questions. Because I had no one here.

Finally, the music ended. My gaze remained on the floor as Mistress Rendell gave us a last speech, her words not even an echo in my mind. How could I stand in a room full of people and be invisible? Once class was over, I snatched the dagger out of my hair, staring at the purple gemstones. I swallowed my jealousy as I watched Faelle leave, that familiar urge to talk to her under the surface. She disappeared through the doorway without a glance back. I chewed my cheek, looking at all the middlings and Mistress Rendell one last time. This would be the last time they thought I belonged here.

In a fog of my own thoughts, I made my departure without a goodbye—not that anyone would notice. I headed straight to Wisptale Commons to wait for Alana. The hollowness in my gut rendered focusing on anything else nearly impossible. It followed me from the class all the way to the Commons like a shadow growing longer and deeper in fading light. I heard Nevma's voice in my head as he buzzed around me, but I plunged myself deeper into the shadow. This was all wrong. I was all wrong.

I was forced to dig myself out of the hollow of my thoughts by a sound. The door handle to my right rattled from the inside, and three frustrated thumps pounded on the door. I stumbled, staring at the door and then up at the Keepton's house rising high above the others. The rattling moved from the door handle to the window.

The window in the alley banged open, and a figure in white climbed out, reaching back to retrieve a pack. He locked eyes with me for half a second before throwing on his belongings and sprinting down the dock. It took me all but five seconds to recognize him as the Elowynnite from the street two weeks ago. Had he been staying with the Keepton this whole time? I blinked, remembering what Appa said. Anyone who attempted a pilgrimage to The Lost Garden could be locked up. It was forbidden.

The urge to tell Alana what I'd witnessed sent me sprinting down the street to Wisptale Commons. I stopped, panting, in front of a confused Alana standing outside of the school. I returned the confused look when I saw Yemma and Appa standing with her. Appa usually worked until dinner time at the wheel shop, and the box he was holding under his arm made me all but forget about the Elowynnite and the Keepton's house.

"Did you take care of my daggers?" Alana's confusion shifted into a smile, a smile that brought out the slyness in her eyes. She knew something. Alana was only slightly less easy to read than Yemma, who was nearly dancing with anticipation. I held the daggers up so she could see them as I crossed the last ten paces.

"How was your last day?" Yemma chimed in. A storm of emotions beat against me as I remembered what lay ahead.

"Fine. I'm glad to be done with it."

"Well, you aren't." Alana blurted out.

I blinked, startled. "What?"

"You aren't done." Appa's face was mischievous as he handed me the box from under his arm. "Open it."

Hesitantly, I took the wooden box from him. It was smooth, made of red oak and engraved. *Made Anew.*

"Made anew?" I squinted at Appa in the afternoon light.

"Turns out pearls have meaning as well," Alana said. Pearls have meaning. I remembered Noura's words as I lifted the lid from the box and stared at the two daggers wrapped in velvet that lay inside. There, in each handle where three gemstones should have been, were the pearls. My pearls. I opened my mouth, but I did not know what to say.

"I talked with the Herald. He agreed to relax the rules this time. There should be no problem allowing you to perform at the Summer Festival, as long as you complete your Gilding before the end of summer," Appa said, his eyes crinkling with a smile.

I swallowed against the lump in my throat. "Thank you." I pressed my lips together, afraid my voice would betray me if I said more. My fingers tightened around the box. What had signaled to the Gilding magic that Lindi was unworthy? Had she received a word like *made anew* that held no power? Or had she failed the Gilding? Because I had done both.

"It can just be temporary. Until you're ready to try again." My heart sank at Yemma's words.

Nevma clung to my sleeve as we walked towards home, but I wasn't looking at him. I was looking at dark wings fluttering around my head.

Moths. A strange sadness clung to me like a wet cloak in a storm. My failure threatened to banish any semblance of joy I might cling to. Nevma didn't move to attack the moths this time, as he had on the boat when I first spotted them. Instead, a warm breeze swept the black creatures away, and I heard the music once more, a wild melody drifting like honeysuckle through the trees. *A song from the beginning forever abides. An echo of all the beauty ever known.* Reluctantly, I let it melt the clouds of despair away.

NOURA CRUMPLED THE PAPER THAT had wrapped her now-eaten meat pie and tossed it on the table, settling back in her chair facing Dion. Her tea shop bobbed just out of sight, a *closed* sign hanging over the side. Normally, she ate her lunch on her boat in between customers, but Dion had requested her help today. She pressed her lips together. He'd also asked for her help a week ago, cleaning the place he'd chosen to take up residence. She grimaced, glad that they were not sweeping up cobwebs and chasing away rats today.

Dion took another bite of his second meat pie, and Noura wrinkled her nose at the sound of his chewing. She shifted, crossing her ankles and tapping her fingers on the table as a breeze ran down the dock. Crumpled brown paper and crumbs were not the only thing on the table. A board lined with figurines took up most of the space. Blades and Bows. Dion's favorite game. A sign rattled against the edge of the table. It read: *Two pints of mead if you beat me*

Noura shook her head, watching her brother. He'd been challenging anyone who walked by all morning and still had a pouch full of coinlets.

"Why are you playing games with these people again?" Noura asked.

"I told you—I'm looking for something."

"Looking for what?" Noura motioned to the empty seat beside her.

Dion set his pie down with a huff. "Do you know how much I can learn from a person in just one game of Blades and Bows?"

Noura scoffed. "You could try just talking to people."

"That's *your* job," he clarified. "I can't define how their mind works—if they're pragmatic or idealistic, if they can make hard and decisive decisions—from one conversation."

"And I can?" She asked.

"No." Dion hesitated, cornered into complimenting his sister. "You can sense people. Their souls. I might be able to find an intelligent mind, but I need more than that."

Noura only raised her eyebrows. Dion hadn't fully explained why he was here. She didn't think he knew much more than she did.

"So you're looking for *someone*, not something," she mused.

"Hopefully more than one. I can't be the only one ready when the time comes."

When the time comes. When the darkness breaks it bonds. Noura held back a shiver at the thought. She chose to venture beyond the Rim, and she would face the growing darkness, however it chose to reveal itself.

"Two pints?" Someone spoke from behind. Noura glanced back at the lanky, auburn haired boy. He scratched his head, considering the offer.

Dion grinned, setting down his meat pie. "Two pints. What can you lose?" he motioned for the boy to sit down in the chair across from him. Noura leaned back in her seat, watching them. He was as tall as she was, dark red curls brushed out of his eyes. He glanced at her watching him. His young face had a magnetic appearance, reminding her of the charismatic boy from *Star-Dancer*, an avarish fairytale, who charmed even the naiads into loving him.

Dion straightened the pieces of the game. "Have you played before?"

"Not often," the boy sat down, studying the board. It was spaced into rows of squares and triangles. The figurines consisted of different animals—a lion, a bird, a dragon. The biggest pieces rested in the middle. Mountains.

The first game ended quickly, Dion settling back in his chair with a smirk. Noura rolled her eyes.

The Lore Wielder

"Again," the middling said, rubbing his chin, still not taking his eyes off the Blades and Bows board.

Dion nodded appreciatively and glanced at Noura, but she only scratched her head. What was he doing? And what was she supposed to sense about this boy?

This time, the boy was ready, and they sat there for nearly twenty minutes, moving the pieces around. Noura was lost. She knew only the basics of the game, since it was played most often by the Guardians she knew.

The boy chewed his lip, his hand hovering over his last few pieces before making a decision. In one quick motion, he swapped his piece for Dion's and had his lion on the other side of the mountain. Dion gaped, and Noura straightened. He'd just won. This boy had actually beaten Dion.

The shock on Dion's face morphed into excitement. "You're the first person to beat me today. Where'd you learn to play like that?" Dion smacked the middling on the back, still grinning.

The boy shrugged. "From the first game. Once I understood your strategies, I knew how to make my own."

Dion cocked his head, his eyes dancing. "Usually, new players copy what they've seen other players do. You didn't."

The middling grinned, two dimples framing his smile. "Of course not. You'd see that coming."

Dion considered this, tossing the figure of the bird in one hand. Noura sat up. He'd discovered what he wanted to know about this boy, but she hadn't.

"What's your name?" Noura asked.

"Alius," he answered, giving her a one-dimpled-smirk. She opened her mouth to ask more when words flickered through her mind. *He will burn bridges to defeat armies and raze towns to rout darkness. Yet he and the Reconciler shall build them up again will by will and stone by stone.* Noura blinked, realizing

Alius was still waiting for her to respond. But she had none. Dion had been right that Noura could sense things about people, but she had never received a clear prophecy before—not here where everything was real. What role would this boy play in the coming unrest? And who was the Reconciler?

Dion set his elbows on the table, fixing his eye on Alius. "Can you win two games in a row?"

Alius's eyes narrowed, flickering back to the board in front of him. "I can."

Noura believed him. She sat motionless and for once, wordless.

Dion studied Alius, unsatisfied. He shifted, sitting back in his chair. "What about ten?"

Alius shrugged, and Dion set the pieces up again, nodding for him to go first. Noura bit her lip, holding her arms close. What if she hadn't been sent here for one reason but two? A soul quest paired with a prophecy... amid the darkness rising.

Six

THE SUN BROKE OVER THE MOUNTAINS like any other summer day, but I squinted at it, resentment rising in my chest. It was just another day for the sun, but not for me. A small, innocent part of me pushed against the resentment, but it was too meager to acknowledge. Too weak. The Summer Festival began this evening, and no matter how confident I was in Lore-wielding, knowing that I had to do it in front of the whole village without true gems exposed my weakness.

After my morning chores, I slipped a book off the shelf in the living room and wandered outside. I ran my fingers along the cracked spine of *Star-Dancer* before settling myself under a tree. I opened the cover, my eyes dancing with the anticipation of being lost in a story that was not my own.

Before I read far, a furry brown creature waddled up through the forest and sat down next to me.

I grinned at the otter, reaching out a hand to gently touch her nose. "Aya, Muna." She was our family's mail carrier and usually retreated to the river that emptied into Snow Cap Creek beyond the edge of the woods.

A glass bottle dangled around her neck on a leather strap, and I set my book down to reach for it. As soon as it was free, she shook, spraying river water all over me and my book.

"Muna!" I drawled, ducking behind my hands with a laugh. When she finished, I dropped them, smiling. I couldn't be upset with her—she was far too cute. Muna looked at me with large round eyes as if she knew this before waddling back towards the river. I uncorked the bottle and slid the letter out, curious as to who it was for. I inhaled sharply when I saw my name written in sloppy handwriting on the outside.

Scout,

Are you ready? After tonight, we will either be victors or failures. There's no turning back for either of us. At least you can take courage in the fact that you don't have to run for leagues and rappel down a cliff. Anyway, I just wanted to wish you luck and remind you not to trip on stage!

P. S. Save me a dance

I bit my lip, rereading it once more. *Save him a dance?* Did that mean he was going to ask me? A cluster of unwanted butterflies settled in my stomach. I folded the letter and pressed it against my racing heart. As I peered around the gatherings of the forest, every color—the blue sky, the vibrant grass, even Nevma—glimmered brighter, especially the color in my cheeks. Yet the letter held me hostage. I couldn't think about dancing with Alius without the dread of the performance creeping in. I tucked the letter into my pocket and snatched up *Star-Dancer* once more, only to stare at the pages without absorbing a single word.

The Lore Wielder

Grass prickled between my toes as I circled my sister. Alana had agreed to help me practice one last time. If I could focus on what I needed to do—what I knew I could do—maybe it would work some of the dread from my body. It did not help that my sister made me wear the traditional costume either. The shirt and skirt, crafted of rows and rows of small bones and white shells, was hot and heavy. The overskirt fit over my pants around my waist, its tinkling shells a meager layer of protection against enemy blades. Its weight made every step harder, but it had its purpose. Not only would it deceive an assailant into assuming I was unable to move swiftly, but it also tricked my own body. Once the skirt was loosened, a new lightness and swiftness would rush through me.

I moved around clumsily, the familiar clang trailing me. Alana stood next to me, free of the cumbersome overskirt. She moved through the steps of the dance gracefully, and I followed. It had only been a few years since she completed her training, but it felt right to be beside her again. I missed her—I missed her being in the class with me, acting as a shield between me and the other middlings. In a flurry of thoughts, I spun the wrong way, tripping Alana. She tumbled to the ground with a thud, and I lost my balance, falling on top of her in one ungraceful heap.

"Opi!" she cried, shoving me off.

"Sorry!" I reacted, rolling off her and laughing. She gave me a look, holding back her own laughter.

"Come on, focus. I can't have you tripping any of the other girls tonight!" Alana spun, trying to land a blow, but I side stepped her and backed away, finding a new balance in my feet. That was Alana—laughing with me one minute and telling me what to do the next, chasing me away but never letting anyone else exclude me, and stealing my daggers before lending me her own.

"Girls!" Yemma's voice greeted us from the door. "Come inside. I need your help." My sister and I glanced at each other. We knew what awaited us in Yemma's kitchen. It was piled high with apples—delicious-smelling red apples. They were the first harvest of the summer.

During the festival, which went through night until morning, we heated a large iron pot over the fire. In it, we cooked apples, maple sugar, and spices. The apple syrup would then be divided out to each family to take home at the end of the celebration.

Alana and I groaned. It was tedious work cutting all the apples, but it had to be done. We were not the only family in charge of the apple syrup. The task was given to multiple families each year, but unfortunately, it was the same five yemmas who volunteered their children each time.

"We need to start; they all have to be cut an hour before sunset." Yemma instructed, handing us each a knife. I sliced into the apple.

"Well," Yemma began again, "are you ready for tonight?" She looked at me with eyes full of anticipation. I wrinkled my nose at the thought.

"She's still a little clumsy, but she'll do all right." Alana poked my side.

"Aye! Thanks for your vote of confidence," I flashed her a hurt look, but I knew, without even meeting her eyes, she believed in me.

Yemma eyed my hands. "You're dripping sticky apple juice on my counter."

I gave her a mischievous grin.

The Lore Wielder

"You know your appa and I can't wait to see you up there," Yemma continued as if I had answered her question. "If you get nervous, just look for us in the crowd."

"I don't think that will help..." I commented, stabbing the next apple.

The sensations overwhelmed my body all at once. The stuffy air in our home, the heavy, scratchy weight of my shirt and skirt, and the searing pain in my head. I closed my eyes as they watered. If Alana saw just how much she was hurting me as she tightly combed my hair back, she would only tease me.

"Sit still," my sister asserted in a distorted voice, the hair ribbon clenched between her teeth. "If you squirm, it won't be smooth."

I bit my lip, doing my best to not move. The traditional hairstyle was simple. One tight ponytail that was braided all the way down and then wound into a bun.

"Please, tell me you are done," I begged, tapping my toes on the ground. She ran her fingers through my long ponytail and began the braid. I sighed, the worst part over.

"There. Done." She held out her hand to me. "Just give me your dagger."

I picked up the freshly polished glass blade and handed it to her in its sheath. It looked beautiful—complete and sparkling ever so gently. I was the only one left incomplete as the ghost of my failed Gilding lived on. I clamped my eyes shut as she poked it through my braided bun.

"Stand up, let me see you," Alana said, and I stood as she spun me around, making sure everything was in the right place. She handed me my other dagger, and I slipped it into the sheath strapped to my thigh.

"You look beautiful!" She grinned. "I bet Alius will think so too." She winked.

I gaped. "What?" How did she know?

She rolled her eyes. "You can't keep something like that from me. Besides, you've been far too smiley lately." My face reddened despite myself. I'd wanted to tell her, but this was why I hadn't. Trying to be friends with Alius was hard enough without being teased about it.

I narrowed my eyes at her. "Appa told you, didn't he?"

"Maybe," she shrugged. "Just take this as a lesson. Older sisters know *everything*."

The evening's warmth danced with my fear as we set out for the festival. I sucked in a breath, welcoming it in with all of me as we took the well-worn path to town. I recognized it, this joy. It didn't have a name but was inexplicably tied to home—to Wisptale clothed in spring blossoms, our home drenched in the smell of apple syrup and summer rain, and to Misty Lale rolling with fog. Nevma flitted on the summer breeze ahead of me, and I knew he sensed the pure warmth too. If I could just hold on to this feeling, to this strange beauty of belonging, maybe I would be all right. No matter what had happened or what would happen, I was still Avarish and still a part of Wisptale. My home.

The sky shone, a dazzling throne on which the sun prepared to watch us dance, laugh, and rise like beacons in the night. Appa took up the rear of our tiny caravan, pulling the cart with the many apple slices piled high in buckets. Yemma walked beside it, giving him a sharp look every time the cart bounced.

"Gracious!" She threw a hand over her heart, her voice carrying to Alana and me, who were well ahead of them. "And look out for the bump too. Here, I'll walk behind so that if the buckets fall—"

The Lore Wielder

"They'll fall on you, my dear!" Appa finished her sentence with only a hint of vexation. Alana and I gave each other a look that only siblings give when they overhear their parents.

Wisptale was awakening like it only did once a year. A large courtyard, once the town center, spread out above the cliffs, blazing with torches all around. It peeked over the marina and Misty district down below and opened into a large grassy square where there was a stage and path circling it, perfect for a festival celebration. The flickering of a large fire fought with the setting sun, and four fat, juicy sheep roasted over it. The smell of crackling meat and smoke enveloped the festival grounds. I breathed it in, clinging to that evasive joy as music, sweet and familiar as the breeze, embraced us with an invitation to sing with the stars. We were here, and we were alive, intertwined with the beauty of our world.

After eating far too much, someone near the stage started a beat on the drums. The sun had set, and the fire roared a short distance away, the smell of apples and roasted lamb lingering. Cheering and whoops of excitement joined the chatter of the evening as two people appeared next to the drums with their instruments. The dancing had begun. When a middling boy whisked Alana away for a dance, I laughed. She and her dance partner weaved in and out of the others who'd gathered on the grassy dance floor. Ilynn whirled past them, and I couldn't help but smile at how much fun they were having. I picked at the grass, trying to find contentment in living through them, but my thoughts kept wandering to Alius. I hadn't seen him yet. I leaned back on my hands, refusing to search the crowd.

Just outside the festivities, a man stood silhouetted against the fading light. Beside him sat a wagon. He leaned against it, gazing at the dancing. I straightened, watching him. I knew him. The iceman didn't come often to Wisptale, but he never missed the festival. A woman approached him, and he spooned out his famous frozen berry-cream into a bowl for her. I tilted my head, curious. No one knew where he came from or even his name. It was rumored he'd lived in the wilds above Wisptale for a hundred years. When the woman left, he settled back into his place against the side of his wagon. His buckets of cream berries would be empty before twilight.

When the song was nearly over, I rose and approached the fire, its warmth and vigor reaching towards me. I tapped my foot along with the music. I didn't have to wait to be asked to dance to enjoy myself. I was here, and I was alive, and life was sweet.

"Aya, Scout," came a low voice over my shoulder. My soul nearly left my body.

"Forsake all, will you stop scaring me!" I hissed at the boy who stood behind me—the boy who had found his way into my affections without even trying. Alius's dimpled smile made me second guess that last thought.

"Dance with me." He ignored my reaction with a simple request.

This time my soul really did leave my body. I hesitated, forcing myself not to clasp my hands behind my back. When he offered me his hand, I took it, and we found a place on the outskirts of the dancing crowd.

"You aren't nervous, are you?" Alius stepped towards me. We were only half an arm away from each other when the music started.

"No," I replied, meeting his eyes. That was only half true. We moved away from each other, following the steps of the dance before coming together again.

"Good." His eyes glinted mischievously in the light. "I wouldn't want you to trip."

"What?" I reacted without thinking. Our hands met briefly near our shoulders as we switched sides. "You're the one who ran into a tree."

"Aya, that really hurt," he responded, rubbing the phantom injury on his arm.

I shrugged as I moved backwards in the dance, twirling away from him as the festival spun on around us. Maybe, in its diversion, I could be myself. The thought brought a smile to my face.

"Have you danced with anyone else?" Alius's question caught me off guard.

"I—no." My voice faltered.

"The other middlings must be intimidated." His smirk greeted me as we passed each other once more in the dance.

I gaped. If I was surprised by his question, his comment nearly made me choke. Intimidated? What was he playing at? His gaze sparkled, full of amusement.

"Aye. You look different tonight. I can't be the only one who noticed." He spun away from me, and I was glad. My only response was to blush.

As soon as the song ended, Alius bowed, then disappeared into the crowd, leaving me standing alone on the outermost edge. I reached over my shoulder to fiddle with my braid, but it was still wound in a tight bun. I searched for a familiar face. The moment was gone, and the crowd closed in around me. The butterflies in my middle retreated, unnerving me as hollowness carved its way in.

I weaved my way through the dancers towards the fire. Only once before had I danced with a boy at the Summer Festival. I still cringed at the awkward memory. Yet dancing with Alius was different. I tried not to look for him, but I found myself scanning the crowd. Where was he? Alana and Ilynn still danced, laughing and spinning with their partners. When my gaze finally found Alius, he was whispering to another girl. I recognized her as one of Ilynn's friends. Sileigh beamed before he took her hand and they disappeared into the dancing. I chewed the inside of my cheek, refusing to stare.

The flames of the fire rippled and reached towards the sky like divine fingers, etching into my vision, but I didn't look away. I never seemed to be the wanted friend. For Ilynn, I was just there, loved out of proximity. And for Alius... I wasn't sure what I was.

The noise of the festival no longer stirred anything in me. I was on the outside looking in. Again. I dared to glance up, and there, on the other side of the fire, I saw someone else. Her red hair seemed to reflect the golden light as fiercely as the flames cast its light at her. Faelle. Yet her face... There was something in it that I recognized. Sadness. Loneliness. I never noticed it before. The part of me that wanted to be her friend stirred.

Tell her she's not alone, I thought. I couldn't know why she was sad, but I knew how it felt. A cold isolation with no way out. But my feet remained firmly in their place. I couldn't.

Behind the music and feasting, I hid my fear and disappointment. It almost worked until time ended my game, and my cup of mead was drained. Alanna, breathless from dancing, dropped onto the blanket beside me. The girls were gathering near the stage for the performance. I rose reluctantly from my place on the ground.

"You're ready for this, Opi!" Alana rose with me, straightening my shirt.

The Lore Wielder

"Look for us in the crowd. We're so proud of you." Yemma cupped my face with her hand.

I breathed in, preparing to make my way to the stage along with the other girls. I was one miserable step closer to belonging.

"Four hundred years ago," Keepton Thorn's words echoed from the stage, "our beloved region of Avarlyn was under threat from our enemy, the army of Da'Shinar. The men battled on the frontlines, and instead of our women shying away in the towns and villages, those who could, made a brave commitment—to protect their homes despite being the last line of defense. The bravery of those women, who chose to follow Winnie of the Wildedge and learn the art of Lore-wielding in the months before the Battle of Wisptale, are honored here tonight. We present to you all the passing on of this glorious heritage to the next generation."

I let the other girls gather before me as I tried to calm my racing heart. *Just breathe. It will be over soon.*

"It's okay, Opi. Go on," the Herald encouraged from beside the stage. His presence, standing tall and confident nearby, should have offered me comfort, but it didn't. I returned a weak smile as I ascended the steps. *Breathe. Just breathe.* As we found our places along the stage, the drums thudded, familiar yet jarring. The moment I acknowledged the sea of people watching me, I would freeze. This was it. The beginning—no matter the trembling in my clasped hands. As the drum beat shifted, awaiting accompaniment by the lyre, I drew in a steady breath. I was on the edge of belonging.

A whirl of wings descended, moths fluttering in my face, and I stumbled back, batting at the creatures. Smoke snaked around me as I lost my footing. The girl next to me caught my arm, preventing me from falling, if only by a knuckle. I glanced up at Faelle as I set myself right once more.

"Thank you," I murmured, and she gave me a swift nod. What happened? I blinked, eyes burning. The moths vanished, but the smoke lingered, and I peered at the crowd through its haze.

The music stopped, its echoes caressing the night, empty and foreboding. I didn't have time to think before an old, cracked voice shrieked from the crowd.

"She's been ousted!" A gasp rippled through the crowd, and I nearly stumbled again. Everyone was looking at me. My eyes unfocused and faltered. What did he mean *ousted*?

Keepton Thorn was on the stage in a moment, arms outstretched. "Peace." He spoke to the crowd before peering at me. His face didn't carry alarm but curiosity. "We could not have anticipated what just happened, but I may be able to offer an explanation." He paused as everyone held their breath. "I believe Master Devn is correct. She has, indeed, been ousted by the magic of the Gilding." Another murmur swept through the crowd. Keepton Thorn grabbed my arm, pulling me until I stood next to him, the other girls backing away from me. Mistress Rendell dashed up the stairs, shielding the other girls, staring at me with wide accusatory eyes.

"We all understand the magic of the Gilding," Keepton Thorn continued, and my eyes snapped back to his bearded face as he towered over me. "It exists to weed out those who are unfit to be Lore-wielders—those who don't have a word of power spoken over their lives. Yet it hasn't been seen in eighty years, has it Devn?"

The old bent man nodded. "My great aunt was the last." He was talking about Lindi. Lindi the Forsaken.

The Keepton's grip on my arm tightened, but I hardly noticed as the pit in my stomach deepened. Unfit. I was unfit to be a Lore-wielder. My cheeks burned not only with shame but anger. Hadn't I known this all along?

"Why the old magic has chosen to awaken this night, I do not know, but the implications are clear. Opal, as of right now, is unfit to graduate as a Lore-wielder." Keepton Thorn faced me again, shadows flashing in his eyes along with the flickering light. His breath reeked of mead. "I hereby revoke your daggers before these witnesses, until you find your redemption at the Gilding tree." Keepton Thorn held out his hand. I blinked, moving as if through water as I removed the daggers from my hair and thigh. Even though the blades and handles were made to be light, they were like stone in my hands, and the glint of the pearls, a spear to my middle. I laid the two leather-clad blades in his outstretched hand, staring with blurred eyes at his chest. The edge of a wing inked on his skin peeked out from his shirt where it should have been buttoned. I blinked, the image fading from my mind as I stared back at the crowd, numb. My failure, gilded in the flickering light for all to see, stunned all of Wisptale into silence.

The Keepton nudged me towards the steps, and I all but ran off the stage, choking back a sob as the nightmare caved in on me. Unfit failure. Every desperate, lonely thought I'd fought back was true. The edge of belonging crumbled beneath my feet, and I fell, silently yet swiftly into the rocks and waves waiting below—waiting to break me apart.

I clenched my trembling hands as I approached the crowd, but there was no disappearing into it. The people parted, wide eyes and open mouths staring at me.

"Opal! Opal, where are you?" My yemma and appa's voices cut through the silence. What would they say? How could they possibly help me? I inhaled one shaky breath, tears trembling on my lower eyelid.

"Yemma, is she cursed?" A little girl a few arms away asked, tugging on her yemma's sleeve.

I swallowed as her words burned me like salt in a wound. There was no hope for me. With one last glance at the stage, I tore through the crowd, shame and dread biting at my heels. I had to get away. I couldn't bear the weight of the truth any longer.

When a familiar frame flashed in my vision, I nearly ran into it before skidding to a stop. Alius's green eyes bore into me. Another sob rose in my chest. He took three steps back, recoiling as if from a flame. I swallowed my sob, knowing I didn't have to guess what he thought of me. The half-smile that lived on his face was gone, the twinkle in his eye, muted. He opened his mouth, but I didn't wait for him to speak—to spew his words of condemnation. I ran.

The mark on my chest tingled, and I tore at my shirt, throwing off the decorative coat and shedding the overskirt. They clanked to the ground as I ran blindly into the dark. I had to hide, had to run from the shimmering lights that bared my soul for all to see.

The music I knew by heart, meant to bring us together, patronized my ears as the performance went on without me. Wisptale was rising while I was sinking. That fleeting joy, killed—crushed and ground into the dirt.

The voices of my parents, Alana, and Ilynn chased after me, but I couldn't face them. They weren't failures. They weren't *cursed*. The outline of a tree rose before me, and I grabbed onto the lower branches, swinging myself up as the darkness and leaves embraced me, hiding me. I climbed as high as I could before another sob escaped my throat. Tearing the ribbon from my bun, I let my hair fall around my shoulders and into my face, which was salty with tears. The ribbon swirled to the ground and disappeared in the darkness, just as lost as I was.

Seven

LOOK UP. NEVMA'S VOICE DRIFTED into my scourged thoughts. **Look at me.** I clenched my eyes a moment longer, buried beneath my shaking hands.

"I can't," I whispered. The heaving ache in my chest was now a sore throb.

Have you become so busy worrying about yourself that you can't *see*? Have you not learned to open your own eyes?

His words were so pointed that my hands dropped from my face, and I gaped in shock.

I know you're broken. It feels like the end of the world, but it's not. There is redemption left for you. Hope.

I sniffed, my blink faltering as I searched for Nevma. He clung to a leaf mere knuckles from my face. Tightness rose in my throat once more. Redemption. My redemption at the Gilding Tree. I shook my head, fresh tears streaking down my face. "I can't," I murmured again. "I am ousted. I'm *alone*."

Alone? Who was it that ran?

You don't understand. I screamed in my head, squeezing my temples and tearing my eyes from him. *Everyone thinks I'm cursed.*

The Lore Wielder

Are you?

I was right. I am unworthy. What happened tonight was proof.

Nevma flitted down to my shoulder, his voice softening. **Your worth rests outside of other's perceptions of you, even your own perception of yourself.**

I let my eyes linger on the small creature, not sure what to do with his words. All of life was permeated by other's perceptions. Only a fool wouldn't see that.

"Fair evening, my fellow Avarish brothers and sisters..." The Herald's voice drifted towards me. The commotion since I ran away had stopped, the whispers swirling away on an empty gale. I exhaled a shaky breath, tightening my grip on the tree branch. "Although the night has already been eventful..." He hesitated. I winced, waiting. Would my ousting be addressed? "It is with great anticipation that I usher in what we have all been waiting for—the competition."

Relief and confusion pressed me closer to the tree trunk, and I closed my eyes. My family had given up on finding me. And since I'd vanished, Wisptale still hungered for entertainment. My eyes flew open, and with one last glance at the safety of the branches hiding me, I slipped out of the tree with a soft thud. I ran my fingers through my tangled hair and crept closer to the stage, still lingering in the shadows.

"Would the contestants of the reenactment step forward, please." The Herald motioned towards the crowd. Alius went forward, and I glanced at him, an arrow piercing my heart. Dancing with him seemed ages away, not mere hours. Now that I was cast out, he would never speak to me again. I bit my cheek, forcing myself to look at the other contestants. Our friendship was over. The only two I didn't know stood at the very end of the line up. One lowered his head as if he wanted to keep a low profile. The other was slight and wore a tightly wound scarf around his head and face. Whispers spread through the crowd. Who were they?

"As you well know, the first challenge that must be completed is the felling of a tree on High Tor. This was the first trap the brave men in the Battle for Wisptale set. Any enemy soldiers who came down the path would be crushed by felled logs when they were sent rolling down the hill..."

The story was beyond familiar—a cavalry of horses sent by the Emperor of Da'Shinar creeping single file to- wards a village they thought was unaware. With the steep hillside to their left and the cliffs only a few arms to their right, the frightened horses backed away, only for their hooves to find loose rock. They plummeted into the darkness below with the logs barreling down upon them. Then came the arrows, swords, and spears from the villagers hiding in the woods. A chaos that broke two hundred men. Chaos that kept the town safe. A chaos we celebrated.

But Da'Shinar's army didn't retreat. A fleet of ships hid just around the coast, ready to attack our shores. They had captured the city of Madrielle months before coming for my ancestors nearly four hundred years ago. Madrielle was coveted as the city built around the river created by the Heir. Little did the Shinarish emperor know, the water had long ago lost its sweetness. They had sailed north-east in search of more land to conquer. Wisptale had gotten wind of the scheme, and fourteen brave men had dashed into the night to set traps where we were most vulnerable to attack. The path along the cliffs, the port, and the shore on the far side of the lake.

Another echoing clash sounded from the cymbals, and I watched the group disappear into the woods below High Tor.

The Lore Wielder

Each had a partner to man the tree saw, row the sculling boat, and roll the large stones into Snowcap Creek.

If I lingered here much longer, I'd be found. I bit my lip and folded my arms tightly, a tear winking in my eye. The mark under my shirt tingled again, and I scrubbed at it. I didn't want to watch the competition. The image of the moths and smoke suffocated me, and the voice of the girl whispering *cursed* seemed to take my final breath.

I glanced up at the people making their way down to the marina and the ferry. Each event could be watched, though not many people went to see the tree felling. Most went to see the contestants rappel down the cliff and row across the lake. By the time the ferry, full of onlookers, reached the cliffs, the contestants would be done felling their trees.

Alana was among those headed for the ferry. How long had she looked for me before giving up? *Who was it that ran?* Nevma's voice haunted me. Brushing the hair from my face, I made a decision.

Eyes damp with forgotten tears, I trailed the crowd, keeping Alana's braid in view. The path clogged with people, and the torches still blazed, banishing the subtle twinkle of the stars. Finally, I stepped onto the edge of the ferry. Alana was just ahead, and I ducked and weaved through the people until I was close enough to touch her. Before I could reach a hand out, she turned, and I realized with a shock that the girl was not Alana. My hand recoiled, and I threw myself away from her, all my hope of comfort bleeding out of me. My sister wasn't here. I was alone, this time not by choice. Shoving the sob rising in my throat away, I dashed back towards the gang plank. I was too late. The plank lifted, and the ferry cast off. I stumbled. Where was my family? Why had they left me? I staggered to a corner of the ferry, away from any prying eyes.

Not only was I cast out from the Lore-wielders, but now, I was separated from anyone who cared about me. I took a shaky breath. I was forsaken.

When the ferry arrived at the cliff, I didn't turn around. I ran my fingers along the wood railing, feeling the roughness of it as I stared into the black water below. The stars and moon winked back at me, trying to reach out and offer me their light as they reflected gently in the water. But the deep feeling in my spirit was a blackness that enveloped light, not a blackness that could be chased away by it.

Voices echoed over the water as the contestants appeared, and dark figures moved faintly atop the cliff. They anchored their ropes and threw them over the daunting edge. High Tor loomed seventy arms tall, dark and foreboding. The light from the moon highlighted the figures as they rappelled down the craggy rock face. My eyes unwillingly found Alius as he worked the ropes between his hands and navigated the perilous cliff. The only one ahead of him was a dark, brawny form. One of the unknown men.

A sharp yell pierced the night air as one of the contestants lost control and began plummeting towards the water. Quick as lightning, the strange man caught hold of the falling man's ropes. He grunted under the exertion as he gripped the rope, and the other's fall was broken with a terrible jolt. The unsettled figure swung helplessly for a few moments before finding his footing and clinging to the rocks. The thought crossed my mind that no average man could have done that. And I wasn't alone in my assessment. Whispers about the man who had saved the other falling contestant floated through the spectators.

Unsurprisingly, he was the first man to touch down, and he snagged his partner's rope to aid their descent. Alius reached the cliff's bottom second and did the same. The moment their partners touched down, they jumped into the sculling boats bobbing nearby.

The rowing course stretched to the other side of the cove, but the task was not simply to get to the other side. Two ships waited for them anchored in the harbor. It was about speed and accuracy, and the two sculling boats disappeared into the dark night in only a few moments. The others followed not far behind, but most heads turned towards the ships floating, waiting for the show. Fireworks.

Of course, the original troop had not set off fireworks. To bolster the port long ago, two of the biggest ships were sunk, creating an underwater barrier that enemy ships could not sail through. In the dead of night, the troop of men had rowed as fast as they could towards where the ships were anchored. The explosives were already in place, and they had set the ships ablaze with flaming arrows—hence the reenactment of fireworks.

The only other remaining access point to Wisptale was on the other side of the cove. The teams would race there once they hit their target.

The ferry brought up its anchor and set off at a menial pace after the sculling boats. The water, upset from the race, still drifted in circles around us like a wary invitation to follow. Some of the boats were neck and neck. Once they were a bow shot away from the ships, we could see where each pair was bobbing by the little glow of light coming from their flaming arrows. Each team could not leave until they struck the target.

I gripped the edge of the boat tighter as the first firework burst into a million sparkling lights, dazzling everyone except me. The ferry, no longer chasing the boats, rocked gently a safe distance from the ships. The fireworks were a thousand fiery jewels sparkling off the black water, but the blackness in my spirit only consumed and extinguished the light.

Nevma landed gently on my hand resting on the railing. **Light always shines. It is not defined by the perceptions of others, but functions exactly as it was made to, whether it is surrounded by darkness or day.**

"I'm not like light," I murmured to him.

"Aya, isn't that the girl who was ousted?" a voice from my side tore me from my thoughts. My knuckles paled as my grip on the railing increased. I dared a glance in their direction, my face burning. Two middling boys peered at me, one pointing an outstretched finger.

"Aye, it is," he confirmed, eyes wide. The other boy grabbed his arm, pulling him away. They stumbled into two others.

"Watch it," one of them complained.

"But it's her! The girl!"

I swallowed, my lip quivering as I stared back. What might they do to me?

"Take your curse somewhere else!" The first boy spat at me. I caught my breath. Nevma buzzed in circles around me, but they couldn't see him.

"Let her alone," the eldest middling chided, ushering the other boys away. "You're not scared of a woman's curse, are you?"

My grip on the rail didn't relax until I saw them vanish into the crowd on deck, my mouth parted in shock. This was how I would be treated now. Anytime I showed my face, whispers and accusations would haunt me. I hugged my arms around myself, returning my gaze to the water where no one could see my tears falling. Where no one could see *me*.

The Lore Wielder

If this was how living felt, I wasn't sure if I wanted to keep living.

The ferry docked once more at the marina, and I blinked in the light of the torches as I followed the cluster of people back to the old square. Alius would have reached the other side by now.

Once those faithful ships long ago were on their way to their honorable demise, the troop had set out to dam up the river, only to be released if a unit of Shinarish soldiers attempted to invade from the west and cross the empty riverbed.

The moment I reached the courtyard where the bonfire's embers glowed, Appa and Yemma stood waiting for me, faces screwed up in worry. All the pain in my chest burst when I met their eyes.

"Opal, are you okay?" Yemma threw her arms around me. All I could do was shake my head, burying my face in her shoulder.

"Where were you? We thought you ran home." Appa pulled Yemma and me into his hug. They hadn't given up. They'd run all the way home searching for me.

Yemma pulled my face back, swiping my sticky hair from my eyes. "It doesn't matter. What happened, doesn't matter."

"We shouldn't have made you go up there," Appa added, brushing my cheek. "You weren't ready."

"Do you want to go home?" Yemma asked, tucking my head into her shoulder again. Go home. An end to this infernal night. But it was half a league away.

I shook my head. "Where is Alana?"

"She and Ilynn went to search in the surrounding woods," Appa answered. My heart ached at the thought.

I rubbed my eyes, exhaustion settling in. "I just want to rest." A part of me longed to tell them about the pain inside, but something held me back. What if they thought something was wrong with me? Something *was* wrong with me, I remembered. I held the collar of my shirt closed.

I lay down on the blanket a few arms from the fire and closed my eyes. Yemma shifted to sit next to me and put my head in her lap as she stroked my hair.

"Are you okay, Opi?" she whispered. I nodded. I knew she was looking down at me and that Appa was listening. It was an invitation to let them in, but I chose to shy away from it as I kept my eyes closed.

"Wake me when they return," I murmered, turning my face away. Yemma tucked a blanket over me, and I gratefully slipped into the oblivion of sleep.

A gentle hand shook my arm. Consciousness immediately returned to my body as the sun was returning to the world. My eyes opened to a gray sky that was just beginning to bleed streaks of light, smothering the stars.

Sleepily, I sat up, rubbing my eyes. I leaned my head on Yemma's shoulder as we both looked towards the Southern Mountains.

This was where myth and history became muddled. As many men as possible were needed to be in the village, manning the archery and catapult towers. In those days, according to the story, pegasi roamed the mountains. Though they contributed to our salvation that day, their contact with humans was their ruin, and they vanished from our country many moons ago.

I blinked the blurriness from my eyes. There, so far away they appeared as mere specks, we saw the contestants returning on the air. As the specks grew, I could make out the large wings that glided on the wind.

Since Pegasi were no more, we'd invented wind-riders. Having never seen a flying horse, a wind-rider looked just as magnificent to me, with its large triangular wing stretching out to lift the rider above the gale. They approached at an alarming speed, faster than any ship could sail or boat could row, the riders strapped in a horizontal position on the contraption below the wing.

I watched as the first wind-rider flew over us and made a wide circle around the square. I squinted my eyes. It was not Alius. His confidence had only carried him so far, and it was not far enough. The unknown pair landed safely some ways off and jogged back towards the town square. When they reached it, the second team was just now making its wide circle around the square before landing. The larger man quickly brought out water and gave it to his partner before drinking any himself. The other removed the scarf from their head, and a long braid fell over their shoulder. I gaped as I recognized her.

Noura.

Eight

IN THE HUNDREDS OF YEARS since The Battle of Wisptale —not once had a woman entered the competition, much less won. It was not a written rule; it simply never happened. Noura took everything as gracefully as she always did, though I could see a gleeful smile pulling at the corners of her lips. She and her partner stood side by side before the crowd, faces glowing with their accomplishment, reveling in the people's shock. Waving, with grins splitting their faces, Noura and her companion bowed their heads as Keepton Thorn crowned them with garlands of green leaves. A pendant, engraved with a pegasus, was pinned on their cloaks before the crowd applauded them off the stage with one last sleepy cheer.

All my questions would have to wait until I saw Noura again. As Appa loaded up the cart with our blankets and other belongings, I wished I could ride in it with my sister as I used to do when I was small. Now, Alana had to be roused from sleep. She had rejoined my parents after I fell asleep and had sufficiently covered herself in her blanket.

The Lore Wielder

I reluctantly shook the Alana-shaped blanket in front of me. She let out a long and frustrated grunt before picking herself up and following behind us, still wrapped in her blanket.

"Opi." Alana's voice caught my attention from behind. What would she say to me? I hesitated before turning.

Wordless, she blinked sleepy eyes and held her blanket open for me to join her. If I welcomed her embrace, the tears would return. I tucked my loose hair behind my ear and let out the breath aching in my chest. Alana's eyes turned up in a smile, and she threw the blanket over my shoulder. I leaned my head against hers, and we walked home together.

I awoke to the smell of warm, bubbly yeast wafting through the house. Somewhere, there was a glorious loaf of bread baking. Although my body was exhausted from the night before, I cracked my eyes open. The bright sunlight pouring into my room revealed mid-afternoon. Even though sleep brought some restoration to my tired mind, gloom settled over me. It lingered like a cold hand clutching my spirit, insistent on devotion.

Nevma glimmered in the light as he darted happily around my room, light and free. He landed on my damp pillow. I was crying and had not realized it. Nevma laid his head down where the freshest tear had fallen. No, *he wasn't light—free*, but not light. For a moment, I fought the urge to keep up my walls. Could I let him see the depths of my grief? But his spirit nudged mine, and I let go a little, expecting him to speak, but he didn't. He simply continued to lie there on the pillow with me, and as I looked at him, the gloom swirled from black to gray. He was drawing it out of me like poison.

Every festival, Yemma baked fresh bread for us to enjoy, smothered with the apple syrup and spiced with the previous night's affections. I covered my face with my hands. The thought of facing my family again was ice in my bones.

You cannot run from this, beloved.

I uncovered my face, blinking slowly at Nevma. He was right. Hiding had done nothing but prolong my misery.

I slipped out of bed and crept down the hall past Alana's room. A soft snore drifted from the cracked door, and I lingered there. Facing my parents would be easier if I wasn't alone. My eyes flickered away. But I was alone.

I stretched my hand as I entered the living room. It still ached from cutting all those apples. Appa entered the back door, and my heart leapt into my throat. What would he say to me? What did he think of me now?

"Ah, one of the sleeping bears is awake!" He promptly removed his boots. His eyes smiled through his evident fatigue, melting the layer of dread clinging to me. He tucked me into a reassuring hug. "I have some news for you all!" he continued. Yemma peeked her head from the kitchen, and I exhaled, long and slow. He had news, not questions or accusations.

He settled down at our low table and crossed his legs on the floor cushion before he began. Yemma poured him a cup of tea. "I know who won the competition, and—" Appa began. He stirred a chunk of fresh butter into his tea slowly, enjoying our anticipation. "—who is running the lighthouse. They are one and the same."

"What?" I gaped at him, the kettle mid-pour over my cup.

"I was just as shocked as you. At least we know who the man is now and that he has a proper job here." Appa sipped his tea thoughtfully. "I do think it's high time there was someone running the lighthouse. All this unfounded fear about it being haunted is silly. What has a port town come to without a proper lighthouse?" The old story of the lighthouse being haunted had always scared me, to the point of keeping me awake some nights.

Forty-some years ago, the lighthouse keeper had taken in his orphaned nephew. A year later, the uncle's body was found in the water. Some were suspicious that his death had something to do with the boy, but others believed he'd fallen from the cliff. The orphan was apt at running the lighthouse, so he was allowed to stay and eventually fell in love with a girl from the town. The love was rumored to be unrequited, though, and after the girl was engaged to someone else in another town, the orphan killed himself. The legend claimed his spirit still resides in the lighthouse, trapped by his obsessive love.

"Do you know who the woman was?" I was not sure if my parents had recognized Noura and remembered she was the one who had healed my hand.

"Aye," Appa answered. "Apparently she is also a newcomer, and when they described her to me, I realized she must be your friend, Opi."

My friend. I sipped my tea even though it burned me. Did I have any friends left after last night? I traced the knot in the light wood of our table that stood a few arms away from the wide archway to the kitchen.

"She doesn't seem the type to enter a competition like that," Yemma commented from the kitchen, but I smiled, remembering how she'd protected the Elowynnite. She seemed exactly the type.

The door of the woodstove squealed as Yemma bent down to remove the bread. "I certainly have no desire to do anything of the sort. All those herbs must have gone to her head." She gave us a serious look as her curls drew up in the steam from the oven. She crossed under the archway from the kitchen to where we sat and placed the steamy golden bread on the table. Appa reached for it, but she batted his hand away.

"Not yet! It has to cool first," Yemma chided, and I bit back a smile. Maybe all my worry about facing my parents after being ousted was unfounded. A small knot clenched in my middle though. They didn't know everything. I ran my fingers along the collar of my nightgown.

The heaviness from the festival lingered on my mind over the next few days, accompanied by my strangely careless curiosity about the moths. There was something satisfying in their darkness. At least they found me and saw me in my own darkness. Nevma bristled anytime my thoughts turned towards the creatures, but I suppressed him. The first time I saw one was after I failed the Gilding. I grimaced. *Made anew.* I wasn't sure which I despised more, the idea of attempting the Gilding again or that word. *Made anew* mocked my deepest fear—that I was broken. Only broken things must be remade. I should be glad to be rid of my daggers.

I continued to skim *Poems from the Sea of the Suns* as I sat at the desk in my room, but my mind had already been churned to mush. I shut the book and tossed it on top of *Algebraic Equations, Level 2*. Alana was at Wisptale Commons today with Ilynn, and I was studying alone. But I couldn't focus. Failing my Gilding was nothing compared to this. What was left for me now that I was ousted? Now that I was marked? I bit my lip and leaned back in the chair at my desk, staring at the two books tossed there.

Yemma and Appa had done their best to assure me that what happened didn't matter, but they were my parents. They were supposed to love me no matter what.

I swiped my pen and rolled it over my knuckles. No, I had to find a way to undo this if I was to be accepted. I sealed my eyes, knowing the answer. My redemption at the Gilding Tree. Maybe the Gilding would erase the mark on my chest. As much as the idea sent spikes through every part of me, it was my only hope.

"Yemma!" I called, pulling on my boots. I hadn't seen her for an hour, and the house offered up a silent reply. There was no one home to tell where I was going. With one last shrug, I left, cutting across the pasture and into the woods. The trees danced to a dirge in the wind, welcoming me into their shadow with their mossy arms outstretched. But it didn't feel like a shadow reaching to block out light. Nevma joined me, the buzz of his wings somewhere overhead. The shadow of the tree was like a covering. I only wished I could take that covering with me. If I was going to attempt the Gilding again, I had to practice. I had to be sure I could swim through the tunnel.

Sweat beaded on my neck as I jogged through the rough path in the woods down to our boat tied up in the river. I untied it and climbed in, paddling to reach Misty Lale faster. How long did Alana say the tunnel was? Eight arms?

The river carried me swiftly to the cove, the warm summer air inviting me into the cool of the water. I dipped my hand in, feeling the ripples rolling over my skin. The coolness of the early summer lifted weeks ago, and the lake's chilly temperature had finally succumbed to the sun's rich rays. With a firm grip, I steered the boat towards the shore before the current pushed me out in the middle of the lake. I hardly noticed my arms burning as I dragged the front of the boat onto the rocky shore. The only thing I needed for this was determination. My breath left me in anticipation as I waded into the clear water. My training ground. A tree on the shore was my marker. Eight arms was all I needed. Eight arms and a strong mead to banish my nerves.

Don't forget. You are Avarish. Nevma circled above me.

I allowed myself a smile. He was right, as always. I was Avarish. I was practically born on these waters. Filling my lungs with the sweet summer air, I plunged under the water, pushing it past me, the bubbles rolling over my body in a race to reach the surface. Usually, Alana, Ilynn, and I spent hours swimming here, but this year was different. They were busy preparing for the next level of education at Arlo's Fellowship, and I was afraid. But I couldn't give up, not if this was the only way to get rid of the stain on my skin. Waiting another year to graduate would be agony, but it would be easier to bear if I could shed *made anew.*

I sought out another mark on the shore and swam back. This time, I made it just past my goal. Not enough to instill confidence, but enough to bring a smile to my face. I could do this. As long as I didn't panic in the middle.

I don't know how long I swam, but I practiced over and over again. Swimming back and forth under water until I made it past my goal every time. I was born on these waters. Surely, they would not betray me again.

It's not the water that will save you. Nevma alighted on my shoulder, but I merely shook my head at him as I waded out of the lake onto the shore.

"That's not what I meant."

Are you sure? I ignored his voice this time. I didn't need his questions right now. What needed to be accomplished today was accomplished. A breeze made the hair on my arms stand up and sent a shiver through me. I shook my wet hair out of its braid and faced the sun. I squinted at the lighthouse, fear and curiosity fighting in me. I might know who lived there now, but it didn't change the possibility of it being haunted.

A sound from behind made me spin. The cove was usually empty. My eyes flickered over the shore and edge of the woods, my pulse pounding. Movement caught my eye, and I followed a rope that snaked into the water. A moment later, a fishing trap skidded onto the shore.

Someone else was here, pulling the rope. I rung out my hair, backing towards the cliff. *Take your curse somewhere else.* The words of the middling boy from the ferry echoed in my head.

When Alius appeared from behind one of the boulders, rope in hand, I froze. Not him. Not now. I tucked myself further into the cliff, watching him approach the fishing trap and kneel down. What was he doing here? Shaking with cold and dread, I clutched at the rock face. A chunk broke off, thunking to the shore. Alius whipped around, searching for the source of the noise.

When his eyes clamped on me, he rose to his feet. I didn't move, wet clothes still clinging to my skin. He glanced away and knelt down again to check his trap. Pain welled in my throat. I had been right. Now that I was ousted, he didn't want to even speak to me. I let out a slow, shaky breath before crossing my arms and heading for my boat.

With a grimace, I shoved it into the water and climbed in, clutching the handles of the paddles before realizing I'd be rowing upstream.

"*Harfares,*" I cursed under my breath as my cheeks colored. I pulled at the oars, but once I neared the river, the boat slowed to a mere crawl against the current. I cursed again, trying not to glance up at Alius.

He shook his head, what appeared to be condemnation visible on his face even though he was twenty arms away.

"Wait," he called over the water, dragging his trap back into the lake and approaching my boat. I caught my breath, wishing I could disappear. What did he want? To make fun of me? I dug the oars deeper into the water.

He scratched his head and sighed. "Do you really plan to row upstream by yourself?"

I clenched my jaw. No. I *didn't have a plan at all.*

He studied me a moment longer, one hand in his pocket. "I'll help," he finally spoke.

Help me? My fingers tightened around the oars. I opened my mouth to speak, but nothing came out. I didn't want his help.

He splashed into the water and caught hold of the side of the boat. "Opal, your only other option is to leave it."

A *perfectly good option.* I swallowed, watching him. He didn't want to help me. There was no smile on his face or twinkle in his eye.

"You don't have to. I know what you think of me."

He glanced away, leaning an arm on the boat until it tilted towards him. "Do you want my help or not?"

I shook my head, blinking back tears. Why would he even offer?

When he met my gaze again, his face softened. "Is that a yes?"

I chewed my cheek, nodding. *Let him help. He can't hurt me anymore.*

Alius climbed into the boat, and I brushed past him to sit on the opposite side. The only other time we had been so close was when we danced. I shut out the thought, letting silence swirl between us as I stared down at the water. He gripped the oars, guiding us towards the river mouth. He was helping me for his own conscience' sake, not because he still considered me a friend. I shivered, wishing I had remembered to bring dry clothes.

"What were you doing, anyway?" Alius fractured the silence.

I glanced up, surprised. "I was practicing." My pulse quickened, that familiar urge to tell him everything rising in me. I cleared my throat, trying to ignore it. It was dangerous.

"Practicing? For?" He raised an eyebrow.

I sighed, studying my hands, which lay idle in my lap. "The Gilding. I failed before."

"I gathered as much."

I glanced back at him, but he wasn't looking at me. Sweat glistened on his face, but he continued rowing us upstream without complaint. Of course he'd guessed it. "I understand if you don't want to be my friend anymore." I pushed on. I couldn't make things worse between us.

He scoffed, looking away. "It's not that, exactly."

"Then what is it?" I pressed, folding my arms.

His green eyes darted between mine a moment longer. "Why did you fail the first time?" he deflected. "It can't be that hard."

I stared, open mouthed. "You don't know anything about it. And I almost drowned, if you must know."

Alius's gaze faltered before something curious settled behind his eyes. "I'm sorry. If it's any consolation, I'm glad you didn't." He studied me until I looked away.

"How courteous of you," I mused sarcastically.

He gripped the oars again, rowing with more determination now, a twinkle back in his eye. "Aya, I am rowing you back upstream, Scout," he said with a grimace as he fought the current.

I shook my head. "I didn't ask for your help." Did he want me in his debt?

"I know. I wanted to," he answered between his heavy breaths.

"Why?" I laughed cynically, flickering my gaze away from him.

He hesitated. "You're still my friend. And I can't leave a girl in distress." His half-smile returned, and I watched him a moment longer, fighting with the butterflies swirling in my stomach. Could I trust him again? My heart beat quickened as I realized just how much I wanted to. A thought that had begun to slither through my mind played on my lips. *I wouldn't mind dying.* Did I dare say it?

I tightened the strings on the front of my shirt, the loose-knit cotton finally drying. It wasn't a thought that scared me. Maybe because I knew it was passive. Yet it was heavy all the same, and the thought of sharing that heaviness with someone else, someone who chose to be my friend, glimmered like a beacon before me.

I uncrossed my arms, holding on to the seat beneath me, the breeze dancing through my hair. The pink of my cheeks deepened when I realized my hair was still down. I pulled it all over my shoulder and began braiding it. When I glanced at Alius, he was smirking at me.

"What?" I demanded.

"Nothing." He shrugged. "I like your hair down."

My fingers only froze a moment before I finished my braid and threw it over my shoulder. Why did he have to say such things? He would never feel anything more than friendship towards me. I knew it as plainly as I knew the color of the sky.

"Aya! There you are!" Alana's voice shattered the moment and I whirled around, looking for my sister.

"What's going on?" Ilynn joined in. Both she and Alana were walking down the path trailing the bank of the river. "We were looking for you." Ilynn was talking to me, but staring down Alius. They both were.

He wordlessly rowed the boat to the shore and took a breath before calmly answering. "She needed help getting the boat back upstream. I was checking my traps in the cove."

They both continued to stare at him, considering his answer.

"And what were *you* doing in the cove?" Alana interrogated me.

I huffed, looking away from her. "I was… practicing for the Gilding."

"By *yourself*?" both Alana and Ilynn exclaimed.

"You weren't home." I reminded her.

"Aye, but we would have helped you, Opi," Ilynn remarked.

I shrugged, searching for a way to redirect the conversation. "What are you doing out here?"

Ilynn's eyes lit with mischief. "We're headed to the lighthouse. After what your appa found out about the lighthouse keeper, we wanted to have a look. And see if it's really haunted."

"Really?" Alius said in surprise.

"Are you coming, Opi?" Alana ignored Alius.

The idea terrified me. No bone in my body wanted to find out if the legend was true or not. But what would I miss out on if I stayed behind? I glanced at Alius.

"Ugh, you can come too, I guess. Just don't get us caught," Ilynn said, folding her arms.

Alius considered Ilynn's offer, clearly about to turn it down before meeting my eyes. There was something mischievous behind his look, too, but I couldn't put my finger on it. "You know what? Why not? Let's do it."

The boat was hardly big enough for all four of us, but Alana and Ilynn squeezed in, being sure to push Alius to the seat farthest away from me. Once we reached the cove and the boat was tied up, we started up the steep bluff. The vastness of Misty Lale seemed to swallow up the other half of the world.

"So... you were checking your fishing traps?" Ilynn glanced at Alius over her shoulder. She and Alana walked a few paces ahead.

"Aye. I've been trying out different spots around the lake since we moved back here. The cove isn't too shabby."

The top of the lighthouse appeared over the trees, bright in the afternoon sun. Its dingy disrepair whispered of the forgotten keeper, but the daylight quieted it.

"Maybe we should have come at nighttime," Ilynn joked, squinting at the silver glint.

"No, daytime time is good. I like daytime," I replied quickly before anyone suggested coming back at night, the idea making me shiver even in the summer warmth.

"Don't be a ninny." Alana shot a look back at me. "Do you really think it's haunted?"

I shook my head, but the chiding didn't dispel my fear. We found a neglected path reclaimed by the forest floor leading directly to the little door at the bottom of the lighthouse. Everything was quiet. There was no sign of the new keeper, but we still crouched down at the edge of the woods, the sound of our heavy breathing setting me on edge. Emptiness swarmed the woods in a chilly welcome.

"All right. We've seen it, now let's go!" I hissed. My request was met with laughter on all sides.

"Come on. There's no one out. Let's get a closer look! Maybe it's even unlocked." Ilynn grinned.

"Ilynn, no!" I cried desperately.

"I'm kidding! Someone lives there now. You're lucky we didn't come up when it was still abandoned," Ilynn said.

I sighed, stuffing down my alarm. It really didn't look haunted in the daylight, its white walls gleaming against the summer sky. But I couldn't get the story out of my head. Two people had died here, one possibly murdered.

We stayed at the edge of the woods, walking around the clearing. The door and windows were made of new wood. Noura's friend was already making repairs, his tools carefully leaning against the walls of the small building in the back. But where was he?

Alius wandered farther into the woods. A platform was built into a sturdy tree with something leaning against its trunk. He bent down, picking up a quiver of arrows. "I've never seen a bow like this," he commented, examining the weapon. A strong gust of wind bade the trees to dance, and fear gripped me once more.

"Can we go now?" I jerked on Alana's sleeve, flashes of a murdered ghost hovering before my eyes.

"Shhh." Ilynn's eyes danced as she grinned at me. "Hear that?"

My stomach dropped. I didn't want to hear anything. I wanted to go home. A soft, low whistling greeted us on the breeze, playing on the leaves above my head. Why had I agreed to come? I was worse than a flighty horse. The next gust of wind cradled another whistle.

"Come on." Ilynn stepped out from the cover of the trees. "I think it's coming from over there." She pointed to the small building at the back of the lighthouse. Alana moved to follow, but my legs obeyed my instincts.

"Are you coming?" Alana glanced back at me, but I shook my head. Even if I wanted to, I couldn't move. "Well, just stay there. We'll be back."

"Wha—no!" I cried, but they were already leaving. I ducked under the tree next to me. Alius was still enthralled with the exotic bow somewhere behind me. I was alone. My hand gripped the tree branch as the quiet woods stirred to life around me. Sunlight crawled through the treetops casting me in unfamiliar shadows as squirrels tore through the trees, and insects landed on my skin, out for blood. Losing sight of Alana and Ilynn, I stumbled backward with a small yelp into a spider web. I whirled around, fighting off its sticky fingers, frustration burning inside me. Why did they leave me? As I stumbled back, a fallen branch sent me sprawling, and I shrieked as I tumbled down the hill. A muffled yell escaped my lips when I landed with a thud and then a splash at the bottom. Cold water from a stream snaked around me, my teeth chattering.

"Opal!" Alius's voice echoed from the trees. "Where are you?" he asked, and I wanted to cry with relief as the forest's eeriness receded.

"Down here!" I rose, dripping from the water, before he came into view. I shook my boots with a grimace as I took in the stream.

"What are you doing down here?" he asked, stopping at the water's edge beside me, one eye brow arched.

"Going for a swim," I retorted before pointing to the river. "Look." Instead of the creek continuing on towards the lake, the water disappeared. A large hole appeared a few arms away, and the creek water poured into the ground below.

"What is this place?" Alius wondered. He edged closer to the hole, and I followed him. Cracking twigs alerted us that my sister and Ilynn found us.

"Good find, Opi!" Ilynn grinned and poked my side. I batted her hand away. She smirked at me, hands on her hips, as she took in the oddity of the river before us. "We didn't find anything up there, but this—" She stepped closer to the hole.

"Where do you suppose it goes?" Alana wondered. They'd found no answer to the whistling noise. I shivered.

"I don't like it. It doesn't seem natural." I took another step back from the water, though my shoes were already soaked through.

"Someone's redirected the river. I wonder why." Ilynn peered into the hole, the water rushing down into the sinister blackness below. Cut stones, nearly smothered with moss, were stacked around the hole in a semicircle. Alius rubbed some of the moss off, and the strange foreboding seeping into me only grew stronger. Beneath the rock's green layer and carved into the stone were strange letters.

Ilynn stepped closer. "I've seen writing like that before..."

"What is it?" I asked tensely.

"I'm not sure what it's called, but I saw it in one of my appa's old books."

"Helpful..." Alius joked.

"Well, can you read it?" Ilynn glared back.

I peered at the letters again, words drumming through my head. *A song from the beginning, forever abides. An echo of all the beauty ever known.* I blinked, the tune clearly rustling with the breeze through the trees above us. *Its melody guides you home.* I caught my breath, throwing a glance at the others. Could they hear it too?

"I wanna know where it's going." Alius jumped up, scanning the trees. Alana and Ilynn didn't seem aware of the music carried by the trees either. I shivered, wrapping my arms around myself.

Alius untangled a vine nearby and gave it a good tug. It snapped, and he stumbled into the river. "Good thing I tested it." He rose, dripping from the water, and unwound another.

"You're not going down there, are you?" I asked.

"If I can handle High Tor, I think I can handle this..." Once the vine was free from other branches, he pulled on it in all directions. This one held.

"Is it long enough?" Alana asked, concern crossing her face.

"I guess I'll find out." He shrugged, securing it around his waist. "It's just in case my grip slips me," he said, eyeing the way down carefully before finding his first hand and foot holds and disappearing along with the water. I held my breath.

"What do you see?" Ilynn asked.

"It's so dark—" he said after several grunts.

"*Can* you see?" I asked, my alarm growing.

"There's some light at the bottom. Only a few arms left to go..." His voice echoed against the cave walls. "Almost—" The vine jerked against the tree branch and Alius hit the bottom with a splash.

"You all right?" I asked warily.

A groan met us in response. "Aye..." More splashing sounded from the hole. Was he hurt?

"Well, what's down there?" Alana asked.

"It's a cave. There's an opening. It must be in the cliffs... I think y'all need to find the way inside—" Alius was cut off by a harsh voice echoing from above us.

We spun to face the speaker, our own voices fleeing like hunted prey. "Did someone go down there?" The speaker questioned us with dark eyes as he splashed into the water. We stared at the vaguely familiar figure we knew from the festival. Short hair and a beard hid half his face, and he wore a dust-colored jacket that did a poor job of concealing the two knives on his belt. He met our stares with a serious set in his jaw, despite him appearing no more than ten years our elder. The new lighthouse keeper.

"Aye," Alana murmured.

"We were just—" Ilynn searched for words.

"Explain yourselves after we get your friend out." He peered into the hole. "You hurt?"

"Aye, my ankle..."

"All right. Stay put. I'll get the boat—coming through the cave entrance." The man brushed past us. "Come!"

We jogged to keep up. Ilynn, Alana, and I all looked at each other, not knowing what to do other than follow. I wished one of them would say something, but we ran on in silence. He led us to a steep pathway down the cliff's edge to the rocks below where his boat was tied up.

"Watch yourselves," he said over his shoulder as he descended at an alarming pace. Alana looked a little green, and my head spun, but Ilynn had a hand for each of us.

"At least we'll get to see inside the cave!" Ilynn grinned.

"Oh wonderful. Just what I wanted..." I gripped her hand a little tighter.

"Cheer up. I'm sure he's fine," Alana added.

"It's not—" I began but stopped. They wouldn't believe me. It wasn't Alius falling that unsettled me. It was this place. They didn't know it would keep me awake at night for weeks.

We rowed swiftly to the rocks.

"Where's the entrance?" Ilynn remarked when the man tied the boat next to a long rock that came out from the cliff, making a perfect dock. In fact, it was a little too perfect.

"Up there," he responded. We scanned the cliff in the direction he pointed.

"The entrance was completely blocked off with rocks. I just opened a hole up there a few days ago."

"Why?" Ilynn wondered, eyeing the small hole.

"Same as you, I expect. I wanted to see where the water went." He waited for us to clamber out of the boat onto the stone dock before scaling about five arms up where he had cleared a man-sized hole.

"Wait here. I'll be back with your friend," he called down with a quick glance back. Ilynn waited for him to disappear inside before scaling the rocks herself.

"What are you doing?" A bad feeling stirred inside me.

"I didn't come this far to not see what's inside!" Ilynn said.

"Come on. It'll be worth it," Alana added, only hesitating a moment before following suit. I released my breath, at the same cross roads as before. Ilynn and Alana disappeared through the hole.

"Wait for me..." I muttered, pulling myself up with a grunt. I stretched as far as I could to reach the rim of the hole, ignoring the pain in my arm as it scraped against the rock. Panting, I peered inside, blinking while my eyes adjusted to the dimly lit cavern. My sister was just inside, clinging to the rocks.

"Didn't I tell you to stay?" The lighthouse keeper shook his head at Ilynn who was already at the bottom of the rocks. He was halfway across the cave, wading through the water towards Alius. I blinked again. Alius was making his way down from the rocks, trying to hide a limp. When he took a second look at the man, his face hardened. He must have recognized him from the festival.

"Alius! I didn't expect to find you down here," the man said, a smile softening his face. "Where are you hurt?"

"I'm fine." Alius pressed his lips together, refusing to look up. The man shrugged it off. My gaze didn't stay on them for long as my eyes followed the water up. It poured through the hole, splashing into a large pool at the bottom and running over into smaller pools and waterfalls. A beautiful cascade, shimmering a little bit golden in the light from above.

"What is this place?" Alana's thoughts spilled into the void.

"Do you really want to know?" The man smirked with his untold knowledge.

"Why wouldn't we?" Ilynn took a few steps farther inside, turning around to take it all in, the cave's ceiling twelve arms above us. Alius finally made it to the bottom and met my gaze. I shook my head slowly at his "all good" look. He still had to climb up and out.

"I thought you didn't take too kindly to Elowynnites."

"Is that what this place is?" Alana said, scrunching her nose.

"They made it, yes." The lighthouse keeper's eyes watched our faces turn from curious to disgusted.

"But why?" Ilynn dipped her hand in one of the overflowing pools.

"I think it must have been part of a ritual," he answered, and she quickly withdrew her hand from the pool as if it had bitten her. Rituals. I shivered at the thought.

It was quite a feat, getting Alius out of the cave. He accepted as little help as possible. I didn't know whether to laugh or feel sorry for him. Once we were all in the boat, the lighthouse keeper gripped the oars against the tide.

"I'm not one to chide, but you do realize that could have ended a lot worse, right?"

"Aye..." Ilynn shot Alius a look. "Thank you for helping us. We are in your debt." She nodded in thanks.

"I don't keep debts. I won't even tell you not to come back. It is a curious place. Just be more careful." A thoughtful expression crossed his face. "And maybe come with a more open mind. Am I rowing to town or where?"

"Our boat is tied up not far from here. Near the cove." Alanna pointed back the way we had come.

"I will take you to your boat then. My name is Dion by the way," he said, waiting for us to introduce ourselves.

"You can take me to the shore. I don't need any more help." Alius ignored the introduction. We all looked at him with raised eyebrows.

"You really shouldn't walk on—" the lighthouse keep- er started.

"I'll be fine. It doesn't even bother me," Alius mut- tered.

"Well, we are fortunate to know you, Dion. I'm Ilynn," Ilynn redirected the conversation.

He nodded his head, but his gaze settled on me as Alana introduced herself. I'd initially thought his eyes were too harsh, but, while they held intensity, kindness rimmed them.

"And I'm Opal," I added, averting my eyes.

"It's a blessing to meet you," Dion replied. When I glanced up, his gaze still lingered on me.

Dion rowed Alius to the first landing.

"Alius..." I said quietly as he rose from the boat. He glanced at me briefly before climbing out. I couldn't let him go alone. My cheeks warmed, but I ignored it, refusing to look at Alana and Ilynn's faces. If today was a test of friendship, Alius had passed it.

"I'll come with you." I clambered out of the boat and onto the shore. I watched a moment as the boat rowed away, wishing Alius was not so stubborn.

"How far is your house from here?" I asked.

"About half a league."

I frowned.

"You can go. I don't need—"

"Don't be absurd. I'm your friend. I'm not leaving you to limp home by yourself."

"And how are you going to help?" he asked, amusement returning to his face as he looked over my small stature.

"I'll find you a walking stick. And we can get back on the road that goes to the lighthouse. It'll be easier than fighting through all this underbrush."

Alius smiled, nodding his head in consent. I put all my focus into my search for a crutch. *Just help him get home.* Once I found a proper stick and the road, we started the long walk back. Alius tried to put his weight on the stick, but it made a poor crutch.

"How bad is it?" I grimaced, pity reflecting in my eyes.

"Don't look at me like that. It's not your fault," he assured me before his smile faded a little. "Did you know he was the lighthouse keeper?"

"Maybe..." I glanced away, afraid he was upset with me.

"Oh, okay. I see how it is." He shook his head, his messy curls falling into his eyes. "Now he's going to think I was sneaking around up there because I'm a sore loser."

"Aren't you though?" I tried not to laugh.

"No. I can lose to someone better and, not to mention, significantly older than me," he replied, his eyes softening again. "Besides, I still beat everyone who is actually from Wisptale. Not to mention, I destroyed Dion in five games of Blades and Bows."

"You what?" I laughed, taken aback.

"You know, the game. Blades and Bows. Dion was challenging anyone who walked by, and I beat him."

I knew about the game, but hadn't played since I was a child. "I wouldn't have pegged you as a Blades and Bows fanatic."

He laughed. "Me either. I hadn't played in years, but everything came back to me. He was actually impressed."

"Then why are we walking home? You beat him, he beat you. You're both even."

Alius shook his head. "I just didn't want his help anymore."

"Like I didn't want yours earlier?"

"Aye, you did," he mused, giving me a dimpled grin.

I rolled my eyes.

The sun was starting to dip lower, and we still had a long way to go. Alius was not able to move very quickly with the stick alone.

"Do you think we'll make it before dark?"

"Honestly?" He paused, leaning on the stick and studying the sun's position in the sky. "It'll be close."

I looked at him for a moment, his face and arms scuffed up and bruised from the fall. He needed my help.

"Come on," I said, taking his arm and putting it over my shoulder so he could lean on me.

"What are you doing?" he asked, a smile tugging at his lips.

"Getting you home."

Nine

NOURA FINGERED THE SHINY PENDANT of the pegasus pinned to her dress, smiling to herself. She didn't often humor her competitive nature, but as soon as she'd learned about the reenactment, she'd begged Dion to enter it with her. She smirked. It hadn't been a fair race though, not with Dion by her side. It was rare that anyone outside the Rim could match a trained Guardian.

The festival hadn't all been light and games though. Noura shut her eyes, remembering Opal standing on the stage. She looked so devastated. Noura inhaled, knowing pieces were falling into place but not entirely sure what to do with them. Just because she'd grown up in a place protected from brokenness didn't mean she was perfect. Her father didn't need her to be. He would gather up the broken pieces she brought him and make them new. Still, Opal's pain pierced her heart.

She glanced up at the figure balancing on the Keepton's window in the dead of night. "Be careful!"

"Shh!" Dion's voice floated down to her. He cracked the window open, wincing at every creak. Once the space was wide enough, he slipped through. Noura folded her arms, lingering in the shadows on the street, holding her breath. Whatever happened, they couldn't be caught by Keepton Thorn. He may have let Dion revive the lighthouse, but he was wary of them both.

A scuffle above her brought her mind back to the mission before them. Dion reappeared in the window, a box in his hands.

"Catch!" he whispered with a grin, and when she stepped forward, arms out stretched, he tossed the box into the night. She cursed as it fell, losing it in the dark for a moment before catching it. Dion squeaked the window shut before lowering himself from the sill and dropping to the ground.

"I never thought I'd see the day you cursed." He took the box from her, and they jogged away from Keepton Thorn's house.

She laughed. "I've been away from home too long."

"Ah." He flashed her a grin as they slowed to a walk. "Now you understand me a little better."

"I will never understand you," she joked, pocketing her hands. He huffed at her but didn't reply. Dion was three years her elder and had been away from home that much longer. He'd also chosen a path she had steered away from. Fighting and swords were not the future she wanted.

Even though her father had prepared her for this, it was harder than she'd imagined. The darkness and lies that permeated the world outside the Rim weren't just a veil over the people. They were twisted vines intertwined with truth, and untangling them was a tedious and discouraging business. The mess between the Elowynnites and Refiners was a vivid picture of it.

She glanced up at the bright light glimmering on the cliff half a league away. The beacon burning in the lighthouse. It wasn't a coincidence that Dion had set that light shining tonight. The lighthouse was her reminder to keep shining, and to not only hold on to the truth she knew, but to hold it up for those who were lost to find their way home. Opal was foremost in her mind, but Faelle lingered there too. Noura caught her brother's arm, the weakness in her reaching for his steady strength. Not many first missions hinged on two souls, but hers did.

"You all right? We're almost to the boat." Dion slowed his pace.

Noura sighed. "I just hope I can keep holding up the light for them."

Dion pulled her into a hug, understanding passing between them. "The light shines even behind the darkest of veils."

THE PREVIOUS DAY'S EVENTS KEPT a smile on my face that wouldn't fade, even when I tried to hide it. And I wanted to. Alana kept rolling her eyes, and Yemma was looking at me sideways.

"Opi." Alana's address met me at the door the moment I walked inside. "Why are you so smiley today?" She plopped down in the sitting room with a cup of tea and patted the seat next to her. My face burned as I kicked off my shoes.

"I'm not..." I crossed the thick carpet and reluctantly joined her on the floor cushion. I didn't want to talk about it, but at the same time, I did.

"Look. I don't mind Alius as your friend. But I just want you to be careful," my sister said.

"Be careful of what?"

"Opi… I don't want you to be hurt," she explained, studying me with a look only an older sister could give. I stared at the fabric of the cushions, waiting for her to continue. "Just remember that you are not the only girl he talks to."

"He's my friend. That's all."

"Make sure he proves to be a good friend." Alana watched my face until I met her eyes.

He would, I thought. He would prove it.

"On another rope, will you be all right tomorrow?" Alana asked, leaning back and sipping her tea. She, Ilynn, and the rest of their class were leaving tomorrow to tour Arlo's Fellowship for ten days. My heart jumped and sank at the change of subject. It was a subject I had been dreading for weeks.

"Are you all packed and ready?" I reached for the teapot and poured myself a cup of tea. The question was heavy on my chest.

"Almost. I wish I were more certain about it."

"Well, isn't that why you're going on the tour? To see what the fellowship is like?" I added.

"True. And it'll be a fun trip since I've never been to Madrielle before," Alana considered, tapping a finger on the side of her cup.

I sighed. "I wish I could go with you."

"You want to go to the Fellowship?" She raised an eyebrow and set her cup down.

"No." My answer was quick. The Fellowship was something I pushed as far as I could from my mind. "But I'm missing out." Arlo's Fellowship meant Alana and Ilynn were leaving me. It was inevitably intertwined with growing up.

"You'll have a chance to go in a few years..." Alana said.

But with who? She and Ilynn would be gone, and Alius was a year ahead of me. I would be going alone if I chose to go at all.

Appa returned home from the wheel shop a few hours early. He came through the door, two dead chickens swinging from his arm.

"Yemma! Where are you?" he called, making his way towards our kitchen.

"What are you doing with those chickens?" I followed at a distance, wondering at Appa's curious disposition. He placed them on the counter before giving me an answer.

"Opi, get the house ready. Today, we are having guests. One of whom I suspect you'll like very much." Appa winked as he exited the kitchen and searched the house calling for Yemma.

"Yemma is outside! Probably trying to sweep the dirt out of the garden," Alana joked. Appa chuckled his thanks before heading out the door. I followed, unable to banish my growing anticipation. Who was coming for dinner? My mind went to one person, but my feet had been brought back to solid ground on the subject. I quickened my pace, unwilling to let my imagination run away with itself.

Only the top of Yemma's head—or hair, I should say—could be seen over the green leaves as she bent down to pick the cucumbers. Appa reached the gate, and I slipped in quietly behind him.

"Aya, Yemma," Appa said in the sweetest voice he could contrive. He knew springing a surprise of two slaughtered chickens on her counter needing to be stuffed should be disclosed strategically. "I hope you've had a delightful day so far, my dear."

Yemma stood up quickly, cucumbers tumbling to the ground, eyeing Appa suspiciously. "What did you do?" she asked intuitively.

Appa grinned slyly, considering his next words. "I may have... invited a couple folks over for dinner." He took a step closer to her.

Yemma let out a sigh and pushed the curls out of her face before answering. "May I ask who I will be cooking for?"

"Oh, yes—sorry, my love," Appa stammered. He cleared his throat. "In town, I ran into the new lighthouse keeper and felt it only right to welcome him to Wisptale by inviting him to dinner. Your stuffed chickens are famous. And Noura, Opal's friend, will be joining us as well," Appa added. At Appa's words, a sense of relief mingled with disappointment washed over me. And then fear. We hadn't told Appa of our adventure yesterday, nor who had been with us.

"But we haven't got any chicken prepared," Yemma said in frustration. Appa approached her and took the basket of cucumbers, gathering the ones that had fallen.

"It's all taken care of, my love. I brought two prepared chickens from town."

"Yemma, I'll get Alana and we'll start on the house," I said. "Don't stress. It will be a lovely time."

Yemma nodded at me as I dashed out of the garden and back to our house. Having something to occupy me would do a world of good for my wandering mind, and I welcomed the task of hosting the two newest residents of Wisptale.

After our home had been put in order and our messiness sufficiently hidden, both Alana and I plopped down on the floor cushions to rest.

"I need a cup of tea!" my sister commented, stretching her legs out.

"Oh, me too," I agreed, hugging a pillow. Drinking tea seemed to be the thing to do that day to quell the confused butterflies in my stomach. We both stared at each other for a moment, waiting for the other to agree to put the kettle on.

"I'm pretty sure I cleaned twice as much as you," Alana said confidently.

"You did not!" I countered, but, in the end, I lost. Yemma eyed us drinking our tea suspiciously at first, suspecting the house was not up to her standards, but after she gave it a walkthrough, she decided there was nothing more to do except finish the cooking.

Our table was prepared, the cushions fluffed, and the house smelled of golden chicken stuffed with fresh herbs. Finally, the sound of voices coming up the path reached my ears. I pulled back the curtain to peek out the window. Appa had gone down to meet them on the path. Noura wore a beautiful green skirt, and her braid was wrapped around her head like a crown, whereas Dion wore many shades of black. He looked directly at the lifted corner of the curtain, a smirk crossing his face. I dropped it immediately, embarrassed, and backed away from the door. Would he be so bold as to mention our excursion yesterday? I breathed slowly, trying to calm my nerves.

"What?" Alana mocked. "Worried he will tell Appa Alius was with us?" She winked at me.

Yemma, who had overheard, mumbled a confused, "What?" But neither of us offered her an explanation before the door opened, and our guests entered.

"Welcome, welcome." Yemma's cheery voice filled the house. Once the initial shock of having to host wore off, she had returned to her usual friendly self. Alana, who was next to Yemma, curtsied, and I followed suit. Noura gave me a pleasant smile as she greeted my Yemma and sister before kissing my cheeks.

"How are you, love?" she asked, searching my face. By the look on hers, I knew she had seen my ousting. My shame only flickered though. If she could stand up for an Elowynnite, I knew she held no condemnation for me.

"This is my brother, Dion," Noura announced, turning to my parents. Alana and I greeted him with a more sober countenance, knowing he knew exactly who we were. Dion, despite his brawny frame and intense eyes, rivaled Noura's gentleness when he was not in a rescue-the-idiot mode. He smiled warmly and, as he was introduced, observed our home with a curious but thoughtful expression. His gaze settled on Alana and me with a twinkle.

"Thank you, again, for having me for dinner," Dion began when Appa directed him towards a cushion to sit on. "Yours is the first home I've been to, besides Keepton Thorn's, since I've been in Wisptale. And I can't say that was much of a welcoming." Dion loosely folded his arms.

"Truly? That is a stain on the good name of Wisptale," Yemma commented, shaking her head. "Would you like some tea?"

"That would be wonderful," Dion replied with a slight inclination of his head.

"Yes, please," Noura agreed. "And your home is charming and so tidy." Noura winked at me as if she was imagining the busy afternoon we'd had preparing for their visit. Yemma welcomed the compliment enthusiastically before disappearing into the kitchen to put the kettle on.

"So," Appa began. "Dion, please tell us how you came to Wisptale. It's such a small town, I'm surprised anyone new comes here at all."

Dion nodded and smiled as if anticipating this question. "Wisptale is not as inconsequential as one might think." He continued when his comment was met with confused looks. "Noura and I were looking for a new adventure, and I've always been fascinated with lighthouses."

"Where are you from? You haven't been sent by Madrielle, have you?" Appa was always concerned that Madrielle was growing too powerful.

"From Madrielle?" Dion shook his head. "We're the furthest thing from Medrians. Noura—" he motioned towards her "—and I aren't even from the Avarlyn Province. My sister wanted to come here first, and when I heard the lighthouse was in disrepair, I couldn't pass up the opportunity."

Yemma came out with steaming cups of butter tea and set them on the table in front of us. Alana and I gave each other a look as we sipped our tea. By all our skeptical expressions, Dion must have noticed that we were not yet content with his answers.

"It's more of a childhood fantasy fulfilled than anything else," he assured us.

Appa set down his tea. "Well, I was just telling my wife how glad I am to see it up and running again. And it's good to know such a fine and capable young man is overseeing it."

Dion nodded, accepting the compliment. "So, you don't believe the rumors that it's haunted?" he mused. Appa raised his eyebrows, and I held onto my mug with a new intensity while Noura shifted.

"I guess you'd have to tell me how you sleep at night before I make a decision on that," Appa joked. "It's got a dark history, that can't be denied."

"Well, so far, I have not run into any ghosts. But I will keep my eyes open." Dion smiled.

Presently, dinner was served, and I was even more grateful that Dion had not mentioned anything about us snooping around the lighthouse. He seemed keener on discussing contentious topics than anything else, as if he wanted to understand the atmosphere of Wisptale from the inside out.

The conversation continued to meander through formalities for the rest of the evening. Dinner ended, and Yemma received the well-deserved praise for her stuffed chicken with a meek smile. Tea was served yet again, and I sat holding my cup close to my face, feeling the hot steam roll over my cheeks. Noura eventually moved to sit next to me.

"How are you?"

"All right." My voice trailed off.

"Are you still worried about what happened?"

I shrugged, but in my head I was screaming. *Of course.* What happened was only the beginning of my miseries. I turned my face away, tears welling in my eyes.

But Noura didn't shy away at the barrier I was building. "All that seems dark ahead of you will be made anew."

I glanced back at her, wishing I could find hope in her words, but a mountain collapsed on me. *Made anew.* The word only reminded me that I could not grow and could not change, no matter how hard I tried—no matter how desperately I wished to be someone else. My change of expression did not go unnoticed. Noura set her cup down, worry creasing her brow.

"Are you all right, Opal?" she asked, but my words caught in my throat.

"I don't know," I said, barely over a whisper. There was no use pretending.

"It's okay if you don't know." Noura hesitated before she continued. "But... don't drown out his voice." She held my gaze, looking for comprehension.

His voice. I did not know how she was aware of him, but I knew she meant Nevma. Because I hadn't heard him speak in days.

~~~

ALANA WRAPPED HER ARMS AROUND me in a hug before she and Ilynn stepped onto the boat. The sun peeked over Mount Nea and spilled into Misty Lale, the lake's mist swirling around me in whispers.

"You'll be all right," she assured me with a smile. But I wasn't assured, and she saw it in my eyes. "We'll be back before you know it."

"We'll miss you!" Ilynn added. I watched them wave as Yemma pulled me away from the marina.

"You'll have your turn in a few years, Opi. Let's get out of the damp." She put her arm around me and grabbed hold of Appa's hand. Maybe this was hard for her too. Her oldest wasn't leaving for good yet, but she would all too soon.

"Aya, I know what will cheer us up!" Appa steered us towards the town center. "Anyone else want cake for breakfast?"

"Really, dear?" Yemma said, shaking her head but also not refusing. Appa held open the door to Rosin's Rum Cakes.

"What better way to wash away the sadness than with a sugar coma." Appa grinned.

The shop was nearly empty, a sleepiness still clinging to its walls as we entered. Yemma and I sat down while Appa brought our sugary breakfast.

"Are you trying to eat away the sadness too?" The Herald approached our table from the corner of the shop, a rum cake in hand. Ilynn's appa. "Can you believe they are off to
~~~

Madrielle already? Weren't we just watching them both learn how to walk?"

"I know! And for ten whole days. They've never been gone for that long before..." Yemma's voice faded as I took the rum cake Appa held out to me. I stared at it, my appetite faltering. Ten days. What was I going to do without them?

"Opi." The Herald addressed me now. He'd picked up my shortened name from Ilynn, but I didn't mind. "I hope you are faring all right."

I swallowed the bit of cake in my mouth and wiped a crumb from my chin. What did he want me to say?

The Herald took my quietness in stride as Nevma buzzed around his head. "I hope you plan to attempt your Gilding again, despite what happened at the festival." He paused, a thoughtful expression on his face. "It will take more courage for you than the other girls after what happened, but I know that courage is in you. Remember." He placed his hand briefly on my shoulder, the hand that had knocked the water from my lungs. "We are never alone, especially when we are at our weakest."

"DION!" NOURA SPRINTED ACROSS THE DOCK. Another piece had fallen into place, but not a piece she wanted. He appeared out of the fog, and she had to grab his shirt to keep from skidding by.

"What is it?" He grabbed her arm, helping her find her feet once more. In any other circumstance, he might have laughed at her mishap, but a fierce stare met hers. "Did something happen to Opal already?"

"Not yet," she assured him, "but we have to find her."

"How? Where is she?" He spun in the fog. Noura grabbed his arm, forcing him to stand still as she closed her eyes.

"You've been away from home too long. *Listen*." She stared into the red-dark of her eyelids, the damp of the mist on her skin and the sounds of the Misty District creaking to life. But that wasn't what she was listening for. Her eyes flew open.

"Care for some sweets?"

"How did you do that?" Dion demanded, blinking. Noura shook her head at him and pushed him down the dock towards Rosin's Rum Cakes.

They slowed to a normal walk before entering the sweet shop. She covered her heart, its pounding fracturing her thoughts. What if this was the last chance? She shut her eyes briefly. *Give me the right words to say, Father.* The kindness that usually resided in Noura's eyes hid behind a fierce determination. She had nothing to fear, not even death itself. She breathed before whispering to herself.

"But you, you should be afraid. You should be *terrified*," she spoke to death as if it were a vision before her.

"What?" Dion murmured back.

"Not *you!*" A smile touched her face once more as she took in the room. Opal was at a table with her parents. "Go," she prompted Dion towards the counter as she slid into a chair. He threw her an annoyed glance.

Noura tapped her fingers on the table. Opal was engaged in conversation with the Herald and his wife, but her eyes were far too glassy. When Noura spoke to Opal at dinner days ago, tears trembled behind the girl's eyes. But now, her eyes were different. The tears were frozen there, unmoveable. Noura waved, catching her attention. Opal tilted her head in confusion before she slowly rose and crossed the floor to Noura.

"Fair morning, Opal." Noura patted the chair next to her. Opal glanced back at her appa and yemma as she made an internal assessment. She forced a smile that twisted Noura's stomach. "Were you sending your sister off?" Noura motioned for her to sit down again. Opal nodded before sitting precariously on the edge of the seat as if she dared not take up any more space. "I know you'll miss her." At this, Opal finally met her eyes. Noura could sense the pain and lies lurking behind her gray irises.

"For you." Dion placed a half-wrapped rum cake in front of Noura before settling at the table with his own. Noura grazed the edge of the paper with her finger. "Opal's sister, Alana, is off to Madrielle for—ten days is it?" She folded her hands, glancing at the girl.

"Aye. Ten days. That's—it's the longest she's been away."

"I know we're poor stand-ins but we'll gladly be around until she comes back." Dion bit into his rum cake, leaning back in the chair. "If you like, that is. Noura's not much fun though." He winked.

Opal bit her lip in an attempt to stifle a laugh. "I—thank you." Her smile almost reached her eyes.

Noura sighed. Swimming around the boat wasn't going to work.

"Are you doing all right with it all, Opal?" Noura pressed.

Opal swallowed hard, slipping back into wordless responses. Dion kicked Noura's foot under the table, but Noura knew it wasn't the wrong approach. Opal didn't need temporary relief from sadness. She needed a warning.

"Do you remember what I said to you when I first came here?"

"I'm not sure," Opal murmured back, meeting Noura's gaze as if searching for a dying hope.

"I know about wounds. And I can see yours isn't physical, but it's in here." Noura motioned to Opal's head. Opal stared at the table in front of her, some of the ice melting behind her eyes. "Opal, look at me. Look at us." Noura searched the girl's face. Slowly, the girl lifted her eyes, watching Noura first and then Dion.

"It's not a coincidence we're here." Dion leaned forward in the chair once more.

"You think you don't belong, but it's not true." Noura paused. "A battle for your heart is coming, Opal." She wanted to continue with, *the enemy is vying for your soul*, but she didn't want to scare her. She drew back, letting the words settle.

"I'm scared," Opal finally spoke.

Fear, Noura thought gratefully. Fear she could work with. "Don't be afraid. You can win this," Noura started, but she stopped, seeing the darkness gather behind Opal's eyes, and she understood what it meant. Opal wasn't scared of the battle. She was scared because she didn't know if she wanted to win.

THE DAY DRAGGED ON IN agony. As if the sky knew my turmoil, it wept large drops of cool summer rain all day, cloaking my loneliness in a dreary, damp fog. I spent the day in my books, pretending to do my studying, but no amount of algebra or *Poems from the Sea of Suns* could capture my mind. Alana was going to leave me. Ilynn was going to leave me. And their absence gripped my heart with icy fingers, wrenching away the joy from my memories. What would I do when they were really gone—really grown up?

A *tap-tap* echoed from my window. I was already on my way to sleep, but I sat up, alarmed by the sound. I had been drifting off to the painful drone of my thoughts but was wide awake now. My heart pounded. Had I imagined the noise? My imagination was a wild thing unsheathed, but when the noise came again, I knew it was real. I shuttered, seeing movement on the other side of the glass. A fluttering.

Not quite frozen in fear, I slipped quietly out of bed and approached my window. I glanced around the room to assure myself that the sound was not coming from inside. Nevma was asleep on my pillow. Silent. The light from the moon lit up the night. Scattered across the landscape, faint figures swayed. *Only trees*, I assured myself.

Then I saw them. One of the black creatures flew into the glass before falling onto the window sill outside. The other shadowy moths fluttered around like mist evading a sunrise. Why were they at my window?

Quietly, I opened it and reached my hand into the night. Nothing else was stirring. I was safe. Two of them alighted on my outstretched hand, their legs tickling my fingers as they crawled along. Once more, I noticed how black their coloring was. A deep blackness that threatened to consume every other color. After a moment, they began to flutter away, and a desire to follow after them rose inside me. Where did they come from, and where were they going? I heard a buzzing behind me, and I spun around in fright, blood rushing in my ears. Nevma was hovering knuckles from my face.

"Oh," I mumbled, "it's just you." I watched as he blinked sleepily at me, but I could sense a warning in his spirit. He flew to the window. The moths had disappeared into the cool night, but I knew Nevma wanted me to close the window. Since the moment had passed, I conceded and sealed myself in, away from the darkness outside.

The Lore Wielder

Don't you want to fight it? I heard Nevma in my mind, but I stumbled back to bed and covered my head with the blanket once more, memories of Noura's words twinkling in my mind. What good would fighting do? If darkness sought me out, maybe that was where I belonged.

Ten

Memoir three

AVARLYN THRIVED FOR THREE HUNDRED *years as a people that arose from those who returned to following the Heir. They built their greatest city around the river the Heir had sent them—the Rema Soul—and shared the water with all. Even people from other lands came to partake of the Sweet Waters. Yet, the time of their testing had come. Teachings and practices that were harmful had arisen, and as a punishment for their waywardness, Da'Shinar, the land across the water, took the city of Madrielle and ransacked it, torturing the priests and Elowynnites in search of the source of the Sweet Water. But the Rema Soul couldn't be controlled. As they exploited the water and searched for its source, the sweetness abandoned the Rema Soul, and its healing properties ceased. It was another hundred years before the Madriens overthrew the occupation and only after 23,000 Avarish people lost their lives. The Madriens waited in anxious hope for the Rema Soul to be restored, since the yoke of Da'Shinar was thrown off, but it wasn't. Though the river was never the same, Avarlyn did its best to remain true to its land's heritage.*

I couldn't remember a Memoir Day without my sister by my side. Her absence was a missing limb as I sat beside Yemma and Appa, completely shut out from the world of the middlings. Is this what it would be like when Alana and Ilynn did leave for Madrielle? I was floundering without anyone else to catch hold of. There was only one other person I could rope my sail to.

I watched Alius from a distance, his dimpled smirk accompanying the chatter of the other middlings. The laughter. Why couldn't I be like them? Every move I made, every word I spoke held treachery. I couldn't risk it. But I was still here, and maybe there was still hope Alius would prove himself this time.

I shifted uneasily beside Yemma as she spoke with Ilynn's yemma all about the possibilities of the Fellowship. I never minded listening, but today, with the butterflies in my stomach on patrol, I was suffocating. I almost didn't care if Alius saw me staring. Maybe it would remind him that I, too, existed. Nevma's scratchy legs crawling up my arm nearly made me jump.

Just wanted to remind you that I, too, exist.

"Do you?" I murmured, the soft breeze catching my stray hairs. It fell in a long ponytail, unadorned by daggers.

You can't tie your sail to anyone else. They will always disappoint you.

I bit my lip, bitterness stirring in my heart. *Then what? Do I just give up?* I closed my eyes tightly, pushing back any tears that dared to escape.

You tie yourself to the truth—to *me*. Nevma landed on my shoulder, but I still refused to look at him.

No one even knows about you. But that wasn't true. Noura knew about him. How, I had no idea.

"You ready, Opi?" Appa joined us, fracturing my thoughts. Crushing them. I nodded to him, Alius's last chance to prove himself was gone. I'd trusted him, almost to the point of sharing my darkest thoughts. It had tried to pour out of me like dark, scary ink when we were in the boat. *I wouldn't mind dying.*

I turned over those words in my mind again. They were still true—dark, but true. Life did not fit, and what did life hold for me if I did not belong?

I gave him one last look. Maybe if I was truly gone, he would realize I was somebody. For a moment, he found my gaze, but instead of seeing me, he looked past me. It was as if he didn't want anyone else to know we were friends. I blinked away my tears. I would not cry over losing a friendship if it had not been real.

The previous day's stormy mood trickled across the pale sky, more clouds rolling in. I looked back as they rose, dark and ominous. Something about their ambiance tugged at the darkness in me. The loneliness. I was the dark cloud surrounded by blue skies. Alana. Ilynn. Alius. Yemma and Appa. Noura and even Dion. Why did I have to be the dark cloud? It only held purpose when the ground was in want of rain, and the sounds of thunder were only a price to pay. And the thundering rolling in my being was deafening.

I clutched a pen in my hand as I sat at my desk, words burning in my mind and a flame flicking shadows on my wall. The ink blotted on the page, shiny and dark. What would I do with the words after I wrote them down? I blinked, my pen hovering a moment longer.

I say you're going to miss me when I'm gone. I say it with my eyes closed. It's easier to pretend that way.

I laid my pen down, staring at the black letters, tears wetting my cheeks. I narrowed my eyes at the words, hating them. Hating that I wrote them and hating that I cared. How could I be so weak?

I held the piece of paper to the open flame, watching the tongues of fire consume the misery I had penned there.

I welcomed sleep like a lost friend, but when it was interrupted by the tapping, I abandoned that friend for a new one. With only a little reservation, I dared to crack open the window another time. Five moths flew inside, swirling over my head, intensifying and validating the sadness that always lingered there beneath the surface. The same sentence rang in my ears, overwhelming any other thought. *I wouldn't mind dying. I don't want to live if living feels like this.*

I was not brave enough to follow them that night. I sealed my window once more before accepting a restless sleep.

My dream flickered, tainted with smoke. Tainted with moths. Master Devn's voice hounded my ears. *She's been ousted.* I trembled, blinking at the muttering crowd before me in my dream. The stage in the festival courtyard creaked under my feet.

"She's been forsaken by the Gilding magic!" Another voice shouted.

I glanced down at the dagger in my hand. Black gems glittered in the handle. It wasn't mine.

"Lindi!" a voice cried from the crowd. My eyes snapped up, and I saw someone I didn't recognize tearing through the host of people. My pulse raced and I dropped the dagger as I backed away. I wasn't just ousted. I *was* Lindi the Forsaken.

I sat up in my bed, covered in a cold sweat. My eyes darted around the room. My daggers were gone. I clenched my eyes shut, afraid to return to sleep.

The next evening, as I sat on the cushions, my hot tea untouched, I watched my parents stirring around me. Alana had been gone for three days, three long days of me being beaten by the wind with no anchor to stay the unbelonging. The quietness suffocating the house and the unabashed fear was what life held for me when Alana truly left me. But the winged creatures, wherever they led me, would welcome me, and the darkest parts of me wouldn't scare them away.

Yemma was arranging the fresh flowers she'd cut and fussing over the leaves and petals that had dropped onto the table. Appa was putting on his boots to finish some evening chores outside, and Alana's place was empty. I was contemplating the relief of death. It felt strange that I could not even climb out of this deep well of depression even among family—who I knew loved me. They would be heartbroken if they could hear my thoughts. But I wondered if their comfort could penetrate the dark veil that had captured me. Yet, the sadness was a part of me now—a hunger and an addiction.

I climbed under my covers with a strange anticipation. Would the moths come tonight? The sound of my breathing roared in my ears as I lay in the quiet stillness of the night. There was almost no moonlight tonight, and the darkness outside the window looked black as coal—a blackness to come and linger in as it whispered to my soul. Nevma alighted on my pillow, next to my watery eyes. His eyes were watery too, and I could feel him pulling at my spirit, reminding me that we could bear the loneliness together. I stared at him through the blur. *No, not tonight,* I thought. *I want to feel it, to know it, and to linger in it.*

If you silence my voice, how will you find your way home? Nevma's thoughts crossed mine.

"The sadness is my home," I responded.

No. Sadness is not a place someone can belong. Death is not a place someone can belong. Don't forget who you are.

I fought the urge to turn over and ignore him.

Then who am I? I screamed inside my head. Nevma stared at me with unblinking eyes that mirrored my tears. **You are mine.**

Noura's words came back to me for a moment. *Don't drown him out.* Don't drown him out. If Noura knew about Nevma and knew that I needed to hear his voice, why had she not explained anything to me? I ground my teeth in determined frustration. It wasn't enough to hold on to—to keep me from embracing the dark.

The tapping began. Gently, then it grew louder. The creatures wanted inside my room. The darkness veiled them from view, but I felt them. Their compounded darkness reached out to mine with soothing fingers. My pulse thudded in my ears as I crept quietly to my window and, with cold, shaky hands, lifted the latch.

As soon as there was space below, the black moths streamed into my room like smoke. They whirled around me in a tornado of wings. Any fear left in me was buried underneath the hunger inside me to make my life matter, even if it ended in tragedy. I reached up, their wings brushing my fingertips, soft and inviting. How could something sinister be soft? Understanding? Noura's words crept through my mind again. *A battle for your heart is coming.* What if this wasn't a battle I wanted to win? I shut my eyes against Noura and Dion's faces. I clenched my teeth at Ilynn's words. *You are loved, Opi...* I forgot Alana's embrace. I blotted out their love with the ink of pain. The only thing that truly wanted me was this darkness. If I was gone, people would realize what they'd lost—that I was worthy of their love.

In one last swirl, the moths dispersed, creeping on the walls, my bed, my books, my clothes—on everything. I watched as my room crawled with the creatures, all my belongings, my mark on the world, buried beneath their wings. A subtle picture of my absence. Maybe when it was too late, I would be wanted. I reached for my cloak and slipped on my boots. Whatever was out there, I had no plans to fight.

The moths trickled out into the night, but I had already decided to follow them. With one glance back at Nevma asleep on my pillow, I stole into the chilly shadow of night, dropping to damp soil beneath my window.

The moon, cold and faint, echoed empty in my mind. Just as Nevma's words couldn't pierce my numb heart. I held my hand out in front me, and my eyes could barely find its shape. Even though I could not see the moths, I knew where they were headed—towards the river, the tributary of Snowcap Creek that ran by our house. I stumbled into the blackness, yet I knew the path so well that I never faltered. Something deep inside of me dared to hope the song might find me, that lullaby singing of a home. I ignored the warm tears that dripped down my face and down my neck in a steady flow.

If there was ever a time for the song to show me the way home, it was now. It was now, when not even Nevma had stirred in my absence. I shuddered, clutching onto an outstretched branch. I couldn't remember a time that he'd ever left me. It didn't matter that I was the one who slipped into the night—he promised to always be with me, didn't he?

I let out a silent scream as I continued to stumble through the black forest. And the forest answered. As if the trees themselves were trying to stop me, their roots grabbed at my ankles to keep me from my next step, and large branches reached out their tender arms to hold me back from my demise. The leaves brushed my cheeks in a desperate hope to dry my tears. Yet I pushed on, drawn deeper into the blackness. The sound of rushing water entered my ears, and I broke into a run, pushed on by an intense urge to get to the water. No, two intense urges to get to the water. The two impulses fought inside of me, yet asked me to do the same thing. Get to the water.

My feet splashed into the cold river, the current pulling at my ankles. I paused in confusion, sensing the two forces inside of me. One wanted me to bend down and drink in the cold, fresh water. The other wanted something else entirely. It beckoned me with a chilly whisper as I felt the soft wings of the moths flying around me. I glanced to the side at its request, and there, tied up, was the boat. I could barely make it out, but I knew it well enough that I could see it bobbing gently in the water, held back from the current by its anchor. I'd followed the black creatures this far; I wasn't going to abandon them now. Wherever they were from had been calling me, summoning me. I had to answer. With one last look at the glistening water below, doing its very best to reflect what little light there was into my eyes—my soul—I turned away.

Moments later, I found the edge of the boat and ran my fingers down the familiar side. It almost felt ironic that this boat that I knew so well would be my passage and gateway into the darkness. As I untied its anchor, I did not hurry.

Everything moved in slow motion as I took in every moment and every decision. How ever black the night was, it did not cloud my mind. I knew and felt everything before me. Carefully, I climbed in and let the boat drift silently down the river, carried by the water. The very water that had beckoned to save me. I stared into the darkness, the trees watching me as I floated past. They rustled, even reached out their arms in one last attempt, but I brushed them away, sustaining my numbness in opposition to their desperate murmuring. They were too late.

The creek dumped me into the familiar cove, but instead of the current fading, it pushed me on. It carried me deeper into Misty Lale. Curious, I leaned over the side and dipped my hand into the chilly water. What was usually so clear and dazzling looked as deep and endless and dark as the space beyond the stars. Yet, the longer I stared, I noticed strange shapes moving all about me. I sucked in a breath, heart racing, as I realized that I was not caught in a current. I was being swept along by the creatures in the water.

Faces, eyes, and hands shimmered up at me. Naiads. I threw myself into the bottom of the boat, the numbness shattering. The moths reacted immediately, landing on my arms and hands, the soothing tug returning. I lifted my head, peering at the night around me. One of the water spirits reached up a glimmering hand and caught one of the moths in its palm. A dim, cold light shone from its hands, and I blinked in awe. What was happening? I leaned once more over the edge of the boat, more in wonder than fear, due to the calm work of the moths. The light dropped into the water like a diamond before spreading out with long chilling ripples into the lake.

As I watched, new shapes appeared in the rippling liquid light, but these were shapes I recognized. I saw myself. I saw

The Lore Wielder

Alana and Ilynn. Gripping the edge of the boat, I drew closer to the glowing figures. We were all together, laughing and talking. Alana was not the favored friend, and I was not the tag-along. We were equal. My chest ached until I thought it would crack. Why could it not be that way? Why was belonging so out of reach?

Before I had time to wipe away any tears, another image came to life. It was Alius, and a coldness spun in the pit of my stomach. He was sitting next to me on a rock by the lake shore, studying me. I watched as I shared with him about the darkness inside me, and he didn't shy away or brush it off. He took my hand in his and drew me into an embrace. I blinked in the strange light, wiping the tears from my face once more. That's all I wanted. I'd simply wanted to be someone worthy of listening to, to be seen for who I was and not rejected.

More shapes appeared before my eyes, but my mind was reeling from the pain. The pain of seeing my deepest desires and knowing they could never be. The boat stopped along with the beating of my heart. The watery light of the images vanished, and I was left in pitch darkness somewhere on Misty Lale, lost. Frantically, I began to search the bottom of the boat for the oars. My initial feeling—that the darkness would be welcoming somehow—was evaporating. I had to get away from here, from this lake and from the naiads.

Something horrible, scratchy, and sharp grabbed my hand. I screamed in terror as large bony wings flapped around me, and the smell of death tainted the air.

I covered my head and ears, throwing myself into the bottom of the boat. I knew what these creatures were. My breath raced as my eyes refused to focus. They were an omen. *The* omen. Harfares of death—twice as big as crows and as bony as skeletons. Their screeches pierced the night, and their black beaks hunted for my eyes. *Hafares go for the eyes.* I snatched up the oar and swatted at the featherless creatures, screaming. One of their talons sliced my arms and I fumbled with the oar, eyeing the water. If I jumped from the boat, naiads would surround me. Another Harfare swooped towards me, but the boat tipped, and my head smacked against the side, the oar clattering out of reach. I rolled to the bottom with a groan. The rocking intensified, and I realized with a shriek that the naiads were capsizing my boat. I was going into the water whether I wanted to or not. Trembles cascaded over my body. *This is not where I belong.*

"Nevma," I whispered through tears of terror and the cry of prey from the Harfares. "I'm so lost. Help—"

My words were cut off as the boat rolled over in one powerful motion, and I was met with the cold embrace of Misty Lale. No, it wasn't Misty Lale. It was the embrace of naiads. I resurfaced for only a moment before the underworldly hands caught hold of me and yanked me back under into their prison. I held my breath as they dragged me deeper into the blackness. I struggled against them, blinking burning eyes, expecting a realm of darkness. Bubbles rolled from my lips, and a cold glow below grew stronger as I was pulled deeper. I struggled against the hands and arms made of water. Their forms rippled and shifted eerily as the water moved them, and their eyes shone hollow as if they themselves had been tortured. My mind flashed back to sitting in the living room with my family. I would never see them again. The relief of death was a lie.

My lungs burned under the crushing pressure of the water. The dim glow grew but my vision faded with my breath. I knew this feeling. Terrible pain was coming and then that chilling calm once I accepted the water into my body. Just before my world went black, I glimpsed something writhing at the bottom of the lake against bonds made of reeds. Its glowing eyes bored into me, and an inhuman beauty shone from its face as its form shimmered in the water. A naiad.

Chills tore through me as the naiad strained at the lake reeds, the creature in desperate want to catch hold of me. At the naiad's beckoning, the long, slimy lake reeds reached their fingers and wrapped themselves around my body. Cold, hateful touches of death pulsed through me before water flooded my lungs, and a sense of torment I'd never known before overcame my body.

My life above, outside in the warm sunlight, wasn't the source of my torment. It was this. This evil darkness had not only drawn me into its claws, but it infested my soul. I was its host.

Eleven

MY EYES FLEW OPEN AGAIN, and a flash of silver glinted in the dark water. A knife. But how did I return to consciousness? For a brief moment, I saw myself floating in the water, mouth parted and eyes glazed. Helplessly, I watched as a hand skillfully slashed through the deathly cords that bound me. The only words reeling through my foggy mind were, *is it too late?* My vision reentered my body with a jolt as my rescuer gracefully swam around me, slicing through the thick, slimy reeds. But the water around us whipped into a violent swirling current. The naiad at the bottom, burning holes in me with his soulless eyes, spun the water in his rage. He would not let me go. I writhed, screaming against his power. The knife bearer swept away from me in one powerful current, but she caught my hand, refusing to let go. She locked eyes with me, and I realized with a shock that it was Noura looking back at me. Her grip tightened, and I thought my fingers would be crushed, but a conviction gripped me. I could not let go of that hand, or I would perish.

In one final effort, she cut my last bonds, and we spun into the torrent, flipping through the rushing water. The current wrapped me in its arms, sucking me down into the depths, into the clutches of the creature sentenced to suffer there. My hope of escape had died, but the terror of that beautiful, haunting being caressed me as its face drew near. Its rage dimmed, its hate hidden. He soothed my emotions, that familiar sensation of belonging in the dark still an ember in my soul. But with Noura's hand firmly in mine, I knew beyond a doubt that there was no belonging in the dark.

But Noura's grip on my hand loosened. Her fight against the current ceased as her hands stilled and the light in her eyes winked out. What tears I did shed were lost in our watery grave. *Not Noura*, I cried from within my soul. When I relented to the shadow's summons, I not only sentenced myself to death but her as well. What had I done?

"Nevma," I gurgled as I spun deeper into darkness. Why didn't I listen to him? But death would not separate us. That, I knew.

A glow pierced the darkness from above before swirling around us, silencing the currents. The shimmering shape of a horse swam towards us and gently lifted us onto its back. The tail swished, and the mane brushed my cheeks as I looked down in shock at the graceful creature. It was shining, bright as the sun in my eyes, under my pale, lifeless hands. I tried to hold on, and I realized with a shock it was holding on to me. In some mysterious way, it embraced me as it galloped up towards the surface at a liberating speed. I fixed my gaze on the light above, refusing to look back at the blackness below. Noura grasped my waist so tightly my ribs threatened to crack—physical pain. Relief fractured the deadness of the realm around me.

We broke through the surface a stone's throw away from the shore, and I gulped in the cold night air. Noura coughed and sputtered as the waterhorse trotted us towards land. A swarm of Harfares attacked, but Noura slashed at them with deadly precision. They fell like rocks into the black water around us, their bodies leaking yellow liquid. It crossed my mind that this was their true form, not the light soft-winged creatures that allured me. The tears absorbed by the lake now fell freely as the horror of what happened reached me. I had been in death's grasp. I not only felt it but saw it face to face.

As soon as my feet hit the rocky shore, I collapsed. Not even the sharp rocks could incite me to move. My body was numb, and I gratefully accepted the lack of pain now that the smell of sand and rock assured my senses. The danger of the water had passed, and I dug my fingers into the sand as a boat grounded behind me.

"Noura, there's no time!" a familiar voice cried in earnest. It was Dion. "Get them to the cave—now!" *Them?* Strong arms wrapped around me as Dion lifted me from the ground. *What cave?* I looked up just in time to see a beacon of light streaming from the cliffs above. The lighthouse.

My eyes lulled and my chin sank against my chest. I could not have been afraid even if I tried. My body held no capacity to feel anymore. Dion swiftly crossed to the entrance of the cave and laid me down.

"Are they breathing?" Noura whispered, her voice breaking.

"We may have been too late," Dion said in a soft voice.

They both collapsed on the ground, and Noura, slowly and carefully, lay a tiny something next to me. It took a moment for my vision to focus before I recognized the shimmering blue body and delicate wings. Nevma. With quivering hands, I scooped him up and brought him close to my face. Why wasn't he moving? My throat tightened as I stared at his perfectly still form.

The Lore Wielder

"Nevma, no—don't leave me," I sobbed, shuddering as something deep inside me, deeper than my desire for death had been, snapped. Why did I answer the darkness's call? I meant for me to die, not anyone else. A gentle hand rested on my shoulder, and I looked through blurry eyes at Noura's face.

"It was him, Opal. Nevma saved us. He was the waterhorse. I couldn't save you no matter how hard I tried," she said, smiling painfully at me. "He carried us."

The weight of his body was lead in my hands. I had not merely led him into danger—he risked himself to save me. Now he was dead. Unable to speak, I blinked at his limp body cradled in my hands, all the breath in my lungs deserting me.

"Opal, listen to me," Noura continued. "He's not dead."

"He's—not?" I stammered.

"The spirit can't die," Dion spoke up. "But he must be taken back to the source."

My breath came back to me, edged with hope. Nevma was my first memory. The first to listen and hear my thoughts. The only one who always understood me and never left my side, even when I ran away from his. I owed him my life.

Resolution filled my heart, and I couldn't tear my eyes from his still form. Wherever this source was, I would climb the highest mountain to get him there.

"Where is the source?" I asked, not looking up. I felt both Noura and Dion smile at me—at the boldness unearthing.

"Do you trust us?" Noura asked in a low, steady voice.

I swallowed, taking in their intense faces, and slowly nodded my head. Would I be brave enough for what lay ahead? I glanced back at Nevma cupped in my hand. But what reality lay ahead without him by my side?

"You have to get him back to the garden—The Lost Garden. The source is there," Dion began.

"But it's forbidden." I stared back, even as my words rang empty in my ears. It didn't matter, not if it brought Nevma back to me.

"Opal, our home is never forbidden," Noura answered, warmth dancing in her eyes.

"Your—home?" I stuttered.

"Where did you think we came from?" Dion mused. My eyes flickered between them. They were from The Lost Garden. My mind reeled. How? I rose to my feet, not looking back at the lake behind me. The pilgrimage was forbidden for me, but what other choice lay ahead? My blink faltered as I spoke. "Show me the way."

"An old path leads up from Wisptale into the mountains. It was used by pilgrims in the past and has lodging along the way. It's a few days' journey."

"Can't—will you come with me?" I asked, but I knew the answer. Both Noura and Dion shook their heads. My hands trembled. A journey into the mountains alone. All my desire to welcome loneliness evaporated in the chilly night air. My pulse thudded in opposition, but my love for Nevma offered a steadiness I didn't know I had.

"Dion and I have another task ahead of us," Noura relayed, regret rimming her eyes.

I forced myself to take a few deep breaths, my sore lungs burning, before resigning to my fate. "Where is the path?"

"It's in here," Dion answered. "It's always been here in this cave." He slid his pack off his shoulders and handed it to me. "Take this—it has food for a few days, some supplies for the journey."

I shoved down the whirl of ice that rose in my gut and numbly took the pack from Dion. He returned to the boat to retrieve something as Noura pulled me into an embrace.

"You can do this, Opal. Only you can do this," she whispered.

"And you might need these." Dion's boots ground on the pebbles as he appeared behind Noura. I gasped, staring at the box in his outstretched hand.

"How did you get that?" I cried, my hand twitching at my side. Should I take it? My daggers had been revoked for a reason.

"Take them," Noura whispered with an encouraging push on my shoulder. I clenched my fist a moment longer before accepting the box. A rush of memories tore through me. Failure. Longing. Being cast out. But what echoed loudest were the words *made anew*.

Dion settled his hands on my shoulders. "Wear them. Use them. They are yours." He pulled me into an unexpected hug.

A haunting screech echoed off the water. Dion released me, taking a step towards the exit, his face hardening.

"What is it?" I whispered even as realization hit me.

Dion unlooped a slingshot from his belt and snatched up a handful of rocks. "Harfares cannot be killed. Not truly. And they already have your scent." He cursed under his breath before bounding towards the cavern's exit. "Stay on the path!"

Noura's hand met my trembling one. "Opal, you have to leave now."

"What about my family?" I asked as another screech haunted the night. We both stiffened, staring at the exit where Dion vanished.

Noura clenched her eyes shut as a shiver ran through her. "The Harfares are hunting *you*. The farther away you are, the safer your family will be." Her grip on my arm tightened. "I will tell them what has happened. I promise."

She led me towards the back of the cave, throwing a glance behind her towards the lake. Water poured in from above from the redirected river, hiding the crevice marring the cavern wall behind it. When I reached its edge, a strange greenish glow trickled through the dark tunnel like veins.

"They are cognizant vines," Noura said breathlessly. "They only glow for true pilgrims."

I'm not a true pilgrim. I'm just a desperate girl trying to save her best friend.

I retrieved my daggers from the box and handed it to Noura along with Nevma. I buckled one sheath around my thigh and wove the other dagger into my hair. Noura cradled Nevma in the velvet before tucking him inside the box and placing it in my pack.

"Are you ready?" she asked.

"What happens if I fail?" I murmured, "to Nevma?"

She hesitated. "He will never wake."

Dion's shouts clashed with a harfare's piercing cry, and something splashed into the water.

Noura's gaze tore from mine to the cave mouth. "Only travel under the cover of trees. If you see any flying-creature of the dark, hide yourself, and *do not move.* Now *go!*" She shoved me into the tunnel. "And don't forget to listen!"

I stumbled as I entered the darkness, my chest pounding. What was there to listen to in here? I gathered my breath and held onto the pack until my fingers ached. What if the Harfares found me again? I cursed.

I chose not to look back at Noura for fear my confidence would wane. The pit in my stomach deepened but I put one shaking foot in front of the other until the opening behind me vanished. The only thing that stayed my feet on the course was the limp body of the dragonfly I carried. And the knowledge that I was being hunted. The Source in The Lost Garden was the only thing that could help us now.

The Lore Wielder

The tunnel's rocky walls, reaching a few arms over my head, crept with green vines. I reached up a hand to touch them as I ran along the tunnel. When I removed my fingertips, they sustained some of the glow. A *true pilgrim. What did that mean?*

Deeper, I traveled into the cliff side until the rocky ground turned to dirt and my breath deepened. The incline changed. I was going up into the mountain. The pack made my back ache, but the terror beating at the edges of my mind would not allow me to rest here. Not in the dark, deep, earth where I could see no way out. It may feel safe from Harfares down here, but I knew they made their nests deep in the caves of the world. The miserable thought crossed my mind that this might be the entire journey, buried beneath the ground for days. I shivered. There had to be an end to the darkness of this infernal night.

Eventually, the tunnel became so steep that I had to use my hands. I climbed at a steady pace for nearly forty minutes in the dark, wiping the sweat from my forehead and blinking tired, strained eyes. I dug my fingers into the vine-covered dirt and hoisted myself up again. Where was the end? On my next climb, I grasped roots, and I breathed in relief at the feel of their sturdy wood—their tangible comfort sent from the world above. A weak light reached into the tunnel, and a burst of energy washed over me. Hope.

With one last effort, I pulled myself out of the tunnel and collapsed, exhausted on the ground. I blinked, taking in the canopy of dark leaves above me. The tunnel led me to the base of a huge tree. A soft yellow light mingled with the pale sky, and I turned my weary eyes towards the east. A halo of gold fought back the last whispers of darkness. Night was over at last.

NOURA INHALED AS IF IT WERE the last breath she might ever breathe before sinking to the floor of the cavern. Dion raced to her side and caught her arm, softening her fall. She was exhausted. Her body quaked, and her mind burned with what just happened. The calm exterior she held together for Opal, broke.

"Are they gone?" Noura murmured, clutching her brother's arm.

Dion nodded. "The Harfares are gone. For now." He knelt beside his sister. "You did it. Opal's exactly where she is meant to be."

Noura buried her face in her hands, a shuddered breath heaving in her chest.

"You did what hasn't been done in nearly half a century," Dion continued.

Noura swallowed, gathering herself and lifting her eyes to her brother. "I know," she whispered, vivid images flashing through her mind, but they were not of Opal. She rose to her feet, leaning on Dion's strong arm. "In the Unreal, I failed." Her eyes flickered away as she turned from him. It was a failure she would never forget. One without redemption.

Dion sighed, his brow creasing. "If you hadn't failed before, would you have had the strength to go after her? To keep believing even after all hope was lost?"

Noura shivered, her dress dripping with lake water. "I don't know." She folded her arms, stepping around the many pools of water towards the beacon of light streaming from the lighthouse. Dion trailed her, and she almost wished he wouldn't. This was why the Unreal existed. Failure wasn't new to Noura, even if her mission outside the Rim was. *Fear of death is only a distraction.* She clung to the words she knew so well. If that was true, fear of failure was but a drop in a pail.

"All we're asked to do is follow. Our weaknesses are far less important than we think they are," Dion said from behind her.

Noura nodded, facing him again. "What do we do now? This didn't go exactly as I planned."

"Not as *you* planned." Dion mused before answering. "We get Opal to The Lost Garden."

Noura tilted her head, peering at the light outside before approaching the boat. "I'm going to speak with Opal's parents. They deserve to know what has happened." She paused. "Meet me outside the lighthouse in two hours. Can you manage until I return?"

Dion scoffed. "Of course. But what is your plan? The Harfares will be hunting us now too."

The twinkle in Noura's eyes returned. "Have you forgotten that healing isn't my strongest gift?"

SUNLIGHT PEEKED THROUGH THE LEAVES of the tree, casting little bits of heaven all around me. After losing myself in the shadows of night, my soul drank up the morning like an elixir. I blinked in the light, searching for Nevma flying in the sky before my face fell. I drew the box from my pack and cracked it open. Nevma lay still, swathed in velvet. My eyes grew misty as I thought how truly lonely I was without him. If he did not come back because of me, I didn't think I could forgive myself.

From my place high up on the mountain overlooking Misty Lale, I could see Wisptale far below. It was only a league away, sitting peacefully and innocently on the lake that had nearly consumed me—and Noura. A league would be nothing for a harfare. I had to keep moving.

After finding a handful of dried fruit and nuts in the pack, I shouldered it and stared at the wild woods before me. What in Avarlyn was I going to do now? My family must know of my absence by now. Noura told them. I chewed the inside of my cheek, biting back tears.

A familiar melodic breeze tousled the leaves above me, and I hesitated before following the tree's branches to the old, twisted trunk, its roots bracing the ground for hundreds of years. As I brushed the bark with my fingertips, the memories it bore from all the ages whispered back. Above me, something was carved into the wood. One section was written in letters foreign to me and the other in Old Avarish.

A song from the beginning, forever abides
An echo of all the beauty ever known
Notes that seek and that notes find
From the Sweet Waters mercifully sown
The broken and bleeding-hearted they bind
Listen, beloved, for its melody guides you home

I ran my fingers over the old grooves in the flesh of the tree, recognition flickering through me. On the wind, through the leaves, these words had whispered to me as long as I could remember. I caught my breath, sliding my fingers away. It wasn't an old lullaby but something else—something deeper, more intertwined with our world.

Noura's last words clicked. *Don't forget to listen.*

Twelve

THE SCARED, REJECTED LITTLE GIRL inside me would have to be dethroned if I was to save what mattered most. I had touched ultimate loneliness deep in Misty Lale. I touched a world void of joy and comfort—a world void of Nevma—and I never wanted to experience that again.

I inhaled, staring at the wild path ahead, the unknown before me, all I'd ever known behind. As if reading the poem awoke the song, its music drifted down the mountain towards me. I threw one last look back. The sky remained clear. I adjusted my pack and entered the forest. Dion bought me more time than I deserved.

The underbrush snagged my ankles as the trees swayed around me, and the wind played with my unruly hair like a mischievous fairy. If this was a path, it was one ages ago, any sign of another pilgrim's mark erased by time. I frowned at the word *pilgrim*. The only people who went on pilgrimages to The Lost Garden were Elowynnites. I ducked under a branch, crumpling a leaf in my hand. But I wasn't after a ritual. This pilgrimage wasn't for me. It was for Nevma.

Leslie Montaño

Sweat dampened my skin, and I piled my hair on top of my head, welcoming the breeze across my neck. It had been hours now, hours of hiking in the wild. My feet radiated heat, and as I bent to unlace my boots, it crossed my mind that the path should be leading me south. I slipped my boots off and dropped onto a nearby boulder, keeping an eye on the sky. The Rema Soul flowed from The Lost Garden, as the legends recorded, and cut through the city of Madrielle. But that was south, farther down the coast of the lake.

As it was, the sound of the song continued to tumble down from the mountain. I uncorked my water canteen and eyed the way ahead. If I remembered this mountain correctly, it eventually plateaued into a plain before rising again. This meant, if I had oriented myself rightly, I was going east.

Lacing up my boots once more, I threw the pack over my shoulders again, keeping the tip of Mount Nea in my view. Its white summit glinted red in the fading sun. I was losing the light, and where was the lodging Dion had promised? A giant made of fear grew inside me as I walked, the shadows around me deepening. Goosebumps traced my arms, and I cursed. The dark always opened a well in my mind for sinister things to crawl out of, but this time, the threat was real.

My hand went for my dagger as movement through the trees caught my attention. A whirl of golden leaves drifted by on the breeze, swirling through the tree branches like a maze. I caught one in my hand as I walked backwards to watch them disappear in the wind. It wasn't yet autumn. Where did the golden leaves come from?

My pace for the last hour had been growing slower, and I paused to scan the sky. Even though no Harfares circled it, I backed under a tree. What if they didn't hunt me as Harfares but moths? How could I see them coming? I shivered. Every twig snapping and owl hooting gripped my chest like a vise.

The sun bid me a reluctant farewell, and I threw off my pack and rummaged through it before finding what I needed. Loose cloth and oil. I searched the underbrush for a long stick before binding the cloth around it and soaking it in the oil. My hands shook as I struck the match, and the woods around me turned from gray to orange. I breathed out, sweeping the torch in a circle to ward away the demons in my head. In the light, the summit disappeared along with the stars. *Forsake all.* How could I find my way now?

I gripped the torch, searching for the path again. But instead of the quiet forest floor, my light cast on a huge form. A ripple of muscle moved under gray fur as the form began to stir. I stumbled back, a deafening wild sound ricocheting into the night. I froze as the massive form rose before me, giant horns flashing in the yellow light. I shrieked, dropping my torch and scrambling away.

I was staring at death again, and instead of Harfares, it had sent a horned beast to drag me back. Its grunts filled the void, the beast stepping closer as I continued to cower on the ground. Its horns dipped towards me and I threw my hands over my head, hot breath meeting my neck. Massive hooves shifted in the leaves, and when no attack came, and no claws grabbed me, I slowly lifted my gaze to the long snout, melancholy eyes, and pointed antlers of a great moose. I gasped, breathing hard. Demon or not, it towered over me, more a giant than anything I could contrive. I snatched up my torch and tore through the forest. Stumbling into a tree with arms outstretched, I threw myself further down the mountain.

The sound of my own footfalls roared in my ears, and I squeezed my eyes shut before daring a glance over my shoulder. No giant beast pursued me through the forest. I was alone. I caught hold of a tree branch, skidding to a stop. The sounds of the forest stilled, all except my breathing.

A moose. Dangerous, but not otherworldly. I'd seen them before, but only from a safe distance.

"It was just an animal. You're all right," I whispered into the night, placing a hand on my chest, willing my heart to calm down. But my heart wouldn't slow, and I froze again as the presence of something else in the woods closed in on every side. Something strange, willowy, and without solid form. Its presence behind me conjured shivers all through my body.

I bolted again, ducking under the thickly laced twigs and shoving branches away in my flight. This was no wild animal. I could feel it.

A root caught hold of my boot, and I crashed to the ground. Tears of panic now budding in my eyes, I snatched a dagger from my hair and brandished it in the face of the strange creature before me.

I muttered through my tears as I forced my eyes to focus on theirs. It took me all but a moment to match them with the eyes of the naiads that had tried to drown me. The sounds of my terror bounced off the mountain, and I slashed wildly with my dagger and torch. I would not let them take me this time, whatever they were.

"Opal!" The voice struck the night, a chord in the silence. My well of terror threatened to explode. How did it know my name?

"Don't be afraid." A gentle hand, which did not try to disarm me, took hold of my wrist.

I struggled but it did not let go. What was this thing? I gasped, tears streaming down my face. *Do I run?*
"Broken and bleeding-hearted, welcome," it spoke to me.

The Lore Wielder

I stared at the glassy, translucent eyes of the being gripping my wrist, my fire to fight faltering. The arms of the other creatures surrounding me took their cue, bent their willowy frames and lifted me off the ground and set me on my feet once more. They knew the verse carved into the tree. Were they friends? Or clever enemies?

I ran my finger over a pearl in my dagger as I grasped it tighter, shifting into a defensive Lore-wielding step—useless against them. The feminine figure who spoke pointed in the direction I'd come. I followed her gaze, another layer of dread pumping into my heart. Blackness swarmed a mere stone's throw away, blacker than the night around us. It circled the sky, searching for a way to enter the forest, but something held it back—an invisible barrier. I blinked away the wetness in my eyes.

"The moths cannot penetrate our barrier," she continued. "You are safe for the moment."

Safe? My eyes flickered between them and the swarm of moths, my grip on the dagger trembling. Harfares disguised as moths beat their wings just outside of their barrier.

"What—what are you?" I stammered, shifting another step away from them. They were like the naiads in their form, but as my heart slowed a pace, I realized their feminine presence was something entirely other. They were not hollowed-out slaves to darkness. My mouth parted as I stared, another layer of ice in my chest melting and a feeling I hadn't known in ages peeking through. Wonder.

"We are Mêliades of the Wild Forest." She paused, a stern calmness in her beautiful face as she bowed her head slightly. Mêliades—spirits of the trees. Dryads. I drew in a breath, disbelief swirling with the wonder inside me. Her head was protected with something reminiscent of an acorn, and long, billowy hair spilled from it, tangled with vines.

"You were in danger. We encouraged you to enter our grove before the darkness reached you." A few of the other dryads glided away from her towards the moths beating at their barrier. She stared back at me with leaf-shaped eyes. "You must go on. There is not much time, but we will give you as much as we can." She glanced back as her people drew their own weapons.

My body tingled, every ounce of comfort I had derived from them vanishing. I had to go on. Alone.

"Please," I begged, "how much farther must I go? And where is the path?" I watched in apprehension as the dryad reached out her willowy hand and placed it over my heart. Over the stain on my chest. At the Melaide's touch, my eyes were opened, and a strange green glow cut into my vision. The cognizant vines. I'd forgotten about them.

"You must extinguish your torch to follow them." She confirmed my dread and must have seen it in my face. "You are almost there, young one. But a word and parting gift before you go." She breathed in, reaching her arms gracefully in front of her as a whirl of their leaves encircled me—just like the tiny golden leaf I'd caught earlier. She spoke again, a riddle this time.

"Only a true surrender,
can save from the stream's Guardian Bender."

"Only a *what?*" I began but stopped, watching as the leaves intertwined, covering my arms, shoulders and head. With one last puff, the Melaide sent the last golden leaf sailing towards me from her hand. When it met the others, a spark of magic rippled through the leaves, melding them together. I spun slowly, the newly fashioned fabric shimmering in the moonlight. It was a traveler's cloak.

The Lore Wielder

"I—thank you." I inclined my head towards the dryad, all grounds for cynicism crumbling. The Melaide wasn't looking at me. She was gazing at the path I entered their grove by, a strange, deep melody accompanying the night air.

"It is a battle song. You must go—now!" She waved her arm in the direction of the vines. I took a deep breath and moved to put away my dagger. "No—don't put it away."

I glanced back at her, wishing she said something else, but I gripped the hilt of my weapon tighter as her form rushed away from me in a myriad of leaves and branches to join the fight. A fight against darkness I had brought to their grove.

Shoved up the path by the danger behind me, I hid my face in the deep hood of the cloak, guilt rising in my throat.

After another half hour of walking by the light of the vines, the ground flattened, and I came to the forest's edge. I paused, a grassy plain spreading out in the deep gray of the starry night. Crickets echoed off the mountains, and I stretched my stiff fingers, releasing my dagger into my other hand. Where was the lodging Dion had promised? I scanned the plain again, venturing into the tall grass.

I muttered to the stars. "It must be here somewhere." I pulled the cloak tightly around myself as another breeze ruffled the grass. The vines stopped with the forest.

Relief finally entered my weary bones when I spotted a small shack, tucked away just beyond the forest's end. The first day's journey ended, and even through hunger pains, all I could think about was the safety of those walls.

Wearily, I trudged towards the door set in an uneven frame. Cracks split the dry wood panels, and I wondered if a breath of wind might collapse the whole thing. I continued to grip my dagger, but if I had to use it, I would have to rely on muscle memory. My mind was already asleep in whatever cot was inside.

A lantern hung on a post, and I quickly shook off my pack to grab the matches inside. After a few moments, the lantern flickered to life. I lifted the latch, and the door swung open with a creak. After another calming breath, I entered clutching the lantern, taking in the small room. No windows graced the walls, but a small fireplace stood directly across from the door. A cot was against another wall, and a small table sat next to it. I quickly shut out the night and firmly locked the door. I was half glad for the windowless walls. Nothing could come tapping at the glass. Or scratching at it. I shook out a blanket from Dion's pack and curled up on the cot with Nevma's box, leaving the lantern burning. I was too tired to light a fire. Too tired to eat. The lantern and Nevma's presence pressed against my heart were the only comforts left.

I stared at the shadows on the ceiling, daring them to awaken the fear stirring just beneath the surface. But they calmly flickered with the lantern as the words of the poem carved into the tree drifted through my head.

Thirteen

A SOFT, SWEET SOUND ENTERED my dreams. Something all golden and full of light. Something ancient. Dazzling. I knew I was asleep. The notes danced through my soul, like I was the stanza in which they belonged and delighted to flow through. In this place, in the presence of this reality, Nevma was there, flitting here and there, dancing on the breeze to the sound. And I wanted him to stay there, so I stayed. I pressed my eyes tightly together, banishing the wakefulness a few moments longer.

I awoke with a start to the sound of gentle rain falling on the roof. The lantern burned out in the night, but light crept in through the crack under the door. I hurried to unbolt the door and soak in the newness of the morning. A mist had settled over the plateau accompanied by the soft rain. *Good.* I peered at the whiteness swirling above me. As long as the mist remained, maybe I could shake the Harfares from my trail. I stepped out into the rainfall, letting it wash the sweat from my face and the shadows of the night away. Even through the pitter-patter of the raindrops, a rushing sound in the distance grew.

I stepped back under the cover of the roof and hesitantly approached the box still half covered in the blanket. Unlatching the case, I picked up the velvet-wrapped dragonfly, settling on the cot once more. Nevma looked so tiny. I'd never noticed how small he was before, or how delicately his wings glistened.

"Please," I whispered to him, "wake up. I need you." I was so accustomed to crying that I no longer noticed my tears. "I should have listened to you." I took his little body in my hands. He was warm, and my heart brimmed with a quiet hope. Maybe he could hear me.

"I thought you wouldn't understand. I thought you would condemn me for wanting to follow the darkness." I clenched my eyes shut at the lie. I hadn't truly believed it. Nevma had never condemned me, ever. "I chose the lie and the moths over you..." Guilt gripped my throat as I lowered my face to his. "Please come back to me. I'll never leave you again."

I drew back, studying his limp body, an ache in my chest. Had he heard me? A movement caught my eye. His wings twitched.

"Nevma?" I leapt up, searching his body for any other signs of life. I sighed at his still form, afraid to hope. The Spirit cannot die. *Nevma will not die*, I repeated to myself as I laid him safely in his enclosure once more. After having him so close to me while I slept, I didn't want to return the box to my pack. I scanned the room until my eyes fell on the golden cloak. The sash dangled onto the floor, and I snatched it up, tying it into a loop and slipping it over the lid of the case. I relatched the lid and lifted the sash over my head so that the sash crossed my chest and the case rested by my side.

The Lore Wielder

It may have been raining, but rain was not going to stop me. I had to get Nevma to The Lost Garden. There was no time to wait out the storm. I wound my hair in a braided bun before weaving my dagger into it and sheathing the other on my thigh.

I paused as I ran my fingers over the golden fabric of the cloak thrown over the cot. Even in the little light creeping in from the open door, it still glinted, and I could see the shape of each leaf that made up the length of the beautiful garment. I put it on and pulled up the hood. It was as if the dryads knew I would need their gift for protection from the rain today. *They know a lot more than that,* I realized, rummaging through the pack for food before shouldering it and venturing out into the storm.

The rain increased in the last few minutes, and the ground turned muddy and slick. Before my breakfast turned soggy, I ate it in a few large bites. Yemma would have been appalled. A slight smile pulled at my lips before disappearing. Only the Mêliades stood between me and the omens of death treading my heels.

By the time I reached the river, I was soaked to the bone and shivering in the chilly morning. Summer reigned in Wisptale but here, higher on the mountain, whispers of autumn drifted in the wind. I looked out across the rushing water gradually swelling from the rainfall. The other side blurred in the mists, too dangerous to ford in the storm. I glanced back towards the shack. It disappeared under a dreary veil. But I felt it deep in my bones that I could not go back, not even a step. Onward it must be, even if the *how* was out of reach.

As far as I could see, there was no place that the river narrowed. Yet, that might be my only chance. Discouraged, I moved with heavy, wet boots along the bank of the river upstream. Upstream felt more natural, even though it ran south along the edge of the woods and not east, up into Mount Nea. The song had always descended from the mountain. I could not hear it in the storm, but I knew the direction it had left me with was right—further up Mount Nea.

A shape appeared on the ground beyond me. I wiped the water from my eyes, unsure if I was seeing clearly. Not but a few arms away, a small dinghy lay on the bank of the river. I opened my mouth, rainwater dripping in as I approached the boat. Kneeling, I ran my fingers under the edge and flipped it over with a thunk. Water streamed down my face as I stared at it, hesitating. What if this boat failed me too? I dropped to my knees and felt along the ground until I found a handle nearly buried in the mud. How long had this boat been abandoned here? Rainwater filled the bottom of the dinghy and I searched the wood to see if the old hull had been compromised before trusting it to cross the river. After a few inches gathered in the bottom, I dumped it out and, with a grunt, pushed it through the mud and into the current. The current thundered past, and it nearly swept the boat away from me. I gulped, my white fingers gripping the side, my eyes transfixed by the rushing water. My pulse raced, and I threw a glance over my shoulder once more. Only mist hung behind me. I shut my eyes a moment longer. Onward. I snatched up the oar and jumped in, pushing off the riverbed.

The water churned around me, a muddy brown from the soil that was washing into the river. I gripped the oar, determination steadying my hands. I would get Nevma across this river. Alive.

I bit back my panic as we swept downstream. The current tugged at my oar as I paddled, teeth clenched. When the tip of the boat caught a deeper current, it spun, and I dropped the oar, grabbing the sides of the boat to avoid going overboard. *Harfares.* I snatched the oar up again, thrusting it back into the water. *Please, don't let me fall into the water again.*

By the time I neared the middle of the river, my arms burned, but I did not stop. Pine trees pierced the fog from the other side, their branches imploring me to endure. Nevma's box thumped against my side with every oar stroke.

"This is for you, Nevma," I whispered into the storm.

My boots submerged in water. I gasped, looking at the steady stream pouring into the boat. My eyes darted in panic, and I clutched Nevma's box before pulling the oar back in and trying to scoop out the water. Not only were we sinking, but we were being swept away from Mount Nea. The other side of the river blurred past. I reached for the paddle again, forsaking any attempt to stay the leak. We would reach the other side before the boat sank. We had to. With sore hands, I thrust the oar back in the churning water and pulled the oar over and over until the water was halfway up my calves.

"Forsaken Other," I cursed into the storm. The far shore was still out of reach even if I swam. The only thing I could think of was to lighten the weight. I eyed Dion's pack—all the food and supplies I had. I threw it overboard and watched as it was pulled away from me. I glanced back at the water pooling around my legs. To my relief, it slowed, but not enough. The only thing left was me and what I carried on my person. If we sank, I would have to swim. I pulled off my boots and thrust them into the current as well. I reached for my daggers—beautiful and terrible, desired yet scorned, vital and yet not enough. Reluctantly, I surrendered them to the water and watched them sink out of sight, holding tight to Nevma.

All I had, except the clothes on my back, was gone. And half of those would go as well if I had to swim.

The water stopped rising. Not just a little, but completely. The bottom of the boat carried hardly a knuckle of water now.

"That can't be," I whispered, grabbing the oar and taking my opportunity whether I understood it or not. My arms continued to burn, but I ignored the pain as the little box holding Nevma thunked my side again and again. I had something to fight for. And fight for it I would, even if it meant losing everything else.

As soon as the dinghy grounded, I collapsed on the muddy bank, the river pulling at my bare feet and the torrents of rain washing over my tired, sore body. My struggle against the current did not feel like a fight I won. All I had drifted down the current, and my daggers had sunk into the dark riverbed. I was at the mercy of the wild. And the wild answered.

The rain continued to pour as I trudged towards the foot of Mount Nea. I held the hood of my cloak close. It lost its golden color long ago, stained with dirt. My bare feet were cold, and the muddy ground clung to my toes. Under the cover of the trees, I found relief from the constant drum of the rain. The wet underbrush was less kind to my feet than the grass, and I questioned my manic decision to throw away both my boots. And my weapons. I had sentenced myself to my own demise.

All common logic told me to return home. I was walking towards my starvation and death on a quest of which I could see no end—but I knew the end if Nevma never reached The Lost Garden. I rested a hand on the box, refusing to look back at the river. At home. I had to lay down my own instincts. I had to love Nevma more than I loved myself.

The Lore Wielder

The woods grew dark, and if there was a path, I could not see it. The gray of the storm, however, allowed me to follow the green light of the vines. Here, they crawled along the ground and up the tree trunks in a clear pattern. Wind rushed through the trees, rustling their leaves and branches. My imagination sparked to life. What if the rustling was the sound of all the pilgrims who went before me, cheering me on? I paused, watching the dark fir trees dance. If other pilgrims did it, couldn't I? I blinked, peering at the vines leading ever up the mountain. I might not be as strong as them, but I was as desperate to reach the Source. If reaching The Lost Garden could revive Nevma, maybe it could restore me as well.

The rain ceased, and the soft yellow light of the sun broke through the canopy of leaves. I paused in a ray of sunshine, feeling its warmth on my face and willing it to dry my soaked skin. The light pouring into the damp forest felt like a new beginning—the opening of heaven. I squinted up at the sky and smiled as my eyes caught sight of a faint rainbow. I might have been barefoot and hungry, but I was not forgotten.

The melody of the song led me the rest of the day. My body still suffered, but I clung to hope—the hope that I was not forgotten. I might be alone, but this was my pilgrimage, a journey outside of myself and the discovery that there was so much I had yet to understand.

I hoisted myself up a large boulder and gazed out across the plain I had traversed and the river cutting through it. The gray sky faded into a fresh blue as the sun dried up the land. Home was a distant memory, and even the great and vast Misty Lale had vanished from sight. Beyond the wild forest I journeyed through yesterday was nothing but mountain tops and sky. I traversed leagues above whatever darkness slithered in the depths of the lake, and I felt the distance. It was not that it could not reach me at this height but that its power was revealed for what it was—a deception.

A crash broke through the trees to my left. Instinctively, I reached for my daggers but came back empty-handed. I threw myself behind a mound of rocks. The sound of breaking branches and crunching leaves grew. Every one of my senses honed in, and I peered over the rocks, holding my breath. One hand clutched Nevma's box, and the other searched the ground for a stone. Heavy breathing cut through the noise as a figure came into view. Terrified breathing. It took all my strength to stay put and not run as a wild-looking man drew closer. He was gaunt, covered in dirt and looking as if he had seen a ghost. Maybe he had, but I didn't dare move. My head was visible over the rocks, and I clenched my teeth as the man paused, turning around. My breath caught in my throat. I recognized him, but from where? His eyes stared right into me, my grip tightening on the stone in my hand. But he looked away, as if he didn't see me.

"Down. Surely if I keep going down..." His voice croaked dryly before he broke into another run down the path I had ascended. I let my breath out slowly, watching him vanish from sight.

"What...?" I whispered under my breath. I shut my eyes, the adrenaline bleeding out of me. He must have been lost. But why was he here in the first place?

My eyes flew open. *Hail and Harfares.* I jumped to my feet, peering down the path after the Elowynnite. He had escaped from Keepton Thorn and come up here? The pieces snapped together. He came on his own pilgrimage. Only, he didn't make it.

The Lore Wielder

NOURA PATTED THE SWEAT-STREAKED coat of the horse she rode. She and Dion had pushed their horses hard for the last hour, cutting across the mountain pass and into an open field.

Noura straightened, squinting at the sunlight breaking through the trees, and sighed. If things had happened differently, she would still be in Wisptale. The night she nearly drowned with Opal set in motion something Noura herself didn't fully understand. It also meant she had to leave Faelle. Noura hoped she'd guided the girl enough to find her own way to The Lost Garden, but it felt like another dose of bitter failure. Noura twisted a hand in the fabric of her skirt. Yet, there was redemption here. Hope lived on.

Once the Heir set his heart on saving someone, nothing could thwart his hand. Her heart thumped faster remembering the *Story of All Stories*, sung over her since she was a baby. This world, Nadea, may be the Heir's inheritance, but it wasn't his only inheritance. In the Other, the world so broken and torn apart by evil—the world Noura originally belonged to—the fullness of his inheritance lived on. And his inheritance had been won, not by escaping death, but by descending into its depths and slaying it from within. Death—once only despair and separation—was rewritten into restoration and invitation.

"We should be there by sunrise tomorrow." The sound of Dion's voice drew Noura from her thoughts. "Unless you have any other tricks hidden behind your ear."

Noura smirked. "I might. Depends how treacherous the Rim decides to be."

Dion sighed. "I can't stay, you know."

Noura's heart sank. "I know," she murmured. The task of aiding Opal to The Lost Garden belonged to her. She tucked her hair behind her ear, watching her brother as he rode on the wild horse next to hers. For years, he lived outside of the Rim, hunting for signs of Hesith's return and searching for a way to prepare the brave to stand against the naiad's cunning.

"If what you said about Alius is true, more rests on that boy than we realize. We can't leave him on his own."

Noura frowned as the prophecy came back to her. *He will burn bridges to defeat armies and raze towns to rout darkness. Yet, he and the Reconciler shall build them up again will by will and stone by stone.* "What will you do?"

"I want to take him to the Guardians' Fortress in the Southern Mountains. See what they can do with him."

"Really? And what will you tell his mother? I don't think she will appreciate you taking her son away."

Dion shook his head, a smile edging his mouth. "That the world is ending," he joked. "I don't know. I haven't thought that far yet."

Noura laughed. "The world is not ending. But that would probably make her hold onto him even tighter. Most mothers aren't too keen on sending their sons into peril before their middling years are complete."

Dion threw up a hand in defense. "Hey, I'm just going off the prophecy *you* received. Maybe you should be the one to convince his mother."

Noura opened her mouth to reply but froze when a winged shadow crossed the field before them. Both horses bucked, their nostrils flaring. A chill grasped Noura's spine as a Harfare's screech cursed the air.

The Lore Wielder

"Forsake all," Dion hissed, trying his best to stay on the wild horse. Noura drew in a breath. Her plan was working. The Harfares had been on their trail for two days.

She threw her head against her horse's neck as she drew a dagger from her boot. *Please. We need you. Be more than you were created to be. Be bearers of hope.* Noura sensed both horses fighting her a moment longer before their stamping hooves stopped. *Go. Run!*

They broke into an all out gallop. Dion cursed again, and Noura shrieked as the wind whipped through her hair, and the countryside flew by. She glanced back to see four Harfares dive after them. One screeched and crumpled to the ground ten arms behind them. Noura's gaze flickered to Dion, who was loading his slingshot again. If four Harfares found them, that meant three still hunted Opal.

"Forsake all," Noura muttered as the wind stole the words from her mouth. She had hoped to draw them all away. One of the creature's wings appeared in her periphery, bony and sleek in the sunlight. Noura pressed her knees deeper into the horse's side and gripped her dagger tighter, her locket thumping against her chest. The screech the Harfare released set her ears ringing, and Noura clenched her jaw. The Harfare's talons lowered, sharp and encrusted with dried blood, and Noura jabbed at the skeletal body of the bird. Yellow blood trickled down her arm as the Harfare's scream echoed behind her, and its body crumpled into the field.

Two down, two left to kill.

A wooded hillside flashed before them, and Noura met Dion's eyes as he galloped beside her.

"Go!" he shouted at her, drawing his sword and pointing it at the woods. He directed his horse to run parallel along the woods instead of into it. "Don't wait for me!"

Fourteen

I STARED UP AT MY HOME for the night. It was ten arms above me, perched on a massive tree. This time, I'd reached my abode before nightfall, and I walked curiously around the tree, wondering at the perfectly crafted house. Its roof grew moss, and its walls had small windows. I was grateful at the thought of being so far off the ground while I slept, especially after the scare in the woods earlier today. I shook off the memory of the wild man before scaling the tree.

The tree itself appeared nearly as old as the one that guarded the tunnel, and a feeling of safety calmed me as I rested in its branches. I swung over to the platform on which the little house rested, opened the door, and ducked inside. It was so vastly different from the shack that I gaped in awe. Art covered the walls—beautiful pictures painted directly on the wood.

I ventured to look at the paintings more closely, following them all the way around the room until I was back at the door. The biggest painting of all decorated the door, full of dark, twisted figures. A broken, wounded woman was on her knees, despatched bodies strewn around her. But she wasn't the only one in the picture, not even in the center of it. A brilliantly painted man stood before her, lifting her chin to look into his face. There was no story written, but I knew who the figure was without question, and chills ran up and down my arms. It was the Heir. When I saw a name inscribed at the bottom, my heart faltered. *Elowyn III.*

I stepped back, unsure of what to think. I'd never heard of Elowyn, but she had to be a significant part of the Elowynnite sect. But who in Avarlyn had she been? I sat down on the floor, staring at the painting and the name, bitter thoughts stealing its beauty. Going on this pilgrimage tied me too closely to them already. I didn't need to be reminded of the Elowynnites at every turn.

Since I had nothing to sleep on, I folded up my cloak for a makeshift pillow and lay on the hard, wooden floor. My stomach burned with hunger, but I had nothing. I'd found a few wild berries along the way, but they had done little to suppress my hunger. I rolled over, pressing my hand hard into my belly, redirecting the pain. A soft white light from the moon spilled in from one of the windows, and I took it gratefully, like the gentle presence of someone who cared. Eventually, I drifted off into a light sleep, sore and hungry, but safe inside the tree-sted filled with painted stories of hope.

When I awoke, everything had changed. I sat up, covered by a soft blanket and resting on a thick bedroll. The delicious smell of bread, butter, and steaming tea drifted through the room. For a moment, I wondered if I either died during my sleep or accidentally invaded someone else's home. Alarmed, I leapt from the bedroll, scanning the room for any other signs of life. The room, however, appeared empty. I was still alone. I turned back to the table and saw the most glorious sight. A simple but delicious breakfast spread.

A movement in the window caught my eye. I watched in awe as a squirrel timidly scampered through the window and down to the table, then dropped a piece of cheese there. I stared at it, and it stared at me for a full minute before the mousy face gave me an expectant look and scampered away again. There was no way this was not a dream, I thought, pinching myself.

Yet, I was too hungry to ask questions this time. Whether it was a dream or not, I was going to eat. I took a sip of tea, the hot, rich liquid warming my aching tummy. My restless hand paused over the bread, not because I was unsure of the food but because another thought had crossed my mind. Fasting. In our religious practice, we only fasted on occasion, but my experience with fasting had been thorough enough that I knew eating quickly would render me sick.

I continued to sip my tea and breathe in the smell of food for a few minutes before taking small nibbles. My eyes watered with the pain of waiting. However, making it to the next lodging for the day was paramount, and I could not do that if I was ill. Nevma may have stirred yesterday morning, but now he lay still, resting on the table next to me, the lid of his enclosure open. I took a small bite of cheese, holding back a wave of uncertainty. How did I make it this far? And how would I ever accomplish something as arduous as this?

I looked around the room, solitude and guilt thick in the air. It was my fault that Nevma nearly died. I was the one who led him into danger yet was charged with taking him to The Lost Garden. It was a precarious contradiction. I glowered at my tea that had grown cold. My mistakes thus far were so detrimental, I experienced magical intervention not once, but three times. I shoved breadcrumbs around on the table.

The Lore Wielder

A vibrant bird alighted on the windowsill. I expected to see something in its mouth, but instead, it flitted around the room before resting on a chest in the corner.

"What do you suppose it wants?" I murmured to Nevma as I rose from the table and crossed the room. The bird chirped intently and pecked at the latch. I blinked, curious, and bent to unlatch the chest. I caught my breath. Supplies rested inside. I ran my fingers over the shirt and pants that lay on top. Underneath was a pair of leather boots similar to the ones I kicked off into the river.

"How...?" I picked up the pale green shirt and held it over the night clothes I had been wearing for three days. Green. *That matched my daggers*, I thought before remembering they too were at the bottom of the river. "How did these get here, and who sent them?"

Food was one thing, but supplies? I wasn't sure if I was enchanted by the gifts or if I was being watched. I removed my old clothes and reached for the shirt. I hesitated. My eyes scanned the room. No mirrors graced the walls. With a slow breath, I glanced down at the mark on my chest. The dark purple veins webbed over nearly half my chest now. I rubbed my neck. Had it crawled up to my chin? I swallowed, forcing myself to look at the paintings surrounding me before pulling on the shirt and pants. I couldn't worry about the mark right now.

The clothes were made of warm wool. *Good.* If the path continued up Mount Nea, I would be encountering snow all too soon. I slipped on the boots, lacing them up tightly. One day without shoes was brutal enough; I would not risk losing another pair. I reached into the chest again, taking out a traveling pack and coat. I laid them beside me carelessly. Something else in the chest caught my eye. There, at the bottom, was a set of paints and brushes. I smiled, running my fingers through the soft bristles. These, I could tell, were not new—not like the clothes. They had been used before. Glancing up at the colorful walls, I watched as the stories came to life around me. Though each painting differed, in every one, a hand could be seen—a hand reaching into the brokenness and bringing salvation in the darkest moments. Every pilgrim who had set out on this journey needed help. I surrendered to the realization, my eyes stinging. Though my pilgrimage was thrust upon me, maybe I still belonged here. I would succeed, not because I could do it alone, but because the salvation that was a part of each of these stories was a part of mine too.

As I put my brush to the bare wood, all the careless paintings on the abandoned boat with Alana and Ilynn passed through my mind. This one would be different. I worked black into the wood, a large dark mass. With my fingers, I dragged the paint outwards, creating a swirl. I didn't have to use my fingers, but I needed to, I realized as I stared at the black paint staining them now. With white and gold, I painted a fading light in the middle of the swirl. My soul. But this was not an ode to myself. After rinsing out my brush with water, I chose blue. This was an ode to Nevma. With large, sweeping strokes, I painted his wings encircling me, his body coming between me and the darkness chasing us. A light from the side also pushed back the blackness. The beacon from the lighthouse.

I washed out the brushes and returned the paints to the chest. I'd left my mark, and now it was time to go. I paused in the doorway, a part of me longing to stay in a place brimming with pure magic. How the next lodging would be, I did not and could not conceive. I arrived here in desperate need, alone, hungry, and fighting despair. Now I was leaving, my body restored and dressed in clothes prepared for me, ushered on by the heritage of hope.

I adjusted the pack on my shoulder, pulled up the hood of the golden cloak, and ducked out into the wild forest once more. At the base of the tree, I shut my eyes, listening for the song. The notes gently came into focus in my ears, and I opened my eyes, looking up at the morning sun peeking through the trees, peace settling over me. *Further up*, the melody called. The mountain had grown steep, and the trees were becoming shorter. I dug the toes of my boots into the dirt as I went, and every once in a while, I had to grab hold of a tree branch to steady my ascent. In no time, my calves were burning, and I had to rest. I wiped the perspiration off my face, even though the day was not hot, and breathed slowly to calm my racing heart. I reached into my pack for the canister of water and took a long drink.

"You know, it's a good thing you aren't heavy," I whispered to Nevma breathlessly after I returned the water, and I patted his box affectionately.

The path dragged on, and I was frustrated at how often I needed a break. Even though I'd grown up in the mountains, I was not prepared for a climb of this intensity. It made me wonder what else lay ahead, because I was sure of only one thing. Snow.

It grew colder and colder by the league. I did not know if I would reach the snow today, but I certainly would tomorrow. All I could see right now were the trees hemming me in. They no longer stood tall and wispy but short and sturdy, their branches reaching desperately towards the sun, absorbing the warmth of their short summer.

"I hope you're ready for this," I said to Nevma, breathing in the last day of warmth. "Take it in, because I don't know how long it will be before we see summer again."

I stared up at the jagged cliff in front of me. It was not as steep and treacherous as High Tor of Misty Lale, but it was still daunting. I let out a long breath and rubbed my hands together. Was I sure this was the way? I looked around, hoping to see another path that perhaps led around the cliff, but there was none. The squawk of a large bird echoed off the mountain, and I squinted at the sky. A hawk circled above the cliff before disappearing over the top. Something in me stirred. Did the bird want me to follow?

For the whole journey, the path had virtually been lost to time, but here, I could see man-made handholds—an intentional way up the face of the cliff. The perilous trail did not lessen my fears but merely affirmed that I had to face them.

Bending down, I tightened the laces on my boots and braided my hair. Nothing could get in my way if I was going to attempt to scale these rocks. I walked up to the cliff and placed my hand on it, feeling the notes of the melody surging through it. This was the way, no matter how much I did not want it to be.

"Please, don't let me fall," I whispered before finding the first foothold and pulling myself up. The cliff was about ten arms high before the first wide ledge, and then, it continued up another ten arms. *Just get to the first ledge*, I thought, *and don't look down.*

I was not exactly afraid of heights, but my skin grew clammy, and my stomach clenched in knots. One mistake, and I could fall. I reached up for another handhold, shaky but secure. I was almost on the ledge.

The Lore Wielder

Once I hoisted myself up, I dared to look down, breathing slowly to calm myself. I was above the treetops, and I looked in wonder at the mountain descending down like a magnificent waterfall of green. For the moment, I was safe atop my castle wall. The ledge was about three arms wide in places, and I slowly stood, heart thumping loudly. The sun was just past noon, but its warmth only grazed me. I was not in danger of losing light, but this was not a place I wanted to rest. I turned around to find a way up the remaining cliff face. *If only scaling cliffs was as easy as climbing trees*, I thought, drying my sweaty hands on my cloak. The path up did not seem as clear here. I could not see any obvious markings, but it was also not as steep and not difficult to map out a fairly easy way up the rock face.

With one hand firmly on the rock and one foot wedged into a crack, I pulled myself up the cliff. At first, it was not too difficult, but the farther up I went, the rock began to crumble, and my footholds were not as stable. I grunted, grabbing hold of a rock just as my foothold melted away. I swung for a moment before my boot found something solid. If I thought about my mistake, my whole body would freeze, but it was hard to ignore my shaking hands. I closed my eyes. Maybe I could go back. *Maybe there's another way*, I thought, glancing down. At the same moment, my handhold crumbled.

Fifteen

COLD PAIN GRIPPED MY BODY AS I continued to slide down the rock face, jagged edges cutting me as I reached out desperately for anything to grab hold of. I fell faster and faster until I lost hold of the cliff completely and plummeted towards the ground, my screams echoing off the mountain. I crashed to the bottom, and the pain rolled like shock waves through me. I hardly dared to move. Yet, the thought of Nevma lying helplessly around my neck forced me to raise a shaking hand and open the box.

"Nevma," I groaned, squinting my eyes and trying to sit up. I had to make sure he was okay. I had to know if the fall had destroyed my last hope of saving him. I picked up his still body in my trembling hands. "Nevma, please. Show me that you are all right." I held his body close to my watery eyes, looking for any sign of movement. Had he been injured? I bit my lip, partly from dread and partly to distract myself from the pain spreading through my whole body. I did not have time to see to my own injuries, not until I knew that Nevma was alive. Finally, his tiny body moved.

"Nevma," I whispered again, and this time his wing twitched. "You're alive," I cried, bringing him close to my heart. "You're alive."

Once I was certain he was unharmed, I laid him in the box once more and secured it across my shoulder, letting myself take in my own pain. My head throbbed from the fall, but I must have covered my head with my arm. It ached, a long gash marring my forearm. Gingerly, I stood up, unsure how steady I would be on my feet. My boots protected my ankles, and my legs were bruised but unharmed.

I squinted up at the cliff I had slid down. I had not landed on the ledge, yet I hadn't fallen all the way down the cliff either. Rocks rose around me on each side. I'd slid into a crevice in the cliff, one that could not be seen from the outside.

Blood dripped off my fingertips from the cut on my arm, and cold sweat stung the scratches covering my body. With a shaking hand, I splashed water on my wound, fighting the darkness tinging my vision. It felt like my ears were under water. I knew the signs. I was fainting. I threw myself on the crevice floor, my consciousness waning.

"Not here, not now." I pleaded with the weakness of my own body. Darkness swirled before my eyes until I finally heard the wind. I heard the birds and sounds of the forest. Pain returned with a vengeance. As soon as my vision cleared, I clumsily dug through the pack gifted by the tree-sted. Whatever magic brought it to me knew what I needed before. Maybe it also knew what I needed now.

When my fingers closed around a soft cloth, I pulled it out. I hardly questioned how it had gotten there as I gently wrapped my arm, wincing at the pain. I washed the dirt off my face, blinking the water from my eyes and studying my surroundings for a way out of this rocky hollow. The crevice went on. It narrowed into a black hole behind me, and I breathed a sigh of relief that I had not slid deeper inside. I was all but done with caves. Thoughts of the Gilding and the cave under the lighthouse burned in my mind. But before I turned around, something caught my eye.

The sunlight spilled in and washed the entrance in a dull gray, just enough light so I could see something half buried in the gravel shards of the floor. From here, it looked like a leather scroll holder had fallen in and been lost. The back of the cave twisted away into darkness, but the leather holder rested only about two arms away from where I had fallen. As I ducked in the narrowing crevice, I stepped over a blackened circle. Remnants of a fire. Someone must have camped here for the night.

There, just an arm away, the top of a scroll stuck out of the gravel. I tried to snatch it quickly, but it was buried firmly in the ground. I muttered under my breath, hastily scraping the dirt away with my hands and shaking it loose. The scroll let go of its grave all at once, and I tumbled back, knocking rocks into the tunnel at the back. I winced as I heard them clatter all the way down, but I did not wait. Leather holder in hand, I bolted towards the light. My back twitched with ice and shivers, whispering of a presence behind me. But I didn't look back.

My palms sweated as I put my hand on the cliff face. The fragile rock crumbled beneath my fingers. I clenched my jaw. I had no other choice. I adjusted the pack on my shoulder and crept along the length of the crevice, hugging the side of the cliff.

A numbness trickled through my body and mind. All the magic and wonder of this morning evaporated in the face of the cliff that still loomed like an impassable giant before me. My feet slipped on the incline, and I sucked in a breath. The crevice was leading me back up. I sighed in relief as I climbed the narrow passage.

A rush of flapping wings filled the air, and I froze. My pulse raced as I glanced down. A swarm of black creatures spilled from the cave. *Hail and Harfares.* What had I awoken? Ignoring the trail of blood I left behind, I scrambled up the rock face and covered my head as a myriad of bats flew over me, their wings and claws grazing my skin. I clutched the scroll tightly in my hand, shaking my head. Why had I taken the scroll?

I watched as the bats disappeared into the sky, my breath coming back to me. I had only awoken bats. With another steadying breath, I continued to creep along the crevice, the top of the cliff drawing near.

But another sound echoed from below. A screech I was all too familiar with now. I whipped my head around, trembling, as I clung to the rock face, no more than bait. My hunters had found me.

The hideous creatures flapped their bony wings, covering the distance between us in a matter of seconds. I screamed, swiping for my daggers, but I was still weaponless. The Harfares slashed their talons at me, and I ducked, picking up a stone. I thrust it at one of the beasts as hard as I could but missed.

I huddled on the edge, covering my head with the cloak's hood—the cloak gifted to me by the Mêliades. I pleaded to them in the chaos.

"Help me... please!" I cried as three Harfares dove at once. But instead of gouging out my eyes, they caught hold of my clothes. I shrieked as their talons pierced my skin, and the rock crumbed away beneath my fingers. Their wings beat the air furiously as they lifted me from the ground, and I dangled helplessly in the air. I kicked and twisted against their grip as the top of the cliff rose before me and then disappeared as the Harfares carried me higher and higher. *Forsake all. Where are they taking me?* The cliff was behind me, but the Harfares were making a circle over the forest atop the cliff. They intended to take me back down the mountain. *Not back to the lake.* I wept.

A willowy, dazzling figure flashed in front of me, wielding a spear. I flinched as the dryad impaled one of the sinister creatures. It released its grip on me, and with a jolt, I dropped closer to the treetops. If she killed another, I would plummet to the ground. Something caught hold of my ankles. I looked down with a shriek as another dryad guided me towards a tree by my boots. The Harfares screamed in fury, their talons digging deeper into my shoulders, but as soon as I grabbed hold of a tree branch, they dropped me. Arrow after arrow from the Mêliades pierced their bodies, and they fell to the ground, leaking their sick blood.

I scrambled over the branches until I reached the tree's trunk and sank down on a wide branch, trembling. *Fool.* I had been so focused on getting over the cliff, on getting that blasted scroll, that I forgot what chased me.

"Go!" The dryad nearest me ordered, "Do not linger here. They will return." Without another word, she motioned with her bloodied spear to continue up the wooded path.

I nodded, my lip still quivering, and stuffed the scroll into my pack before climbing down the tree. The cuts on my back stung, but I set my jaw and raced for the cover of the wild forest ahead.

They are hunting you, Noura's words burned through my mind again. I gripped the straps of my pack until my fingers ached. *My family is safe.* Nevma hadn't escaped the consequences of my choice, but at least I hadn't led the Harfares straight to my family.

The branches that reached out to touch my face were a gentle reminder to keep going. *Don't stop.* A reminder that they were commissioned to protect and aid me on this journey. A journey on which I was completely alone—yet not alone at all. I pushed my spent body on, holding tightly to Nevma's box like a lifeline. And he was. Mount Nea was a confusing mess of dark and light, just like Wisptale and Misty Lale. What was this dance with the dark that light seemed to participate in? Could it not eradicate evil instead of allowing it to persist and touch all life? It had been naive to hope that darkness was behind me and only light was ahead.

I glanced at the trees, which grew shorter here, and placed a hand on Nevma's box as I walked. "Nevma, if I keep following the song, we'll be surrounded by snow by nightfall." I sniffed. "But this—" I stared at the summit of Mount Nea piercing the sky, the solitude of the forest mingling with my aching body "—is all for you. And you are more than worth it."

When I put aside all my fear and pain for Nevma's sake, it became a little easier to bear. There was a purpose outside myself to stoke the embers of resolve. If I was on this journey for myself alone, I would have given up on day one. To push myself on, I would have needed to see something in myself worth saving. But there wasn't. It was Nevma who was worth saving even if the path forward was unclear.

Once I was half a league or so away, I slid the pack off my sore back and sat down on a mossy rock jutting out from the forest floor. A moment's rest was all I could risk. The sun stole through the trees, illuminating the rock in a circle of light. After quenching my thirst and re-bandaging my arm, I carefully took out the scroll. Gently, I brushed off the dirt that must have clung to the parchment for some time. It was clearly old. But not remarkably so. I unrolled the scroll and held it under the warm light from the sun.

"What?" I whispered, taking in its contents.

It was a map. But—I leaned in closer—it was wrong. I double checked the compass rose and turned the map around, trying to understand what I saw. I ran my finger along the river that should have been labeled the Rema Soul. It ran through Madrielle and emptied into Misty Lale. That much was correct, but here it was named *Rema va Yuels*. Strange. I shifted the map to look at Wisptale. Snowcap Creek wasn't labeled Snowcap Creek but the Rema Soul. And if I followed it back to its source, there was a land plotted out that I had never seen on a map before. *The Sanctuary*.

I shifted the map again, my eye catching something else unusual. S.F. was scribbled at the bottom of the parchment. Initials. But who was S.F.?

I put the map away in frustration, grabbed my pack and set out once more. According to this map, if I kept ascending the mountain, I was headed towards The Sanctuary. But what was The Sanctuary?

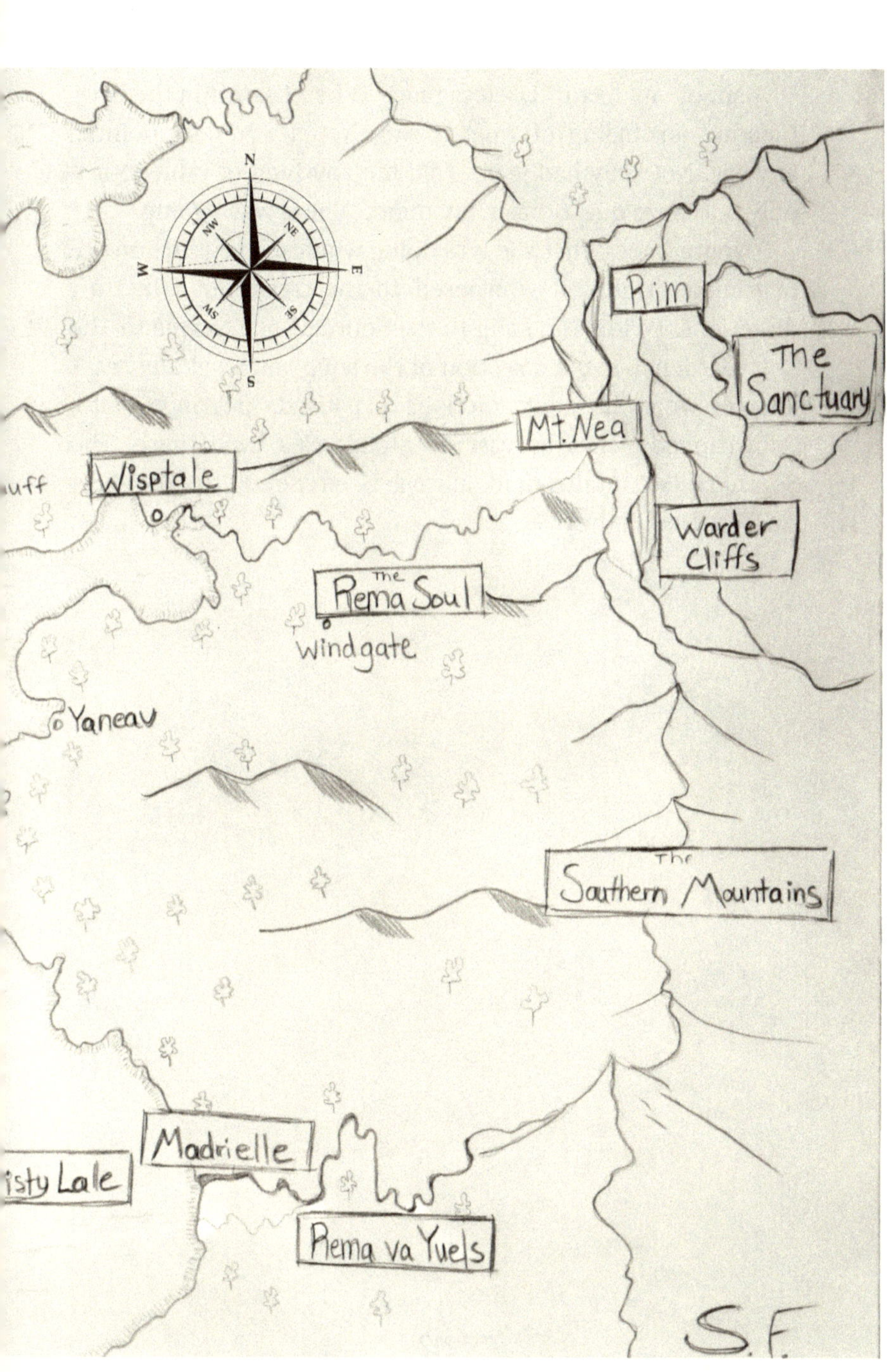

N
NE
NW
E
W
SW
SE
S
Rim
The Sanctuary
Mt. Nea
Wisptale
uff
Warder Cliffs
The Rema Soul
Windgate
Yaneav
The Southern Mountains
Madrielle
isty Lale
Rema va Yuels
S.F.

If the Rema Soul flowed from it through Wisptale... Was it supposed to be The Lost Garden?

I shook my head. "Useless map." When I saw it in the cave, I hadn't an inkling of what it was. Yet, I was disappointed anyway. Not only had it not told me anything of value, but it only put more questions in my mind. Where was I going?

"Noura knew what she was doing when she sent me on the pilgrimage, right?" I whispered to the trees. But I had my directions. Follow the song to the Source. Take Nevma to The Lost Garden. But the direction of the song and what I'd always known were in contradiction. I paused, peering south. Snowcapped peaks as vast as Mount Nea lived there. The Southern Mountains had always been home to The Lost Garden. Hadn't they?

Sixteen

I WAS RIGHT ABOUT THE SNOW. Cold wind tumbled down from the mountain's summit, sending shivers through me. Ahead lay a merciless whiteness, concealing the treacherous terrain. The trees, far fewer here, were strewn across the snow, stubborn witnesses to life.

I gazed towards the South. I didn't have a guide through the Southern Mountains—nothing beyond navigating by the stars. But East, towards what I now knew as The Sanctuary, I had a guide. I couldn't forsake the song, not now.

"Here we go." My boots crunched through the old, icy snow, and I pulled my coat closely around my body. The wind bit my cheeks, leaving them chapped, and I prayed there was a fireplace in whatever shack I would stay in tonight. Neither Nevma nor I would make it very far without the warmth of fire at night. From where I stood, I could not see much beyond the wild forest behind me and the walls of snow ahead. If I felt small in the forest, I was but a speck of dust here, marring the great whiteness that threatened to swallow me.

"At least I don't have to worry about running out of water." I tried to cheer myself up as my thoughts drifted to stories of people freezing to death or being buried in an avalanche. There was no one here to save me. Even the trees feared this place. I paused, my warm breath clouding the air around me, and listened. The melody melded with the wind, not directly down from the summit, but a little to the left. Southeast in fact. I smiled. *It's about time!*

I followed the song, leaving a trail of footprints behind. Just as the white snow shimmered golden, the sun nodded farewell, and a cabin peeked out from a blanket of snow. Even though I was exhausted, I raced towards its welcoming embrace. After being battered by the wind, I wanted nothing more than to be inside its four walls. I stopped a few arms away. There was a chimney. That meant there was a fireplace. But what made me stop was that smoke was billowing up from the chimney.

A fire was already burning. My heart thudded in my chest. Someone was inside. Could the magic of this morning have gone before me? The light was fading around me, bringing on a new layer of ice.

"What should I do?" I wondered, though I knew there was no other choice than to knock. "Please, please, be magic."

I lifted a shaking hand, knocked, and jumped back, afraid of who might answer. What would I say? I hadn't spoken to another person in days. My throat tightened. Another harsh wind stung my face and stirred up the courage to knock again. This time, the door opened. The cabin-dweller wasn't a *who*, but a *what*.

To my astonishment, I was met with two dark eyes, whiskers, and a snuffling nose. An abnormally large white fox stared back, just as startled as I was. He stood nearly as big as a wolf.

"Uh, hello?" I said, thinking a person might be on the other side of the door. The fox studied me curiously.

"You're early."

"I'm—what?" I stared at the creature, unsure if I had hallucinated.

"I got word of your arrival this afternoon. Thought you'd be another hour after that fall you took." The fox stared back at me. "Well, come in, come in." He bowed slightly before scampering around to lead me inside the cabin. I, however, was still too taken aback to move. "Shall I take another form? This one doesn't appear to suit you," the fox added in a low tone.

"No—I—it's fine." *Another form?* What was this creature? Could I trust it, and, moreover, who had sent word that I was coming? "It suits me just fine," I finally replied. "Please, what is your name?" I remembered my manners.

"You're not wrong to be hesitant. However, we can't defrost the entire mountain so, please, come inside."

I stood firmly on the doorstep. "Who told you I was coming?" I had no weapon, other than my good sense. If he was friendly, he would be patient. The fox padded back towards the door.

"The trees, of course. You think you're the only one who can hear their song?" This time, the fox's face softened as he studied my appearance. "Forgive me. It's been a long time since a pilgrim came this way. My name is Tirigan."

I mulled over the information slowly. Even though I heard the song my whole life, apparently, I knew next to nothing about it. It did have something to do with the trees. The dryads. Yet, was that enough to trust him?

"Do you..." I hesitated. "Do you serve the Heir?"

"Longer than your lineage has been alive, kit." Tirigan motioned his head towards the warm fire. "Come. I may not be able to answer all your questions, but no doubt you have a tempest of them in that head of yours."

Knowing I had no other choice and taking comfort in his words, I followed Tirigan into the warm room. My body broke into shivers as I approached the fire, rubbing my hands together. The cabin only had one room, with the fireplace and two chairs next to a tray of food. My stomach growled audibly.

"Eat, kit." Tirigan chuckled. "It's prepared for you." I hesitated only a moment longer before dropping into a chair. Any questions I had faded as I bit into the fried fish and roasted nuts. I hadn't eaten since breakfast, and my stomach curled in on itself. I hardly dared to look up as I filled my belly with hot tea and scraped the remaining food from the plate with my reddened fingers. All my manners melted away like the snow from my boots, which I had cast off by the door

Pictures and books lined the walls of the cabin, dried herbs hung from the ceiling, and a neatly made bed draped in a thick quilt was pushed into the corner. Only a human could have prepared a home such as this. And where was said human now? Finally, I took in the slanted eyes and whiskers of the fox. I'd never conversed with an animal before.

"How is your arm feeling, kit?" The fox asked, curled up in the other chair.

"Fine," I murmured, peering at the red-brown cloth dried to my arm. "How do you know about—"

His nose twitched. "You humans are a bit daft. I told you—the trees."

"Do you mean the dryads?"

"Trees, dryads, nymphs. I'm happy you are at least familiar with the term. Considering your kind tried to erase us creatures." The fox jerked his head towards the kettle. "You need to soak your wound in warm water and put on a fresh bandage. I would help, but I have no thumbs in this form." Again, a soft smile appeared on the beast's face.

"Form?"

"Aye. Fox or feathers. Or something like you. But this fox skin is very apt at surviving in the snow. Hosting, on the other hand..." Tirigan stretched his paws out towards the fire, his white coat glinting gold in the light of the flickering flames. I waited for him to explain further, but he did not. Not wanting to bother my unusual host, I reached for the kettle and poured the hot water into a bowl, staring at the rising steam.

I set the bowl aside, watching the heat being sucked away from the water in mere minutes. Once the hot water relented, I carefully washed my forearm, dissolving the sticky dried blood before attempting to remove the cloth. I winced, running the fingers of my good hand down the jagged cut. I slid more than fell down the cliff, yet my body could still feel the impact of hitting the bottom.

Tirigan interrupted my thoughts. "Most come here beating down the door with questions. But you..." he eyed me. "You either have none or lack the courage to ask."

I averted my gaze. I had questions, but they fled my mind, fear anchoring my words. Yet Tirigan didn't look away, and his whiskers twitched expectantly. I gathered my breath. "Does everyone hear the song, or just some?"

"Ah, that is an important question." Tirigan looked down thoughtfully. "The song of the dryads is not the only way your kind are called. The call can be heard by all who desire to hear it. And all who desire to hear it have already been called upon."

I creased my brow, my hand pausing over the half
-wrapped bandage on my arm. "So others might hear
something else?"

"Hear, feel, know..."

"And what is the call?" I had never thought of it as a call
before. It was calling me and had been calling me my whole
life. But to what, I wasn't sure.

"The better question is *who* is calling. And I think you
already know the answer to that question, kit," he said with
finality. I finished wrapping the bandage around my wound.
Tirigan was right. I did know the answer. My eyes darkened as
I remembered the other summons I had answered. Was I still
worthy of the song of the dryads? Did Tirigan know what I'd
done and what really forced me on this pilgrimage? I was not
like the others who had come of their own accord.

"Well, I was told this was a pilgrimage to The Lost Garden.
And to follow the song. Everyone who has helped me along
the way is a servant of the Heir." I returned to my place by the
fire, watching the burning tongues flicker. "He must be the
one calling me."

"Very good. It is he who has called us all." Tirigan's
whiskers stilled. "Me to guide, the dryads to worship and
protect, and you to himself. To salvation."

"To salvation," I repeated, clutching Nevma's box that still
hung around my neck. I grazed the wood beneath my
fingertips, the pit growing in my stomach. My eyes burned.
"Do you know why I am here?"

"Of course. Do *you* know why you are here?" Tirigan
looked at me with unblinking eyes before jumping down from
his chair, approaching me.

I turned away as a tear fell. "I'm here for him," I said,
opening the box and letting my tears fall onto Nevma's weak
body. "It's all my fault. I—I followed another's calls and—"

"Kit," the fox interrupted me, laying his soft white head on my shoulder. "You are not the only one who has followed that call. And you won't be the last. There is so much more to your pilgrimage than trying to right a wrong. I did not misspeak when I said the Heir's call is your salvation. Not only your dragonfly's, but yours."

"You don't know what I've done."

"Even if I didn't, that would not change the truth." Tirigan tried to comfort my tears that fell more freely now. But he did not know. He could not know what I'd done. I sniffed, drying my eyes with my sleeve. I wanted to disagree with Tirigan—to assure him that what I'd done was too dark, but I anchored my tongue. He wouldn't understand. He wasn't even human. My throat constricted, and instead of asking another question, I reached into my pack and pulled out the map. It was a long shot, but maybe the creature could explain why this map was wrong and assure me of which way to go.

The fox stepped back, taking in the parchment. He walked around it, studying it from all sides, and then smiled fondly. "Where did you get this?"

"I found it buried in a cave," I answered, studying Tirigan's furry face.

"I haven't seen this in nearly forty years," he wondered out loud. "Even then, I was impressed he had it. There hasn't been a true map made of the world in centuries."

My mind raced. "What do you mean? Who had it?"

"Shylo Fletcher." Tirigan spoke in a fond tone, and I tilted my head curiously at him. "Oh, don't mistake my affection. He was in far worse shape than you." He chuckled to himself. I looked down, disappointed, not recognizing the name. "Lost the map before he reached the summit, half-starved and frozen to death because he'd refused to surrender his own provisions to the Stream Bender. Aye, he was the last pilgrim I hosted...You're the first one in a long time, kit."

"You said there has not been a true map in centuries? What do you mean by that?"

"I mean all other maps are a lie. They don't show the true Rema Soul, nor plot the location of The Sanctuary. The Lost Garden, as you call it."

I gaped at Tirigan's words. It made sense. The song had never hinted that I would ever be traveling into the Southern Mountains. Always, it called me East. East, where Snowcap Creek's source lay.

"But..." I turned towards the dark eyes of the fox. "If that map is true, the Rema Soul runs right through Wisptale. Right where I've lived my whole life."

"So it does."

Seventeen

EVEN THOUGH MY BODY BEGGED for sleep, my mind could not stop racing. I rolled over for the eighth time, tugging on the thick blankets, and released an exhausted sigh. Not only was I tired from the day, but also from trying to wrap my mind around what Tirigan told me about the map. It belonged to a pilgrim who traveled here decades ago, yet that alone was not what kept me awake. It was the possibility that Snowcap Creek *was* the Rema Soul. My whole understanding of The Lost Garden and even the world itself was shifting.

My mind kindled with questions, but I was not ready for the answers. If Snowcap Creek's source was The Lost Garden, what had happened to the Sweet Waters? This question was lingering in my heart long before, but it did not seem as paramount when the Rema Soul was flowing through Madrielle, a place so far away. But now, whatever had stolen the water's sweetness lived in my own village. *Perhaps it still dwells there*, I thought with a shiver, visions of the creature imprisoned at the bottom of Misty Lale pressing in on me.

I blinked my eyes in the warm light of the fire. It was morning at last. Apparently, I drifted off to sleep somewhere between my thoughts of the two rivers. I expected to see the shape of the fox shifting in the dim light, but I did not. Instead, I saw a human figure. Alarmed, I sat up in the cot, heart thudding in my chest.

"No need to be alarmed, kit. This is simply my other form." The human answered without turning around. I could see the profile of the hairy face of a young man as he fried the morning's fish in the coals. Though, if this was Tirigan, his young appearance must be an illusion. "You'd have been called upon to cook both our breakfasts otherwise."

"Oh, I could have—"

"Of course you could have, but to be frank, I don't have much faith in your cooking." He plated the fish, took the kettle off the heat, then turned towards me with a warm smile. "After living so long, I get rather set in my ways." It was hard to imagine that Tirigan was hundreds of years old. His eyes were bright, and there were no wrinkles on his face. If I guessed by appearance, he looked no more than five years my elder. Except for the hair. His beard was short but full, and he seemed to have a layer of hair that covered his entire body. An adaptation to the cold weather, perhaps?

"Come, eat." Tirigan poured a steaming cup of tea. My stomach rumbled as I hesitantly climbed out of the bed and took the plate offered to me. I sat down, picking up a knife and fork, my manners coming back to me. Tirigan sipped his mug of tea but did not speak. He seemed to be thinking—hard.

"Thank you for the fish," I said to break the silence. He only nodded in return, the flames of the fire reflecting in his eyes. Since talking was not one of my strengths, I shrugged and continued to eat breakfast.

Tirigan probably always had a lot on his mind considering his life. Who was I to be uncomfortable with someone's silence? Part of me wished he remained as the white fox. In this form, I felt like he was another person to whom I must be properly acquainted. I pushed my plate aside and sipped my tea.

After the hot liquid warmed my insides, I would pack up and leave. My time with Tirigan was long enough, and I could not lose sight of my purpose, even if my world was shifting. Once I stepped outside the cabin door, I would have a decision to make. I knew what direction I must travel. East. Everything pointed to The Sanctuary, and I could not waste any more time getting Nevma to the Source. But the decision must happen in my heart. Resistance spread deep in my bones, whispering that traveling east would be a betrayal to everything I was taught.

My eyes lifted to the strange creature who'd taken me in, though he was not looking at me but at the mountain's summit, visible through the window. It was time to bid Tirigan farewell.

"Thank you, Tirigan, for everything." I strode across the room and pulled my coat and cloak out to prepare for the snowy path that lay ahead of me.

Tirigan looked up with a start. "You do not travel alone, kit. I go with all the pilgrims for their last day on the summit of Mount Nea." I froze mid-button. I was not sure if I was relieved or burdened. Could I bear his uncomfortable silence for the rest of the day? Tirigan continued, "Forgive me for my quietness. Remember, I have not guided someone to the cliffs in half a century... and you are one of the youngest to traverse it."

"It's okay—" I answered, hesitating on the word *cliff*. "The path is to a cliff?" I glanced at him, pain throbbing in my arm.

The Lore Wielder

"Aye." Tirigan's words trailed off as if he were considering them again. "The cliffs are as far as I can take you. After that, you will cross the Rim of The Sanctuary." He rose from his chair, swiftly putting out the fire. Excitement and hope danced through my body at his words. Nevma would be healed, and I could go home. An end to this treacherous mountain with its tors and Harfares was in my grasp. Tirigan threw on a heavy coat and boots.

"So, we are close?" I asked, audible wonder in my voice, but Tirigan chuckled at the question.

"'Close' is a relative term. We are not close, but the path there will be faster than any you've taken yet."

"So, it is easy?" I exited the cabin into the frigid air, and Tirigan shut the door behind me. He looked at me with amusement in his eyes as I tucked Nevma's box inside my coat and adjusted my pack.

"The journey today will test you in a way none other has. It will be one of the most defining moments in your life, whether you go on or turn back." He strode in front of me. His boots left large footprints that I followed behind in.

I swallowed, considering his words as the morning sun peaked over the mountain's summit. The snow turned golden in places, as if it were touched by a brush dipped in pure light. This, however, did not relieve the dread that was swelling in my chest. This whole journey brought me to my limits—to my knees. I had already pushed myself beyond what I ever thought possible. Yet now, I was to be pushed even harder? "Why?"

"Why?" Tirigan answered. I jumped, not realizing I'd spoken out loud. "Do you know why The Sanctuary is hidden at all?" The cold air bit as sharply as his words.

"So people cannot find it."

"No. The Heir hid the garden because it was the only way it would remain a sanctuary. The intention was never to keep his lost children from ever finding it again. In truth, the path to The Lost Garden is meant to be found. But not all who find it, find it with pure intentions."

"So..." I paused, trying to read between the lines. "Anyone can follow the path up here. But not just anyone can cross the border to the Sanctuary?"

Tirigan stood still for a moment, and I nearly walked into him. He studied me with his fox-like eyes. "No, not just anyone can enter the borders of The Sanctuary. And not just anyone can follow the path up here. Anyone with selfish intentions would never have made it across the river. And just like you were forced to decide what was more important on that river, you will have to make another decision today... You see, only those who know their only hope lies beyond the Rim will have what it takes to face what lies ahead." Tirigan began walking again, and I scampered after his footprints.

"What other hope do I have?" I replied in a small voice, clutching Nevma's box. Tirigan glanced back with a kind expression.

"You may be one of the youngest, but you are perhaps one of the bravest." He continued scouting out our icy path, but I bit my lip, my eyes burning at his words. If only he knew. I was the furthest thing from brave.

We were rounding the summit. Mount Nea's barren peak still loomed hundreds of arms above us, but our goal was not its peak but somewhere behind. Some place where a cliff marred our way. The trees refused to grow at such a height, and Tirigan was the only other life that could be seen in the ocean of snow. There was no song here, I realized with an intake of breath. No trees to sway in the wind and no nymphs to inhabit them. Tirigan was my guide because he was the *only* guide. It was lonely, walking with a near stranger in a desolate place, knowing I was headed to the edge of a cliff—knowing a choice lay before me.

Over the past few days, my body had adjusted to the thin air, but my lungs still yearned for a full breath that did not burn with an icy grip. Whenever Tirigan heard me gasping, he would pause in the snow and force me to rest, drink, and eat. Though I'd experienced his kindness, I was still not used to talking freely with him in this form. I'd known him less than a day and had already bared a part of my soul to the creature. But that was while he was still a fox.

"How are you faring, kit?" Tirigan put a gloved hand on my shoulder, concern tracing his eyes. I merely coughed in response. It was hard enough to breathe, much less talk. We'd left the cabin only a few hours ago, but I shook my head wordlessly.

"Come, there is a cave not but a stone's throw away. I'll build a fire for us and put the kettle on." Tirigan brushed a layer of snow off his coat.

I shook my head again in protest. I did not want to waste any more time, but my objections rolled off Tirigan like the powdered snow that began to fall. Dark clouds tumbled through the sky like billowing mountains of ash. Without a glimpse of the sun, there was nothing to pierce the ice, and the cold became unbearable.

Once we were inside the cave, Tirigan worked on lighting the fire. It was a relief to be out of the bitter wind. When we entered, I was surprised to see a stockpile of wood stacked against the cavern wall. *It must be common for pilgrims to rest here*, I thought, observing how familiar Tirigan was with the place and the blackened circle in the middle of the cave where he worked.

Moments later, a flame sparked and wrapped its glowing fingers around the wood. Tirigan let out a deep sigh and glanced at me.

"Come. Warm yourself, kit." He smiled, but I noticed how he twitched restlessly. Was taking me to the cliff not as easy as he would have me believe? I slid off the rock I was perched on and squatted down, embracing the warmth of the fire. My body accepted the heat with violent shivers, willing the flames to grow stronger and the warmth deeper. It had been a long time since Tirigan brought a pilgrim this way. Why had they stopped coming? He cleared his throat, shattering my frozen thoughts.

"I know you resisted my words earlier," Tirigan began, "but you are brave, kit."

Words stuck in my throat. I swallowed. "I'm not." My eyes lingered on the dancing flames, unwilling to look up at his bearded face.

"You're here. You braved the journey thus far—"

"Others came because they wanted to," I interrupted. "I had no choice."

"Kit, to believe you had no choice—indeed, to believe you are solely here because you were in error is to misunderstand the Heir's beckoning." Fire burned in his eyes as he continued. "And it does not make you any less brave than all those who traversed here before you."

The warmth of his words was as powerless as the tiny flames that tried to rid my body of the ice inside me. Talk of The Lost Garden did bring me hope. But it was hope for Nevma, not for me. If he and I were restored, nothing else mattered. Tirigan's boots ground on the gravel floor as he rose.

The Lore Wielder

"I'm going to fetch some snow for the kettle, but I will leave you with this." He paused. "All you've done that brings you shame will melt away in the glory of what lies across that border. You must stop doubting why you are chosen to be here."

I did not look up as he ventured out into the storm. My aching fingers burned before the fire, but I didn't move, not even to swipe away the tear frozen on my cheek.

A soft thud came from behind. I spun as a low snarl reverberated off the rock walls.

"Do you pretend to believe the beast?" A low voice caressed my ears. A slinky figure paced towards me on soundless paws. "You know who you are and what you've done. You know the truth." The snarly mouth of a snow leopard bared its teeth.

I rose to my feet, gripping a rock, pulse racing.

The creature crept closer. "Is it not better to cease pretending the Heir chose you?" Its cat-eyes narrowed. "You've already been chosen by something else. Summoned to death as surely as your little friend. *Owned* by death." It purred soothingly. I squinted, one hand on Nevma's box and the other tightening around the rock. I stared at its dark eyes, a bottomless pit. I knew those eyes—knew the hatred behind them. The feline had told one too many lies.

"He's not dead!" I flung the rock toward the leopard and snatched a burning stick from the fire as it pounced. "Tirigan!" I gasped as the creature's claws bit into my flesh. Arms raised, I fought to keep its fangs away from me. My coat shredded under its claws, the cat's hot breath knuckles from my face. The stick snapped. *Forsaken Other, why had I lost my daggers?*

With two heavy paws, it pinned me to the cavern floor. I whimpered, waiting for its fangs. But no teeth met my flesh. I cracked my eyes open. It stared at me, mouth drawn back in a snarl. *Let him win. Give up. Even if I save Nevma, I still have to live with what I've done.* Its eyes softened as I stared back, and a familiar calm settled over me—the calm of drowning. My blink faltered as my muscles relaxed.

A *thunk* cracked the silence, and the snow leopard crumpled off me with a whine. Tirigan bounded between us, but the cat scrambled to its feet once more. It hissed, fixing its eyes on Tirigan.

"You again." The leopard pounced at Tirigan, and he narrowly avoided the claws. "Come now, neither of us can die. Let me have her."

"Run, kit!" Tirigan pulled out a knife from his boot. I lay on the cavern floor frozen, warm blood staining my coat, all the breath evaporating from my lungs. Tirigan grunted. "I said *run!*"

My eyes snapped to his as my breath returned, and I scrambled to my feet.

"Where? I don't know the way!" I reached for my pack, trembling. The leopard pounced again and caught Tirigan's leg with its claws. I shrieked as blood streamed from the wound. Tirigan stifled a howl, managing to land a hit with his own knife before giving me one last look.

"The—map—" he shouted as his enemy shook off its wound and began to stalk its prey again.

The map. My thoughts raced as I ran towards the entrance. Towards the snowstorm alone. It didn't matter if I trusted it, the map was all I had now.

"You will never have her!" Tirigan's words echoed from the darkness of the cave. I caught my breath, glancing back at the two figures fighting around the flickering fire. I left him to fight a battle that was mine. I ground my teeth, stumbling into the storm. My blood stained the freshly fallen snow. Snarls and shouts still pursued me from the cave mouth. *I dare not waste a second Tirigan bought me.*

Fine snowflakes berated my face as I ran. With a grimace, I cursed at the tracks behind me. I could only hope the beast who tracked me would be Tirigan. He was my sole protection on the summit of Mount Nea. I was beyond the reach of anything else.

My smarting wounds echoed the wounds that had been unearthed by the leopard's words. He had spoken of truth, yet his truth had contradicted the truth I knew to belong to another—the one who threw himself between us.

"But why? Why is the lie so much easier to believe than the truth?" I stared up at the gray clouds, the snow swirling down around me. I'd tasted death, and I knew it hated me. Yet I'd been tempted to give up again.

Brave. I jerked on my pack's strap in frustration. I wanted to scream. I wanted to hit something, but there was nothing here but me. Tears stung my eyes.

Once I was well away from the cave, lungs burning, I blinked frosted eyelashes at the summit. It cut through the snowstorm, marring the whiteness surrounding me. I lowered my chin below the collar of my coat, teeth chattering. What now? Had I even run in the right direction?

I pulled out the map. My only landmark was the daunting tower of the summit, and I stood in its vast shadow. And there, on the other side of the charted summit, lay the coordinates for my destination. The Rim of The Sanctuary. *The Warder Cliffs.* Whatever lay at the bottom of the Warder Cliffs had not been mapped. I blew the snow off the parchment before rolling it back up and tucking it away in my pack. The way forward was east. It had always been east.

Leslie Montaño

I crunched forward in the snow, noticing a subtle descent. I was going down—away from the frigid summit. My eyes flickered to it one last time as I stood in its shadow. I was sick of its tricks and treachery.

The sun broke through its ashy barrier, and the cliff's edge glinted in cold light. The end of the known world spread out before me. I inhaled slowly, taking in the stark drop-off lying two stone throws away. Beyond it was misty oblivion.

Eighteen

THE SNOW CRUNCHED BENEATH MY boots—the only sound accompanying my breathing. Here, standing on the edge of the charted world, nothing lived as far as my eyes could see in any direction. It was an end solely of bitter winds and icy ground. I glanced back at the summit, so hostile that even the snow escaped its jagged cliffs. I returned to what lay before me. If I had approached the Warder Cliffs at night, I would have walked right off the edge. It was only from the sunlight swirling in the mist that I could see where the land ended and the clouds began. I crept closer, hoping to spot a path or even the bottom. But everything was a consuming white. The clouds causing the dense mist hovered only beyond the cliff. In the sky above the mist, blue shimmered through. The snow clouds hung behind me, trapped on the summit of Mount Nea. I paced the edge. Did the elements respect the border?

The cliff ran unnaturally straight in either direction, like the rock separated from it was a deliberate severing.

I continued to pace along the edge, heading north, for east would be a fall to my death. And south, a temptation. What if the map led me to a dead end? My breath condensing in the air threatened to become a mist of its own as my lungs throbbed. The south spoke to an older part of me. The me who did not trust the map. It wanted the map to be wrong.

I paused, watching a bitter wind stir up the powdery snow and send it over the cliff's edge. If the map was wrong, it would realign my world. I looked up, conceding to the reality that going north had brought me nothing but another edge. And no path down.

"Where are you, Tirigan?" I chattered through my teeth. "You told me to follow the map, and this is where it led me. A forsaken cliff." I sighed, my cracked lips stinging. But my heart was not in my accusation. Defeated, I sank to the ground. I was lost—beyond the reach of any vines and even the song. My chest grew hot despite the cold. "Forsake all," I muttered, before digging my gloved hands into the snow and hurling snowballs into the white oblivion. The heat in my chest finally burst.

"Why am I here?" I screamed, my voice echoing off the mountain. A void carved into my middle, and I buried my head in my hands. "I'm sorry, Nevma." I wanted to cry, but I didn't.

The ground trembled. My eyes shot up in panic as a rumble and crack rolled off the mountain. Fog billowed from the summit.

"Hail and Harfares," I whispered in horror. My voice was distant, a million leagues away, and my heartbeat thundered. I froze as the avalanche cascaded towards me.

There was nowhere to go. I was trapped between the avalanche and the cliff's edge. My boots caught in the snow, and I stumbled, cursing. *Run*, was the only word resounding in my head. I scrambled up again, racing along the edge. Run, run, *jump.*

Jump? I shoved the thought away. Jumping was the surest way of dying. Yet the word would not leave me alone. I threw a glance behind me. Millions of bales of snow streaked down the mountain towards me, engulfing it in a thousand glittering stars tossed against the gray sky. *Jump!*

"I can't!" I screamed as the air around turned white. Just before the blue sky vanished, a hawk flew overhead. Just like the hawk I'd seen before.

Tirigan's words flashed in my mind. *"Fox or feathers. Or something like you."* How long had he been guiding me?

The mountain roared, and the air swirled like smoke. I jumped. And I fell. Fast. Faster than I thought possible as I plummeted through the mist. I was going to die. I clutched Nevma's box and squeezed my eyes shut.

I slammed into the surface of the water below, propelled downward at a sickening speed. I clenched my jaw to keep from screaming. Pain crackled through my legs and side where I'd hit the water. Did I die? I stopped sinking and opened my eyes. My world was a warm blue. I flailed my arms and legs, fighting the downward motion to reach the surface—if there was one. The weight of the cloak and coat pulled me down, and I fought my way out of them, my lungs burning. I came up, gasping for air and shaking, reeling from another brush with death.

I spun in the water, searching for the mountain of snow, waiting to be buried, waiting for death to finally win. My panicked breath hung in the air like a cloud. The avalanche never came.

"Impossible," I murmured through bleeding lips. It was as if the snow had disappeared. As if...the elements respected the border.

Quickly, barely keeping my head above water, I poured the water out of Nevma's box. The water was warm. A mist still hung above me, obscuring my view of the Warder Cliff's edge, but it must not be far. The fall did not break my bones, and the air was still cold enough to take my breath away. Yet, hot water drifted around me, thawing the days of coldness that had settled in my bones. Blood swirled like red smoke from my shirt, the water washing it green once more.

Cliffs rose on every side. I swam, one arm holding Nevma above the water, towards a rock I could grab onto. It was too slippery to pull myself up and out of the water, but I had to check on Nevma. And find a way out of here. I scanned the rock face, breathing hard.

"Come on," I muttered weakly, seeing no way of escape. It was like a prison made of pillars on each side. I blinked the water from my eyes, not sure if it was from the pool or pain. Had I crossed the border the moment I jumped? Excitement and confusion jolted through me as I clung to my hold on the rock. If this was The Sanctuary, if I crossed the border, what good had it done? I'd traded one dead end for another. My hope of finding a way out of here hung like the steam rising and swirling from the pool. I could see it, feel it, but never grasp it.

Finally, my eyes caught sight of movement. The water bubbled and swirled across the pool with a soft gurgling sound. *Of course.* The water had to get in somehow. And out. With Nevma safely on the rock, I plunged my head back under the water and opened my eyes. Across the pool, there was a crack in the rock and a current of water feeding it. I swam towards it, the water growing warmer and warmer before resurfacing into the cold air. I had to find where the pool emptied.

The Lore Wielder

I let myself relax and float. All the sensations in my body came flooding back in full force. Every knuckle of me hurt, like I had slammed into a brick wall. I clenched my jaw against the pain as the subtle current carried me towards the far rock face.

When I reached it, I submerged again and saw a cave a few feet below the surface. The current drew me closer. A green glow twinkled through the tunnel. Cognizant vines. My heart thudded in my chest, and I pushed myself upwards, wiping the water from my face as I met the air, my breath joining the steam rolling off the water. The only way out was to swim through the cave—an underwater tunnel.

I returned to the rock where Nevma waited for me, my anxiety building. Flashes of the last time I tried to swim into an underwater tunnel burned in my head—the darkness and terror of it, but most of all, the failure. If I could not do it before, how could I brave it now? I breathed out slowly, trying to calm the storm in my chest.

"Nevma, I can't... I never could. I never should have been charged with taking you to The Sanctuary. I was bound to fail you..." My eyes flitted away from Nevma's weak body, still glistening with water. "Nothing has changed," I whispered, my chest aching. I blinked the steam and tears from my eyes, guilt threatening to pull me under. My grip on the rocks loosened, and I let my chin graze the water's surface, my body stilling. By the skin of my knuckles, I'd gotten this far. Not by skill or pure intentions, not by faith or might. My head dipped back, and I shut my eyes. Until a voice answered.

You've changed. The voice I had been waiting for broke through the silence haunting me. My eyes snapped open, fingers digging into the rock once more.

"Nevma?" I gasped, scooping him up and holding him close. My head fell back once more but this time with uncontainable joy. "I can hear you. *I can hear you!*" I sang, smiling through a new stream of tears. "You're alive!" Breathless, I waited, eyes flickering with new light. Merely crossing the border stirred life in him again. Nevma did not lift his head or try to crawl; his legs brushed against my hand, and his wings fluttered.

My smile faded, and I set my jaw, eyes still on Nevma. The last time I refused to listen to him, I led us both into unspeakable darkness. But not this time.

I needed no other prompting, not even another word from him. The reason I'd fought my way here flooded back.

I tucked Nevma safely back in the box. "Hold on. Just a little bit longer."

The first time I tried to swim through a tunnel had been for myself. But now, there was something far more important than gems to find. The Source, The Lost Garden—hope. Holding tightly to the box, I dove into the water. The thud of my heart drummed in my ears as the warm water drew me into its current. I swam through the clear water, a pebble-strewn floor glittering up at me until the green glow from the cave embraced me like a long-lost friend. The light was dim, yet enough to reveal the way. I hesitated before the entrance, bubbles dancing over me. My muscles sparked, edging forward yet pulling me back. It was now, or never. The comfort of the vines and the words from Nevma propelled me into the darkness. I couldn't go back against the current, even if I tried. I was leaving behind the light and the air. I was leaving behind *myself*.

The current pulled me into the softly lit tunnel. Daggers of fear stabbed at my mind, and I felt every stroke they slashed, but I clung to the green glow, swimming farther, deeper.

A yellow light bloomed before me, just as my lungs threatened to burst, and I swam towards it with everything in me. I broke through the surface, sucking in a long breath of damp, cold air. The underground river pooled around me as a sob escaped my lips, echoing off the cavern ceiling. It was done. Despite my fear, despite my failure.

I clutched Nevma's box to my heart. "I did it."

My teeth chattered and I swam towards the yellow light in the cooling water. It flickered on the shore of the underground pool, casting moving shadows on the walls, taunting me with tales of its warmth. The pool grew shallower, and I stumbled through the water, nearly falling onto the rocky shore.

Movement caught my eye. A *fire doesn't build itself.* I splashed back into the pool. Its coolness gathered around my ankles as I stared at the figure. Instinctively, I reached back for my dagger, but my fingers returned empty. I cursed, shivering. I was bleeding, bruised, and weaponless. The border into The Sanctuary was penetrated. I was at its mercy now. I sucked in the cold air and raised my eyes to the figure that stood beside the flickering fire light. It took a step towards me, and I was shocked to see it was but a child, no more than nine or ten. A halo of gold danced around long cinnamon curls and bounced off dark, warm eyes.

"What—" I searched for words. "What are you doing here?"

"Waiting for you." A radiant smile broke across the young girl's face, and my fear melted away. She was waiting for me? "Come, sit by the fire." She approached me and held out a small, innocent hand, one that shimmered just like Noura's had when I first met her. I stared at it for a moment, still clutching Nevma's box, teeth chattering. "Come on. What's holding you back?"

"I... Nothing." I shivered, releasing my death grip on Nevma and taking her hand. She closed her warm fingers around mine, and I was surprised at how strong and sure her hold was. She may have been a child, but she was not feeble. A familiar strength exuded from her. She led me to the fire and bade me sit.

"Who are you?" I asked, the heat from the fire reaching into my bones and warming my cheeks until they burned. It illuminated just enough of the cavern that I could see a small shelf in the corner filled with mugs and bottles. The shape of a door appeared just past it, and a kettle was simmering on the fire.

"Ciela." Her answer was short but bursting with energy as she gingerly removed the steaming kettle from its place. She looked at me with almond shaped eyes and a dimpled smile. "Ciela, Guardian of the Rim. Or... I hope to be one day." Her eyes strayed away in a momentary daydream. She held out a steaming cup of tea, and I accepted it gratefully.

"Can you tell me where I am?" I blew on my tea, the hot steam condensing on my chilly skin.

Ciela grinned. "I can tell you everything, Opal of Wisptale, bearer of the Green Pearls." She giggled when I looked at her with shock. I started to ask how, but she merely continued. "Despite all, you climbed all the way up Mount Nea and have crossed the Rim to The Sanctuary. You have found what was thought to be lost. And all for your dragonfly."

I stared at her, not sure if I should be alarmed or grateful that I did not need to explain anything. Her eyes crinkled gleefully at me over the fire's golden light.

"May I see him?" Ciela motioned towards Nevma. Guilt began to slither its way back into my chest as I glanced down at the box. I opened it, blinking at the small blue body that had suffered so much because of me. Carefully, I placed him on my palm and held him closer to the light. She tilted her head as she studied him. "Do you trust me?" Her low voice floated over the heat rising from the fire.

"Trust you?" My pulse quickened as I considered what she was asking me.

"Yes. You must trust me. Here." She held out her palm. I drew Nevma away.

How could she ask this? I risked my life to carry him here. I was not going to allow someone else to take him from me.

"Opal." Her voice sounded far away and my head swam. "I know what Nevma means to you. And I know how to help."

How did she know Nevma's name? My stomach twisted in knots.

"Opal." This time her voice was close. She sat down next to me, and I let her lift Nevma's tiny body from my hand. "Trust me," she whispered again as she cupped her hands and brought them to her lips. She peered at me, her eyes glowing in the light before returning her gaze to her hands. Quietly, so quietly that I could barely hear, she whispered. It was not a language that I understood, but the words sounded like music, and Ciela's face glowed as she spoke to Nevma.

Ciela laughed until her dimples showed, and she opened her hands. A shimmering blue body shot out from her open palm and flew in exuberant circles around the firelight. I leaped to my feet, my mouth open in astonishment.

"Nevma!" I cried, holding out my hand for him to alight on. "But how?" This was a magic beyond anything I had hoped. Every broken knuckle of my spirit began to mend the second his legs tickled my hand, and he looked into my eyes.

What a journey it's been, dear one. His voice sung sweet and strong in my ears. Ciela clapped her hands and twirled around us.

"I will never leave you, ever again," I said fiercely, new tears streaking my face. Nevma flitted to my shoulder and tickled my ear. "How did you do it?" I turned to Ciela. Who was this child? She grinned at me.

"Oh, I hardly did a thing. He just needed to be woken up."

"What?" I said in disbelief, my mind racing back to the words Dion had spoken. I knew that the Spirit could not die, but what about the Source? Did he not need to be taken to the Source?

"I don't understand... the Source..."

"Opal." Ciela looked at me thoughtfully. "He needed to be taken to the Source because *you* needed to be taken to the Source."

Nineteen

I FROZE, STARING AT THE dancing flames, completely mystified. Dion had not said anything about me needing the Source, yet weren't there moments I'd hoped—hoped for restoration not only for Nevma but for myself? Nevma might have had a broken body, but I was the one with a broken spirit. I brushed at the mark on my chest, refusing to look at it.

Ciela slipped her hand into mine once more. "Come. It's time to leave the Rim. It's time to enter The Sanctuary." I looked from the mysterious, brave little girl to the doorway that promised to take me into the heart of The Lost Garden. Nevma still rested on my shoulder. My coat, and my pack from the tree-sted now rested at the bottom of the pool. I had nothing to hold on to, nothing to carry with me except myself. My shivering, bleeding, broken self.

"Ciela, I don't know if I'm ready." I glanced down at my green shirt that now bore rips and stains. My hair hung in wet clumps, and my lips were cracked and bleeding from the relentless cold and suffering I had endured. My voice dropped. "I don't know what to do."

Ciela squeezed my hand. "Everything is ready for you. Just enter in." She took a step forward and then glanced back to see if I would follow. Finally, I nodded and let her guide me towards the door. It was old, hewn of stone, heavy and broad. Ciela let go of my hand and took a step back.

"Knock." She grinned again. I looked at her apprehensively, unsure how my small knock could be heard through the thick stone. "Knock. The door will open for you."

I let out a slow breath, raised my hand and knocked. A bright trickle of light darted across the door, revealing the curves and grooves of a script. I ran my fingers over its markings, the new light source dancing beneath my fingers. The script was like the poem engraved on the tree from the beginning of the pilgrimage, and I held my breath for a moment before slowly sounding out the letters.

"*Not one of mine is lost,*" I read, and my pulse skipped. The Lost Garden was never lost. *I* was never lost. The door opened with a loud crack. A low light spilled into the cavern from behind the door, revealing what lay beyond. A narrow passageway cut through the rock, straight and sure. I would have groaned at the prospect of another tunnel, except to this one, there was an end. Not but a stone's throw away was the most beautiful sight. The glow of light—the glow of the sun. I stepped forward, Nevma circling my head, Ciela by my side.

"If you still don't know what to do, I think walking will do the trick." Ciela winked at me and stifled a giggle. I let myself laugh, smiling down at my young companion. I had not thought of who I might meet at the Rim, but this bright and brave little girl by far exceeded my expectations. I took a deep breath.

The Lore Wielder

"I'm ready." The words felt strange on my lips. How could I be ready? Mere minutes ago, I thought my sole purpose for coming here was Nevma. The light grew stronger as we neared the end of the tunnel, and my heart grew warmer. I ran my hand along the smooth wall, feeling the cool rock and the cumulative touch of pilgrimage. It was carved so elegantly without a scratch or loose rock to be seen.

"I hope you're not afraid of heights." Ciela flashed a smile and ran ahead, disappearing through the exit.

"Aya, wait!" I called after her, all hesitation leaving my body, as I ran towards the light.

Always run towards the light, Nevma remarked before disappearing as well. I blinked in the warmth of the sun and spun looking for Ciela and Nevma, the cave all but vanishing behind me. A magnificent, bewildering landscape spun in my view, and I dropped to the soft green grass that met my boots as I took it all in.

A range of snow-capped mountains encircled me, and a delicious green valley spread out, filled with trees and swaying grasslands. But what made my jaw drop was the island. I gaped at the enormous rock that hung over the grasslands, and my gaze slowly took in the layers of rock, clay, and dirt. Waterfalls plummeted down its surface, pouring from somewhere overhead. I took a step back, straining to see the lush green fields and hills that covered the very top of the rock. It was as if someone had plucked an island out of the sea, foundation and all, and suspended it over the valley. It hung hundreds of arms above the valley, its great shadow streaming over the grassland like a black lake in the afternoon sun. Even though the snowy mountains were not far, it smelled of early summer—fresh, dewy, and new. One of the waterfalls glistened in the light, and my eyes followed its flow to what lay above.

Gleaming white structures rose from the hillsides that were lined with trees and dotted with wildflowers. Never had I seen something so colorful and full of life, and I held my breath as my heart and mind thudded together. The Lost Garden. The Sanctuary.

"Aya, Opal!" Ciela's voice broke my trance. What met my eyes was almost as magnificent as the suspended garden. A graceful horse with a shining coat and a shimmering mane walked beside Ciela. The beauty of the creature itself was enough to draw anyone, but what almost made my heart stop were the great wings that stretched out from the horse's back.

My skin prickled. "Is that—"

"A pegasus? Yes." Ciela's eyes gleamed, and she reached up and patted its side.

"But I thought they were gone—extinct."

"Nothing is ever truly lost, not here. Come, he wants to meet you." Ciela motioned for me to approach. I steeled myself. The pegasus was no small pony. He stomped his hooves impatiently, likely wondering why he'd been interrupted from eating the sweet grass. I exhaled and approached warily, holding out a hand.

Ciela smiled. "He's quite gentle." His warm breath met my hand as I rested it on his nose, and I peered into his large dark eyes. He blinked slowly at me and neighed, sending a puff of air over me with a sweep of his enormous wings. "See! He likes you already. And that's good since he is our ride." Ciela cast her gaze up, and I followed it.

"You mean, we're going to fly there?"

"How else would we get there?" Ciela replied, but I was rendered speechless.

Was I afraid of heights? I scoffed, glancing at the girl. Sweat beaded on my hands, and I scrubbed them on my damp pants.

The Lore Wielder

Did it matter if I was? Excitement laced through me, weaving all my fears and wonders together into something I could hold onto. I pressed my lips together, looking back at the pegasus, into its glassy, steady gaze. I, Opal, bearer of the meager green pearls, was *flying* to The Lost Garden.

"Are you ready?"

"Aye," I answered finally. "I am ready."

The pegasus bowed its head, as if to confirm his readiness as well, and trotted over to a boulder from which we could mount its back. Once I helped Ciela scramble on, I hoisted myself to the boulder, glancing back at the tunnel that led us here. It was but a dark opening in the side of a grassy hill that stretched up into the clouds at a remarkably steep incline. We were leaving the Rim. When I'd crossed the border, I had not had time to process it, but now, as I looked back, I wondered at it. The Rim had warmed my soul and given me Nevma back. It had reached its wise hands into my journey and changed it to what it was always meant to be. If the Rim had changed so much, what might The Lost Garden hold for me?

I swung my leg over the pegasus's back behind Ciela. His warm sides and gentle pace calmed my spirit. Ciela caught my hand.

"Hold on!" Her voice echoed through the valley as the horse broke into a trot and then a gallop before pumping his wings. The air rushed past, and I blinked watery eyes as my hair whipped over my shoulder. I was not sure when the pegasus's hooves left the ground, but within minutes, we were sailing over the green valley, riding the wind. It was the most tangible taste of freedom I'd ever known, and I threw my head back, closing my eyes, cherishing the wind and light as they danced around me. Ciela's laughter mingled with mine, pure and strong in its essence.

"Keep your mouth closed. Bugs!" she said over the wind.

The rocky foundation of the island flew past us, turning from gray stone to clay and dirt as we rose higher and higher towards the heavens. The higher we flew, the warmer the atmosphere and the bluer the sky became. Soon, the trees and wild grass that clung to the edge of the island drifted by with the clouds. The pegasus soared up and over the land, as if he too was coming home. His wings ceased pumping, and we glided, the breeze poignant with the sweet smell of fruit trees and wildflowers as the land grew closer and closer. I closed my eyes as the sound and feel of hooves pounding on soil brought me back to the ground. When the pegasus slowed to a trot, I nearly bounced off, reaching for Ciela to hold onto.

We both tumbled off onto the flower-strewn hillside, jostled but uninjured. The horse turned around and trotted back, putting his nose in our faces to assure himself we were unharmed.

"Aya, we're all right! We don't need your drool in our faces." Ciela guided his face away from ours in amusement. As if that was all he required, the pegasus bowed his head once more and galloped off out of sight.

"What a strange creature," I remarked. "Oh, and sorry about the fall."

Ciela stood to her feet and brushed herself off. "It's not the first time." She held out her hand to me, her windblown curls bouncing around her face. "Welcome—" she paused, stars in her eyes, "—to the beginning."

Twenty

I CAUGHT HOLD OF CIELA'S hand and stood, my senses thudding with goodness. The honey-infused air mingled with the chatter of rivers and bird's songs—and best of all, the sound of life itself. Over the breeze, laughter and shouts of excitement tumbled from the estate ahead, as if the most thrilling game of hide and seek were happening.

Ciela directed me to a dirt path that ran along the edge of the woods, drawing us towards the sound. The trees bowed their branches, the bright green leaves dancing like paper jewels in the wind, untouched by disease or drought. Butterflies fluttered above us, and Nevma left my shoulder to join them as they darted in and out amongst the flowers.

"He looks happy." Ciela held her hand out and one of the butterflies landed on her finger. I watched Nevma as he played.

"Aye." My voice came out frail. "It's as if he belongs here." Nevma did belong here, in this place of beauty and perfection. A place safe from me. Ciela gave me an amused smile.

"Don't you know where he belongs?" Ciela turned towards me, scaring the butterfly away. I watched its wings as it made a beeline away from us. Almost as Nevma had done.

"I think he belongs where he is safest. Happiest," I answered slowly, wincing at my words and the pain they brought me.

Ciela scoffed. "Being safe is overrated."

The dirt path became cobblestone as we neared the estate, and a river cut in front of us, bubbling and swirling with crystal clear water as it disappeared beyond the tree line. A bridge arched over the river, but instead of leading me to it, Ciela brought me to the edge of the water. A pail bobbed in the water, attached to the bridge by a rope.

Ciela pulled it towards us and scooped up the water, holding it out to me. "Here. Drink and wash your face before we go inside." I gratefully accepted the water, my thirst rising at the sight of it. I hesitated. What would it taste like? I drew the bucket to my lips, the tales of the sweet water dancing through my mind. The water spilled over me and trickled all the way down my empty stomach and into my bones, sweetness tingling on my tongue—as if the stream had been infused with honeysuckle. I drew the bucket back, peering at the water sloshing inside. It was real. I laughed, closing my eyes and breathing it in. *The sweet water is real.* Chills raced down my arms.

I returned the bucket to the stream and dried my face with my shirt, dirt and blood still rubbing off my skin.

"You might want to do that again." Ciela's voice startled me as she dropped next to me beside the river. "Can I braid your hair? My sisters just taught me how."

The Lore Wielder

I reached back, feeling the dirty clumps of hair that I had once been proud of. "Sure." I splashed more water on my face and scrubbed my hands and arms another time.

Ciela sectioned my hair as if braiding it were the most important thing in the world and began to slowly braid my long, tangled strands. Whenever she pulled too hard, it reminded me of Alana. I smiled. It was strange how I could think of her here and miss her, but not feel sad about it.

"Ciela." I had so many questions, and I was not sure where to start. "Who—who lives in this estate?"

"We live here," she answered. "All the children." As if her words were a summons, the gate beyond the bridge opened, and a group of children trotted out onto the path. I smiled at the young toddlers running along with their clumsy legs and blushed at the middling-age children, even more aware of my appearance. Ciela finished with my braids and jumped up, waving.

"Aye, over here—"

"Ciela, no!" I hissed. I couldn't meet anyone, not like this. After spending so many days alone, the thought of talking or explaining myself even to children made me quake. Ciela turned her twinkling eyes on me, ignoring my plea.

"Come on!" she yelled at the children, still holding my gaze. "There is someone you've been expecting!" Nevma landed on my shoulder and tickled my ear with his wings.

Breathe, dear one. I'm here.

I swallowed and stood to my feet, running my fingers over my braid for comfort. My hand closed around the collar of my shirt, knowing what still lay beneath. Was the mark visible on my neck now? My eyes flickered to the trees. But there was nowhere to hide.

The white and gold of the children's attire flashed in the light as they ran down the path towards us, joy incarnate. I breathed in, a wave of it crashing over me. Ciela dashed across the bridge to meet them. I hesitated, running my hand along the smooth railing of the bridge to steady myself as I crossed the river. Before I reached the path on the opposite side, Ciela and another girl took both my hands to pull me along faster, and a middling boy taller than me set a green garland crown on my head. I freed my hand to graze the tender leaves and opened my mouth to protest, but the sight of Nevma made me pause. I blinked. If they were expecting me, then I did not need to justify myself or mutter how unworthy I was. All I needed to do was receive.

I let out a slow breath and squeezed Ciela's hand as we approached the gates, the others crowding round me with smiling faces as they chattered amongst themselves. The gate was thrown wide open, each side a beautiful piece of metal work glinting gold with a handle shaped like a tree. A low wall ran along each side, covered in vines.

"Are those cognizant vines?" I pointed towards the wall as we passed by.

"They are. But here, they have another name," the middling boy who'd given me the garland answered. I returned my gaze to him to ask him what it was, but he was already disappearing past the gate, a mischievous expression on his face. Compared to myself, covered in dirt and scratches, he was fresh and beautiful. All the children were beautiful, with not a trace of hunger or disease on them. As if they were perfectly safe and loved their whole lives. And perfectly shimmery like Ciela.

When we passed through the gate, belonging wrapped its arms around me. I was home. I couldn't begin to explain it, but I knew it. This place of beauty, safety, and love was what I was created for. My eyes misted, but I did not cry as I took in the gleaming white walls of the house and lush green vines creeping up them.

The house stood five stories high with large cathedral-like windows peering down at us, trimmed in a bright sea blue. Trees draped their graceful branches over the walls and the archways, loaded with all manner of fruits. The breeze was saturated with sweetness, and the air buzzed with the sound of bees delighted in their work.

"And this is only the courtyard," Ciela whispered as we came to stop beneath a trellised garden. Delicate white flowers crept down the vine, and butterflies drank their fill of the sweet nectar. A fountain bubbling with water stood at the center of the courtyard.

"Is it—is it sweet too?" I asked, stepping closer to the fountain, marveling at the sculpture in the middle.

"Of course. All the water here is sweet." Ciela sat down on the edge of the fountain's pool. I braced myself on the marble, leaning closer. There was a circle of beautiful flowers in the middle, but what caught my eye was the inside of the circle—two hands reaching out from an array of flowers. In each palm, there was a hole clean through the middle. As if it had been pierced. And cupped in the middle was a tiny form. A baby's form, like one still in its mother's womb.

Curious, I reached my own hand out and touched the wounded hands, remembering the beginning. The beginning of our world, always meant to be a sanctuary for those souls who were too full of light for the Other. The Lost Garden was more beautiful than I could have imagined.

I stood in front of a mirror, drying my long hair, contemplating what to do with it. Ciela had brought me to the girls' chambers where I would be staying, and I immediately jumped into a hot bath, trying to wash the pain from the journey away. The wounds, though, were there to stay.

Smarting red lines from the snow leopard were slashed across my chest, stomach, and arms. They were not serious or deep, but that did not stop them from stinging. I winced as I ran a finger along one near my neck. The mark on my chest had fingered its way past my collarbone. I chewed my cheek. It had been visible to Ciela and the others the whole time. My stomach chilled.

With a sigh, I forced myself from the mirror. A tray of fruit, sweets, and tea lay on my bed, and as soon as I wrapped myself in a white robe, I sat down to eat. Even though the room could house around five girls, I was alone. Again. Except for Nevma. And surprisingly, it felt good. Nevma tickled my cheek with his wing before resting on my shoulder. I smiled, turning my head to see him.

"I can hardly believe you're back." I shuddered with the emotions of losing him and of pushing myself beyond what I ever thought possible to save him. Now, having him back, right here, sitting on my shoulder looking at me, felt surreal.

What have I always told you? Nevma's voice sounded in my head, and a smile pulled at my lips.

"Believe. You always told me to believe."

And you did. You believed, not in yourself, but in the hope you would find. I nodded, still not comprehending how he had returned to me fully. I lay down on the soft bed, closing my eyes.

Opal, you are brave when you have faith. I let myself fall asleep with Nevma's words drifting through my dreams.

Ciela came back only once to bring me a hot meal and to assure me that I did not have to join everyone for dinner. It took nearly half my energy to eat before passing out in the bed again. I was safe. I had accomplished my mission, and now I could fully embrace the deepness of sleep.

Ciela burst into the room as soon as there was morning light. I heard the other girls groan, but they were not the ones with a young girl bouncing on their bed.

"Wake up, *wake up.*" She pulled on my arm, and I joined in with the other girls' groans. When I fully opened my eyes, I expected to still feel the aches and pains from yesterday's journey, but after a good night's rest in a real bed, I was amazed at how restored I felt.

"Come on, the Heir is waiting for you!"

"The—what?" I stuttered, tumbling out of the bed, one leg still tangled in the blankets. All the sleepiness left my body in an instant. I wasn't ready. I did not know exactly what I was expecting, but it was not this.

"Ciela, I can't meet anyone like this." I motioned to my tangled hair and nightgown.

She dismissed my concern with a wave of her hand. "Don't be ridiculous. He's been talking about you for weeks!" She pulled on my arm, her eyes twinkling. "And you've finally come."

"Aye but—" My head spun. Meet the Heir of all things? It was beyond anything I could conceive.

Ciela threw a clean bathrobe over my nightgown as if that would improve my appearance. "You have two minutes to fix your hair. Then we're leaving." Ciela's voice was surprisingly commanding, but then again, she did want to be a Guardian of the Rim.

I tied the robe around my waist, glaring at the girl, unsure what to think. Hastily, I threw my hair into a braid and splashed water on my face.

"You know this is for you." She tapped her foot impatiently, and I bit back a smile before a myriad of butterflies migrated through me. I peered into the mirror hung on the wall opposite the bed. My smile faded, taking in the web of dark on my skin. Ciela appeared in the mirror next to me. "He doesn't care what you look like."

I sniffed. "I just want it gone." I dropped my hand to my side.

"I know. Why do you think I'm taking you to see my father?"

I froze, breathless. "You—you think he will heal me?" I searched her face, clutching her arm to keep my hand from trembling. Was this why I was brought here?

"Of course!" Ciela rolled her eyes. I released her arm and covered my mouth as I gaped. *I can finally be free—free of this mark. Free of not belonging.* Ciela tossed her hair. "Can we go now, please?"

I nodded, closing my robe over the mark once more. The Heir was going to help me. My fingers shook, still clutching my robe closed as I followed Ciela out of the room. He was going to wash the stain of failure away.

We walked at quite a pace on a dirt trail that wound up the mountainside behind the estate. It was the only mountain on the island, and I hoped we did not have to reach the top. The sun was rising from the east, highlighting our strange position in the sky. The light spilled over the orchards and glades, shimmering off the waterfalls that plunged down into the plain rolling far beneath us. I bit my lip, my skin tingling. What had haunted me was nearing its end—restoration within my grasp.

The path grew steep, and we were both panting from the exertion, but my smile never left my face. When I saw the pavilion ahead, fluttering in the morning breeze beside the top of the waterfall, I knew we were close. I could feel it in the air, like its very elements sung from being so close to its maker. I paused, breathing it in, a song stirring in my own heart. Tears of joy shimmered in my eyes. How could I, one who had never belonged, be here? In this beauty? In this wonder?

The ground leveled out as we approached the glade where the pavilion sat. Wildflowers bloomed in every direction. Ciela stooped and began to pick the flowers. "For your hair. Since you're so worried about how you look." She winked. I lowered myself onto my knees so she could reach my braid and let her weave the flowers into it. When she began on the part over my shoulder, I noticed with a twinge that she was using dandelions. I opened my mouth to speak but decided to swallow the words instead. They were the very words Alius said to me about dandelions.

"Thank you," I said when she finished. "Are you coming with me?" I asked, pulse thudding.

"Oh, no. This is between you and Father." Ciela stopped walking beside me and motioned that I should go on. My knees threatened to buckle as I turned in the direction ahead of us. The wind caught my hair, its scent breathing calm into me.

"Go on," Ciela murmured from behind. As she spoke, a figure stepped out from the pavilion. I blinked, steeling myself to see some wonder beyond my comprehension. But instead, I saw the young boy from the gate. He motioned with his head for me to follow. I gave one look back at Ciela, but she ran away, chasing the butterflies. A slow breath passed between my lips as I turned to follow.

"I'm Neo, by the way," he said over his shoulder as he led me through the wooded hillside.

"Opal," I murmured, trailing behind him.

He laughed. "I know."

We came to a large pool. Beyond it, the tip of Mount Nea pierced the clouds, bathed in morning. I approached the top of the hill where it tumbled down before us in small cliffs and boulders.

"Wait for Him by the pool," Neo said before disappearing. Filled with curiosity, I approached the edge of the pool, my heartbeat drowning out all other noises. I was about to meet the Heir. I clenched and unclenched my hands, pacing. My chest tightened. I could barely breathe. I peered into the water. It was perfectly clear and nearly still. When I leaned over the water, my stomach plummeted to my toes. A body lay perfectly still under the water's surface, golden hair swirling around her. I covered my mouth with my hand and stumbled backwards.

Think, dear. Nevma's voice shook me like thunder. Flashes of the journey went through my head. The night I followed the moths, the terrifying boat ride, the Harfares, and the water. I stopped on that memory. How long had I been underwater? How long had I been nearly lost in the bowels of Misty Lale? My mind raced. The crazed Elowynnite on the mountain ran right past me. I thought it was because he had gone insane, but what if he couldn't see me? I held my hands in front of my face, shaking. Were they real? I cursed, daring to look at the body again, lying still and pale before me under the glassy water.

"Am I dead?"

Twenty-one

"FEAR NOT."

I whirled around at the voice, my spirit stumbling within me. Nevma leaped into the air from my shoulder as if seeing an old dear friend. I caught my breath as I followed his bright blue body darting gleefully through the air towards the figure who had spoken. I did not know what I was supposed to do, but when I finally met his eyes, I fell onto my knees, shaking. But not from fear. It was something else. Something powerful, and I could not stand under its weight. Glory. Wonder. All thoughts about what happened to me faded like mist.

"*Listen, beloved, for my melody guides you home.*" His words floated like incense over the air and beckoned my gaze upward. Upward towards the Heir himself. The Father, as the children called him. His eyes gleamed with something divine. Something ancient. Something lovely. He was a man—or at least he looked like a man.

"Be not afraid," he repeated.

"I—I'm not afraid," I said, surprised at my words, a drum of wonder sounding within me. How could I not be afraid?

"I know." He smiled and approached where I was still kneeling, his long white garments flowing behind him, glowing in the morning light. Ciela was right. Hearing his voice and meeting his eyes, I knew him. I couldn't explain how, but it was true.

"I don't understand," I murmured, glancing at the pool once more. "Am I...?"

The Heir's eyes shone glassy as he knelt next to me. "It is true. You are dead. Noura couldn't save you. She was too late. Your body was brought here two days ago. It was your spirit alone sent on the pilgrimage." Quietness settled between us as he studied my face. The watery haze in his eyes faded, and he smiled. "Ask your questions, dear."

I took a deep breath. "If I am dead, why did I feel everything—hunger, exhaustion, pain—" I held out my wounded arm.

The Heir gently touched the wound on my arm before his gaze returned to mine. "Because it was real. You endured every bit of the pilgrimage as if your body had. This is something misunderstood about death." He rose to his feet, his face turned towards Mount Nea. "Some believe it is an escape from pain, but it's not. The spiritual world is just as real and painful as the physical world."

I released my breath, still reeling. Knees too weak to stand, I dug my fingers into the grass before me. "Is this... is this why I was brought here? Because... I'm to stay?"

"No, my dear child." The Heir turned to face me again, laughter in his eyes. "It is not the time for you to stay... Come and walk with me." His infinite eyes twinkled as he held out his hand and helped me to my feet. I staggered for only a moment. While all anxiety slipped away, awe hung over me, but it wasn't a heaviness that was unbearable or unnatural. It was a heaviness of wonder that melded with my spirit, overwhelming what did not belong. "I have a feeling there is much to be said... and much to be asked." Though His face was fixed on the mountains ahead, with those words, he set free the questions exploding in my chest. The dam broke.

"Nevma—he was gone. And now he's back, and I don't understand." I blinked through blurred vision, unable to speak another word. Nevma was back, and everything was right, but nothing made sense.

The Heir looked at me with his gentle eyes, amused. "Ah, the wind blows where it wishes... Nevma saved you, and you fought your way up here to save him. Only he never needed saving." The Heir settled himself on the grass, and I joined him, grateful to relieve my shaking legs. "It was always about saving you. Even after you were pulled from the lake." The last bit hung in my mind, but I was still focused on Nevma.

"Ciela said he was asleep..."

"In a way, he was. But the Spirit is clever. He knows exactly what you need, even if it hurts sometimes." He spoke slowly, answering my next question before I could ask it. "You couldn't hear his voice because you stopped listening. You stopped listening because you didn't like what he was saying." I blinked back tears at his words. Even if Nevma had only been asleep, it was still my doing because I listened to another's voice. The Heir continued earnestly. "What Nevma did in allowing his body to grow weak was exactly what you needed to give you the courage to come here."

My breath trembled. "Then it's all my fault. I listened to another voice and—and..." I could not finish my thought. All the brokenness and confusion and guilt collided with my overwhelming joy that Nevma was alive. The moment the Heir put his arm over my shoulder, I buried my face in the shelter of his embrace. Neither of us spoke as I wept. Neither of us had to.

"If you had not listened to that other voice, you would be the only one in the world to have done so," he whispered as my weeping stilled.

I wiped my glistening cheeks, drawing back. I'd made the wrong choice, but the Heir never gave up on me.

You are brave when you have faith. The voice spoke in my mind, but it wasn't Nevma. It was the Heir's voice. Nemva was so much more than I ever dreamed. I'd begun to think he was a remnant of the Heir's spirit, but no. An ancient unity flowed through them both as Nevma rested on the Heir's arm. The Heir met my gaze with knowing eyes before reaching in his pocket and bringing out a flute. As his hands grasped the instrument, I noticed them for the first time. They were pierced with old wounds, just like the hands in the fountain. His voice tore my eyes away from his scars.

"Nevma may have pushed you on the pilgrimage, but it was the music that guided you." He pressed his lips to the flute. A soft, beautiful melody pierced my heart as he played. It was the same music I'd heard my whole life. I was about to respond when the trees around us echoed the tune, carrying it down the hillside, as far as the Heir wished it to be heard.

"It was you—not just the trees? You played every time? For me?"

"Yes, beloved. *Every time.*" His words sent a wave of emotion through me, and I thought about every time the song guided me. Touched me. Saved me.

"But why *me*?"

"Because you're mine," he answered simply with a shrug. "Your dandelion—" He continued, and I followed his gaze to a dandelion dangling precariously from my braid. It seemed to wink at its maker. "I made this flower full of goodness, something to be used to soothe and heal the body. A source of nutrients and beautiful to behold, whether in its yellow bloom or its white seeds. Yet, almost no one sees it for the way I created it to be. And here is my question to you. When others do not see its values, does that change anything about the dandelion? Does it render the flower worthless or steal its beauty?"

I furrowed my eyebrows. "Well, no..."

"Opal, just like the dandelion, you belong because you're mine, and I made you as such. No one—no one can ever take that away from you."

I closed my eyes as the warmth of his words spread through my chest. Along with guilt. I had belonged all along, I just couldn't see it. I'd refused to open my eyes. I scrubbed my nose, glancing at Nemva. He flaunted his metallic wings at me.

"There is one more thing, Opal. I want you to close your eyes. Remember the faces of your family. Your friends."

At the mention of them, knots gripped my stomach, but I breathed in slowly and clamped my eyes shut. The faces of my parents, Alana, and Ilynn flitted in my mind. The Heir's voice continued gently in my ears. "You know that you are loved, even if it is hard to believe sometimes." And he was right. I swallowed the ache in my throat. I was seeing with a mask stripped from my eyes for the first time. They had never stopped loving me or valuing their relationship with me. Things might be changing—they might not always understand me—but that did not mean I didn't matter. I had been blind, only thinking about myself.

My mouth parted as my vision blurred. "They love me... but I have been so selfish." The pit in my stomach twisted. Had I done anything to love them back? With a shudder, I forced myself to look at the Heir once more. "How can I be like a dandelion if I have nothing to give?"

"What makes you think you have nothing to give?"

One tear slipped down my cheek. I hesitated. "Because I *don't* give."

The Heir reached up and wiped the tear away. "Can I let you in on something? After this journey, I think you'll find just how much you have to give. A flower can only bloom outward. The only way to become what you were created to be is to reach outside of yourself, even when it's hard and scary."

I fingered the edge of my robe. Bloom outward. Was there really something in me worth growing? I stared at the cloud-riddled sky. "Is that the reason you brought me here? To show me that I had something to give?"

Nevma alighted on my shoulder. **That's the reason I brought you here.**

The Heir's eyes shone again, not with sadness but inexplicable joy. He rose to his feet and approached a patch of bright red flowers.

"This is not an end, but a beginning." He stooped down and picked one. My heart skipped a beat. I'd nearly forgotten during our conversation.

I was dead.

He tore the bright red petals off the flowers and began to grind them between two smooth stones. Crush them. Slowly, a paste began to form. Something reminiscent of blood. The flower's blood.

"Are you ready?" He looked at me, a joy brimming on his face that I did not understand.

I rose to my feet, my knees wobbly. "Ready for what?"

A flicker of pain passed over his face as he stared at the red paste on the stone in his wounded hand. "When the darkness sought your life, it did not realize I was also inviting you." His eyes snapped back to mine. "An invitation into my own death."

I stared at him, my head spinning. Death's greed had held a hidden invitation. The battle the darkness had waged against me had been absolutely routed. My legs threatened to collapse again, but I refused to sink to the ground. Because this time, I was ready.

Nevma rested on my shoulder, and I could feel him pulling on my emotions again, steadying me for what was coming as we watched the one clothed in white wade into the pool.

Gently, the Heir lifted my lifeless head out of the water. I watched, a strange eeriness creeping through me, seeing my own body limp and far away. I was detached from that broken and stained body. He closed his eyes, dipped his finger into the red paste, and anointed my head with it, whispering words I did not recognize. "*Talitha cumi.*"[1]

---

[1] "Little girl, I say to you, arise!" Mark 5:41

Twenty-two

I EXPECTED FIREWORKS BURSTING THROUGH my muscles—lightning bolts shocking me awake. At his words, my sight vanished, though not a drop of fear resided in me as Nevma's power intertwined seamlessly with the Heir's. It started as a trickle, warm and lovely. It flowed through my whole body, whispering to each cell as it passed. Whispering words I did not understand, but words permeated with the power that created the world itself.

My nerves awoke. Water surrounded me, and delicious breath filled my lungs. Light beckoned to my tightly closed eyes, and I timidly answered its call, my vision blurry at first, until my eyes focused on his. The Heir. He was laughing, deep, beautiful, joyful tones that sang in my ears. Nevma tickled my cheek with his wing.

"Welcome, beloved, to the beginning." The Heir's eyes were glassy but exuberant.

Welcome to all that was prepared for you, Nevma added, soaring around us, as if this—restoration, *creation*—was the desire of their very essence. I threw my arms around the Heir's neck, joy spilling out of me.

"Thank you!" It was the only thing I could think to say to them. And it was enough.

With a thick blanket over my shoulders and Nevma buzzing gleefully around my head, I followed the Heir back down towards the pavilion. When we reached the edge of the waterfall, we stopped and looked down over the hillside towards the estate. My mouth dropped open in shock when I saw hundreds of faces staring up at us.

"And now, we feast!" As soon as the words left the Heir's mouth, sounds of celebration erupted from the hundreds of children below. Shouting, dancing, running and laughing. The lingering child inside me jumped at the chance to escape, and as soon as Ciela grabbed my hand and began pulling me down the path towards the chaos, I let go of all my resistance.

Nevma floated on the laughter of the children. And I—I was alive again. Truly alive. And standing in the middle of the chaos was the last person I expected to see. I ran towards her, overwhelmed by the sight.

"Noura!" I threw my arms around her, and she embraced me with the love and care of an older sister. Her tears fell on my neck, and she drew back to look at me. "How? I thought you had something else more important..."

"The more important thing was *you!* Dion and I had the task of bringing your body safely here. I've been waiting for you to arrive for two days!" She wrapped me in yet another hug.

"Is Dion here too?" I searched for him, but Noura shook her head, a sad expression flickering across her face.

"He was needed elsewhere, otherwise he would have never missed this. But he sends his greetings." She smiled through her tears.

When we finally arrived at the gate in front of the estate, I beamed at the sight before my eyes. Blankets lay on the ground piled high with fruits, fresh breads, cheese, and anything one could possibly want for breakfast. It was the most marvelous picnic I had ever seen.

"Nice pajamas," Ciela whispered before disappearing amongst her friends. My cheeks burned as I looked down at my old and battered clothes that were never meant to be seen in the light of day, much less in The Lost Garden. Yet, the embarrassment faded as I glanced around at the deliciously wild and free pandemonium that was the feast. Many of the children were watching me, but I saw in their faces only delight and continuous wonder.

I sat down right in the middle of the group and joined the feasting. It did not matter that I had yet to meet anyone other than Ciela and the Heir. After all, this was home. And I could not feel like I did not belong if I had finally found home. Even though, and it was strange to think, this body never made the pilgrimage, I drank two steaming cups of tea to rid myself of any lingering remnants of Mount Nea and ate so much buttered bread I thought I would never hunger again.

I ran my fingers through the lush grass just beyond the blanket and breathed deeply, that sweet smell drifting through my whole body like the most delicious tonic. My eyes drifted around the feast until I found the Heir. And I smiled. He sat on the grass, three tiny children bouncing on his lap and poking their fingers in his face and smearing food everywhere. And he was delighted to bear the careless, sticky caresses of each. He was their father after all.

"Opal! Over here." Ciela's voice pulled me out of my daze. I followed her voice and saw her running towards me, a young woman in tow. "Here! This is Mavis." I stood to my feet, brushing the grass from my clothes, and bowed my head in acknowledgment.

"Ciela wants me to give you a tour of the place," Mavis commented, an amused look on her face. Ciela bumped her shoulder into Mavis's arm. "And take you to the Dome of Beauty."

"First," Ciela added with a grin.

"Yes, we'll go there *first*," Mavis conceded and ruffled Ciela's honey-curls. Ciela protested but the deed of endearment was already done. The young lady, perhaps seven years my elder, led the way. I followed behind, admiring her vast locks of auburn hair that reached her knees. We wound our way through the courtyards to a gate on the east side of the estate. Once through, we met a beautiful green slope where one of the rivers flowed and another pavilion sat at the bottom.

"This is the Dome of Beauty." Mavis stepped beside me, taking my arm in hers. My eyes returned to the pavilion which rose gracefully from its peaceful surroundings. Its fabrics walls were painted in stunning designs and blew gently in the wind as young girls and women stirred inside the tent.

My hands and feet soaked in a lovely smelling liquid as Mavis ran a brush through my hair. The inside of the pavilion was as grand as the outside and filled with every comfort someone could want after a long day—hot baths, soft cushions, massages, beauty oils. I sank back into the cushion, completely relaxed even though I was surrounded by strangers. Everything was different about this place. It was so... free. In my own world and culture, there were so many expectations to meet to be accepted. Expectations to know what to do and what to say. We had to justify ourselves with every other breath. But here, I simply was.

Once I was properly cleaned and rubbed down with oils, Mavis brought out a cloak. I gasped as I recognized the golden leafy fabric.

"Is that—"

"Of course. A gift from the dryads should never be lost." She beamed. I reached for the cloth, my fingers closing around the fabric. It was the same, but different. The cloak was embroidered all over with green. The same soft green as my pearls ran in leaves and curves all over it, and white flowers peeked out from the swirls.

"Come on. Put it on," she encouraged. I slipped it over my white tunic, and Mavis fastened a wide leather belt with two buckles around my waist. She led me in front of a mirror. I hesitated to look, fighting a strange thought. What if I looked different? There was something inside me that wished to look different. More beautiful—more like someone else. But I took a deep breath, shoved the idea from my mind, and let my eyes slowly rise to the reflection staring back at me. Even to that thought, I must die.

"You look wonderful," Mavis whispered, leaning on my arm.

And I did. I was most emphatically still myself, robed in clothes that felt far too beautiful, but there was something about my face that was lighter. An inward peace glowed beneath my eyes. Joy restored. Light taking up residence. I glanced down at my hand, noticing the soft shimmer beneath my skin.

"The scars." My hand flew to my chest when I noticed the soft white lines beneath my skin. "But how?"

"Because everything was real. Your body did not experience the journey, but your spirit did, and you bear the proof. The shallow ones will fade with time."

As I studied the glow beneath my skin, I realized the mark was gone. I drew in a breath, and a smile tugged at my lips. I'd forgotten about it. What had haunted me for so long was nothing more than a dying star that had burned out a millennia before.

Ciela, Mavis, and I left the Dome of Beauty. My fingers clung to the soft fabric of my cloak as we continued the tour. My hair tumbled over my shoulder, loose and free like how most of the girls here wore their hair. There was freedom in venturing out with my hair down and no daggers. Those were the outward signs of where and to whom I belonged—to Wisptale. Here, they were not forgotten or erased but simply lifted.

We returned through the courtyards and passed through the open gate. I turned back, admiring the vast and beautiful estate behind. So full of beauty and life. A space only someone like the Heir could create. A space void of everything I had run from and completely removed from the fingers of darkness. Paradise.

"Can you guess where we're taking you?" Ciela squeaked, a skip in her step as we crossed the bridge of the first river of Sweet Water. I returned her enthusiasm, breaking into a skip of my own.

"No! Is it one of your favorites?"

"Oh yes! It's one of the Domes of the Guardians. Where they learn how to fight." Her eyes glimmered. "I cannot wait until I'm old enough to train there!"

"I'm not so bad at fighting myself," I said, immediately wishing to take back those words.

"You? You don't seem like a fighter." She scrutinized me.

"I'm not a fighter. Actually, we prefer the term defender," I explained. "Where I'm from, every girl learns a specific type of fighting—Lore-wielding."

"Lore-wielding?" She giggled as we entered the woods. "Show me, show me!" The top of a dome rose above the trees in the distance.

I frowned, eyeing the dome. "Show you? Maybe another time..."

But she insisted. I took a deep breath and closed my eyes, remembering the night of the festival and everything that I'd lost that day. My limbs surged with memory even without music, and I began the precise steps of the dance on the well-worn path of the forest floor. A smile danced on my lips. I didn't realize how much I missed embracing this part of where I came from. Even if it was born of tragic times, the history flowed through my blood.

The air rushed by, and my loose hair flew around me wildly. I improvised the ending, never forgetting the loss of my daggers. The result was less impressive, but when I landed, my ears filled with the sounds of shouts and cheers. My eyes flew open, and I stumbled back to face twenty new faces watching me. Both Ciela and Mavis snickered.

"Not bad, not bad," Neo said, stepping out from the crowd. "Maybe you should train with us." He was the one who had given me the crown of leaves. The one who led me to the pool this morning. My cheeks, which were already red, grew even redder. This was a group coming back from Guardian training. If they were anything like Dion, whatever show I had put on was nothing compared to what they could do.

"I don't know about that, but I do think she should have a chance to redo the ending for us." Noura stepped out from the crowd. "I think it's time you have these back." She reached inside her cloak and brought out two daggers. Two daggers with green pearls embedded in the hilts.

I gasped, staring. "But I lost them in the river..."

"Or did you surrender them to the river?" She winked, afternoon light dancing through her hair. "Take them."

I hesitated, two rivers colliding inside me—one of awe and one of loathing.

"I don't... know if I want them back." The pearls had haunted me. They marked me. "I don't want to be who I was."

"What? A dandelion?" Noura gave me a knowing smile. "Take them. And remember what your pearls mean."

Chills raced up and down my arms as I touched the handle of one of my daggers. Green pearls. Made Anew. Nevma had guided me to them, not as a substitute for something better, but as what I was meant to have all along.

Slowly, I lifted them from Noura's outstretched hand, the light glinting off the blades. A new affection for them entered my body. They were mine. An extension of myself. My hands tingled as I grasped the hilts. Ciela pulled on my arm.

"Come on, I want to see the dome!"

"Ciela, you come here almost every day!" Mavis chided her like an older sister would.

"So?" She ran ahead through the gathering of Guardians, entrusting me entirely to Mavis.

"I have never seen a more passionate nine-year-old!" I said, laughing.

"She's been talking about being a Guardian at the Rim since she could walk."

The crowd of Guardians parted, though Noura and Neo followed behind Mavis and me as we continued to the dome. Ciela had all but disappeared, but we trailed along the wooded path behind her. The Dome of the Guardians was not like the Beauty Dome at all, which was more or less an overwrought tent. The West Dome of the Guardians was a low tower situated on the edge of the island. The trees gave way to another wide, grassy land used for training. Ciela plopped down on the ground, face resting on her hands, keenly observing the sparring.

"Well, this is it." Mavis motioned to the tower. By her lack of enthusiasm, I guessed that she must not have any interest in the art of being a Guardian. She knelt beside me, pointing to a group paired off, sparring. "Those are the Guardians. Everyone else here has never left the garden before."

It was easy to pick them out from the rest. Not only were they the eldest present, but there was something about their eyes. Something I recognized in my own that I had yet to encounter here beyond the mysterious eyes of the Heir himself. It was suffering.

"I don't know why anyone would leave," I said quietly, more to myself than my companions.

"What!" Ciela immediately responded.

"We're all meant to leave," Mavis added over Ciela's excitement. "We belong to the story of this world as much as anyone else."

"The story of suffering?" My eyes met hers for a minute, expecting to find only innocence. I blinked as a deeply buried pain flickered in her eyes.

"We are here *because* of suffering. We may live in paradise, but we never forget where we come from." As Mavis said this, she fished a locket out of her tunic and opened it. At first, as I peered inside, I saw nothing but pale blue. Then, faces appeared. Faces that resembled hers.

"Are those—"

"My parents. My siblings."

"But where are they?"

"Another world. One day. One day, I will get to meet them. I don't claim to know what it's like, being from the other side of the Rim. Not yet anyway. And I can't say I've experienced suffering yet, but I know there will be a new joy—a joy I've yet to know—when I finally meet them."

Another world. Of course. It was just as the Heir explained so long ago in the *Book of Memories.* He returned to The Sanctuary after binding Hesith in the lake in order to care for the little lives brought from the Other—*those too full of light for the brokenness of that world.*

I furrowed my brow, remembering the locket Noura always wore. "Do you all have lockets?"

"Oh, yes!" Ciela answered, pulling out hers and proudly introducing me to her family. I smiled as I recognized Ciela's almond-shaped eyes in her yemma's face and Ciela's curls that matched her appa and brother's hair.

"Thank you for sharing them with me. They're beautiful." We sat in cherished silence for a few moments, our eyes turning back to the action before us, though not really taking it in. A gentle breeze drifted past us, warm and refreshing. It didn't take away any of the weight we felt but simply whispered of a goodness beyond and a goodness to come—hope.

"An Avarish girl? This I've got to see!" Someone's voice drifted from beside me. I furrowed my brow, turning to see someone walking towards us with Neo. My hand dropped to the grass in alarm. He was speaking to me.

"I'm told you're a Lore-wielder from Avarlyn. Come, I wanna see what you've got!" He smiled and brandished his practice sword playfully.

"How did you know?" I stammered, my cheeks warming.

"The daggers. And Neo told us."

"Come, we want to see what you can do." Neo grinned, offering me a hand up.

I already made a fool of myself on the walk here."

"Hardly." Neo dropped his voice, and I took his hand as two more Guardians approached. "It's more for your benefit than ours. Trust me. This isn't your normal training ground."

I gave him the most confused look I could muster, but the older Guardians had already gripped me by the elbows and were pushing me to their sparring ground. This was absurd. I turned around to protest again, but they were all watching me. Waiting. I shifted uncomfortably, running my fingers over the smooth pearls. How in Avarlyn could this be for my own benefit? I'd been pushed outside of myself quite enough already.

Carefully, I tucked the blades into my belt and wound my hair up. If I was going to do it again, I might as well do it right, I thought, slipping a blade out again and weaving it through the bun in my hair. I took my stance, and to my amusement, I heard a familiar drum beat. It was Noura. I smiled at her as I allowed the crude beat to accompany me.

"Are you ready?" Neo joined me.

I hadn't sparred very often. Memories of practicing with my sister carried me as Neo and I circled each other. He carried a dagger as well, made for practicing. He advanced, cutting towards my left side. I side stepped but felt the wind of the pass. Lore-wielding was deceptively defensive, and I refrained from grabbing my daggers as I danced around Neo, evading his blade. I breathed in sharply when one of his hits grazed my wrist. It blazed with pain, but the pain stoked my focus. It was almost time. I found balance in my feet, preparing to spin into a kick when I realized something was accompanying me. A wind. It was warm and strong, yet somehow gentle, and I knew it came down from the trees. It did not flow as normal wind but swirled around me, breathing into my movements. I was stronger and more sure-footed than I had ever been. At the same time, Neo ducked, and my kick flew over his head, not that I actually intended to hurt him. But as I landed, new parts of the dance infused my steps—steps that were forgotten or ones that were simply too hard for me to master before.

When I finally unleashed my daggers, they met his blade, and he stumbled back.

"There it is." He smiled, circling me more cautiously now. His fighting style was wildly different from mine, relying more on his weapon than the movements and balance of his body. When I attacked again, he was ready with a thrust, but I parried and knocked him off balance with my foot. He caught my wrist, steadying himself before leaping away from me and conceding the fight.

I couldn't help but reel with bewilderment. What happened? I scanned the Guardians in front me. They were all smiling, not with smiles of mockery or even of admiration. But smiles of knowing. Finally, my eyes found Neo again, and I opened my mouth to speak, but nothing came out.

"I told you," Neo answered.

"But—" I had to catch my breath. "How?"

"Any good thing brought into The Sanctuary is strengthened. Even if you were to learn a new way of fighting here, you would always be strongest as a Lore-wielder."

My eyes darted between his two dark ones. "And if I leave? Will it fade?"

"Only if you let it." He returned his knife to the pile of practice weapons before meeting my gaze again. "But I advise you, don't let it fade. There is more waiting for you outside our Sanctuary, you know."

It took all day for Mavis and Ciela to show me the main areas of the garden. Everything was perfect and beyond beautiful, as it should be. But my favorite part was the Garden of Crimson at the very top of the Island, among the wispy trees that swayed there. A wall surrounded it, and no one was allowed to venture inside except the Heir. But I wasn't disappointed by this. It felt too sacred for anyone else to enter. It received its name from the red flowers that bloomed inside. The same kind of red flower that the Heir had crushed for me. But these were not meant for crushing.

I bent down to peer through the gate at the ones growing near the wall. Inside the petals was a small form growing. Just like the form held by the hands in the fountain. This was *the* garden—the heart of it all. I was looking at the next generation of light that would grow up to be Healers and Guardians of this world. Tears of awe mingled with a strange sorrow spilled down my cheeks. Not sorrow for the babies. They were safe. But sorrow for those in that other world who had to bear a lifetime without their children's presence. All I could think was how much that world must need their light, yet for some reason, it was my world that was made all the brighter because of them. Brighter and better because of their bravery to share their light outside the shining walls of their sanctuary. Where their story ended in the other world, their stories would be told here.

I rose slowly, heavy with the weight of waiting for restoration. But there would be beauty in the waiting. Purpose in the sorrow. Dignity in the life that would be.

Remembering the girls who stood behind me, I quickly wiped my eyes. Was it odd that I would weep over something I never experienced?

"Sorry," I mumbled.

"Sorry?" Mavis stepped towards me. "For bearing the weight with us? For caring beyond your own experience? Don't ever apologize for having a tender heart. It's a gift."

The Lore Wielder

I closed my eyes, holding back more tears. A gift... I'd never felt as though I had a gift. The Heir's words returned to me. I ran my hand along the gate, watching the crimson flowers sway one last time. He was right. It was as if this journey had released me from a prison of myself—freed me to bloom outwards and reach others in a way I never could before.

My time in The Lost Garden, The Sanctuary, was coming to an end. I wasn't meant to stay, and though I felt torn leaving such beauty and safety behind, I knew it was right. It was right for me to descend back into the broken world carrying as much of their light with me as I could.

The sun set like a burning fire in the sky, igniting a glow in my own soul. Everything was bathed in the golden light and shimmered under the weight of the glory that enveloped the island. I held my breath, willing myself to remember what it looked like—what it felt like to be in the presence of the sun.

NOURA LAY IN THE GRASSY area outside the Guardian's Tower, a quiet smile playing on her lips. Opal was made anew. She wasn't a different person. She was who she was meant to be all along. Noura squinted at the gilded sun, embracing its warmth on her skin. Her skin was glowing again. Just like Opal's and that of every other child who entered The Sanctuary—humans in the presence of the Divine.

Soft footfalls bade her sit up. She crossed her legs under her skirt as Neo approached. His dark hair glinted with streaks of red, and his amber eyes smiled at her as he plopped down in the grass beside her.

Noura knew he wanted to speak, but his eyes trailed the ground. She was six years his elder and couldn't help but remember the shy yet mischievous boy he had been. He was seventeen now. She glanced away from him, a lump in her throat, afraid of the reason he was here.

"You can wait, Neo. There is no rush," she murmured, resisting the urge to pull him into a hug. She didn't think she'd be able to let him enter the trial if she did.

Neo pressed his lips together before meeting her eyes. "I already talked to Father. And I'm old enough. What better time now that the darkness is rising again?" He watched her steadily while she remained quiet. What could she say? He was right. All the same, the idea of him leaving The Sancturacy was worse than a spear to her gut. "Is it that bad?" he asked, looking for the truth, not comforting words.

Noura crumpled her skirt in both hands. "Yes."

Neo nodded. "But it's worth it?"

Noura gazed at the space on the grass where Opal and Neo had sparred. "You saw it for yourself," Noura answered.

Neo looked away, holding back a grin. "I could have beat her."

Noura laughed, the weight of their conversation lifting. "I know. You've been training here for seven years."

Neo leaned back on his hands. "What is it like?" He nodded his head towards the mountain range marring the land far beyond their island.

Noura sighed, picking at a loose string on her dress. "Even though I know good will win in the end, it's hard to keep believing it at times. Hard when even the smallest things leak pain and corruption. Yet there is something deeper beyond the Rim—what we believe here in The Sanctuary feels like a lullaby to fall asleep to. Out there, what you believe is your lifeline. Light and goodness mean more on the other side of the Rim because they are the only whisper of hope the people have."

"Do you regret leaving?"

Her eyes flickered back to his face. "No. I had a chance to make a difference in someone's life, and that is always worth it."

Neo ran a hand through his hair, his face turning solemn again. "I'm going to enter the Unreal tonight."

Noura sucked in a breath, her stomach chilling. Every child who left The Sanctuary had to enter it, but it didn't make the idea any easier. Noura shut her eyes against the memories of her own time in the Unreal three years ago.

Neo nudged her arm. "I'll be okay. I want to do this. I want to be a part of the good in this world."

This time, Noura couldn't resist, and she pulled him into a hug. "I know. You're ready, Neo. And I'll be here for every step of it."

Noura watched the setting sun with a pit in her stomach. It was always this way when someone she was close to decided to enter the Unreal. Before her own experience, she had only been anxious, even curious. Now though, it made her want to cry. Once one entered the Unreal, there was no returning to the innocence of life before.

She strode through the courtyard and the back gate. Neo was waiting there.

"When did you grow taller than me?" she asked with a smile as she tried to push away the dread.

Neo gave her a half-smile, shrugging. "You don't have to come with me."

"I know. But I want to," Noura replied.

They walked together along the path that wound around and away from the estate. Trees shaded them from the evening light, the sweet smell of fruit wafting by. Noura bit her lip, remembering her walk here. She had been twenty. And she did not return from the Unreal the same.

The path dipped downhill, towards a grove of white trees. Their branches were so thick, it was almost as if they themselves were a wall.

"Any last pieces of advice?" Neo asked, approaching the small opening between two trees. Their branches had been directed away to leave an entrance. Noura stared past him to the mirror floating in the middle of the grove, her pulse thudding. It glinted in the light, which was the only reason she could see it. No grass grew in the circle beneath, and all the light was cast in shades of green from the leaves of the trees. Neo was about to face his deepest temptations and fears. One night in the Unreal had burned ten years into her soul.

"Once you step through, you won't remember that it's not real," Noura said barely above a whisper. "But what you can remember is every good and beautiful thing you've ever known here. Hold us close to your heart, Neo, even when it breaks you."

To her surprise, Neo reached down and embraced her. His heart was racing too, and when he let go, his eyes held fear. She squeezed his hand as he turned away, entering the grove from which he would return, never the same.

THE MORNING THAT FOLLOWED WAS glorious, but solemn, as Mavis and Ciela oversaw my preparations before meeting the Heir at the gate. I pulled on my boots—the same ones that had come to me in the tree-sted—over pants and a tunic gifted from the Dome of Beauty before throwing on the embroidered cloak and fitting the leather belt around my waist, where I tucked my daggers.

Not many words were spoken. The sorrow of parting had to be embraced. We walked quietly through the girls' apartments and the courtyard towards the gates. The two trees—artworks of metal—glinted their goodbyes as I passed through. Quietness hung as the morning blinked its sleepy eyes in a dusky blue light. The journey back through the mountains had to start early if I were to reach Tirigan's cabin by nightfall.

Ciela tugged on my sleeve, "I don't want to say goodbye."

I blinked hard. "I don't either. But maybe this isn't goodbye forever."

Ciela grinned. "I know it's not. One day, I'll be on the other side of the Rim, battling evil by your side."

I laughed through my tears. "Battling evil? I hope not," I said, pulling her into a hug. When she let go of me, she sniffed, sticking out her bottom lip.

"There are many ways to battle evil," Mavis added, putting an arm around my shoulder. "You'll find yours."

I leaned my head against her arm, looking at the path winding away to the bridge. "Thank you," I whispered.

Two figures stood on the bridge, and I smiled when I recognized Neo talking with the Heir. Maybe I would have a chance to say goodbye to him as well.

Mavis nudged me forward, and I gave Ciela's hand one last squeeze. Neither Neo nor the Heir looked up as I drew closer. The Heir put a hand on Neo's shoulder as Neo stared at the ground. He didn't stand tall, like the boy I'd met two days ago, but let his shoulders sag. Was something wrong? I hesitated, not wanting to interrupt.

"Come, Opal," the Heir said without looking at me.

Neo leaned back against the railing of the bridge as I approached. When he looked at me, I paused. No. *His eyes.* The innocence was gone

"Leaving so soon?" Neo asked, a half-smile playing on his face.

I hesitated, studying his brown eyes that now held suffering. Pain. "Someone once told me that I have more to do outside the Rim." I shrugged.

Neo's gaze glimmered and a genuine smile spread across his face. "I know you do. The world needs more people like you." He crossed his arms, still watching me.

I scratched my head. "Like me?"

"You're the first pilgrim any of us have ever met. That has to mean something."

"I guess," I answered, tucking a loose strand of hair behind my ear.

"Well, if you won't believe me, maybe you'll believe him," Neo said, gesturing towards his father.

The Heir smiled. "Are you ready, child?"

I nodded, turning my back to Neo.

"Opal." Neo hesitated. "Don't let it fade."

I glanced over my shoulder, something aching in my heart. "I won't."

He nodded before uncrossing his arms and walking back to the estate.

"Walk with me," the Heir said. I caught my breath, suddenly fearful of what lay ahead. Nevma alighted on my shoulder, and I felt them both look at me with knowing eyes.

"Will I be safe?" I managed to get out. All the difficulties of my journey here flooded my mind. My heart faltered. The Heir continued to walk down the path towards the bridge as he spoke.

"Is it safety you're after?"

The Lore Wielder

I hesitated. "No." I was surprised at my answer, but I meant it. Though the journey was painful, it had worked something in me and given me a depth I did not have before.

"That is wise. I cannot offer you that outside of my sanctuary. Not in this life." As we walked farther, my heart quickened. It wasn't just safety that concerned me. Who I was in this place was different. New. And I didn't want to lose myself. Not again.

"But what if I go back?" My voice trembled at the words, at the remembrance of the darkness that had gripped me. Its depths scared me far more than treacherous mountains and hunger. The Heir stopped at the edge of the woods, placing his hand on my shoulder.

"The choice to believe what is true or not is in your hands, Opal." The Heir took my hand in his wounded ones, and I noted the glimmer beneath my skin again. How long would the mark of The Sanctuary remain on me?

You will never be alone, Nevma reminded me, clinging to the front of my cloak.

"Do not dwell on the former things, Opal. My resurrection can never be undone, not even by death itself." His eyes glimmered as if the Sea of Suns itself reflected in them, and love and joy overflowed from his face like an unbridled hurricane. A feeling of spring, as if seeing the first buds after a long winter or witnessing robins hop about in the softened soil after the melted snow, bloomed warm and wonderful in me. I belonged. *Forever.*

The soft beat of hooves caught my attention, and I lifted my gaze as a pegasus came trotting from the edge of the forest, wings outstretched, catching the morning light.

"It is safe to take him as far as Tirigan's." The Heir affectionately patted the creature's velvety nose. "Remember who you are, Opal, and remember who I am. The world outside the Rim will do its best to make you forget. But even moments of weakness don't change what is true." He stood next to the pegasus with open arms, and I ran into them, love as pure as light lifting me from the ground

"I don't—I don't want to go," I mumbled into his embrace, tears welling in my eyes.

"I know." He kissed the top of my hair before lifting my chin so I had to meet his gaze again. "But you are never alone, Beloved. Never. Your life out there is not finished. Do you trust me?"

The Heir waited for me to let go and step away. I released my breath, looking at the Rim beyond. Did I trust him? I glanced at Nevma perched on my shoulder once more. He saved me. Spun my death into new life.

"Yes," I whispered. "I trust you." When I looked back, the Heir was gone. "Farewell, Father." I blinked through my tears, letting them fall freely. It was time. I breathed in the heavenly air, savoring its sweetness one last time. If only I could bottle it up and take it with me. While the air might not be containable, I had filled my canister with water from the fountain. I did not know what I would do the day it ran out. With one last glance, I took in the wonder of The Sanctuary before mounting the pegasus that would carry me back home, to a home that was no longer my true home.

Twenty-three

MY FINGERS DUG INTO THE creature's mane, my heart rivaling the beat of its wings. The icy wind tore through my hair but was not the source of the chills rippling through my veins as we sailed over the great rolling plain that spread out beneath us. I looked over my shoulder, squinting in the ever-deepening sunlight at the massive island suspended in the air, its waterfalls like fire and its mountains like giant guardians.

My chest tightened as The Lost Garden grew smaller and smaller, and I turned my gaze forward once more, a struggle rising within me. Leaving was like a knife in my heart, yet the desire to return, to face my home outside the Rim as a new person, bloomed small but determined. There was more. There was more for me to do, see, and *be* outside the Rim.

"Take me to the mountains. I'm ready," I whispered to the world. Ahead, the Rim rose like a wall of soldiers, shields raised and ready for battle. The rock formation traveled around the great plain, slicing it off from the rest of the world as far the eye could reach. And beyond, whiteness. The only way forward was over the jagged peaks. I tucked my head lower as the wind bit my cheeks, and I looked along the base of the mountains for the tunnel I had entered by, but it could not be seen at this height. The ground below was but a blur of green.

On I rode, and the journey to the Rim seemed far longer than it had the first time. I was alone once more, facing the icy slopes of Mount Nea. The loneliness after being around so many children in the presence of the Heir threatened to drag both me and the pegasus down. Something tickled my neck, and I glanced down, remembering what clung to my cloak there. Nevma. I smiled. He didn't have to say anything. A spring bubbled in my soul, and I gratefully drank in the reality that Nevma was back—for good. I would never lose him again, never leave him again or ignore his words. He was a source from The Sanctuary itself. He was in the song echoing from the garden that was never meant to be lost.

As we approached the tooth-like peaks, I felt the pegasus shift upwards in the wind, and I squeezed my knees into his side to keep from falling off. My vision was full of tangled mane and laid-back ears, and I shut my eyes, Ciela's words coming back to me. *You're not afraid of heights, are you?*

"Go ahead and add that to my list of fears, Nevma." I tried to laugh but choked as the pegasus finally leveled out and spread its wings wide, gliding on the frosty gale. Slowly, curiosity pried my eyelids open, and I gasped at what I saw. Petrified trees dotted the rocky landscape, but even more surprising were the arches, towers, and pillars. It was a ruin. Movement caught my eye in one of the towers, and I drew in a sharp breath at the thought of ghosts before remembering that I had passed this way as one myself.

The Lore Wielder

My calm returned when I realized it was being used by Guardians from The Sanctuary—friends. I smiled, thinking of Ciela taking her place there one day. Yet, it seemed strange to have a guard post so high up in a place that seemed untouchable. What in our world could be a threat up here?

The rock formation dropped off, and the blue sky paled as we flew closer to the fog. Below, countless jagged rock towers reached towards us with greedy fingers, but the Rim was gone. Behind us. My stomach gnawed on itself, and I remembered I had yet to eat breakfast. Pure whiteness lay ahead, and I did not know how far it would be until we found a place to land. After spotting a wide rock for the pegasus to land on, I guided him towards it. We skidded to a stop, closer to the edge than I would have liked. Loose pebbles hit the bottom far below, and the fog was already swirling around us. I slid off the creature's back and, with stiff fingers, untied my pack. I settled down on a large stone and started in on a meager breakfast. It was nothing like the feasts I'd had in the garden, but that was behind me now, just like the Rim.

From my position on the pinnacle of rock, I could still see the tower across from me and a few of the Guardians walking about the perimeter.

A terrible echo rolled off the rocks, shooting ice into my blood. I leaped from the rock, dropping my breakfast, and whirled around, daggers already in my hands. In an instant, the sound became crystal clear.

"Help! Help! Man down!" The Guardians moved like lightning into action as another pegasus weighed down by its load flew past us—nearly on top of us. I ducked, creeping towards the edge. The pegasus drooped under the weight of two bodies, its altitude dropping fast. Finally, it landed, and a man jumped off, continuing to yell and motion for the other Guardians' aid.

"They're back! Asma, she is bleeding. I can't—I can't stop it." The words echoed eerily off the rocks as the Guardians slid a limp body off the pegasus's back. The creature stomped and let out a terrified bray. I blinked and realized there were not only Guardians but Healers running from the tower to help. If Healers were here, at least five, attacks like this must be common. I swallowed as they laid the woman on a litter and bent over her, trying to stop the bleeding. I couldn't see where she was wounded from my perch, but I could see the blood. And a lot of it. A healer rose, his clothes drenched in crimson. My stomach churned. Slowly, the urgency subsided. The Healers sat back, shaking their heads. The man who had brought his friend dropped to his knees, his head in his hands. I covered my mouth as the food I had just eaten forced its way up, and a horrible, unnatural sensation pressed in on my whole body. She was dead. I let myself fall to the ground in weakness, staring up at the swirls of fog above. I just watched someone die.

I opened my eyes to Nevma buzzing around me. All I could think was that we had truly returned. The man's words continued to echo in my head. *They're back.* Whatever was back had killed a Guardian. This was not something I could face. Surely, I couldn't be *meant* to face it. How could the Heir send me out here when he knew the dangers? *I'm a child.* Even in the cold air, my body felt hot, and fear only further clenched the tightness in my throat.

Child, Nevma whispered.

I stared at him, my eyes glazed with hurt. Betrayal. What could he possibly say? I'd just witnessed death and was being forced to face whatever had done the murdering.

Death is part of this world—an ugly unnatural part, but don't forget the hope you have.

"The only thing I want is to *forget!*" I didn't have to point to the motionless body being carried to the tower. "Hope." I shook my head, my eyes burning salty. "What good is it here?"

Whatever is out there, you cannot face—not alone. But you are not.

"Who's with me?" I wheeled around, tears of anger dripping down my face. My lone voice echoed through the fog, validating the scream of hopelessness bursting in my chest. The Heir's question echoed in my mind. *Is it safety you're after?*

"Right now, yes..." I muttered. Ignoring Nevma's attempt to rest on my shoulder, I determinedly packed up my things and mounted the pegasus. I was going back to The Sanctuary. Any hope the Heir offered felt vague. It felt cheap in the face of mortal danger. And why was going back wrong? Why did Nevma want me to face whatever was out there?

Opal, Nevma's voice thundered in my head. **You already died. What are you afraid of? Your allegiance has changed. It is no longer to fear or to yourself.**

I continued to avert my eyes, warmth rushing into my cheeks. My allegiance. It had been to myself. I swallowed, lifting my eyes to Nevma's. The despair, the rasping Harfares, the haunting water. That allegiance had led to death. Pain spread through my heart. The truth hurt. Nevma landed on my shoulder, and I forced myself not to turn away.

You don't face this in the hope of living, but in the hope of the one who created life itself.

The pegasus shifted uneasily. He wanted to return as badly as I did. I shut my eyes and clenched my teeth.

"I don't understand *why* I must face this. Does the Heir want me to suffer? Do you?" My voice cut through the air, and I was surprised by its coldness.

Nevma did not move or flinch. **The weight of waiting for restoration is heavy. Unbearable. Yet there is beauty in the waiting. Purpose in the sorrow. Dignity in the life that will be.**

I blinked slowly as my own words came back to haunt me. They had been spoken over a completely different circumstance. From the outside, I could see the beauty and purpose in the Garden of Crimson. But from the inside of my own fear and sorrow... from the inside, finding beauty and purpose was like grasping for mist. How could I hold on to it?

"I... can't," I whispered, and I meant it. My limbs were like lead. Even if I wanted to go onward, I didn't think my body would respond. Before I could think of another reason to fear, another sound broke through the fog. The pegasus, exasperated from waiting to be attacked, took the lead. He bolted off the rock. I bit back a scream as my stomach plummeted with us into the ruins below. Nevma clung to my cloak, tucking himself away from the wind. The pegasus was out of control with fear. I knew it was feeding off my own, but the stomach-turning ride made it impossible to have any other feeling.

The pegasus dipped and darted between the rock towers, and I pressed my head against its neck, holding on with all my strength. The fog was thickening. It was nearly impossible to see, and the rocks seemed to appear out of nowhere. I was less afraid of what living thing might be out there than the immediate danger of being dashed to death. That is, until I heard a sound. It was strange and eerie, like the cry of a small child. My teeth ached from the tightness of my jaw.

The Lore Wielder

Then I saw it. Through the tears, through the fog, suspended above a rock that had just appeared in front of us. The pegasus dove, but I had just enough time to see the creature dive after us, its eerie cry of prey pursuing us. A thousand needles ran up my spine from the presence of something behind me, but I shouted the pegasus on without looking back. Something flashed to my left, scaly and shimmering.

Out of the corner of my eye, a fish-like tail and fins cut through the fog—no, swam through the fog as if it were water. When the torso, gangling arms, and face came into view, my heart nearly stopped beating. This was no mystery creature. Immediately, I could feel where cold, slimy hands had once gripped my body, dragging me down into the lake. The creature swimming through the fog was a naiad, or something like them. When it vanished, I realized I had no idea where we were going. We flew low, the rock formations towering above us, and I was certain I could glimpse the ground below. We were lost in a maze on the Rim of the world.

A dark human shape, huge and distorted, appeared on a pinnacle. I met its eyes, and they radiated a hatred so deep it felt as if I was staring into the eyes of the Hesith himself. Yet something was wrong. It was wounded. The giant clutched his arm, a sticky substance pouring from it. The pegasus veered away but not quickly enough, its breath coming in terror-filled snorts. As we passed by, quick as lightning, the giant's good arm hurtled a blade at us. A sharp pain jerked my head sideways, and I clutched at the pegasus's mane to keep from tumbling off into the fog. I hardly dared to open my eyes. The channel of adrenaline cutting through me overwhelmed any sense of injury.

The creature jumped off the tower and shifted in the fog. Its human legs twisted around violently until a scaly tail took its place. When its transformation was complete, it dove after us through the mist despite its wounds, baring sharp, horrible teeth. Something like a sob and a prayer bounced off the accursed terrain as I ducked my head and reached for my own dagger.

"Save me," I whispered as I slid the dagger from my leather belt. But this time, as I looked behind, I saw two great wings sweeping the fog back. A light glowed around it as the shape of a pegasus and rider appeared. For a moment, I thought the creature might leave us alone in favor of the other, but it did not stop its pursuit.

I twisted back, my sweaty hand gripping my pearl-studded dagger, hoping beyond hope I would not have to use it. Yet the whipping tail and snarling face came faster and faster through the fog. I could throw my dagger, but my aim was poor at best, and I couldn't risk losing them again. In a wild effort to retaliate against the attack from behind, I twisted around on the pegasus's back so I could face the creature. It was on top of us now, and I slashed wildly at it, forgetting everything I knew. I struck true though, before its teeth could find my neck, and I thrust it off. A strangled cry escaped its lips as it tumbled off and crashed into the ground. A moment of relief passed through me until I realized we were next. I tightened my knees and gripped the pegasus's back as he skidded to a stop on the Rim's floor. I tumbled off and hit the ground hard. Sharp pebbles dug into my arms and hands. I winced as I sat up and brushed them off.

The light from the other rider pierced the grayness of the fog, and I scrambled to my feet, the slashing of a sword cutting through the air along with furious curses. I staggered around to see what was happening.

The Lore Wielder

"...go back to the pit, you filth! You child-slayer!"

The other rider, who I realized was a Guardian, spat a new insult at his enemy with every slash. Finally, satisfied with his work, he heaved a heavy sigh and turned a mournful face towards me. I went to take a step nearer.

"Don't. This Spawn has done enough harm today. Let it be forgotten." His voice was familiar. As the guard stumbled towards me, the fog thickened around the body of the creature, concealing it completely.

"What—what was that?"

"A Spawn. Half Naiad, half human. It was they who brought ruin on this city. They, who caused the fog." I glanced around, seeing more clearly now that the ruins ran all the way from the top of the Rim to where we stood. Even on the map, this city did not appear.

"A child-slayer?"

"Child-slayer. Child-hunter." The Guardian stumbled past me, to the pegasus who stood stomping and snorting behind me. "They will eat any human. But on one from The Garden, they will feast..." He paused, looking at me in warning. "You had a close call." He motioned towards my head. Only then did I remember the sharp pain that had burst through my head after the Spawn's blade. Timidly, I raised my hand, afraid of what I would find. But instead of blood, my fingers brushed short hair. My hair.

"What—" I exclaimed, my hand searching for my long braid. But it was gone. Sheared off by the blade. My hair fell down just to my shoulders. The Guardian turned away, continuing to attend to the pegasus. At his touch, its breathing slowed, and its hooves no longer pawed the ground. He took its face and whispered something into its ear.

"You need him to get out of here." He turned to walk back to his own mount.

"But how?" I cried after him. "We're lost!" I wasn't as afraid of being lost as I was of being left alone again. What if another Spawn attacked?

"There won't be another attack today. Not if I can help it." His face was hard as stone as he seemed to read my mind, and I marveled that he had ever been an innocent child brought up in The Sanctuary. It was only then that I recognized his voice. It explained the fury with which he had killed the creature.

"Thank you—for coming after me. And... I'm sorry. About your friend," I said, surprised at my boldness.

He paused, his back towards me. "So am I..." he whispered to himself. "West is that way. Stay away from the ruins. The higher you fly, the thinner the fog."

"Thank you..." I replied again in barely a whisper as I watched him mount his pegasus, and I turned to my own. I found a large stone and clambered onto the pegasus's back as quickly as I could. I did not want to stay in this place a moment longer, even though I knew the Guardian wasn't really going to leave me. He had saved me and avenged the friend who died in his arms. I trusted his words. There would not be another attack today.

Twenty-four

THE MIST ROLLED AWAY LIKE waves as the pegasus's great wings cut through it on our way up. My hair and skin glistened with water droplets, and the dampness combined with the cold air sank into my bones. Up, up, up we flew, smothered in the whiteness. At least, I hoped it was up.

Even though the words of the Guardian comforted the creature bearing me, he still danced on the edge of bolting. Yet I had to trust his senses. I blinked as the whiteness softly shifted to a pale blue, and my heart flew nearly as high as we did. It was the beginning of the end of the mist—the confusion and blindness the Spawn had somehow brought on the city below. The higher we went, the more glorious the blue. It bled through the veil, a declaration of its perpetuity against the frailness of mist.

I glanced back at the swirling mountain of white below and then at the sky and the world beyond. The snow-capped mountains rose in front of me before dipping into beautiful green forests to my right and left. The fog had seemed so endless—so consuming, cloaking the reality that the rest of the world still lay beyond. Yet, that is all it was—a cloak of despair. True horrors lived there, yes. But they had their limits. They had their end. The blue sky ahead did not.

The sun was still behind us, rising in the east. The snowy mountains sparkled brilliantly in the golden light, and I had to squint. Apart from recognizing the summit of Mount Nea, the sun's position made our direction clear. The sun was not exactly behind us. We had veered south during the attack. As the mountains drew nearer, I took in the massive cliff that plunged into the fog below. From this distance, the cliff face was so smooth, it appeared as if someone had sliced it off from the mountain with a gigantic knife. So much about the Rim felt unnatural. Old, yet wrong.

On and on we flew, making up for the detour we had taken. The strangeness of the Rim was not the only thing on my mind. The coldness in my stomach spread through my body. Little daggers of shock. Though blue lay ahead, darkness pressed down on me like a millstone. The panic-filled scream from the Guardian, the blood, the face of the Spawn. Even the slashing of the sword that had ended the creature filled my mind. My throat threatened to close as I fought to keep the blood and fiery eyes at bay, fought to keep the blue sky not only in my vision but in my mind's eye. I repeated what the Guardian had said over and over. *Let it be forgotten.*

No one forgets death. They only learn to grow around it, Nevma whispered. I let the wind dry my tears as they came. How could any of this could be turned into purpose and beauty? I swallowed the words. They stirred bitterness in my chest.

When I saw the fog from the cliff's edge days ago, I thought it was another element to conceal the garden.

The Lore Wielder

Everything had seemed so intentionally hidden, and maybe it was. But not by the Heir. He never attempted to wall himself and the children away. Whatever the reason that our maps were changed, we'd unknowingly been in alignment with our enemies. The Naiads and Spawns. I shivered at their level of deception.

Green flashed before me as we flew over the cliff. It was a weak green, but it told me just how far from the summit we truly were. Yet I wasn't entirely worried. After all, this time I was flying and would make it to Tirigan's well before sundown.

The pegasus quickly dropped altitude. He needed a rest. I slipped off his back as soon as he came to a stop. Riding bareback was not the most comfortable way to travel. I limped to his face and gently stroked his nose as the Guardian had done. The beast was serving me and risked its life for no other reason than that the Heir had told him to.

"Thank you. Truly. I'm indebted to you just as much as the Guardian."

The pegasus shook his head in response and trotted off to a patch of green grass. What he really needed was water. And so did I. I quickly pulled out my water canister and took a big gulp. The sweetness trickled through me like a fountain, and I wondered why I had not taken a drink before. It even trickled through my mind, not erasing the pain I had seen, but bearing it with me. My hands shook as I screwed on the top again. My mind was calming, but my body still buzzed from the danger.

Once the pegasus had his fill of grass, he wandered on, and I followed at a distance. I was still unfamiliar with the wild creatures. Not only that, but for me, it was as if they had returned from the pages of history. I wanted to watch. To wonder. His ears twitched this way and that before picking a definitive direction. The terrain was rough and rocky, and the trees clung to the hillside with exposed roots from the melting snow that washed the soil away. After a moment, I could hear what the creature could, and the soft chattering of water entered the silence of the nearly lifeless landscape.

As soon as the pegasus saw the stream, it plunged its head in. I slowly approached the bank, dipping my hands in the water and washing my face. Even though it was bitterly cold, I felt as if I needed to wash whatever was left of the fog off my skin. I unwrapped a bit of bread from my pack and sat down on a rock, teeth chattering, anticipating a warm fire and fried fish at Tirigan's cabin.

My anticipation and meager meal were interrupted as a new sound broke the silence. I whipped around as screams and the sound of running feet echoed down the hillside. The pegasus jerked its head back and began trotting away. I dropped my bread and raced after it, trying to catch hold of its head to calm it.

As soon as the pegasus slowed, I turned its head and guided it back as the sounds grew louder. There was a thicket of trees between us and the commotion, and I hid us inside it, watching and waiting, my hand on the daggers in my belt. My breath fogged in the air as I scanned the hillside, hearing the shouts and footfalls approaching. My feet said to run, but I forced my mind to hold steady. What else would I have to face today?

Something up above the scant trees caught my eye. It hovered over the forest before dispersing into countless crows. The birds of prey dove, and the sounds of their squawking pierced the air. A human scream mixed with the sound, and I ducked, reaching back to grab hold of the pegasus, ready to mount it in a moment. A hawk dove towards the swarm of birds and snatched one with its long claws. It was just like the hawk that guided me over the cliff's edge during the avalanche.

"Tirigan…" I whispered. I waited, watching, but the screams kept coming. The hawk was doing its best work, but it was outnumbered. "Come on, Tirigan. Please don't need help…" But even as the words came from my lips, I knew that it wasn't true. I was standing here, hiding with a weapon as someone else was being attacked. I shook my head as I pulled out my daggers. The pegasus jumped back, startled by my movement.

"It's okay. It's okay, old friend. I need you to stay here. Stay and wait," I pleaded with him, lowering my weapons. With a stroke on its nose and uncertainty flooding my body, I stepped out from the thicket, searching for the source of the screams. There, across the river, a small shape swung two long sticks, and red hair flew around her. The hawk took out another bird, but the others were still swarming the girl. I dashed across the shallow river, my daggers raised.

"Get away from her!" I yelled, running into the madness. The crows' sharp beaks and talons sliced my arms before one fell by my blade. Yet, in the chaos and painful stinging, something entered my body. It was the same familiar yet old knowledge that had filled me at the Tower of the Guardians. I struck and slashed true, not quite sure how I knew what to do but doing it. The birds fell, their bloodied corpses littering the ground. I found myself, to my own shock, employing the same tactic as the Guardian in the fog, finding a curse and insult for every bird I struck.

Finally, when the air cleared, and the beasts ceased coming, I stepped back, looking around. I had no idea how many I killed on my own, but at least twenty black birds dotted the ground. I heard a soft cry behind me and spun, remembering the girl. She was covered in cuts but still held on to her stick, a number of birds at her own feet, her red hair sticking to the blood on her face.

"Faelle?" My voice came out hoarse. She met my eyes, and I knew it was her. We had barely spoken before, but I knew her. What was she doing out here? She stood up slowly, wiping her face with her sleeve. She looked awful, but I probably looked just as skinny, tired, and rattled when I arrived at Tirigan's.

"Where's Tirigan?" I remembered, searching the sky for the hawk. Surely, he would not have left? I darted to a clearing near the stream and squinted at the noon-day sky. There, not too far away, a hawk flew back towards the summit. Only, something was wrong. Tirigan was injured.

"Who is Tirigan?" Faelle finally spoke, staggering towards the water. I put away my daggers and hurried to help her sit down.

"Tirigan. The..." I realized I didn't know what he was exactly. "The Guide. From the cabin?"

"What cabin?" Her brow creased, and as I looked into her tired eyes, I realized there was no way Tirigan would have sent her out in this condition.

"You... must have come another way. His cabin is farther up, near the summit of Mount Nea." She didn't answer as she stared at the rippling water. My cheeks burned pink as the familiar sense of not knowing what to say crept in.

"I'll be right back." Nimbly, I jumped off the rock we rested on and trotted across the river. "Please don't have bolted," I prayed as I approached the thicket, looking for the large shape of the pegasus. I held my breath for only a moment before seeing the creature about thirty arms from where I left him, stamping nervously.

The Lore Wielder

"Steady," I talked to him as I approached, keeping my demeanor calm. As I drew nearer, his eyes widened, and he shook his head when I reached for him. He still did not care for me, but he must have been bound to me somehow.

Once I coaxed the pegasus to follow my lead and located my pack, we returned to the creek. Faelle still sat where I left her, staring blankly.

"Where did you get that?" She quickly stood to her feet.

"It's a long story." I smiled, prompting the pegasus to cross the creek with me. When I reached the other side, I searched my pack, certain it held something to care for wounds inside. While I did find some clean cloth, there was nothing in the way of ointments.

"It's a pegasus." Her voice almost stumbled over the word. "They're extinct."

"Aye." I smiled. She seemed to be handling it better than I did. "Here." I dipped a piece of the cloth into the stream. "Let me help."

"No—" Faelle jerked away. "I mean... thank you, but I can do it myself."

"Sure," I replied, watching as she washed off the nasty cuts from the birds. Thankfully, most did not seem too deep to be concerning. There was one on her arm, however, that was particularly nasty. I snatched another cloth from my pack to wrap her arm, and my hand brushed the canister of water—what some long ago had called healing water. "I wonder..." I said to myself, partly curious and partly wanting to conserve my supply. Nevma had only to tickle my ear to remind me that the water was meant to be shared.

"Can I try something? I think it will help your arm." This time I moved toward Faelle more slowly. She was still shaken from the attack.

"What is it?"

"Just... trust me," I said, not quite sure yet how to explain the water, let alone the pegasus. Nervously and carefully, I tipped the canister, and a small trickle of water splashed onto her wound. I bit my lip, not sure what I expected to happen. Faelle looked from the cut to me and then back. A moment before I lost hope, the red cut slowly disappeared, replaced with new, healthy skin.

"It's working!" I cried, full of awe before nearly choking on my words.

"I don't... I don't understand," she said, breathless. As her cut healed, and the white scar appeared, I glanced at my own arm. Curiously, I lifted my sleeve and held it next to hers. We both blinked in surprise at our twin scars. The placement on our left arms, the size, and shape of the scar were all the same.

"I don't understand. What did you put on my wound?" "Water. Water from The Lost Garden," I answered. Faelle continued to stare at me. Not sure what to say, I continued. "And the pegasus is from there too."

"Were you attacked by the birds too?"

"No. Well, that's not how I got my scar. That, I did to myself. Falling," I grimaced, remembering the crevice. It was strange, the two scars. They looked the same but were caused by completely different things.

"So you actually reached it? The garden, I mean." She fingered a pebble, averting her eyes. "I was beginning to doubt it was real." She looked at the stream again, thoughtful. "But it must be. Not just any water can do that." She motioned to her arm.

I shook my head at her, smiling. That was the most words she had strung together thus far. "No. It can't."

Faelle's gaze settled on the Pegasus. "What's it like?"

"The Garden? Is that where you're going?" I asked even though I knew the answer.

"Aye. I just have to know that it's really there."

"Well, I can tell you..." I paused. "But... only you can choose to believe if it's real. And I think you already know the answer to that question."

She continued to stare at the stream. "Tell me."

"Well..." I furrowed my eyebrows, struggling to put The Sanctuary into words. "It's like nothing you've ever seen—the most beautiful place you can imagine. It's a place you can't truly be sad in. It's like crossing into real life from a dream. I never felt I belonged in this world. But there—there it was home. And the water..." I paused, reaching for the canister again. "Taste it."

She hesitated and then took a small swallow.

"Can you taste it?" I asked, excitedly.

"I'm not sure. Maybe." She wiped her mouth with the back of her hand, averting her eyes. I blinked, tucking my hair behind my ear. Could she not taste it?

She is afraid of being disappointed. Nevma darted over the water.

I dragged my hand through the dirt for a moment, searching for words. "What brought you here? To this mountain?"

She hugged her knees and tilted her head towards me. "The butterflies. White ones. They've always been around me when..." She trailed off. "I followed them up here for a while, but I got lost. For the past two days, I can't seem to find which way to go. Every time, I find myself staring over the same cliff with no way to get down."

I shivered, remembering my meltdown on the cliff's edge and the avalanche that forced me to jump. Faelle's journey was clearly different from mine, but she had to face the cliff too.

"Do you know what I did?" I said, holding back a smile. "I jumped."

"You *what?*" Her eyes widened.

"Well, I was *forced* to jump... I might have caused an avalanche." I squinted at her, watching her reaction.

She shook her head at me in disbelief. "I don't understand."

"I don't either." I shrugged. "But I don't think we have to understand everything."

A welcomed silence rested between us, and I breathed in the cool air, relishing it before I entered the bitter cold that lay ahead. *Lost.* We had both gotten lost. I, on the way back. She, on the way to The Sanctuary. And yet somehow, we'd gotten lost in the same place.

The pegasus raised its large head, dripping from drinking the icy water, and stretched its wings. I drew my legs to my chest. What would a world be like if pegasi still roamed freely?

"Faelle! You don't have to find a way down." I jumped up, my heart beating to the drum of wonder inside of me. "You just have to find a way *over.*"

"You would let me take the pegasus?" she asked, rising to her feet and brushing dirt from her hands. I laughed again, realizing she was a step ahead of me.

"I was lost too! On the way here." I closed my eyes, hesitating to think of it—of the creatures. "That's why I was chased by the Spawn," I said under my breath so that Faelle did not hear. To steer me in the right direction to find Faelle. Would she have to face them as I did? But I couldn't think of that. There would be no answer. "Our lostness brought us together. Take him. It's why I was given the pegasus in the first place. I know it."

The Lore Wielder

Somehow, without Nevma even saying a word, I knew that this was another gift I was supposed to share as I reentered the world.

"It was given to me, not only for my own sake but to help you as well."

"How can you know that?" Faelle was measuring every word I spoke, and I couldn't blame her. Instead of answering, for I didn't have an answer yet, I reached into my pack and brought out a piece of my bread.

"When was the last time you ate?" I asked, noting the way she pressed her hands into her stomach.

"Yesterday," she answered, her eyes on her feet. I nodded at her answer, remembering what it felt like to go without for more than a day, and pushed the bread into her hand. It became hard to think straight. And Faelle would need a clear mind if she was going to enter the fog.

"Eat. Do you think you have the strength to continue on today?"

Faelle didn't answer as she took a bite of the bread. My eyes rested on the pegasus once more, munching on the grass and looking nearly refreshed himself. I did not want to think of the journey that lay ahead of me that I would have to traverse on foot. But if I was right, and I was supposed to give Faelle the pegasus, this was the plan all along.

I watched as Faelle tried to maintain some composure while she ate. Her green eyes darted, scouting for any trouble. Another attack. How many times had she been attacked? I didn't ask. After all, we weren't exactly friends. We merely knew each other. Yet, I felt a certain confidence that we were safe, for the time being. Tirigan would not abandon us if more danger lay ahead—not really. I glanced down at the scars from the snow leopard.

My daggers still gleamed with blood, and I knelt to wash them in the river. I shivered as the sickly blood from the possessed birds swirled into the water and disappeared down the stream. Instinctively, my fingers ran over the shimmering green pearls. Made anew. The meaning wasn't a disappointment or a burden now. It was a hope—a hope I was meant to have and explore as I reentered the broken side of the world.

"You're lucky you still have yours," Faelle finally spoke after finishing her meager meal. "Mine are gone."

"It's not luck, Faelle. Mine were gone too." Carefully, I slid them back into the wide leather belt, turning towards her. It was the only place for them now that my hair was shorn off. "The things we surrender that are truly good often come back in a new way." Self-consciously, I fingered my hair. It was going to take a long time to get used to not having my braid.

"Why did you cut it?"

"I didn't. It was cut in an attack. At least it was my hair and not my head." I shifted my feet, trying to make light of nearly being struck in the head with a blade. I couldn't deny that it made me feel different—like a part of me and a part of my connection to Wisptale was severed. Every other dagger bearer in Avarlyn had long hair. I couldn't think of any who wore their hair short, other than small children.

"Does it feel weird?"

"Very." I shook my head, sitting down next to her once more. I couldn't help but admire her long, red braid, dirty and messy as it was.

"The sun," Faelle said, squinting up at it. "It's well past noon now."

"Are you up for another journey today?"

"How far is it?"

The Lore Wielder

"It should be shorter than the time it took me to fly here. I was flying in from the southeast instead of directly from the east. That's your direction, you know. East."

"I figured as much. I think I am rested enough to continue. Thank you for your help," Faelle said, a soft smile on her face.

"You're welcome," I smiled back, a warmth towards her spreading in my heart as I thought of all the times I wanted to speak to her but didn't. And here we were, thrown together on the slopes of Mount Nea.

The pegasus lifted his great head from grazing and trotted towards us as if summoned. I shook my head as he approached Faelle, and his allegiance transferred before my eyes. He was wild, after all. Only truly belonging to the Heir. I would miss him.

Faelle rose to her feet to meet the pegasus. He stopped in front of her, unfurling his wings. The movement sent a puff of wind over her. Faelle raised a tentative hand to his neck and stroked his coat.

"How does one get up?" Faelle asked, glancing back at me. "He didn't seem so big until now."

I smiled. "I usually find a rock, or maybe there is a fallen tree somewhere near."

As I watched Faelle scramble onto the pegasus's back and give a solemn wave, another thought brushed my mind.

"Faelle!" I exclaimed before they trotted away, "I think... I'm going to wait for you. Then we can travel back to Wisptale together."

"Really, Opal? I wanted to ask, but I wasn't sure... I would like that."

While we were still talking, the pegasus decided he had waited long enough and turned his solemn head eastward.

"I'll be waiting at Tirigan's," I cried as I watched them leave, Faelle just as helpless to control the creature as I had been. She motioned with her hand that she heard me before disappearing from my view. A strange feeling settled over me as I watched the place where they vanished. It was just Nevma and me once more. And Faelle was right. It was well past noon, and I had to reach Tirigan's before nightfall—on foot.

Twenty-five

BY THE TIME THE SWIRL of smoke from Tirigan's cabin appeared, the sun was nearly down. My teeth chattered as the last of the light shrank in the graying sky, and I buried myself in my coat. The warmth from the garden was a distant memory, and the cold in my bones threatened to make me forget what warmth was. I staggered in determination towards the lighted windows and smell of smoke through the ice-encrusted snow.

I wondered if Tirigan knew I was coming. Was this the usual path back of the pilgrims? The assurance of the uncomfortable silence that awaited me sent a wave of butterflies through my stomach. But the thought of escaping the cold and having a warm meal pushed me onto his front step, and I pounded on the door with a sleeve-wrapped fist. Awkward shuffling sounded on the other side, and something crashed to the floor. *What was that?* I stepped back as the door swung open, not sure if I should show my alarm.

"Greetings, kit." Tirigan stood, leaning heavily to one side, in his human-like form. "Come in, come in." He limped out of the way so I could enter. A small table had made the crash, and he stooped to set it upright again.

"Thank you..." It was hard not to stare. How could I not inquire about what happened to him? But surely, it would be more respectful to wait. I ignored my concern as the warmth in the cabin embraced me, and I settled into a chair by the fire.

"That was some clever fighting earlier. For a moment, I wondered if you would come out of hiding," Tirigan commented with a half-smile and poured a cup of tea. He pushed the steaming cup towards me and leaned back in his seat uncomfortably with his bad leg outstretched.

"So did I," I replied, tentatively picking up my tea. It was too hot, and I quickly set it down again, resisting the urge to suck on my red fingers. Tirigan overlooked my blunder.

"You were very brave—as I think I've said before." He returned his gaze to the fire. "Nasty things, possessed crows. I haven't seen those in years."

My heart thumped at the thought of what that might mean, but even more so at the question I held. I shifted uncomfortably.

"Why did... Why did you leave?" The thought of him leaving after the attack still baffled me. Especially after the way he had protected me in that cave.

"Because I was instructed to," he answered plainly. He rearranged the burning fire with a poker. "I did not know Faelle would be following so closely behind you... I watched over her for days from the sky."

"But why?" Why would he leave her unaware of who was watching over her?

"I wasn't the one that was supposed to take her to the cliff. You were," he answered with a solemn expression.

"You knew I would be there?"

"Of course," he answered, picking at a bowl of nuts and offering some to me as well. "But I wasn't anticipating the possessed crows." His eyes trailed the ground as he frowned. "Either I'm growing slow, or something unusual is after her. After both of you." He glanced down at his leg.

My pulse jumped. "Both of us?"

Tirigan sighed. "I don't pretend to understand it. It is rare that two pilgrims' fates are intertwined in this way." His gaze flickered over me as he leaned back in his chair. "You chose a good place to wait for her to return."

I reached for my tea again, unsure what to say or think. What could he mean that our fates were intertwined? My head spun, thinking of how clearly I had known what I was supposed to do—protect Faelle and help her find her way over the cliff. I clenched my fingers around the cup, staring at its contents. If Tirigan had stayed there to fight, I would never have come out of hiding.

I took a sip of the bitter tea. "And your leg?"

Tirigan's mustache twitched in a smile. "Ah yes, that—well, a very capable fighter abandoned me in a cave with a vicious snow leopard."

My cheeks warmed, and I squirmed even though I knew he was joking. He had told me to run after all. I opened my mouth to speak, but he waved his hand.

"It's not the first injury I've received, nor will it be the last. I am a Guide after all," he resigned, his thoughtful expression aglow in the fire light. I was only just beginning to understand the dangers of his position. The dangers of *my* position. What else lay ahead of me? I raised the tea cup to my lips again, staring at the dancing flames, before letting my next question enter the quiet of the cozy cabin.

"Will Faelle have to face the Spawn?"

"That is a question that must wait for her return." Tirigan pulled hot, steaming potatoes out of the fire. "But I think not. After all, the Heir wants her to *get* there," he added with amusement in his eyes and gave me a lump of salted cheese to go with the potato. I accepted it gratefully.

"One of the Guardians—the one that came back to save me—said they were half-naiad, half-human. Do you know anything more? About them or the ruins?"

"Now that is some dark history," Tirigan said between bits of potato and cheese. "The naiads, like the dryads, were here from the beginning. The Spawns, however... They want to claim history, but they can't. Even my kind are older than them." At the mention of his kind, I wanted to ask more, but my curiosity about the Spawn won. Maybe if I understood them better, they wouldn't haunt my dreams. I shut my eyes. Or they would become my definition of a nightmare.

"But what *are* they?" I shifted forward in my chair, my wide eyes searching for the steadiness in the Guide's. "And why do they hate us so much?"

"They are half breeds. Humans who mixed with the naiads and betrayed the Heir. They hate you because you belong to him." Tirigan refreshed his cup of tea and settled back in his chair, finished with his meal. "Tell me, what does the Heir look like?"

My lips parted in confusion at his question. "Well... he looks ancient, but without a wrinkle—"

"No, no. What kind of *thing* is he?"

"Well, he looks human." It seemed strange to consider what the Heir was other than divine.

"There we are. More accurately, humans look like him. And you remind the Spawns of him."

The words from the Guardian in the fog came back. *They will eat any human. But on one from the Garden, they will feast.* I picked at my potato, staring at the glow beneath my skin. Was I marked? The glow that marked my new life—was it also a signal to those who wanted me dead? Even in my hunger, the face of the beast baring its teeth burned in my mind. I shook my head, afraid to ask any more about the creatures.

"And the ruin? It didn't appear on the map."

"It wasn't there when that map was made. Or, more truly, when the original copy of that map was drawn by Elowynnites."

Blood drained from my face, and I averted my eyes. The map had been charted by Elowynnites? That means they were right about something, and we were... wrong. I sank lower in my chair.

Tirigan continued. "Even I remember a time before the fog, and the land was bare. You could almost see The Sanctuary from this mountain top. A migration of Elowynnites, after the persecution began, went there to build a city on the Rim. It was a marvelous city that flourished for nearly a hundred years before it was attacked." The light in his eyes faltered.

"Were you—did you see the battle?"

"No. I had yet to be made a Guide to reside on this mountain. But I've heard tales..." Tirigan's eyes wandered to the jumping flames again, and I knew I did not want to see what he was remembering. "The city was overrun, the inhabitants... killed. The city itself rapidly deteriorated, as if the spawn's presence brought decay. That's one demented reason they can claim to be older than even the garden itself. If the stones that built a city and now lay ruined tell an ancient tale, how can you argue against it?"

I frowned. It would be a historian's word against what stood before their eyes. "Why would they do that?" *Older than the garden itself.*

"Claiming to be older, from the beginning of time, gives them power to erase history." Tirigan motioned to the bookshelves he had lining his cabin walls. Maybe that's why he kept them, as a way to stay the erasure. I shivered, thinking again of the erasure my own people had taken part in. I wanted to ask if he knew anything about it, but shame choked back my words. My thoughts returned to the strange creatures that lurked mere leagues away below the Warder Cliffs.

"So, are they... intelligent?" I asked, refusing to shiver. The Spawn who attacked me hadn't uttered a single word.

"Extremely. They aren't just blood-thirsty giants. They have their own languages and rewritten histories. Deception can't spread without a carrier."

My cheeks warmed. Every word from his mouth was chipping away at what I had believed in before. Hadn't we carried a deception? I picked up my cup of tea and glanced at the books.

Tirigan studied my face for a second. "You are welcome to read any of them while you wait. That's what they are meant for."

I nodded my thanks, still keeping my eyes low, my mind overwhelmed. I did not want to believe half of what Tirigan said, but how could I deny it? The map had been true.

~~~

I RAN MY FINGERS ALONG the many book spines. To say I slept badly after my conversation with Tirigan last night would be an understatement. Though I could not recall any dreams in particular, they left me unsettled. The only reason I was able to sleep at all was because of Tirigan's presence.
~~~

Yet, when I awoke to the empty cabin, my only comfort had been the sunlight pouring in.

Finally, my hand rested on a title. *Madrielle, A History.* There were so many books that it was hard to know where to start. I should have asked Tirigan, but shame still hooked my tongue. I wasn't ready to talk about the Elowynnites just yet. I could, however, read about them.

I flipped the cover open as I resumed my place by the fire. The flames were low, and orange sparks danced in the air when I added a few logs.

The book itself was written in a beautiful hand. I chose *Madrielle: A History,* partly because it was a place I recognized. But it was also the place everyone in Avarlyn thought the Rema Soul ran through. Well, everyone except *them.*

In the back, I was surprised to find a map of the city. The Rema Soul was nowhere to be found. Instead, the river flowing through the middle was called *Rema va Yuels.* I squinted at the words, guessing their meaning in Old Avarish. *Va Yuels* brought jewels to my mind. Maybe it meant River of jewels. I would ask Tirigan what it meant later.

After skimming the chapters, I decided to search for another book. I wanted something on the breaking—on the schism. After all, religious sects don't happen without reason. My stomach grew cold as I read the next title. *The Blood of the Saints.* Who were considered the saints? Hesitantly, I picked it off the shelf and read the first line.

Many believe the dark persecution was carried out solely by the Shinarish when they invaded Madrielle. This, however, neglects the long history of abuse perpetrated by the Refiners before the Shinarish set foot in the province of Avarlyn.

I wet my lips, reading on, even though I did not want to. I was a Refiner. My face burned as the words of the book ripped apart what I was taught about the Dark Persecution. Could my people really have done wrong? But there, recorded in the book, were the stories of the Elowynnites. Elowynnite Saints. One chapter told of a woman who invoked the name of Elowyn in public. She was tied to a post for three days and mocked. The accusation against her was ascribing divine power to a saint, a mere human. Another told how the Refiners looked down on anyone who attempted a pilgrimage and even found reason to jail a group of young pilgrims.

I shut the book with a painful thunk. My throat tightened. This was worse than finding Shylo Fletcher's map. I ran my fingers over the cover. Could it be true? Rewritten history... How could I know who rewrote what?

With shaking hands, I threw on my coat and boots and braved the cold mountain air. I *needed* the cold mountain air. My mind had been twisted and bent too far and was going to break.

When the chill hit my face, I sucked it in gratefully, feeling it ache in my lungs, grounding me to what was real and in front of me. The cold. The mountain. The Sanctuary... It was real, and no one could take that from me. I had not only lived it, but, in a way, died to get there. If that was sure, maybe who was right in the schism was not the most important thing. Yet, it still hurt somehow—like a wound that might never stop dripping blood.

~~~

"TIRIGAN. I WANT TO LEARN more. More about the—the Elowynnites." This time, I decided to ask the master of the library where to look for answers.
~~~

The Lore Wielder

We had finished dinner. Where Tirigan was all day remained a mystery, but I didn't mind. It gave me the day to contemplate my discoveries undisturbed.

"Ah, of course. You may have lost the map—a shame really—but nobody finds something like that and can walk away without more questions."

It was true. The map must be somewhere at the bottom of the hot spring I fell into, but it never left my mind. Not after I'd realized its direction was correct.

"It's just so hard for me to rope my mind around. The Elowynnites..." I couldn't finish my sentence. *They were right.*

"Did you doubt it?"

My gaze remained on my folded hands. "Aye—it was the opposite of what I was told all my life."

Tirigan looked at me thoughtfully. "So, what is your question, kit?"

What *was* my question exactly? I had so many. "Well, I guess, how did they know? How did the Elowynnites keep the real location of The Lost Garden when we lost it?"

Tirigan nodded, stroking his beard. "They protected it. And the Sweet Waters. And at a very great cost too. It has been passed down through the elders since the beginning of the Dark Persecution. In truth, most Elowynnites do not know the true location. In their minds, to protect it means a level of secrecy not fully disclosed even to their own. It's all tied to the Pilgrimage. If the elders deem you worthy to make the journey, only then is the real location of The Sanctuary revealed."

"And if they hadn't kept it secret, then Da'Shinar would have found it."

"In a way, yes—things could have unfolded differently if they had not guarded the location so closely." Tirigan paused. "You know, the best place to start is Elowyn herself."

"Elowyn?" I asked, remembering the name beneath the painting in the tree-sted. Tirigan strode over to the bookshelf and pulled out another handwritten book. I stared at it like it was a dazzling viper when Tirigan held it out to me. I already bled, wounded from the other books. Should I risk something that could sink its fangs farther into me?

An uncomfortable warmth trickled through me as I accepted the book with weak hands. It was pale blue with silver lettering on the cover. My thumb brushed over the name, *Saint Elowyn*. She was their namesake.

"Thank you." I swallowed, glancing up at Tirigan. He chuckled.

"You don't have to read it. At least not yet. Tomorrow is another day." He turned his amused smile away before shrugging on his coat and venturing out to retrieve more firewood for the night.

I sat frozen, unsure of what to do. My fingers tingled at the information that rested beneath them, but my mind was like a ship without a rudder—tossed this way and that by a myriad of thoughts. Reluctantly, I left the book and slipped quietly off the chair to retire.

Twenty-six

WITH A STEAMING CUP OF TEA in hand and furrowed eyebrows, I traced the silver letters *Saint Elowyn* one last time before slowly opening the cover. No information inside could be as condemning for my sect as that contained in *The Blood of the Saints*. A shiver trickled down my spine, remembering the accusations against the Refiners so long ago that still felt so fresh—so personal. This book was different, however. It was a diary, with a forward written by an anonymous author. Dated from the year fifty-seven. A mere fifty-seven years from the Garden's creation, 870 years ago.

Elowyn was a young girl, proposed to be even younger than me, at only ten years old. Nothing in the beginning seemed all that different from our *Book of Memories*, except this particular girl's presence. There was the Heir, the creation of the garden, and her birth two generations later. Then Hesith and his deception. What Elowyn recorded began after the days of darkness.

Entry one: The cold... I don't know how we survived. Everything that was green and living froze and turned brown.

Nothing like this ever happened inside the walls of the garden. We should not have left. We should not have listened to Hesith. Now the sun has disappeared, and we will all die.

Entry two: We live in houses made of ice and snow. We never leave except to hunt for food. The new lake is slowly filling with more water. Papa says it's mostly from the ground. It happened one night, but the sound was so shattering that I don't think anybody left their shelters to see what it was. One day, the walls of the garden were there. The next day, it was as if someone took a giant knife and cut the whole garden out of the ground and took it somewhere else. There was nothing left but a gaping hole in the ground. It is so deep I can't see the bottom and so big that I can't see the other side.

The rest of the story went on, and the more I read, the more I understood why the Elowynnites respected her so much. It was baffling to me why I had never heard of her. How could my sect have missed such an important piece of our heritage?

I set down my cup of tea, now cold, and closed the book. When Tirigan came through the door, I jumped. He had five gutted and skinned squirrels slung over his shoulder and a wide grin on his hairy face. I wrinkled my nose at the look of the fresh, bony meat.

"Today is a day for a feast! Your friend returns." He set his catch down, glancing at the book in my lap. "Ah, I see you started *Saint Elowyn*. And how is she treating you thus far?"

I set the book down and let my eyes wander to the hopping fire. "I feel as if everything I know is being shaken."

"Is that a bad thing? The things that are true will continue to stand, despite the shaking."

"I suppose. The things I am certain about are the most important." I paused, remembering the feel of new life gently spreading through my body, the cool water rolling off my skin as the Heir lifted me out of the pool. "But it also hurts."

"That is the only way to learn. Here." He held out one of the squirrels skewered on a long stick. I took it hesitantly, still eying the meat.

"You trust me to cook it?" I asked, amused. Tirigan chuckled and settled himself by the fire.

"Oh no. That will be yours. I'll cook mine and Faelle's." He crumbed some dried herbs retrieved from the ceiling and rolled the two squirrels in it before setting them to cook over the fire. He pushed the leftover herbs towards me. As I sprinkled the herbs on my impaled meat, thoughts of Faelle's return weighed on my mind. We were going to journey back together. I was glad of the company, but also anxious. The only friend I'd ever had was Ilynn. And had I even been a good friend to her?

"I guess Faelle did not meet any Spawn on her return," I wondered aloud, hindering the silence only accompanied by the crackling fire. The hour was still early, much earlier than when I arrived on the mountain. I couldn't help my question. Even though other thoughts had occupied my mind the past day, a chill clung to an instinctive part of me, frozen there by what I'd witnessed in the ruins.

"Let's hope that she didn't. Poor girl had a rough enough pilgrimage already." Tirigan eyed my inquisitive expression. I averted my gaze, a vision of crimson Healers before me. My stomach turned again, but I choked down the urge to vomit as squirrel drippings sizzled into the hot coals. I knew I would never forget what happened. I also knew the ache to understand why I was here and not in The Sanctuary was like a ghost that would haunt me if I let it. What if more suffering lay ahead? I stared at the impaled squirrel.

"At least I have someone to travel back with." I fumbled for a distraction from the question of suffering. "I was not looking forward to journeying alone."

"It can be difficult," Tirigan replied, attuned to my need for a new subject. "I was mostly alone the past forty years before you two came along. And who knows when the next pilgrim will be brave enough to set out."

I watched the solemn face of the Guide as he rotated our dinner over the coals. Immortality must be lonely. "Don't you—don't you have friends?" I asked, still studying his face. He glanced back with a weary smile.

"I do... just not too many friends I can have a conversation with," he answered, and as the flames reflected in his eyes, I could see the animal side of him flickering. "That is not to say my whole life has been lonely. But that is a tale for another time, kit. You needn't worry about your friendship with Faelle. Everything will come with time. And remember, you are not the same as you were. Friendship isn't merely about quelling your own loneliness. It's about giving—learning from each other." He blinked dark eyes at me, and I wondered how he had sensed my fear of new friendship so keenly. It was true; I had always thought friendship was simply a means to not feel lonely. A friend was a person with whom you felt happy and accepted. A smile tugged at my lips. Ilynn was that but more.

"I want to be a good friend. I just need to learn how," I ventured, my shoulders relaxing. Tirigan gave me a nod as he turned over the squirrels once more.

"I think the more you open your heart, the more you will find that you have already learned."

His words wrapped around my mind as I stared at the flames. I had experienced true friendship. I experienced selfless love in Alana and Ilynn. What if my journey back with Faelle held more than keeping loneliness at bay? I clenched my eyes shut at the doubt creeping in. I had to reach outside of myself to become who I was meant to be.

Tirigan's eyes twinkled. "She's here."

My brief confidence quivered, and I opened my mouth as I watched Tirigan throw on his coat and approach the door. I followed, not wanting to be left alone by the fire.

The cold wind was like needles as it pricked my skin, skin that had grown used to the warmth of the cabin. The sunlight danced off the snow against a clear blue sky. Tirigan paused, looking back, first at me and then the world beyond. I followed his gaze. Gray clouds mounted in the north, a haze swathing the horizon.

"There—" Tirigan pointed in the direction of the cliff. I tore my eyes from the clouds to the magnificent sight before me. Faelle was still a ways off, but the giant wings of the pegasus swooping through the air and the graceful head were all but mesmerizing. My heart ached knowing that the time when the creatures lived with us was lost.

Faelle lifted a hand, and I waved back, warmth towards her spreading in my heart once more. The pegasus landed gracefully, and I couldn't help but grin when I saw the dagger glinting in Faelle's hair.

"Welcome, kit!" Tirigan said, though he did not approach. He could sense her wariness, and I remembered that she had yet to meet him.

"Thank you," she said with a smile. She looked beautiful, and the glow of The Lost Garden still radiated off her. Her clothes were new and fresh, all the dirt and tears from the journey washed away, and her vibrant red hair braided. I found myself touching my own short hair, ignoring a pang of jealousy. My hair would grow back. I did not need to know why she was allowed to keep her braids while I lost mine.

"Aya," I said quietly, and she gave me a nod and smile in response as she slid off the pegasus's back. I slowly walked towards the creature; my hand brushed its nose.

"Thank you," Faelle began. "I don't know how I would have reached the garden without him."

I glanced at her before returning my eyes to the pegasus. "It was all him. We are indebted to you, my friend." He looked down at me with big glossy eyes, and I leaned my forehead against his nose. "I will miss you." He put his velvety nose on my cheek, not as if to say the same thing, but in recognition of what we had experienced together. And then, he was gone, his white and gray wings pushing back the air as he flew towards the sun. This was, perhaps, my last glimpse of the wild creature.

"Come, the fire is crackling, and the food is ready." Tirigan beckoned us to follow. Faelle gave me a curious look, and I walked closer to her.

"Don't worry, he likes questions," I assured her.

It was true, even if his answers were vague. I still wasn't quite sure what sort of creature he was, but I had a feeling he liked to remain a little mysterious. The warmth and smell of the cabin surrounded us the moment the door opened. Faelle let out a sigh of relief, her wind-chapped cheeks glaring angrily. Even if the ride had not been perilous, it had still been bitterly cold. I shed my own coat and crossed towards the fire.

Tirigan removed his coat and boots before retrieving the meat from the fire. I couldn't say it smelled good, but it certainly stirred our appetites. The kettle whistled shrilly.

"Tea first, kits. The squirrel must rest a good five minutes before eating," he said, proud of the feast he had prepared—three steaming cups of tea, the squirrels, flatbread, and a bowl of nuts. Faelle's eyes widened as she took in the impaled animals, but she took it all in stride and settled into one of the chairs.

"It looks wonderful." She picked up one of the sticks, looking over the meat before setting it down again and reaching for her cup of tea. "So, you are Tirigan."

I reached for the nuts, wondering if I could learn anymore about him through Faelle's questions. She already seemed more forthright than me.

"And you are Faelle," he said with a subtle wink.

"I was told you helped me on my pilgrimage. I don't remember seeing you though."

"That's because you didn't. Opal here has had the privilege of seeing me in all my forms." Tirigan paused to bite into his squirrel.

"Forms?" Faelle turned towards me. I shrugged my shoulders and bit into my own piece. I was not going to let Tirigan evade telling us what he was so easily.

"To be a Guide up here, I must be able to cover long distances in a short time and survive the cold. I could not do that in this form only," he answered, and I rolled my eyes. That might be the most we would get out of him. I leaned towards Faelle. "He flies. Do you remember seeing a hawk?"

"Oh, yes. The last few days," Faelle continued, one hand hiding her chewing. "Was that you?"

"More or less," Tirigan said, mouth full and no shame.

"So you're some kind of shape-shifter."

"I haven't always been, but, yes, I was given the ability as a gift," Tirigan replied, but he redirected the conversation from himself. "So, do you have any questions? Any *other* questions?"

Faelle looked thoughtful as she took small bits from her squirrel. The taste really wasn't bad. Nothing to complain about, especially if one was hungry.

"I do. Why don't you want to say more about yourself?" Faelle asked.

Tirigan shook his head. "Kit, a life of nearly a thousand years warrants me much I wish to tell. But my trust in humans is weak."

"Oh." Faelle tilted her head, taken aback.

Tirigan sighed, weighing what he was about to say. "I wasn't a human given a gift..." His nose twitched as he stared at his hands. "Because of that, we were hunted down by your kind. Most of us live in the uninhabitable places of the world now. Our homes are ice, our light—colors streaking the sky. Our food—only what dares to swim in the coldest waters." He looked at us, eyes softening. "But I will say no more. To keep my kin safe."

Faelle conceded, glancing at me, but I was still looking at our Guide, shame spreading in my chest. As if it could hold anymore.

"You didn't deserve that." My eyes stung, but I blinked the sting away.

"No. Not when we were meant to give aid to your kind." He set his food down. "But I don't hold you accountable for the sins of your ancestors."

I lowered my head, staring at my half-eaten food. What had we done to his people, and why had we done it? The accusation seemed to include all humans. There was no shirking the guilt. I released a breath, looking up once more. The source of so much suffering wasn't black skies or divine negligence. It was us.

Tirigan's ear twitched. Even in his human-like form, they appeared big and fox-like. He was listening. My grip tightened around my tea cup as a distant melody mixed with crying whistled through the cracks of the cabin. Faelle turned, mouth parted in question, but I put a finger to my lips.

A gust of wind slammed into the cabin. My eyes snapped to the creaking window. Tirigan jumped to his feet, peering out the north window as the walls around us wailed and shook.

"What is it?" I scrambled up as Tirigan turned around. His eyes darted between us and his mustache twitched.

"If we don't leave now, we'll be buried here. Look to the north." He jerked his head towards the window.

I blinked at him before peering through the frosted glass, Faelle beside me now. My fingers trembled on the cold sill as I took in the frozen world outside. The low mountain of clouds was nearly on top of us now, and a stormy gale whipped the snow into senseless fog.

I didn't want to say it.

"Blizzard," Faelle whispered by my side, her green eyes cast in the shadow of the storm.

Tirigan doused the fire. "Ready yourselves. We leave as soon as possible." Thick smoke swelled into the room. Both Faelle and I coughed.

"We?" I sputtered, staring at the Guide. His face was calm, though a twinkle flecked his eye.

"I will take you as far as I can before nightfall," Tirigan said, wrapping his scarf around his neck.

"Wouldn't it be safer to stay?" Faelle asked, wringing her hands.

Tirigan shook his head. "It would be weeks before we could dig ourselves free. My food supply is meager—no, we must leave now. The trees were whispering. This is no normal storm—" he paused, one hand gripping his coat as a smile broke across his face. "And I intend to outrun it."

Saint Elowyn: entry three

The night is getting lighter. I can tell. At some point, the sky turns from black to a grayish-green before turning black again. Some say we are going crazy. Others see it too. I think it means there is hope and the Heir has not left us. But the others... They think it is something Hesith is doing to save them from the darkness. I don't know how they can believe it. Don't they remember what it was like to walk with the Heir in the garden? I don't think he caused the darkness. No. Maybe it was just that the earth itself broke from sadness without Him.

Twenty-seven

THE SUN WAS NO MORE than a flame on a windless night, the remnants of its soft orange glow melting into a starless sky. Noura ducked her head lower as the wind ripped through her hair, hollowness creeping into her. She glanced tear-stained eyes at the long wings of the pegasus bearing her towards Wisptale once more. The wonder that had swelled in her the first time she had flown in circles over the town hidden in twilight was a burned out coal.

Noura dreaded what awaited her on this side of the Rim, but she couldn't tear her thoughts away from Neo. Neo, that sweet boy who would never be the same. Noura buried her cold fingers in the pegasus's mane. She'd waited outside the grove of trees, refusing to move until he returned. A chill that had nothing to do with the cold laced up her spine.

She'd stumbled out of the Unreal torn apart by what she'd experienced. Dion had caught her, tucking her head against his chest in a rare embrace as she wept. She'd passed the tests, but felt anything but victorious.

Neo had no brothers or sisters. When he'd stepped out, shrieking with his head between his hands, she'd jumped to her feet to comfort him.

"It's okay. It's over. It's all over," she whispered.

Neo melted into her hug as he'd done as a child. "You were right," he murmured. "I feel as if I've been shattered into a million pieces."

Noura released a breath. "You were shattered, but—" she paused, "you were also remade."

Neo let go of her, returning his gaze to the mirror. "I don't regret it," he said breathlessly, straightening to his full height. Noura blinked away her tears. He was picking up the pieces as the Unreal faded to memory, just as she had done. The memories that were his only taste of the world beyond the Rim.

"What—" Noura hesitated. "What did you see inside?" The Unreal held any number of horrors, but one always carved the deepest hole into their beings.

Neo's gaze flickered back to Noura, and he hesitated, a new depth behind his eyes. "I saw her."

"Her?" Noura furrowed her brow.

Neo searched the ground in front of him, words trembling on his lips. "I saw Opal."

A swell of orange burned into Noura's vision, pulling her back to the present as she squinted against the wind. Gray smoke fumed in the sky before her, burning her eyes and throat. She steered the pegasus away from the fire glowing a hundred arms below them. She'd hoped to reach Wisptale before night completely settled in, but now she would have to land leagues away.

The town on fire forced her mind back to the prophecy. Back to Alius. *He will burn bridges to defeat armies and raze towns to rout darkness. Yet he and the Reconciler shall build them up again will by will and stone by stone.*

Noura clenched her eyes, the pit in her stomach deepening. Alius was one reason Dion had returned to Wisptale. When she'd shared the prophecy with her brother, he'd been speechless. It was one thing to find a boy with the potential to lead armies, but it was quite another to realize that need was upon them. Darkness was no longer stirring. It had already snapped its bonds.

Noura and the pegasus landed roughly in a mountainside pasture. She slid off his back, drawing her hand along his neck until it rested on his nose. She pressed her forehead against his, his soft hair and smell calming her.

Go. I wouldn't see you harmed for the world.

The pegasus blinked slowly before dipping his head and trotting away from her. Noura gathered her breath, facing the dark forest before her and the burning world ahead.

"I AM SORRY, FAELLE," TIRIGAN said with a half-smile. "You deserve to rest, but alas, the mountain had other plans."

Faelle gathered her few belongings that still lay bundled up by the door. She hadn't even had time to unpack anything.

As soon as I realized I would be the one slowing us, I scrambled to shove my belongings into my pack, strap on my belt and daggers, and throw on my coat.

Tirigan took a rope, tying one end to my arm and the other to Faelle's. "I'm confident we can outstrip the storm, but if we should find ourselves otherwise..." he tugged on it before straightening. "Do not get separated. Meet me outside when you are ready—lock the door behind you—and let us face the adventure ahead." Tirigan's hairy face turned white as he transformed, and he disappeared out the door.

Faelle shifted nervously, her boots already laced up. I fumbled with my own laces before jumping to my feet and giving her a ready nod as I tucked Nevma into my scarf. The thought of outrunning the blizzard set my legs trembling, but the prospect of reaching home a day earlier than expected set my heart ablaze.

Home.

Where you've always belonged. Nevma spoke from inside his cocoon.

The whispers of the storm wrapped talons around us as I pulled the door firmly shut and stepped off of Tirigan's front step. It took a moment for Faelle and me to spot Tirigan once we retreated from the cabin. His white coat all but vanished in the snowy terrain. He was running—scampering back and forth, ears twitching and nose in the air. He glanced back at us with a wild look before taking off down the mountain at a trot. I let go of my breath, glancing at Faelle.

"How are we going to keep up with him?" Faelle murmured, flakes of ice already forming on her eyelashes.

"He won't leave us," I said, stuffing my hands into my pockets and burying my face in my scarf as the blizzard edged closer. "I don't think."

The icy snow was heavy against our boots as we followed Tirigan's big pawprints down Mount Nea. More than once, the wind nearly flattened us.

Faelle was silent as she jogged beside me, her cheeks bright pink and a cloud of foggy breath dissipating behind her. My eyes flickered to the north, watching the storm. We traveled ahead of it, but the snowfall blurred everything except what was right in front of us. There was nothing to do but run. Breathe and run.

It was not long before we both had to stop, panting. Tirigan sensed that we no longer followed and scampered back up as another gust of wind spit snow in our faces.

"I'm—sorry—" I began between breaths.

"Drink your water. Rest a moment," the fox said, a pink tongue dangling from his mouth. His low growl made me start until I realized he was laughing. "I haven't had this much fun in a long time."

"Fun?" I gawked as Faelle and I wrenched the tops off our water canisters.

"I don't usually have an excuse to test my limits unless I'm outwitting something with claws or fangs. Not with company, at least."

Of course. I kept forgetting we were the first pilgrims in half a century.

The Sweet Water was cold, but it did not add to the burning in my lungs. A trickle of warmth spread in my chest, and my breathing steadied. Tirigan had been alone until I'd showed up at his door six days ago. Faelle tucked away her canister, and I did likewise just as Tirigan darted down the path again. I plunged my boots into the snow once more, a new strength swirling inside me as we descended homeward. Nevma tickled my cheek from his cocoon in my scarf.

Home. I ached for it deep in my bones. If we could outrun the storm, it would be there, waiting for me with open arms. As it always had been. I smiled, despite the bitter wind and pelting flakes of ice. The Sanctuary was only the beginning for me. Neo's words echoed in my mind. *There is more waiting for you outside our Sanctuary.* The only way to find out what it was, was to live.

Night invaded before we reached the tree-sted, but it didn't matter. Tirigan's eyes glowed before us, and the blizzard howled from its prison at the summit. Faelle untied the rope connecting us.

Icy rays of moonlight crept through the glittering tree branches, yet it wasn't the only light. A soft glow split the darkness. It spilled quietly over the forest floor before rising. Faelle abruptly stopped, and I ran into her.

"Sorry, sorry!" I grabbed her arm to keep her from falling. My grip on her tightened. Something else was out here. I caught my breath. Tirigan's shadow shifted, silhouetted against the light coming from the creature. He did not run nor snarl.

"What—what is it?" Faelle whispered, breathing hard. "Greetings, Hena. Do you bring more news?" Tirigan's voice crossed the frosted distance between them.

As my eyes finally focused, my grip on Faelle slackened. The glowing form was a dryad. A friend.

"She's a dryad. It's okay," I whispered to Faelle. The creature was beautiful, with long, flowing leafy locks, but not quite solid. She must have traveled far from her tree. "I see you braved the storm with the young ones." Her glowing eyes drifted to Faelle and me before snapping back to the fox. "There is much stirring in the valleys below. I come to bring you a new command. You must go, at once—" Her willowy voice lowered so that we could not hear. After a moment, Tirigan stepped away and her form shimmered in the wind. "I will bring the young ones safely to the tree-sted." She fluttered closer to us.

My heart dropped into my stomach. Tirigan was leaving us? He bowed, acknowledging her authority. My breath fogged in the air. There was a whole world out there. Faelle and I were safe, only a two-day walk from home. Someone else needed him more than we did.

"I will go. Immediately." Tirigan turned towards us, the light creases on his face deepening underneath his fur. "I know you will take care of them. They are important. Together," he added, pinning us each in turn with his gaze. "They were driven together for a purpose, and whatever that purpose is, the world is better for it."

The dryad did not answer but inclined her head. I clenched my fists buried within my pockets.

Tirigan fixed his eyes on us. "I am sorry I must leave you here. The tree-sted is not far now. You will camp there tonight and continue your journey in the morning." His ears perked up, taking in the sounds of the night. "The journey home may be harder." He paused, looking thoughtfully at the moonlight glinting off the snow. "Hold on to what you know. Only what is tested truly becomes a part of you."

"Thank you for everything." I nodded towards Tirigan as Hena drifted closer.

"Aye," Faelle added, her gaze still trained on Hena. She didn't trust her, but then again, Faelle didn't seem to trust anyone.

"I am sorry I could not be of more help to you, Faelle." Tirigan studied her for a moment before turning to us both. "Farewell. The Heir be with you."

He disappeared into the dark night. I moved closer to Faelle. I wasn't afraid of the dryad, but I certainly did not feel the same care coming from her.

"Come, young ones. The way is not far now. I am sure you are tired from your journey." She beckoned us to follow as she spoke.

Faelle's lips were tight, but she moved forward, and I followed. No snow remained beneath our feet. The flicker of strength inside me wavered, and I took another drink of water. It trickled through my hollow stomach, and I shivered despite the sweetness. *Nearly there*, I told myself, dreaming of the tree-sted. Nearly *home*.

"What do you think he meant when he said the way home may be harder?" Faelle whispered to me. I breathed into my scarf, remembering his words, tracing them like a maze in my mind.

"I don't know. But we're almost home now," I assured her.

The dryad moved like smoke, gliding over the ground, her extremities fading into a tangle of branches and leaves. It was strange to think that someone like Tirigan answered to her. Yet, he was tied to the dryads and relied on them to bring messages from the world below his mountain. How much more of this unknown world, full of beings we had turned into legends, still existed? It must be strange to be so real, and intricately a part of this world, and yet be forgotten.

We traveled on for another hour, the night growing colder and colder. I winced, my fingers aching, as I pulled my coat closer to keep out the icy breeze. Summer was at its height in Wisptale. I sighed, blinking frosted eyelashes.

We no longer stumbled now that our feet tread in the light reflecting from the dryad. She seemed to absorb the moonlight and reflect it to all that was around her as she radiated authority. She was not like the Mêliades I had first encountered in the wilds above Wisptale.

When I saw the tree-sted's shape silhouetted against the moon, I wanted to cry out in joy, but all I could do was stagger towards it. We'd made it. The tree-sted might not be as cozy as Tirigan's cabin, but it held something just as wonderful. Magic.

"Here I must leave you." Hena spoke from behind us. "Farewell, young ones," she said as her shape dimmed around the edges.

"Wait," I called out. "Will Tirigan be safe?"

The dryad quivered a moment. "Nothing in this world is truly safe." And then she was gone. We stared, her image still appearing before our eyes as we blinked. We were alone.

"At least she brought us here," I mumbled, scrambling up the lowest tree branch. "Aren't you coming?" I paused. In the dark, Faelle's nod was barely visible, but she followed. I lifted the latch and stepped through the door on the side. The tree-sted was only lit by the silvery light of the moon.

"I'll get a match. Can you find the lamp?" I moved towards the small table, slipping off my pack and pulling out the match box. I fumbled in the dark with stiff fingers and Faelle stumbled around, searching for the lantern.

"Here." She set the worn lamp on the table while I continued to work at making a flame. Finally, a little spark grew. Faelle's face burned yellow in the light, and her messy orange braid spilled over her shoulder. But she was not looking at me. Her eyes scanned the room. It was empty.

Saint Elowyn: entry four

I have to leave. I have to go. Even Papa thinks the gray skies are from Hesith. I may die, but I cannot stay here when I know the Heir is still out there. I know he has not left us. Maybe I can find him. Maybe he will let me back in the garden, and I can leave this terrible place and people behind.

Saint Elowyn: entry five

It's so dark. It seems even darker when I am alone. I'm scared. Terrified really. I can't believe I left. I'm so hungry. I made a small snow house. The lamp I brought gives off enough warmth so that I don't die when I sleep. I don't even know when I am supposed to sleep, but I always try to be awake when the sky turns gray. That's the direction I'm traveling in. I don't know why, but it just feels right.

Twenty-eight

"IT'S EMPTY... BEFORE, THERE WAS—" Faelle looked up at me, eyes weary. "Well, it was like magic." She had not rested from her journey. She was with the Heir this morning only to find herself here, hungry and cold once more. I knelt down on the floor, opening my pack again.

"I know. It was as if this place gave us exactly what we needed. More than what we needed."

"What happened?" Faelle paced the room.

"I'm not sure. But—" I pulled out the food I brought from Tirigan's. "We still have some food. It's not much, but it will be enough."

She nodded, sitting down and accepting the flatbread from me. We munched on our meager dinner as silence settled in. And exhaustion. The pace Tirigan set had drained us. When our bellies were half full, neither of us complained about sleeping on the hard floor. I watched the lantern light flicker against the walls of the tree-sted, the old paintings spreading along the wall like one big story. My eyes settled on the one with Elowyn's name. I didn't know who Elowyn III was, but I did know her namesake's story.

She was the first pilgrim, the only one who still had faith among all her people. She deserved her place as a mother of the faith. My pulse faltered, and I shut my eyes. Believing Elowyn's story didn't make me one of them. *But is being one of them so awful?* I shuttered, looking at another painting. When I found the bright blue and gold of my own, I smiled. Nevma.

Now you know you can be a faithful friend. A friend to the end, Nevma whispered sleepily. I blinked away a warm tear. Whatever the cost, having Nevma back was worth it.

Not far from my painting was another one. One that I did not remember. I studied it in the low glow of the lamp. The brushstrokes revealed dark clouds and rain, doubts and confusion. But encircling it all were white butterflies. Faelle noticed which painting had caught my attention.

"I always felt like everything in my life was hard. Confusing. But those white little creatures, they always stood out against the brokenness in my life."

"It's beautiful." My voice drifted softly as I glanced at her, but she was not looking at me. Instead, she was looking up and smiling as if something was fluttering around her. "They are beautiful... I thought I lost them."

I closed my eyes, fully understanding her words and the emotion behind them. Her pilgrimage might have been different from mine, but the Spirit had led her too.

Sleep played at my eyelids, but I did not want it. Not when there was so much to learn and listen to. Friendship was at my fingertips. A friendship all my own. What if this was what the tree-sted held for me? I readjusted the pack under my head and rested my eyes.

When sleep took me, it was not a restful sleep. Unwanted faces and creatures crept into my dreams. Alius's grin turned cold. I brushed a moth away. Alana was gone, and Ilynn had abandoned me for new friendships in Madreille.

Sadness whispered. "*Come back...*"

A familiar pain crept through my chest. If home held nothing but heartache, why shouldn't I answer sadness's call?

The stage in the festival courtyard creaked under my feet, and I glanced down at the dagger in my hand, black gems embedded in the handle. I stumbled towards the stairs but not before a crowd morphed into view.

"Stop her! Stop Lindi the Forsaken!"

The dagger clattered to the ground as I threw my hands over my ears, tears budding in my eyes. *I am not Lindi!*

I heard the door of the tree-sted creak open through the fog of the dream world.

Soft earth was beneath me, and I dug my fingers into it. Where was I? Everything was dark. Black. Was I still dreaming? A chill blew through me, and the sound of rustling leaves broke the silent night air. I was outside. I was outside, and I was awake. But how...?

I glanced around. The tree-sted was nowhere in sight. A tear slid down my face. I was not dreaming, and wherever I was, I was alone. The stinging smoke of memory clouded my mind. I was meant to be alone. I didn't deserve friendship or love.

"You're right." A soft, cold light appeared in front of me. It shimmered and wavered, peering at me with a mesmerizing face. My breath faltered. I was kneeling on the ground, kneeling before the creature. When I looked again, I saw the leafy locks of its hair. A dryad.

The Lore Wielder

She towered before me, her long, nearly-solid dress sweeping behind her. Her tree grew close. "You don't belong in this world." The dryad's words were smooth, and they struck me hard, though not like a blow. Like the strum of a minor chord in my soul—sad, but right somehow. "Some people are meant to be alone. Why are you fighting it?"

She leaned down towards me, and another dark chord vibrated in my soul, one that pulled and beckoned. I was fighting it? If I was bound by sadness again, hadn't I lost already? Her eyes glistened under long lashes. With a gulp, I tried to stand up, but I couldn't. A force weighed me down, insisting I bow to her. Only, the weight wasn't foreign. I swore under my breath. It was the weight I would bear if I stayed in the world of the living.

"Why are you saying this?" I finally whispered, my voice trembling with the realization that I was thrust into the shadow I had thought was defeated. She straightened and walked around me in a circle.

"Why bother denying it? There is only one thing that will never leave you. Sadness." She paused, looming before me. "Let it back in. You know its touch. And you like it." Her voice had grown to a whisper. A slow, tantalizing drawl.

I squeezed my eyes shut, digging my fingers into the dirt. I was not dreaming, and she was right. The weight of sadness spoke to me. I didn't want it, yet I did. It was safer, safer than believing I could be loved. What if when I arrived in Wisptale everything was just as it was? What if the moths were waiting for me? I trembled, remembering their lure. What had truly changed in The Lost Garden? I was still *me*, and the world was still broken and still breaking me.

I met the dryad's eyes as she held out a hand. My own left the surety of the ground. She was a dryad after all. Shouldn't I trust her? But before my fingers touched hers, a twig snapped from behind. She withdrew her hand and stood to her feet, looking far taller than before. Her mouth curved in a mocking smile.

"We are not alone..." she said under her breath. "Come out, come out, little girl. I see you hiding in the trees, too afraid to join us." The dryad drifted away from me, her face glowing with a light that seemed wrong. I tried to turn my head and look, but I still could not move under the weight of her power. Who else was out there? A dagger flew through the night, finding its mark in the tree in front of me. It had spun clean through the dryad without leaving a mark. The dryad's shimmery form rippled with indignation.

"How dare you?" she growled at the knife thrower.

Fear leapt into my throat as I watched, still unable to stand. The ground beneath me vibrated. A beetle crawled across my hand. I shook it off, but another took its place. The ground shifted and moved as worms reached out their blind faces from every direction. The soil crawled with every living creature from the underworld. I fought to stand up against the weight as the legs and bites of a hundred insects crept up my legs and arms. The night air shook with my screams as the creatures invaded my skin.

"Stop it!" Faelle's voice joined my screams, and from the corner of my eye, I saw her rush towards the dryad. All she had were her daggers to fight against something that was not even solid.

"Please, help!" I sobbed, still pinned to the ground as the insects crawled towards my mouth and eyes. They would suffocate me—devour me alive.

"You have no right to her. Not any longer!" Faelle's determined voice pierced the night as she confronted the dryad, but not with her dagger. "Opal, get up. Get up, *now!*"

The weight forcing me to kneel vanished. I gasped, frantically shaking the spiders and centipedes off as I scrambled to my feet. The ground had stopped vibrating, but it still crawled. When I looked up, the dryad writhed, pinned to a nearby tree trunk. Faelle stood five arms away, hands outstretched.

"Grab the ax!" Faelle shouted, not moving from her position. Somehow, she was holding the dryad. Containing it. Before I could ask where I could get an ax, the light from the dryad glinted off steel a few arms from her. I snatched up the ax. *Where did she get this?* I spun back to the dryad. I knew what I had to do. The only way to kill a dryad was to cut down her tree.

"Find her tree. Cut it down!"

What was happening? How long could she hold the creature? "Will you be all right?" I asked, breathless.

"Go!" Her voice was steady, but her eyes flashed with fear. I hesitated, knowing leaving her with the dryad was the only way, before dashing into the dark forest. I had to trust Faelle.

Where was the blasted tree? *Help me please. I can't do this on my own,* I prayed as I stumbled through the dark. Nevma darted in front of me.

"Where have you been?!" I nearly yelled at him.

Where you left me.

"But I needed you!"

Who do you think woke Faelle? Now, will you follow me? Nevma flew in front at a pace I could barely keep up with. I ran for a minute longer before Nevma stopped.

Here. You will know her tree by its leaves.

"What?" I cried, expecting Nevma to lead me right to it. "I don't have time for this!"

Yes, you do. Only you know where her lies have taken root. Only you can cut down her tree. I gritted my teeth in frustration and whirled around in the dark, looking for any sign of her tree. Only Nevma would give me such vague instructions at a time like this. I was searching for a tree in a dark forest, not rooting out lies.

My throat tightened, and my vision blurred as her words came back to me. *You don't belong in this world. Why are you fighting it?*

"Because!" I answered my thoughts out loud. "I will not serve a liar." This time, I lifted the ax more intentionally as I breathed the cold night air. "I know where you are," I whispered, clenching my eyes shut as something foreign unveiled itself in my heart. And I did know. A pain spread through my chest like a map. The closer I got to her tree, the sharper the pain. Finally, I opened my eyes, standing before what I knew was her tree. The pain pulsed like an open wound, and I let the tears flow down my face freely.   Nevma alighted on a branch next to me as the leaves rustled aside, letting in a strong ray of moonlight. The leaves—they were yellow and brown. Sickly. Her bark rotted off in chunks. The nymph looked beautiful, but she was wasting away. Solemnly, my fingers gripped the ax handle, and I raised it.

"I do belong in this world, and I will fight you until my last breath." I swung the ax. Over and over again, I hacked into her diseased bark. Her brittle wood broke away in large bits. Even so, my breath deepened, and my arms ached long before the work was finished. When it came down to the last swing, I paused, putting my foot on the swaying trunk.

"I don't know why you betrayed the Heir, but you will never lie to anyone else *ever* again." With a grunt, I pushed with all the strength left in my leg until I heard a loud *crack*, and the whole tree crashed to the ground. I let the ax head rest on the forest floor as I leaned against another tree, sucking in air as if it would save me.

Saint Elowyn: entry six

It's been three days now. I think.

I think it's getting colder too. My fingers. I can barely move them, and they are turning red and blue. I can't remember the last time I ate. Please, don't let me die. I'm trusting you.

Saint Elowyn: entry seven

I thought I died. Everything went so cold and black when I fell down into the snow. I was only half awake when the fox found me. He must have dragged me into this cave. Where the fire and fish came from, who knows? I should be scared, but I am too cold and hungry. I would be dead without him.

Twenty-nine

I STUMBLED THROUGH THE FOREST back towards Faelle. Weakness tangled my limbs. Why was I still fighting the same fight, the same lies, after all this time? I thought I was different—new.

It takes time and truth for old patterns to be broken.

How much time? My fingers tightened around the ax. How many renegade dryads were out there?

Before I reached the circle of trees where I'd left Faelle, a shadowy figure crashed into me.

"Opal!" Faelle grabbed my arms to keep us both from falling.

"Is it gone?" My breath came in deep gasps and hers matched mine.

"Aye! It was incredible. And horrible." Her nose wrinkled. Nevma buzzed in a circle around us, and I thought I could almost see white butterflies joining in. I relaxed my grip on the ax. We weren't alone. I would never be alone if I could just *remember*.

"What happened? And how did you—"

"I don't know. It was the butterflies. They woke me, and I followed them to you. They poured out from my hands, a hundred of them, pinning her back to the tree. When they touched her, it was like they burned her. I could feel her hatred pulsing against their barrier, but as long as I focused, she never broke through. Until—until you found her tree…" Her eyes widened, reflecting the moonlight as we walked. "Opal, I saw every stroke. That ax hit her like she was solid. And then she just… melted away."

I released a breath, images of what I'd done flashing before my eyes, the ax heavy in my hand. I wasn't sorry—no. That thing had to go. But it was heavy, killing a dryad, a kind of creature I had grown to trust.

"Thank you," I murmured. "Thank you for coming to find me." I swallowed the lump in my throat. "You didn't have to."

"And you didn't have to help me by the cliff. But you did."

I blinked, staring at the ground beneath my boots though I could see neither. Tirigan had said our fates were somehow intertwined. Maybe we needed each other.

Faelle held out her hands in front of her. "Do you think this is what it's like?" She turned her hands over. "I mean, what the Heir meant about a new life? A new strength to face the brokenness?"

Moonlight streamed through the trees. It touched Faelle's face, illuminating not the girl I'd found lost on the mountain, but someone new. Someone stronger. Someone free. Whether I felt it at this moment or not, the Heir's power over brokenness stood before me.

"Aye. I do," I whispered, my hands tingling with the rush of old knowledge that had filled me in The Sanctuary. It wasn't me, but something that moved through me. Faelle and I were vessels. The Heir wasn't far off, hidden behind garden walls. He was with us in the light and the dark.

I cleared my throat, lifting the weapon in my hand. "Where in Avarlyn did you get this ax?"

Faelle laughed, her footfalls moving along the path again. "That was the easiest part. The tree-sted may have been empty, but the moment I awoke and realized you were gone, I saw the ax in the corner."

"Why does that not surprise me?" I smiled, shaking my head as I relinquished the lead and followed Faelle. A starry sky peeked through the leafy trees on the mountainside. I didn't have the faintest idea where the tree-sted was. *Harfares.* I must have walked in my sleep or been in a trance.

The longer we walked, the more evident it became that we were not going to find our way back tonight. Not in the dark. My heart sank, and Faelle's frustrated sigh cut through the stillness of the night.

"I think we may be lost." She didn't look at me or turn around. A cold wind stole my breath, but Nevma rested on my shoulder, and I smiled at the warmth of his presence, even while we were lost.

"You followed the butterflies to find me. Maybe they can lead us back to the tree-sted," I said, adding in my heart, *please, guide us home. You are the only one who can.* Faelle finally looked back at me and nodded. Nevma leaped into the air from my shoulder. I had so much to learn about him.

Don't worry. It will only take a lifetime.

I could have sworn he winked at me as he took the lead.

Faelle closed her eyes, and her face softened in the dim light. She opened her eyes once more and chose a direction. I couldn't see what was guiding Faelle, even though I knew what it was. Her butterflies. My eyes were on Nevma.

By now, the sky bled gray. I did not know how long we wandered, but morning was breaking. The light was coming. Exhaustion wrapped around my body like a heavy blanket, but I pushed on.

Faelle and I didn't speak. We were too busy yawning. It took all our focus to lift our weary feet and not trip over the underbrush. Finally, once all the stars had winked out, Nevma darted back towards me.

Here it is.

I glanced around, still not recognizing anything. Where was the tree-sted?

"Here is what?" I whispered. As far as I could tell, we were nowhere near the tree-sted. Everything looked faded and uncertain in the groggy morning light. The mountain itself was still cast in shadow. We stood on the edge of a shallow ravine with a creek cutting through its moss-covered rocks. Nevma did not stop though. He hovered over the water, clearly expecting me to follow. I glanced back at Faelle.

"I don't know where we are going, but I know it's this way," she said, pointing down the rocky slope in front of us.

"All right." I nodded, letting her know I trusted her.

We knelt on the edge and picked our way carefully down the ravine to the riverbank. The other side was eight arms away, rising above the glistening crystal water. After a ten-minute walk along the rocky riverbank, the sound of the water changed. It no longer chattered but roared. The calm stream churned to rapids as we scaled two large boulders, and I caught my breath as a fifteen-arm waterfall tumbled down before us.

I hesitated when we reached the base of the waterfall. Why were we led here? I knelt down on the rocks, watching the soft morning spill over the trees. Nevma played in the mist coming off the rushing water before disappearing behind the waterfall.

"Where did—?" Faelle began under her breath before abruptly looking at me. But I was still staring at the place Nevma had vanished. Was I supposed to follow him up there? The wind rolling off the water sent shivers through me, and Faelle shifted on the rock beside me.

I glanced longingly at the golden light gracing the treetops before returning my gaze to hers. "There's nothing to do but keep following." I shrugged. "I have a feeling we aren't going to see the tree-sted again."

"I think you're right." Faelle frowned before scaling the last rock between us and the waterfall. We were careful not to fall into the pool, but as we moved closer, the mist had its way with us. By the time we found the ledge hidden behind the falls, dampness clung to our clothes. The ledge widened, opening into a cave behind the waterfall. We ducked inside, narrowly missing the falls. I blinked as my eyes adjusted to the low light. Faelle knelt down to rummage through her bag and struck a match. A myriad of human shapes flickered against the cave wall. Small but unmistakable. I jumped, and Faelle dropped the match.

"What was that?" Faelle's voice trembled.

"I don't know," I whispered, stepping back towards the falls. Faelle lit another match. I swallowed as the small flame struggled to illuminate what we had just seen. Faelle rose to her feet as I caught sight of a pile of something a few arms away. My boots ground on the cavern floor as I stepped towards it. Candles. A whole stack of them.

"Here." I reached for one and held it to the match. The damp wick sizzled before catching.

"Why are there candles?" Faelle wondered, taking in the cave wall that was dedicated to them. I lit another one, giving it to Faelle, and stepped a little farther into the cave.

"Because," I murmured, holding out the candle as shivers danced along my skin. "It's a shrine." With more light, I could see what cast the human-shaped shadows on the wall. Countless icons of a young woman littered the cave floor and the shelves built into the walls. Faelle stumbled back, and I smiled, surprised that I hadn't recoiled as well.

Kneeling down, I picked up one of the icons. It was strange—different to be around a shrine—a tradition Refiners never participated in. But I had a feeling I knew exactly who this shrine was dedicated to. I ran my fingers over the figure's weathered face.

"Are you sure you should be touching them?" Faelle whispered from somewhere behind me. I held back a smile and set the icon of Elowyn back down.

"They are just figures. I don't think touching them will do any harm." Blowing out my candle, I rose, blinking heavy eyelids. I set down my bag and lay my coat on the cavern floor.

"What are you doing?" Faelle asked. "We can't stay here."

"Why not? We need to sleep, if only for a few hours." I curled up on my coat with my head resting against my pack.

"I don't like it. Isn't it wrong?" Her voice was low as if something else might be listening.

I rolled over to face her. "Do you know who the shrine is for?"

She scoffed. "Does it matter?"

I furrowed my brow. "I think so. Elowyn, at least, deserves to be recognized."

Faelle gasped. "We're in an Elowynnite *shrine*?"

I sat up, blinking wearily at her. "Tirigan gave me Elowyn's diary. She was the first pilgrim. The first one to return to The Lost Garden after the days of darkness."

"But the Elowynnites..."

"I know. But she's only their namesake as far as I can tell. Now, please, can we try to get some sleep? Besides, you are the one who found this place," I said, smirking to myself and closing my eyes.

Faelle was a faithful Refiner, as she should be. The story of Elowyn swimming in my head had finally relinquished some of its power now that it was spoken. I didn't need to be afraid of the truth.

I heard Faelle lie down next to me, and I cracked my eyes open. The candle still flickered on the shelf before us, and as I drifted off to sleep, I wondered if this was the same cave that Elowyn awoke in so many years ago.

Saint Elowyn: entry seven

The fox is following me. To be honest, I am glad because I was so lonely before. It is still dark all the time, even though I am following the direction of the light. It must be light, that grayness. Only light can change the color of darkness, right? My fingers and feet are constantly prickling now. It hurts, but I must keep going. There is nothing left for me if I turn back. Nothing but cold and darkness. And lies.

Thirty

MY DREAMS BRIMMED WITH FLICKERING light and a bright young face. Elowyn's face. Peace swirled through me in her presence. That internal fight between what I was taught and what I knew was still raw, but maybe healing wasn't a world away.

When I awoke, I sat up slowly, hugging my knees as I stared at the shrine. One side of the cave held shelves carved into the wall, which bore countless candles. The one we left lit swayed in the breeze from the waterfall, its wick a few knuckles shorter than before. What I'd told Faelle was easy to accept. I could find a place for Elowyn in my faith. It was much harder to come to terms with the persecution and losing the location of The Sanctuary. I frowned. How much easier would it be to ignore all this? It was far simpler when I believed the Dark Persecution had been at the hands of Da'Shinar.

I glanced at Faelle who lay still, her chest rising and falling in the rhythm of deep sleep. I had a feeling she had fought sleep for a while longer after I passed out.

The hunger pains in my stomach intensified, and I crept soundlessly out of the cave. We'd eaten all of our food last night, and even though this cave was full of mystery, breakfast wasn't anywhere to be found. My eyes ached in the bright daylight as I pressed my back to the rocks and slid away from the rushing water. It was late morning by my estimation, which gave us enough time to make progress towards home. But where were we in reference to Wisptale? We could be days away. I shook the thought away.

Once I descended the falls, and my feet met the solid bank of the river, I searched for pliable switches to weave into a fishing trap. The pool beneath the waterfall swirled and frothed, and I smiled to myself. I'd gotten the idea to catch fish from Elowyn's diary. If this was indeed the same cave, she had eaten fish here too.

My fingers stiffened in the morning air, but I did my best to work quickly, urged on by my hunger. My fish trap wasn't anything like the ones Appa could make, but it would do. I lowered the basket into the pool and went off in search of firewood.

As the day progressed, and the sunlight ate away the mountain's shadow, warmth I had not felt since leaving The Lost Garden kissed my cheeks. I paused, taking it in and letting it mingle with the peace that glowed inside me like the candles in the cave. Mere weeks ago, it was darkness that had taken up residence in me. But now, it was light. My light flickered small compared to the darkness of the world around me, but couldn't even the smallest light threaten the powers of darkness?

I made my way back through the forest to the waterfall with an armload of firewood and left it on the riverbank well away from the mist. When I entered the cave again, Faelle was packing up her belongings. Her braid hung down her back, and her face was washed. She didn't speak when I retrieved the matches.

"I made a fish trap. Hopefully I can catch something for breakfast before we leave." I stood, matches in hand. A dim light lit the cave, even though it was day. The candles had long since burned out, and the lack of flickering and shifting light quieted the eeriness of the shrine.

"I am starving," Faelle said, throwing on her pack and looking quite ready to leave the cave without looking back.

"Let's go check the trap," I suggested, leaving my pack behind as we exited the cave. I wasn't sure why, but I wanted an excuse to return one last time.

My stomach rumbled as I gently pulled up the fishing trap, hoping to see a wriggling trout in its grasp, but it was empty.

"Nothing yet," I said over my shoulder to Faelle, who was standing a few arms behind me. I frowned, lowering it once more.

"Can I see it?" She knelt next to me, and I gladly handed her the line I'd made of vines. "My brother taught me how to make these." Her voice was quiet as she took the basket in her hands. "Maybe you could dig up some dandelion root to go with the fish while we wait?" After studying the fish trap, she searched the ravine for more switches.

I nodded before climbing back up the ravine. When I'd gathered firewood, I came across a meadow not too far away with an abundance of dandelions.

Dandelions. I shook my head in near amusement. When I reached the edge of the meadow strewn with wild flowers, I paused. There had been someone else all along who saw the purpose in dandelions. I knelt next to one, running my fingers over its yellow bloom. I frowned. Its purpose right now was to die. I drew one of my daggers and cut into the soil around it.

"I hope you've had as much success!" I said, sliding down the ravine with two handfuls of dandelion root. When I reached the river, I plunged them in the cold water and scrubbed the dirt off.

"Not yet, but I have a good feeling about this pool. I don't think we're going to leave hungry." She took one of the freshly washed roots and held it over the fire to roast. "My brother always said the biggest trout live under waterfalls."

My stomach gnawed at me again. "Well, I certainly hope he is right. Here." I tossed Faelle another root while I continued to scrub the others. "Can you roast one for me as well?"

She nodded as she looked thoughtfully into the fire. I knew Faelle had a sister, but I had forgotten about her brother. Her family had not always lived in Wisptale. Had I even seen him before?

The dandelion roots crackled and popped in the flames. The smell wasn't exactly nice, but it still stirred my appetite. I piled the other roots onto clean leaves before settling myself next to the fire. Faelle handed me a dandelion root before biting into hers. It still sizzled, but I took a bite anyway. The root tasted of soil and rock, but I was too hungry to take much notice.

Once Faelle fixed my fishing trap, it yielded three glorious trout. We gratefully cooked and ate them, sharing the third one. They were remarkably sweet and not in want of any seasonings.

Faelle doused the fire as I stood, wiping my mouth. The sun shone directly overhead now. Too much of the morning had been slept away, but I couldn't feel guilty for it. Nevma buzzed around my head in a restless whirl. It was time to go.

I scaled the rocks leading up to the cave behind the waterfall one last time to retrieve my belongings. *It is a strange place*, I thought, ducking inside, narrowly missing the stream of water. I could understand the cave being special if it was believed this is where Elowyn stayed. But all the candles and icons... Those I had a harder time understanding.

All the thoughts spinning in my mind made me pack slowly. Were we brought here for a reason, or simply because it was safe? I shouldered my pack and stood, but something told me I wasn't ready to leave. Chills traced my spine as I lingered before the rows upon rows of icons. They were different sizes, but all the faces had the same peaceful expression. Nevma alighted on one of them, and I picked it up. The paint was nearly rubbed off, but Elowyn's eyes still shone, and her red lips still held their color. My fingertips ran over something carved on the bottom, and I turned it over.

S.F.

I caught my breath, staring at the letters. Was this the same S. F. as the owner of the map? I bit my lip, hesitating before I packed it away in my bag. I had a feeling Faelle would not want to know about it.

I had ventured deep into the cave, and when I turned to leave, I stumbled over something hard and long. I gasped, wide-eyed, at the canoe before running to the cave opening.

"Faelle! Come back up here. I think I found our way home!" I dropped my bag at the entrance and ran back to inspect the canoe. It was small, but just big enough for the two of us. A few moments later, Faelle appeared in the colorful mist.

"What is it?" she asked, keeping her feet firmly outside of the cave.

"A canoe! Come on, let's see if it floats!" We hoisted it up and carried it down the ledge before sliding it carefully down the rock beside the waterfall. It crashed into the water below with a loud splash. I grabbed my pack.

"You think it will hold us?" Faelle asked, jumping down to the rocks at the foot of the waterfall after me.

I splashed into the water, ignoring the chill in my excitement. "It doesn't seem to be taking on water. Let's put our packs in and see if they hold." The bottom stayed dry with the weight of our packs, so I pulled it towards the shore and climbed in. One oar lay in the bottom, and I plunged it into the water to keep from drifting down the river.

"It's working!" Faelle cried, breathlessly.

"Are you ready?" I asked, grinning. Home whispered just beyond the horizon.

"Yes." Faelle nodded, throwing one last glance at the waterfall before she climbed in.

As we drifted away from the falls, I gripped the oar, navigating the canoe through the rapids until the river widened. In the calm, I laid the oar across the boat and sighed, finding a strange contentment in the touch of the noonday sun and the hope that we would reach home soon.

It seemed a lifetime ago that I left, but it was a mere ten days. Ten days without Alana by my side. I bit back a smile. Seeing my family again would make everything worth it. This side of the Rim might be scarred with brokenness, but I was glad I hadn't stayed in The Sanctuary. I had people to love and a life to live. I dipped the oar in the calm water, watching the swirls. How had one ripple in my life changed so much? A ripple that began as a curse but was turned on its head—thwarted. I blinked away a tear. Above it all, working in ways deeper and more mysterious than even the vilest naiads, was the one who had orchestrated everything. All so that I could not just have a life, but a new life worth living.

The rush of rapids broke the silence, and I sat up, gripping the oar. Foamy white lay ahead like angry clouds as the river churned over the rocks. Faelle shifted uncomfortably, flinging her braid over her shoulder and shading her eyes from the sun as she took in what lay ahead. The whole river churned white around large boulders. The rapids were nothing close to falls, but if we had learned anything from living by a lake, it was not to underestimate the force of moving water. Especially when rocks were involved.

From the front of the boat, Faelle pointed to the right. "That should be our path, through those two big rocks." She squinted back at me as I settled myself on the seat and gently directed us in that direction. The calm water swirling around my oar vanished, overtaken by churning water. Faelle gripped the sides of the boat as the current caught us. I let out a long breath. Once a path was chosen, there was no going back. We would have to ride it out.

As soon as the two rocks came fully into view, both Faelle and I looked at each other in alarm. The water was pouring over an edge, but we could not see how far the fall was.

"Hold on!" I shouted, plunging the oar into the water as we began to spin sideways. I held it firm against the current, forcing us straight again as the falls came on faster and faster. Before we tipped over the edge, I dropped the oar in the boat and grabbed the sides of the canoe to keep from keeling into the river. With a jerk and a crash, we rode over the rapids and spun out into the white water.

"Nice choice of direction," I joked, grinning at Faelle as she released her grip on the sides of the boat.

"Aye, we made it, didn't we?" She shook her head, returning a smile. "Next time, I'm steering!"

"Gladly!" I said, holding out the oar to her as we accepted the embrace of the glassy water ahead. Faelle sighed, the excitement draining from her face, and set the oar down.

"I was so scared, you know. Last night, with the dryad." She slipped off the bench to sit in the bottom of the boat and tucked her chin in her arms, watching the forest drift by. I opened my mouth to answer, to apologize for leaving, but she continued. "It was all so familiar—what was after you—what that dryad was saying." She swallowed, hesitating to continue. "I haven't been happy for a long time. The sadness does feel like my only companion sometimes." A twinge of guilt plucked through me as I thought of all the times I wanted to befriend her but was too worried about what to say—too worried about myself. My heart pumped a little faster as Nevma, resting on the oar handle, stretched his wings.

Often, others are too busy worrying about themselves to look someone else in the eye. His words from so long ago came back to haunt me. How many times had he told me to open my eyes?

I cleared my throat. "I need to apologize, Faelle." I hesitated. "I can't tell you how many times I wanted to be your friend, but I didn't know how." It was hard to admit out loud. What might she think of me? I continued. "What the dryad said about sadness was a lie, not just because that creature said it, but because I'm not going anywhere." I searched her eyes, blinking back tears. "You're not alone, Faelle. Not anymore."

My pulse faltered at my words. I was scared of them. Scared of what a new friendship meant. What if I didn't go anywhere, but she did? I felt Nevma's weight on my hand and glanced down at him.

Friendship cannot be built on fear.

The Lore Wielder

I swallowed to clear the tightness in my throat as more words burned on my lips. "We were lost so that we could find each other. Lost in more ways than one, I think."

Faelle smiled before closing her eyes. "It's hard to believe all of it was real on this side of the Rim. What if things don't change at home?" She met my eyes again with a glassy gaze.

"I don't know." I shrugged. "Some things might be the same," I said, and this time I looked away. "But we are not the same. *We're* what's different," I said, a burning coal lit within me. A new fire, but one that was familiar. The desire to bind our friendship with truth wasn't just coming from me. It had been cultivated in me. By Ilynn. I pressed my lips together, holding back a smile.

Faelle nodded, pointing her face towards the sun. "Well, I'm not going anywhere either." She glanced back at me. "Even if we're still broken and still sad sometimes, at least we can be broken together."

The current picked up, growing stronger while we talked. Wind played through my unbound hair as I scanned the river ahead. The calm water spread out before us, but the sound sent a dagger into my middle. The river roared.

"Opal..." Faelle murmured, sitting up abruptly. I stiffened. The afternoon light glinted like flames off the water, blinding me. Faelle stared at the river ahead. "That's not a rapid."

I snatched up the oar and dug it into the water, paddling against the current. The force of the water gripped the boat mercilessly as it pulled us towards the edge.

"Faelle, I can't! It's too strong!" I yelled over the thunder of the water pouring over the falls.

"Hail and Harfares," she cursed, throwing herself into the bottom of the canoe. I tossed the oar, lying down beside her, gripping her hand.

Leslie Montaño

"Cover your head!" she yelled against the pounding water
as the boat tipped, and we plunged feet-first down the falls.

Sain Elowyn: entry eight

I saw it. I saw The Lost Garden today. From the top of the mountain. It... was different, floating in the air. I don't understand it, but just seeing it makes this all worth it. It disappeared when I climbed down, but I feel certain I will reach it tomorrow!

Thirty-one

I DIDN'T REMEMBER HITTING THE bottom. When I opened my eyes again, I was lying down, my body aching. Green jewels shimmered in the canopy above me. Leaves. Something soft was beneath me, and a murmur of voices entered my ears. I tried to rise, blood rushing to my head, but a hand pushed me back down.

"Stay down," a low voice ordered. I relented, all feeling returning like a vicious bite. My leg throbbed mercilessly. "Come on, girl. I know you can do it. I see it in you. I can feel it."

"But I—I can't. I don't know how." Faelle's voice was weak. Shaking.

"Faelle?" I whispered, opening my eyes again, trying to find her. Was she hurt too? Who had found us?

"Yes, you can because it's not you. It's him." The man's voice was clearer now. Tirigan? It couldn't be. Gentle hands touched both my ears, but my eyes couldn't focus. The hands holding my head warmed.

The Lore Wielder

"Wha—" I tried to speak, but a throb in my temple shut my mouth. The warmth strengthened, swirling through my head like breath. It trickled down my body, searching for injury until it found my leg, growing hotter and hotter. And then the pain was gone.

"Is it—did it work?" Faelle asked.

"I told you I could feel it." A gleeful tone swelled in the man's voice.

I gripped the blanket, fighting the darkness crowding in, but sleep won.

The moment my consciousness returned, my eyes flew open, and I sat up. All traces of pain were gone. I opened my mouth to ask how, but closed it when I saw the man sitting on a stump two arms away. My fingers rested on the dagger hilt in my belt. He glanced at me, warm eyes meeting mine under a tangle of white curls. He calmly blew out a puff of smoke from a pipe.

I gasped, recognition hitting me. "You're the iceman," I whispered, and I rose to my knees, my fingertips leaving the hilt of the dagger. The mysterious man who brought ice to sell in Wisptale.

"Aye. Folks call me Wilder." He shifted on the stump he was perched on, almost laughing as I continued to stare back. "That wasn't enough for your friend either." He pointed the end of his pipe in Faelle's direction. She shrugged as she sat by the fire, poking it with a stick. Her face was pale, but she looked unharmed. My eyes snapped back to Wilder when he spoke again. "I live some leagues from here. I'm making my way to Fairbluff. I stopped to eat when I saw you going over the falls." He chewed his pipe, shaking his head. "Nasty fall you had. Your friend... I don't know how she came out unscathed."

"He pulled you from the water, Opal. I was trying but..." Faelle's voice caught in her throat.

"Thank you," I murmured, edging closer to the fire, my clothes still damp. "How long was I out?" The sun was still bright.

"Not too long. How are you feeling? Better now, I bet?" Wilder asked.

"Yes." I stretched out my leg. There wasn't even a scar. "But how?"

"I'm sure she'll tell you when she's ready." Wilder gave me another smile. Chills trickled along my arms. The iceman. Wisptale held him at arm's length, yet he pulled us from the water. It was strange to find him here and to imagine he had a life beyond cutting ice. An abundance of lines and wrinkles creased his face, but he didn't seem old. Just weathered. His tangled white hair was knotted in a bun at the back, but strands still clung to his face. He didn't wear boots but soft leather moccasins and a forest-colored cloak. I saw no weapons, but that didn't mean he didn't carry any.

"If you're up for it, I'm happy to take you downriver." Wilder shifted back, shaking one knee as he rested on the stump. "I'm headed to Wisptale to catch the ferry to Fairbluff."

I looked at Faelle. Her eyes were a swirl of emotions. Fear. But it wasn't fear of Wilder. He saved us from the river. Could we trust him? I would let Faelle decide. She tossed her blackened stick, rising to her feet.

"Thank you," Faelle murmured before looking at me, her eyebrows raised in question. I glanced once more at Wilder before nodding. Our boat smashed to bits in the falls. Wilder was not only the fastest way home, but he also knew the way. Faelle relaxed, turning back to Wilder. "I think we will take you up on your offer."

"Then it's settled." He sat forward again. "Are you recovered enough to travel?"

I nodded, standing up tentatively on my leg.

Wilder emptied his pipe. "We'll break camp and get on the river as soon as we can then."

Faelle folded up the blanket, and Wilder doused the fire. I watched, mouth open and full of questions, but not one word would form properly. Maybe I really had injured my head, I thought, wondering about Wilder. A necklace hung from his neck, part of a geode. Why did he live out here away from everyone?

"My boat is this way." His voice cut through my curiosity as he threw his camp supplies on his back, leading us to the riverbank. Faelle and I snatched up our soaked packs that must have been pulled from the water and followed. His rowboat was tied up, swaying against the current, and he climbed in swiftly, nodding to the wide seat across from him.

"Come on, if we're going to reach Wisptale before nightfall."

"There aren't any more waterfalls, are there?" I clambered in beside Faelle. Wilder laughed, but I frowned, completely serious.

"No, no more. Some pretty wicked rapids, but no more falls." He smiled.

I gripped the side of the boat tightly and squeezed the pack between my knees. My body might be healed on the outside, but it still knew fear. Faelle and I should be dead. How badly was I injured, and how did Faelle escape unharmed? Nevma zoomed through the tree branches dangling above us. I smiled at his shimmering body. He could have warned me about the waterfall, but he didn't. And I might never know why, but the journey thus far had proved I could trust him. I narrowed my eyes as he rested on a leaf. If only trust meant I wouldn't end up with a broken leg every now and then.

"What were you doing out here anyway?" Wilder folded his arms, letting the current take over for a while, sweat beading on his forehead. Faelle and I looked at each other. We hadn't discussed what to say. We trusted him enough to take us to Wisptale, but beyond that, I wasn't sure. Tirigan's warning flitted through my mind. *Only what is tested truly becomes a part of you.* What testing still lay ahead of us?

"We got lost," I offered.

"On Mount Nea," Faelle picked up where I hesitated. "We've been on a very long journey, and we're headed home to—"

"Remember what Tirigan warned," I whispered. Faelle gave me a confused look, her mouth still open.

"Tirigan?" Wilder grabbed the oars again in surprise. "You know him?"

"Yes. How do you know him?" I replied, just as stunned.

"How do I know Tirigan?" He huffed as if fending off an offense. "I knew him well before either of you were alive. He and I are of the same nature." He shook his head, eyes brimming with memories of some far-off place. "We're both—" He paused, searching for the word. "Hermits, hemmed into the same mountains. Of course we know each other." He pulled at the oars, watching the forest drift by. Faelle and I stared at each other, shocked, and I wished I could speak to her alone.

"People are harsh," Wilder continued. "They don't like folks who are different. I don't live up here because I want to. Though, the peace and quiet is unmatched—don't get me wrong. But I've experienced enough grief and alienation for a lifetime."

The Lore Wielder

The hard seat and ache in my back almost went unnoticed as my thoughts circled. Wilder had saved me from the falls. Why? He and Tirigan felt the same way about humans. Could he be a Guide too? I tucked my hair behind my ear, glancing at Wilder. But what *were* Guides? From this side of the pilgrimage, it seemed surreal that I missed so much of the Heir's touch brushing the world. It was right before my eyes the whole time, not dancing with the darkness as I had once thought but undermining it. Nevma alighted on my shoulder and crawled into the pocket of my shirt. I smiled, watching him. Of all the Heir's touches, he was the best of all.

The sun sank in the sky as we drifted down the river. Summer's glory reached us once more, and I almost smiled when I noticed the sunburn on my arms. Summer still reigned in Wisptale. I turned on the seat, looking back at Mount Nea. The frozen summit glittered against the afternoon sky.

"Do you know what *nea* means?" Wilder asked.

I furrowed my brow as the word *light* flashed in my mind, but I shook my head. "If I had to guess, it's Old Avarish for *trials and horror.*"

Wilder's eyes crinkled as he chuckled. "It's not Old Avarish. It's Alandre. *Nea* means light."

My mouth parted, and I shivered. How had I known? Mount Nea was anything but light.

"Alandre? What's that?" Faelle asked.

Wilder nodded. "It's like Old Avarish's grandmother. I'm sure you know the name Rema Soul."

"That's Alandre?" I gasped.

"It's become so familiar that most have forgotten its roots."

I scratched my head. How long had Wilder been dealing in ice? "But who would name that mountain *light*?"

"The first person to reach its summit," Wilder replied.

I paused, refraining from asking Wilder if it was him. He couldn't be that old. The only other person I could think of was the first pilgrim. "Was it Elowyn?" I asked.

Faelle wrinkled her nose, and I nudged her arm. She would have to get used to me talking about Elowyn.

"Aye," Wilder answered.

"But why light?" I questioned.

Wilder shrugged. "Maybe it has nothing to do with the journey, but the fact that it's the gateway to the Rim."

I sat back, clasping my hands together. A gateway to the Rim. A light to The Lost Garden.

It must have been nearly six hours since we set out, and my eyes burned from the brightness of the water. I shut them tightly.

"Aya! Look!" Faelle nearly jumped out of the boat. I yelped, steadying myself as the boat rocked and Wilder gave her a mildly stern look.

"What is it?" I wondered, my heart thumping. Was something wrong?

"Look! Around!" She pointed wildly, shifting the boat again as she sat back down in her excitement.

I squinted to see what she was talking about and gasped. The trees, the rocks, the hills, and the river—I knew them all like the back of my hand. This was Snow Cap Creek. We were home.

"We made it!" I nearly jumped out of the boat myself. "We're home." The words felt as sweet as honeysuckle on my lips as new tears warmed my cheeks. It wouldn't be much longer now.

Wilder's eyes lit with amusement. "Even if you both rock the boat like a hippo, it was worth it to see that." He chuckled as we both bounced on the seat of his boat like children.

The Lore Wielder

"What's a hippo?" Faelle asked, covering her mouth as she laughed, and I joined her. Home was where we could be children again. Neither Faelle nor I was ready to abandon the sanctuary that was family.

"Never you mind," he replied, grabbing hold of the oars again.

I breathed in the air of my home, its familiarity embracing me. The moment glittered with magic, and everything I had endured to get here faded in its beauty. We weren't simply returning, but returning whole. I studied the relief in Faelle's face as joy spun around us, knitting hearts together.

Sliding off the seat and into the bottom of the boat, I leaned over the side and dipped my fingers in the water. This wasn't just Snow Cap Creek. It was the Rema Soul. I blinked slowly, resting my chin on my hand, staring at the water. Was it sweet? My pulse raced. The sweetness healed, but it also drew ruin to the Province of Avarlyn. Wherever the Rema Soul flowed, danger lingered around the corner, waiting to exploit it, like Da'Shinar had done so long ago—occupying Madrielle and killing 23,000 Avarish people. What might have happened if they found the real Rema Soul? I bit my cheek, forcing the thought from my mind.

"I bet we will see the top of the lighthouse just over that ridge," Faelle commented, squinting against the low sun. The thought made my heart fly. Whether it was haunted by a ghost or not, once the lighthouse appeared, it would only be an hour or more of floating until we reached home. Ten whole days away, and home was finally here. Finally close enough to touch. What I would say to my family, I had no idea, but at this moment, I did not care. Just to see Appa's grin and Yemma's curls bouncing as she ran to give me a hug was more than enough. And Alana. She might even reach me before Yemma.

I let the joy of it all wash over me as I settled back down in the boat and closed my eyes. My fingers ran over the pearl-studded hilt of my dagger. The lies were revealed, the change in me had begun, and—I glanced back at Faelle—I was no longer alone.

"Aye, what's that?" Wilder fractured the silence that rested between the three of us. "Anybody expecting a letter?" I straightened and peered over the side of the boat. There, not far away, was an otter. It swam towards us, against the current. As it drew closer, I recognized Muna, our family's mail otter. When she reached the edge of the boat, I leaned over and pulled her inside. She flopped on the bottom, exhausted from the swim.

"Muna. What are you doing, girl?" I asked, petting her head. She shook, water spraying us, and held up the bottle for me before collapsing again. I grabbed it from her tiny paws. *Forsaken Other, I hope she hasn't been looking for me this whole time.* I uncorked the bottle and slid the paper out. Muna didn't jump back into the water but curled up in the boat, shaking.

"What's wrong?" I whispered to her as I unfolded the paper.

Opal,

I don't know if this will reach you, but Wisptale isn't safe any longer. I've sent Yemma to Madrielle to be with your sister, and you must get yourself there too. I'm staying. I can't abandon our home.

-Appa

A dark smear stained the bottom corner. Blood.

Saint Elowyn: entry nine

He found me. The fox who never left my side kept me warm all night, and when I awoke, the Heir was standing over me. He was waiting for me.

Thirty-two

"IS EVERYTHING ALL RIGHT?" FAELLE asked, shattering my thoughts. My lip quivered as I stared at the letter.

"No. It's from my appa." I paused, my voice betraying me. "He says Wisptale isn't safe anymore."

"What?" she whispered, grabbing my arm.

"What happened?" Wilder's face hardened.

I took a shaky breath. "I don't know. He didn't say."

The lighthouse topped the trees, glinting pink in the sunset. I clenched my teeth against the streaks of orange and pink dazzling the sky. How dare it write beauty into this moment?

"What now?" Faelle asked.

"We get out of the river where we are no better than sitting ducks," Wilder said, splashing into the water and tying up the boat.

Heavy footed and heavy hearted, we clambered out. I picked up Muna and set her on the riverbank. She blinked at me with wild eyes before disappearing into the forest. The air had a tinge of smoke in it. Something was burning.

"I don't like the smell of that." Wilder shouldered his pack and started into the woods. "Come on. We'll be safer under the cover of the trees."

"Where are you taking us?" I asked, stumbling after him, fear for my family thrusting me towards whatever danger lay ahead.

"I'm taking you to the lighthouse," he answered, his eyes scanning the woods for any danger. "Where I used to live."

"What?" I grabbed Faelle's arm, my head swimming in confusion. She stared back at me, mouth open.

"I used to run it, maybe forty years ago." He turned back to make sure we were keeping up. "Come on. Don't straggle behind."

"Forty years ago... But nobody's run it since then," I answered. My body chilled, but I continued to chase after the tall white-haired man. "But the last keeper, he—" The word *suicide* streaked through my head, but I held it back. "—he died."

Wilder turned around, a mysterious glint in his eye. "Yes. He did."

I froze. "Who are you?"

But my question lingered, unanswered.

The thud of boots running through the underbrush made us all pause. Wilder rolled his cloak over his shoulder, dropping to the ground and flashing us a look to do the same. I dropped with the dread in my stomach, digging my fingers into the soil. Faelle pressed her head into my shoulder, shaking.

"Don't move," Wilder mouthed, reaching for a hatchet looped under his cloak as he glanced around the tree in front of us. He drew it silently, scanning the woods for what had made the sound. I forced my eyes to stay open. I had to know what was out there—what my appa had stayed to face.

Smoke stained the sky as a figure appeared only twenty arms away. A bow lay across his chest, and a short sword thudded against his thigh as he ran. Red waves clung to his sweat-stained face as he neared us. Wilder's grip on his hatchet tightened.

"No!" I hissed, reaching a hand towards the old man. When I looked back towards the figure, he was gone. I rose, peering around the tree before me.

"What are you doing?" Wilder hissed back.

I glanced at him, holding a finger to my lips. Before I could scan the woods again, a hand grabbed my shirt, jerking me out from behind the tree. I shrieked, slamming my hand into their arm before cold metal grazed my neck. I stared back at his green eyes and snarled mouth, my own mouth gasping for breath.

"Forsake all, Opal!" Alius dropped the sword point from my neck and stepped away from me, panting. I collapsed against the tree, staring in shock. With a grimace, he lowered his head for a moment before his eyes snapped back to mine. "What are you doing out here? Don't you know what's happened?"

I shook my head, trembling.

"I don't know where you've been," Alius continued, sheathing his sword and approaching me again. "But you can't go back. Not now."

"What's happened, boy? Can you tell us?" Wilder rose from his hiding place and stepped towards us, the hatchet still clutched in his hand. Alius stiffened, stepping between me and Wilder.

"Wisptale was attacked two days ago. The whole Misty District is gone," Alius relayed before turning back to me. I couldn't breathe. Wisptale *attacked*? He wiped the sweat from his brow, searching my face. "I'm on my way to Windgate for aid."

"Attacked by who?" Wilder asked.

Alius's hand returned to the hilt of his sword. "Da'Shinar."

Sneak Peak

book two

The Lore Wielder

It was slick. Rain beat down on me as I carried the fire wood inside and shoved my back into the door. It slammed shut with a *thunk*, and dim light met my eyes as Faelle came into focus. She sat cross legged on a rug before the stove.

I sighed. "I don't think it'll be much good." I kicked off my wet boots and crossed the floor to pile the wood next to the iron door of the stove. "The rain came on so fast."

Faelle picked at the rug. "He's been gone for hours," she whispered and my stomach slipped into knots.

Wilder was gone. He had disappeared into the gray whispers of the morning with not much more than a murmured explanation. Faelle and I were nearly snapping in two from the anticipation of his return and the news it would bring. That is, *if* he returned and wasn't killed or captured by soldiers from Da'Shinar. Wisptale crawled with them. I shivered before sinking down to the rug across from Faelle.

After Alius had disappeared up the river, we spotted a Shinish soldier from a distance in the woods. He carried a double-ended spear, and a Harfare was scrawled across the front of his uniform. I found myself picking at the rug too, remembering the confusion swirling in me as I watched Alius go. I glanced at the window. It would be a miracle if he made it to Windgate; a miracle we desperately needed. Yet, I wished the task hadn't fallen to him. Alius's gesture of standing between Wilder and me when Alius thought he was a threat, wasn't lost on me.

Thunder crashed outside, and both Faelle and I flinched. The lighthouse was a strange lodging. Dion had made it livable but it still fell apart in places from the years of neglect. We stayed in the keeper's quarters, not the lighthouse itself. The stove crackled before us, and the locked door marred the wall behind us. Pots and pans hung from hooks on the walls, and a vase of dried flowers stood on the small table in the corner. Perhaps Noura's touch? I blinked quickly as an ache spread through my chest. Where was she now? Noura wasn't one to stay in The Sanctuary when the place she called home for months was burning.

She had come to Wisptale for us. Dion on as well. Yet we had found the lighthouse empty. A part of me hoped we would find them here—Noura's bright smile and Dion's solemn but kind face—peering at us from the door. But Wilder had to practically break in yesterday.

I scoffed to myself. The man also did not explain his comment yesterday, and I knew it was haunting both Faelle and myself. Wilder *was* the lighthouse keeper. But how could that be?

"You don't think. . ." Faelle mercifully pulled me from my thoughts. "You do think he is alright, and not. . ." Her eyes flickered to the ground, fear tracing her irises.

"I don't know," I murmured back. "I think Wilder knows what he's doing. I *hope* he does... " I pulled the sleeves of my shirt over my hands and sat closer to her. No words could describe what surged through Faelle and me, playing with our attempt to disassociate from everything that happened to our beloved home. Did our homes still stand or were they burned to the ground? My throat threatened to strangle me thinking of Appa. I knew Alana and Yemma were safe but what about him? Faelle hadn't heard anything about her family. Her hope was a dying ember.

I leaned back on the couch we both refused to sit on and stared at the ceiling beams.

"Opal. . ." Faelle's voice trembled. She rested her head next to mine on the edge of the couch. I turned towards her, studying her as she stared at the ceiling. She blinked her light eyelashes slowly.

"How do you think Da'Shinar found out about the river? I mean, that the real Rema Soul flows through Wisptale. Not Madrielle." She dared to turn her head towards me, her array of freckles appearing stark against her pale skin.

"I... don't know." My voice cracked. That question wasn't new to my mind but it hadn't been at the forefront.

"What if. . .someone followed me?" Faelle resumed staring at the ceiling.

"What do you mean?" I sat up straight realizing the implication. *Followed her or followed me.* Until I remembered I'd been invisible to humans. Regular humans at least.

"I don't know, exactly. But what if someone here followed me up the mountain and found out where The Sanctuary was and that the maps were changed. It's the only thing that makes sense."

"But why would anyone betray us to Da'Shinar?"

"Money. Position. Maybe they were a spy and not Avarish at all."

Faelle's theory chilled me and one thing was certain—someone *had* betrayed us.

Noura

Noura washed the blood from her hands and leaned back from the still body in front of her. The countless wounded haunted her. She dried her hands before placing a cool palm on the man's head. No fever, but his breathing was weak. She had done what she could, but she was a healer by method more than miracle. It took her more effort and time than other healers from The Sanctuary. This man would make it, but he needed more time.

"I'm sorry to interrupt, but we have another wounded." came the camp leader's voice. Dalon. Dark circles marked his eyes.

Noura instinctively rose. "Yes, of course. I'm ready." She forced her wearily legs from the tent. "Where is he?" she asked, following Dalon through the camp.

"Just over here," Dalon answered.

This had been her reality for the past three days—do what she could for one man before rushing to the next. Had she even slept? Noura wasn't sure. Even though she had seen the Misty District burning from the sky, she did not imagine this much death, not yet. Da'Shinar had come with one thing on its mind—find and control the sweet water no matter the cost. Noura's jaw tightened as she steeled herself. This may be her first real war, but it wasn't her first time in the trenches in her memory. Her mind drifted to Neo. He might already be on this side of the Rim. She bunched her skirt in her hand.

Dalon glanced at her before sweeping back the tent flap for her to enter. Noura ducked inside, blinking as her eyes adjusted. The sun had sunk lower in the sky, making the tent even darker. Auburn waves darken with sweat framed a pale face.

"Wounded from an arrow," Dalon said in a low voice, and Noura glanced back at the captain. Those were often the hardest to heal. Though Dalon's statue was tall, he didn't look it. Not anymore. Unkept hair and beard covered most of his face, and he stepped back out of the tent, leaving Noura alone with the young soldier. She gathered her breath before kneeling beside the pallet. When she recognized his face, she gasped.

Wistptale 40 years earlier

The Lore Wielder

Shylo Fletcher

I shouldered my pack and wrapped a cloth around the lower half of my face and lifted the latch on the door. The light from outside stung my eyes as I squinted. Would she be there today?

It had been the heart of summer when I first encountered Tulsi Rose. I saw her hair first—mountains of shimmering curls tumbling down her back in a loose braid. When she spun around at the sound of her name, I spilled my tea. Her face would be burned in my mind until the day I died.

That had been six weeks ago, and the last time I'd restocked my supplies. A breeze tugged at my scarf, but I tucked it around my face snuggly and buried my hand in the warmth of my pocket once more. Murmurs of autumn tinged the leaves golden and burnt sunlight and summer faded, no more than a memory torn away in the wind. It whipped off of Misty Lale, bearing the vengeance of the world. I blinked as a sudden ache broke through my usually numbness. Moments like these stirred up memories of my home in the south. Summer might still be clinging to the valleys. I shuddered beneath the mid-morning sun, imagining it tenderly tucking its warm ray over Rainwen right now and shielding it from the coming autumn. But there was nothing left for me there. My family was gone—dead...I breathed into my scarf as my eyes flitted over Old Town before descending the stairs. She wasn't in Rainwen either. Tulsi was in Wisptale.

A shiver of wind upset my hair as I creaked onto the new docks of the market. It now sat so close to the marina that the fishy smell clouded every good and delicious one trying to peek through. I found the shop quickly and stepped inside out of the breeze that fought with Misty Lale. A draft blew through *Ignolian's Fares*, but the warmth still hit me in the face, and I lowered my scarf. Ignolian's son recognized me. This was one of the few shops I dared to visit. The boy gave me a kind nod. Was it genuine or just good business? Though the Keepton had declared me innocent of the crime, I knew no one in Wistpale believed it.

"The usual?" The boy slipped off his stool and reached for the extra large bundle of tea leaves. I always bought the largest portions to lessen my visits to the Misty District but now, even though my wits told me it remained the wise thing to do, I no longer wanted to wait every six weeks. I wanted to come everyday. I tapped my fingertips together in my pocket.

"Yes but—" I cleared my throat from the cold. I also hadn't spoken to anyone in six weeks. "But the regular size this time. I... want it to stay fresh." My eyes flitted briefly over him, noting his surprise. But he couldn't guess my reason. Nobody could. Not even the girl with the face that didn't fade even when I slept. Ignolian's son stepped around the counter, and I realized I could have gotten the brightly packaged tea bundles myself. They rested on the shelf not two arms away. I blinked, searching for the flour. As many times as I had set foot in here, I hadn't paid enough attention. It was the first place my uncle brought me when I arrived five months ago. He had asked for large portions as well, never gathering the items himself.

"Hail and Harfares," I muttered, my ineptitude glaring at me. Sacks of salt and sugar, and bunches of garlic, brooded as I scanned the shelf for flour. Where was it?

"Is this what you're looking for?" The boy dodged my arm as I spun around, and he lifted the sack of flour off the lower shelf in front of me.

"Oye! You're a saint if there ever was one," I commented, a smile of relief breaking over my face. The boy flinched, and I swallowed the dread clutching at my throat. *Forsaken Other,* why did I say that? It was as good as scrawling *"heretic"* across my forehead to mention anything about saints here. The boy recovered his composure, but his reaction lingered—a staunch reminder that even people who helped me were not my friends.

"Will that be all?" the boy asked, resuming his place behind the counter. I stared at the two items. I could take them and head back. But I didn't want to. I needed a reason to stay.

I glanced around the shop. Spread out on a table by the door were colorful handkerchiefs.

"One minute." I strode to the table, letting my fingers embrace the soft fabric. They were silk and printed in traditional Avarish patterns—leaves intertwined with the stars. But what color? I cleared my throat again. "Do you have a—a sweetheart?"

"I'm eleven... " the boy answered flatly, and I chided myself. Of course he didn't have a sweetheart. He was probably just now realizing girls existed.

"A sister then. Do you have a sister? What color would she like?"

"I do. She might like the purple and green. Or the blue and pink."

"Blue and pink... " I said before whispering to myself, "Blue would match her eyes."

"Do you want me to add one? They come at a pretty price. My father said they are genuine silk."

"Yes. Yes, I'll take the blue one." I approached the counter once more with the delicate handkerchief in hand, ignoring the color in my face. She deserved something pretty. She deserved *all* things pretty.

I tucked my purchases under my arm and entered the fresh autumn mixed with the fishy aroma once more. The handkerchief was wrapped safely and finished with a bow. I hadn't asked for that but the boy was intuitive. Once the sounds of the market greeted me, uncertainty weakened my knees. A few stares from passersby made me hastily return the scarf to my face, and I chided myself again. The fog of my thoughts about Tulsi rendered me careless, and I couldn't afford to be careless, not here.

Tulsi should be here somewhere. She worked in the market with her older brother. They sold tree-syrup and honey but often in different places around the market. They set up their wheeled-cart where there was available space.
I usually bought tea and a cake from Rosin's after my errands, but this time I needed something stronger.

After warming my belly with a pint of spiced-mead from the pub, I wandered the market again. Maybe they had sold all the syrup for the season. Disappointment washed over me. I adjusted my bundles and pressed my finger tips together again. I shouldn't stay any longer. I didn't have a good reason, not really. I tried to banish Tulsi from my mind as foolishness. She would hate me like everyone else in this blasted town. It was better and safer for me to not exist in her mind. Where was that numbness I clung to? But as I reached for the familiar numbness, I couldn't find it. Not when a reddish braid caught my eye.

Pronunciation guide

Alandre (a-lán-dree)

Avarlyn (a-vár-lin)

Alius (áy-lee-us)

Ciela (see-e-la)

Da'Shinar (dá-shin-ar)

Dion (dée-on)

Elowyn (él-o-wen)

Elowynnite (él-o-wen-nite)

Faelle (fáy-el)

Harfares (hár-faers)

Hesith (he-sith)

Ilynn (ée-lin)

Lale (láy-l)

Lindi (lin-dee)

Mêliades (ma-lee-dees)
Nevma (nev-ma)

Noura (nór-a)

Tirigan (téer-i-gan)

Glossary

Avarlyn: The province that includes Wisptale, Fairbluff, Yaneav, Madrielle, and Windgate. They are united by language and religion, but do not form a country.

Da'Shinar: The country across the sea who attacked Madrielle in the year 325 in an attempt to control the sweet water.

The **Gilding**: The Lore-wielding rite of passage where the wielder must swim through an underwater tunnel and retrieve geodes from the cave in order to decorate her daggers with gemstones.

Harfares: Corrupted birds of prey who arose after the rebellion. They consume Freebirds and are an omen of death.

The **Heir**: The divine being to whom the world of Nadea belongs and who planted the garden.

The **Herald**: An Avarish religious leader who leads the town in memoir readings each week.

Hesith: The possessed naiad and former keeper of the sweet waters in the garden.

Lindi the Forsaken: The last ousted Lore-wielder in living memory, who disappeared from Wisptale not long after.

The Lost Garden: The garden planted by the Heir that disappeared after the rebellion.

Mêliades: Dryads of the wild woods whose spirits are from fruit trees.

Memoirs: the recorded history from the beginning of the world.

The **Rema Soul:** The river of sweet water sent by the Heir as a gift to the people who returned to him.

Spawn: Half-human, half-naiad beings that live mainly in the ruins on the Rim.

Acknowledgements

"For we are his workmanship,
created in Christ Jesus for good works,
which God prepared beforehand,
that we should walk in them."
Ephesians 2:10

Without Christ, this story would not exist. It is He who took a lost, lonely girl and reclaimed her as His own for the good works prepared for her.

The Holy Spirit walked with me every step of the writing process, and I am beyond grateful that God allowed me to be the vessel to write *The Lore Wielder*.

I am incredibly thankful for my husband, who is a wonderful sounding board for ideas, and most importantly, who never doubted me for a moment!

To all my beta readers, whether you are family, friend, or acquaintance, thank you! Your encouragement and feedback was invaluable—the push for more detail and clarity, the dual perspective suggestion, and raising the stakes—my book is better because of you!

A special shout out to my sister, Carolina, who not only inspired Alana, but was the first to read my book and brainstorm with me! And to Hannah and Emily—your initial feedback on the story was vital. Emily, thank you so much for advising me on the book cover!

I also want to thank my editors, Leah Taylor and Genevieve Mumford. Your work truly elevated this book to the next level!

Meet the author

Leslie Montaño lives in Virginia with her husband and two children. She wrote her first historical fiction at the age of twelve and hasn't stopped writing since, whether she is chasing a new story idea or writing about her personal experiences.

The Lore-Wielder is her debut novel, and she plans to continue writing fantasy as well as bringing to life a historical fiction set in the Byzantine era. When she is not writing, she is teaching art, baking sourdough, reading, and spending time with her family.

You can reach her at **author.l.montano@gmail.com**

www.ingramcontent.com/pod-product-compliance
Lightning Source LLC
Chambersburg PA
CBHW051256130726
47987CB00004B/1554